For Dominica

Acknowledgements

I could not have written this book in its present form without the help of several people who generously assisted me Some helped me with my research. Others offered me encouragement when I needed it. Some called my attention to errors and reduced the likelihood that I would be embarrassed by my production.

First and foremost among these people was my wife, Dominica, who consistently encouraged me to move forward with the book. Dominica was not only an early reader, my copy editor, and a wise critic of the manuscript, she also correctly urged me to change the book's title from its original title in its early drafts to *Mandarin Yellow*. Dominica proved, too, to be an invaluable and tireless sounding board, permitting me to constantly bounce ideas off her.

Another early reader was my mother-in-law, Josephine Thomas, who provided me with valuable corrections to the manuscript. I'll always be grateful for her help and encouragement. Other early readers (who read the book before I changed its title) whose suggestions I valued were Sue Cohen (proprietor of Brenbooks in Rockville, Maryland) and Sergeant Quintin Peterson (a first-rate novelist and playwright, himself) of the Metropolitan DC Police Department [retired]. "Q" offered me valuable insights into DC police procedures and terminology.

I thank Vered Uziel (Washington, DC) who generously assisted me with respect to my web site (www.stevenmroth. com) and with Facebook, Twitter and LinkedIn. Vered also offered me valuable suggestions with respect to promoting my book, and I am grateful to her for having shared her expertise.

I am grateful, too, to Berton A. Heiserman (www.thepenhaven.com - Pen Haven, Kensington, MD) who took in trade a group of Esterbrook pens I did not want for a 1927 Duofold Mandarin Yellow fountain pen I now proudly possess. My thanks, too, to Richard Binder (Richards Pens, Nashua, NH - www.richardspens.com) who created the Mandarin Yellow pen photographs I used in the book and on my web site.

I also am indebted to Paul Pinkham (Washington, DC), a pen collector and friend, who put me in touch with Richard Binder. And I thank Jerry Palazolo (Memphis, TN), Ron Schoolmeester (Washington, DC), Barry Yahr (Atlanta, GA), and Stanley Pillar (Walnut Creek, CA) for their generous offers of help along the way.

Finally, I owe a debt of thanks to Claudia Jackson (Telemachus Press, LLC) who designed my book and who patiently listened to my questions and "complaints" and dealt with them all like the very talented, creative professional she is.

Mandarin Yellow

Chinatown
Washington, DC

THE OLD WOMAN padded across the sidewalk, slowly moving away from the restaurant until she reached the curb bordering 7th Street. She paused and glanced around, rubbed her stomach three times in a sweeping circular motion for good luck, burped loudly, and giggled at her private indiscretion. She seemed remarkably content for a dead woman.

It had rained earlier in the evening, pelting the sidewalk and street with a noisy tattoo of weighty drops. But now the rain was gone and all that remained of it was a blanket of damp, heavy air that shrouded the empty sidewalks and street. No pedestrians scurried along the sidewalk, dodging one another as they made their way among the constellate of neighborhood restaurants and bars; no delivery vans, with their rasping horns and squealing brakes, jockeyed for parking spaces; and no cars raced up and down the street, not even the ubiquitous taxicabs that typically darted through Chinatown's hive of intersecting avenues sniffing out quarry.

Across the street, a few hundred feet south of the woman, a man hunched in an alley and watched and waited with predatory patience. He had come to Chinatown to kill the woman.

The man hummed his favorite Bob Dylan tune, "Blood

on the Tracks", confident in his knowledge that before long he would be able to match the rhythm of his song to the cadence of the woman's final footsteps.

THE WOMAN TURNED her head left and looked north up the sidewalk. She turned again and looked south, studying the thread of pavement as it narrowed and fell away into the dark.

She hesitated and looked back at the restaurant, then retreated a step toward its revolving door, but abruptly stopped. She turned away again and glanced across 7th Street to the sidewalk on its other side.

The woman shook her head and let loose a loud Mandarin curse, mocking herself for her timidity. She sucked in a deep breath, nodded once to offer affirmation to her nascent will, then shuffled across the street. Committed now to the far side of 7th, she headed south along its sidewalk to her rendezvous.

She walked boldly now, as if corroborating her freshly found fortitude, then abruptly stopped not more than fifteen feet from the lurking man. She licked the tip of her forefinger, held it up to test the evening breeze, and adjusted her body to use her diminutive back as a shield against the night's inflowing breeze.

She reached into her silk purse and pulled out a sterling silver cigarette case and a small sterling Ronson lighter. She plugged a *Chonghua*-brand Shanghainese cigarette firmly into the corner of her mouth, leaned down into her cupped hands, and thumbed the Ronson three times before it caught. The wick sparked blue, then yellow, then orange, and finally sputtered out, raining colorful but useless sparks down onto the woman's hands. She straightened up, muttered another Mandarin expletive, and looked around for more effective shelter.

She saw the alley.

The woman pulled in her stomach, swallowed a resolute breath, and stepped into the malodorous, dimly lighted sanctuary. She again fired up the Ronson, leaned forward, and once more lost herself deep within her cupped hands.

—

THE MAN SILENTLY uncoiled behind the woman and spiraled up to his full height, looming unnoticed over her rounded back. He reached out and grabbed the woman by her hair, then wove its course, black filaments among his fingers, bunching the strands in his fist. He yanked hard, snapping the woman's head back, forcing her to face upward.

In one fluid motion, the man pivoted and fast-walked the woman deep into the alley, dragging her behind him. The woman's arms and legs flailed, unable to gain purchase, and her heels bounced helplessly along the littered ground like the soft, stuffed feet of a rag doll being quickly dragged along by its arm.

Without slowing his onward dash, the man flicked his fist forward past his thigh and sent the woman headfirst into a brick wall at the end of the alley. She crashed with a thud and dropped to the ground, rolled over onto her side, and softly moaned. The man leaned in and again grabbed a fistful of hair. He yanked the woman's head back, forcing her once again to look up at him.

The woman's mouth flopped open. Her eyes bulged. She sucked in air and belched it out in short, wasted gulps. Her fetid bursts of bile-impregnated breath were indistinguishable from the foul smelling detritus that littered the alley.

The man placed his knee on the woman's chest and pressed hard to keep her in place while he reached into his windbreaker and pulled a semi-automatic Ruger Mark II pistol from his pocket. He shoved the .22's barrel deep into the woman's mouth, splitting her lips, cracking some teeth, snapping off others.

The woman retched in spasmodic eruptions, jerking her head from side-to-side in convulsive volleys of unavailing denial.

It occurred to the man she might not be the right one, might not be the woman he was supposed to kill tonight. The job had come up so fast he hadn't had time to prepare for it in his usual, methodical way.

He shrugged his indifference. If she wasn't the right one, he'd research the target and come back to Chinatown again, find the right woman, and do her, too.

That settled, the man squeezed the trigger and blew away the back of the woman's head, splattering the brick wall behind her with bone shards and chunks of brain matter.

With practiced efficiently, the man leaned over the woman's lifeless body and fired a second shot directly into her heart, this one for insurance, just the way he'd been taught. Then he picked up the two spent shell casings, placed them in his jacket pocket with the Ruger, and left the alley.

The entire job, from the time the man first loomed over the woman's rounded back until he departed the alley, had taken him just under two minutes.

- Part One -

Chapter 1

THIRTY-EIGHT YEAR old Socrates Cheng stood behind a glass display case in his Georgetown Mall store and read the morning's *Washington Post* while he awaited the arrival of his first customer of the day. The sound of the jingling entrance bell broke his concentration. In one swift, fluid motion, Socrates closed the newspaper, leaned down and placed it on a shelf behind the display case, and put on his best vendor's smile. As he straightened up, he glanced across the showroom at the visitor and immediately lost his smile.

Facing Socrates from just inside the entrance door stood a pencil-thin, octogenarian Chinese man dressed from neck to ankle in an intricately embroidered sage green silk gown with wide sleeves. The old man stood stone statue still and looked hard into Socrates' eyes from across the room.

Socrates cleared his throat and frowned. He could feel his shoulders and neck stiffen.

What's he doing here? he wondered. Socrates' face and neck grow hot. *This can only be trouble.*

Although Socrates typically greeted every arriving visitor by walking over and saying something welcoming, he felt no such inclination on this occasion. He remained behind the display case, he felt safer there buffered by the waist-high glass counter, and studied the old man's face.

He was sure his instincts were correct. *It's Jade's father, there's no doubt about it*. Socrates silently sighed.

Socrates' thoughts were interrupted when the door's overhead bell jingled again and two young men, both with military-style burr haircuts and both dressed alike in solid black double-breasted Asian-style business suits, entered the store. They took positions bracketing the old man.

Socrates also recognized them. They were two of the old man's four sons, the middle brothers, Jade's younger twin brothers. The two known in the Li family as the Twins.

The old man, without taking his eyes from Socrates, said something to one of his sons. The young man turned toward his father and bowed slightly.

Socrates was able to hear what the old man had said, but he wasn't able to translate what he'd heard. The man had spoken in the difficult Shanghainese vernacular that Socrates recognized from his childhood. It was the same dialect his parents and paternal grandparents had often used when Socrates was a child, on those occasions when they wanted to say something in front of him, but did not want him to understand what they'd said.

As Socrates thought about this and smiled at the memory, the old man suddenly started walking across the room, heading directly for Socrates. The man's gown brushed his ankles as he walked, sweeping from side-to-side as he moved forward. His anomalous speed and grace afoot, the attributes of a *T'ai Chi Chuan* master, belied his advanced age.

The old man walked around behind the display case and planted himself directly in front of Socrates. He stood so close that Socrates could smell ginger on the man's breath. Socrates reflexively stepped back one pace and resurrected his dormant retailer's smile and trade craft patter.

"Good morning," Socrates said. "Welcome to my vintage fountain pen store. May I help you select a pen?"

The old man frowned. *"Ai-yah*, he said." His voice was grating, a high-pitched squeal. "Yes, you *will* assist me, Socrates Cheng, by tending to your heritage and recovering the valued stolen writing instrument known in this country as the Mandarin Yellow."

Socrates took a deep breath and tried to process what he'd just heard. He had no clue what the old man's cryptic statement meant.

"Tend to my heritage?" Socrates repeated softly. "I don't know what you're talking about, what you think my heritage is. If you mean my Chinese heritage, then you're wrong. I'm not Chinese, not any more than I'm Greek. I'm American, is what I am, part Chinese, part Greek, but altogether American. That's my only heritage." He nodded once sharply, punctuating his statement a mental exclamation point.

Socrates watched as the old man stiffened, and then as he abruptly changed his deportment. The old man bowed his head slightly, then raised it and looked into Socrates' eyes. When he spoke, his voice had softened.

"Permit me to introduce myself. My name is Li Bing-fa. I am a Celestial being, a Taoist of the Middle Kingdom. These are my sons." He turned toward the entrance door and flicked his hand in the direction of the two young men.

"I know about Celestial beings," Socrates said. He relaxed and smiled. "My father also is from the Middle Kingdom." He paused, then added, "In fact, Master Li, I recognize you from family photographs I've seen in your daughter Jade's home."

"I have no daughter," Bing-fa said. His voice had reacquired its sharp edge.

Socrates tightened up. Bing-fa's persistent denial of Jade as his daughter, and his banishment of her from the Li family because of her ongoing romantic involvement with Socrates, infuriated him, but he said nothing.

Bing-fa stepped in closer. "I intend to engage your services, Socrates Cheng. You *will* help me and you *will* serve your cultural patrimony by locating the thieves and recovering the precious Mandarin Yellow and other stolen treasures. Do not think otherwise."

Socrates reflexively stepped back and resurrected his territorial comfort zone. He still had no idea what Jade's father was referring to.

"It's not going to happen," Socrates said. He shook his head. "I sell vintage fountain pens to collectors, that's all. I don't recover stolen pens or solve crimes. That's for the cops."

He wanted this over. "Let the police handle this, it's what they do."

Bing-fa locked eyes with Socrates. His voice now sounded angry and dismissive. "The Embassy and I will not involve the authorities. You will obey me and help us."

Socrates said nothing. He focused his eyes on a small vein pulsating along the right side of Bing-fa's forehead.

"Do not, Mr. Cheng, make a hasty decision you will later regret," Bing-fa said. "I will return tomorrow. Then we will discuss what you will require to proceed."

Bing-fa pointed his finger at Socrates and touched his shirt. "You *will* assist the country of your ancestors, Socrates Cheng. Do not be so foolish as to think otherwise."

That said, Bing-fa turned away and strode across the showroom and out the door held open for him by one of his sons.

Chapter 2

THE DAY AFTER he dragged the woman into the alley and blasted away her life, the killer sat at his kitchen table drinking coffee, eating a glazed doughnut, and reading the story of the shooting in the Metro section of the *Washington Post*. The headline told him what he needed to know: EMBASSY'S DIPLOMAT MURDERED IN CHINATOWN.

The newspaper's account gave the woman's name, stated that she worked as the cultural attaché for the Embassy of the People's Republic of China in Washington, and chronicled the discovery of her body by sanitation workers in the early morning hours. The article also stated that although there was no known motive for the killing, it appeared not to be a random robbery or mugging gone bad since the woman, when found, still had both United States Dollars and Chinese Yuan in her purse and was still wearing a credible knock-off Rolex watch.

The man finished the article and left the breakfast table, satisfied he had earned his fee and would not have to return to Chinatown.

A few minutes later, the man left his townhouse and drove to a strip shopping mall near his home in North Potomac, Maryland. He parked his car at the far corner of the top enclosed tier of the county's public parking garage, and walked two blocks to the Safeway supermarket to buy a week's worth of groceries. Twenty minutes later, his errand completed, the man hauled two bags of groceries up the interior stairs to the top parking level of the county's garage and stepped out into the concrete parking area. He immediately stopped walking and looked around. Satisfied he was alone, the man squinted into the garage's particulate gloom and inspected his car from across the oil-stained floor.

His vehicle seemed to be just as he'd left it, but he would not walk any closer until he knew for sure that during his brief absence no one had rigged an explosive device to the ignition. He was a professional, and would do this by the book.

The man placed both grocery bags on the concrete floor, then pulled his key ring from his back pocket. He held his arm out in front of him as far as he could reach and aimed the key fob at his car, repeatedly pressing the START button to engage the engine. He silently cursed himself for having again forgotten to replace the fob's failing battery, and focused all his attention on willing the device to work. His intense concentration blunted his usual vigilance.

As the man stared across the garage at his car and repeatedly jabbed the fob with his hostile thumb, a solitary figure, dressed in blue jeans, a plain grey sweatshirt, and a Baltimore Orioles ball cap with the beak pulled down low, stepped out from behind a cylindrical concrete support column, and with several cat-quiet strides stole up behind the man.

In one deft motion, the intruder reached around the man and palmed him under his chin, forcing the man's jaw up and his head back, exposing the man's throat to the intruder's weapon.

Seconds later, the intruder released the man's jaw and let him sink to the concrete floor to bleed out.

Chapter 3

LINDA FONG, THE assistant director of the THREE PROS-
PERITIES CHINA ARTS GALLERY in Georgetown, loathed
her supervisor, gallery director Iris Hua.

Today, as on most days while at work, Fong sat at her desk
in a small alcove that had been created as a work station and
contemplated her persistent disdain for the director, disdain
that often interfered with her concentration as she attempted
to perform the menial tasks repeatedly assigned to her by Director Hua.

Fong's aversion for the director, as deeply felt as it was,
was not the only corrosive element at work. The alcove itself
represented a continuing and malignant irritant in Fong's
work life because Director Hua had deliberately positioned
Fong's junior size desk so it faced north, contrary to traditional *feng shui* rules of good health and mental comfort. This
deliberately provocative physical siting of Fong's desk meant
that when Fong sat at her desk, she faced directly into the in-
coming *ch'i* flowing south.

And that was not all. As yet another thorn purposely introduced by the director into her work relationship with Fong,
Hua had placed her own oversized desk along the north wall
of the alcove so that when she sat at her own desk, she not only
correctly looked south with her back to the inflowing *ch'i*, she

also faced Fong's desk and was able to watch Fong work. This scrutiny did not sit well with the assistant director.

"Assistant Director Fong," Hua said, speaking in Mandarin, "are you still laboring over the insignificant Chow assignment I gave you?" Hua launched a wolfish sneer at Fong as she spoke.

"I expected you would have completed this minor task yesterday. If this assignment is too challenging for you . . . ."

Fong looked up from the open file she'd been daydreaming over. She composed her pinched face, outwardly releasing her hostility. She bowed her head slightly and demurely lowered her eyelids. She could feel her cheeks grow warm in spite of her efforts to appear unflappable.

"I am just now completing this worthy undertaking, Honorable Director." Fong, too, spoke in Mandarin.

Hua thinned her lips and fought against another smile. "Is this project too basic for your under-utilized skills, Assistant Director Fong?" She paused for the answer she knew would never come.

"Is this simple chore I especially chose for you unworthy of your unfulfilled ambition?" Hua paused again. The silence that followed underscored her sarcasm. "I thought this lowly assignment suited you perfectly."

Linda Fong again bowed her head. "You are correct, Director Hua, as always. This elementary assignment rightly suits my undeserving talents. I am most pleased to be given the opportunity to perform this minor task for you." Fong could feel her stomach churn as she forced herself to say these words.

The director slowly rose from her chair and looked down at Fong.

"Assistant Director," she said, "you must set aside your despicable desire to replace me as this gallery's director." Hua nodded sharply to underscore her point.

"If you are so unhappy in your placement as my assistant, perhaps you should request reassignment back to the Embassy, and cede your enviable role to someone who will appreciate the special opportunity it represents to serve me and our country." She paused to let these oft-repeated words sink in.

"I know what you really want, Assistant Director, but it is unpatriotic of you to continue to envy my good fortune."

Good fortune, is it? Fong thought. *In a pig's ass, it is. Your so-called good fortune is that you were related by marriage to the man who was Chairman Mao's First Secretary during the Long March. It doesn't matter you know nothing of our country's glorious history and culture or that you run this gallery like an ignorant Western barbarian.*

But Fong did not give voice to her seditious thoughts. Instead, she again lowered her eyelids and bowed her head, and said, "Good fortune visits those who deserve to receive her visit, Honorable Director. I do not envy in others what I do not deserve to have myself."

And, Fong thought, *good fortune also visits those who invite her in, prepare for her, and are ready to receive her and take advantage when she presents herself.*

Chapter 4

WHEN SOCRATES ARRIVED at his store the next morning, Bing-fa was already there waiting for him, sitting on a park-style wooden bench under an indoor palm tree set in the mall's common area walkway. Bing-fa's sons, all four of them this time, stood like sentinels shoulder-to-shoulder behind the bench, staring over their father's head, facing the store.

Socrates furtively glanced at Bing-fa without turning toward him or otherwise acknowledging he saw him. He hoped to get a few things done in the store before he told Bing-fa he'd thought through his demand and decided he would not become involved. He did not look forward to delivering this message to this head of a notorious Chinatown crime syndicate, a man who already had plenty of reason, from his insular point of view, to dislike Socrates.

Socrates stooped inside the entrance door and picked up the morning's mail from the floor, turned on the lights and air conditioning, and had just draped his sports jacket over the back of a chair when Bing-fa, standing close behind him, said, "You are wasting precious time, Socrates Cheng. I am ready to speak to you."

Socrates turned toward Bing-fa and said, "Give me a few minutes, then we'll talk." As he turned back toward the pile of mail, Socrates thought, *I need a few minutes to jack up my resolve to tell you what I'm gonna tell you.*

Bing-fa glared briefly at Socrates, then turned away and walked across the showroom, over to five framed historic documents hanging on the far wall. He read through them, then walked the perimeter of the store, ignoring the classic pens on display, but stopping from time-to-time to examine other hanging historic documents.

Socrates looked up from the pile of mail he'd been reading and briefly eyeballed Bing-fa as the old man shuffled along the perimeter of the walls.

Bing-fa suddenly turned toward Socrates as if he realized Socrates was watching him.

"You are interested in the Middle Kingdom's treasured documents, Mr. Cheng?" Bing-fa said.

Socrates nodded from behind the display counter. "I was. Not so much anymore. I collected Shanghai commercial instruments when I was in law school."

Socrates swept the room with a lateral toss of his arm. "The ones over there," he said, canting his head toward a row of documents hanging along another wall, "were brought to this country by my grandfather when he and my paternal grandmother emigrated from Shanghai."

"You read Shanghainese?" Bing-fa asked.

"I used to when I was in college, but I've been away from it too long. I still can read Shanghainese with the help of a dictionary, but only good enough to get the gist of it, not good enough to understand every word or nuance."

"You speak Shanghainese then?"

"No. Never did," Socrates said.

"And other dialects?" Bing-fa asked. "Do you speak or read inferior Cantonese or exalted Mandarin?"

"Mandarin, is all," Socrates said. "I studied it in college as part of my course major. I still read it fairly well, but I don't write or speak it anymore."

"These documents," Bing-fa said, indicating with his hand those hanging on the wall behind him, then turning and nodding at the others hanging on two other walls, "why are they out in the open exposed to the light? Such treasures should be carefully rolled-up and stored in the dark until it is time to examine them."

Socrates ignored Bing-fa's words and instead responded

to his implied subtext: *What's a barbarian like you, who does not properly take care of them, doing with these examples of our national patrimony?*

"I used to be interested in nineteenth century commercial trading documents," Socrates said. "My grandfather Cheng, like his father and grandfather before him, was the Comprador for the Taipan of the trading house Jardine, Matheson & Company."

Collecting these was my way of connecting with the one grandfather I knew and loved, and with the Chinese half of my ancestry. Socrates decided not to share this private thought with Bing-fa who, he assumed, would somehow turn it to his own advantage against him.

Socrates studied Bing-fa's face for his reaction to Socrates' revelation about his grandfather's exalted role in British occupied Shanghai, but saw nothing that would suggest awe or admiration, or even approval. He saw no reaction at all.

Socrates continued. "I collected Shanghai documents as a hobby and planned to buy and sell them as a second source of income while I practiced law." He paused and reflected momentarily on that aspect of his life. "It didn't quite work out the way I expected," he said.

Bing-fa moved his arms farther up into his wide silk sleeves, and nodded.

"I didn't have enough capital or a sufficient line of credit to buy high quality collections or to acquire individual rare documents at auction so I couldn't compete with established dealers for wealthy collectors. I eventually accepted this fact of life and gave up." He straightened the bills into a neat pile, put the stack into a drawer, and walked across the showroom to Bing-fa.

"I'm selling off my small collection. That's what's up on the walls. When they're gone, I'm done with historic documents for good," Socrates said, as if to conclude the subject once and for all.

Bing-fa nodded and stepped closer to Socrates. "I will acquire all you have," Bing-fa said, "providing your prices are reasonable."

Socrates could not believe his good luck. He'd never expected to sell more than one or two of the remaining documents, if even that many. He assumed he would be stuck owning most of them for years.

"Are you a collector, Master Li?" Socrates asked, suddenly warming to Bing-fa's presence in his store.

"No. I am a patriot. I will return these stolen treasures to their rightful place, to China. The looting of our cultural heritage by foreigners will no longer be tolerated."

Socrates felt as if he'd just been slapped. He took a deep breath and thought, *Time to deliver the bad news.*

"We have other things to talk about, Bing-fa. Let's get to it."

Chapter 5

JADE LI CLOSED the door behind Bing-enlai, called Youngest Brother in the family, as he left her condo apartment. She was grateful Younger Brother had visited her, but was concerned that their father, who had eyes everywhere, might find out. She returned to the living room to await the arrival of their Eldest Brother, named Bing-wu, who also would now secretly visit her. He had called that morning and said he must speak with her about an urgent family matter. Neither Bing-enlai nor Bing-wu would ever learn from Jade that the other had visited her in defiance of their father's edict prohibiting all contact with her.

As Jade awaited Eldest Brother's arrival, she set aside the exhibit catalog Youngest Brother had brought her, and unrolled its companion poster.

Three Prosperities China Arts Gallery

presents

A SELECTION OF ART, CULTURE AND HISTORIC TREASURES FROM THE SECRET ARCHIVES OF CHAIRMAN MAO

featuring

THE PARKER DOUFOLD "MANDARIN YELLOW" FOUNTAIN PEN

Together with:

Imperial Porcelain Ware
Blue & White Export Ceramics
Painting & Calligraphy Scrolls
Historic Documents
Bronze Vessels
Carved Jade

2178 Prospect Avenue, NW | Georgetown, DC | 202.337.2000

A sharp knock at the door interrupted her. Jade quickly rolled the poster into a cylinder shape and placed it and the catalog in a drawer where they would not be seen by Eldest Brother. She had no desire to explain how she'd obtained them.

JADE SAT AT the kitchen table and moved her eyes from left to right and back again, in an endless loop, as she watched Eldest Brother quickly pace the width of the room. She pushed away the cup of tepid green tea she'd poured twenty minutes earlier, but hadn't touched.

Eldest Brother punctuated his pacing by stabbing the air with a folded copy of the *Washington Post* he held in one hand.

"Our father is despondent," Eldest Brother said, speaking in Mandarin. "This writing" — he jabbed the newspaper with his finger — "has caused him to lose face. He has been dishonored. We are all dishonored."

Ah, yes, Jade thought, *ineffable honor. So difficult to obtain, so easy to lose.* Jade did not give voice to her heretical thoughts. Instead, she nodded her assent.

Bing-wu's bellicose rants no longer frightened Jade, although they had frightened her when she was a child. Frequent exposure had hardened her against Eldest Brother's melodramatic outbursts when it came to matters of Li family honor and concern, real or imagined.

Eldest Brother stopped pacing and cast the folded newspaper across the table at Jade, brushing her cup but not knocking it over.

"Take this, Little Sister. Read it now. You will see."

Jade unfolded the paper and skimmed the first part of the article:

The Washington Post

BURGLARY AT LOCAL ART GALLERY
OPENING OF CHINA TREASURES EXHIBIT
POSTPONED

WASHINGTON, DC
By Washington Post Staff Writer, Jonathon Chow

The much-anticipated exhibit, "A Selection of Art, Cultural and Historis Treasures from the Secret Archives of Chairman Mao," jointly curated by the Honorable Li Bing-fa and the Embassy of the People's Republic of China, originally scheduled to open this week at the THREE PROSPERITIES CHINA ART GALLERY in Georgetown, has been postponed for approximately three weeks because of a burglary at the gallery. Thieves entered the premises sometime early Saturday morning.

Jade set the *Post* aside. "Surely father knows no one thinks the burglary and the exhibit's postponed opening were his fault." She regretted her words almost as soon as she said them. She had just struck a match under her combustible sibling.

Eldest Brother slammed his fist into his other palm. "Fault is not relevant," he said. "It is a matter of personal honor, a matter of our family's honor." He pointed his finger at Jade. "You should already know that, Little Sister."

Jade considered this, briefly thought about how silly Confucian views of honor were, and then unfolded the newspaper and turned back to the article.

Ms. Iris Hua, the director of the gallery, told this reporter that most of the stolen objects had been kept in Chairman Mao's secret archives and have never before been seen by the public. This exhibit was to have been their debut.

Pressed by this reporter for more comment, Ms. Hua talked about one specific rare historic item the thieves stole. This was the Parker Pen Company's Duofold fountain pen known as the "Mandarin Yellow." This pen, she said, had been designed and manufactured by George S. Parker for Chiang Kai-shek, and presented to him in 1927 after Parker returned to the United States from an extended trip to Asia.

Discussing the romantic, cultural and historic significance of the Mandarin Yellow pen, Ms. Hua said that upon his return to the United States from China, Parker caused his company to manufacture a limited quantity of Mandarin Yellows. Parker then returned to China and presented the first pen off the production line (stamped in gold, "No.1") to Chiang Kai-shek. This Mandarin Yellow was inscribed on its barrel. "To Generalissimo Chiang Kai-shek, savior of all freedom loving people in China."

An historic fountain pen, Jade thought. *I should tell Socrates. He would want to know about it.* She made a mental note to mention it to him, then resumed reading.

This Mandarin Yellow eventually found its way into the hands of the People's Republic when, in December 1936, a warlord kidnapped Chiang Kai-shek, ostensibly because Chiang had bankrupted China with his personal greed and corrupt economic policies, and was wasting his army's limited resources fighting Mao Tsetung's Communists instead of fighting the invading Japanese.

The warlord confiscated the Mandarin Yellow and Chiang's other possessions, and delivered them to Chairman Mao. He also delivered Chiang himself to Mao to be executed. Ms. Hua stated that Mao's financial backer — Premier Stalin — and the financier, T.V. Soong, and Soong's sister, Madam Chiang Kai-shek, all interceded on Chiang's behalf and prevented Mao from executing him.

In January, 1937, as part of the agreement for Chiang's release by Mao, T.V. Soong and his sister brokered a temporary truce between Mao and Chiang. The terms of the truce were reduced to writing in a document known to history as the Xi'an Agreement. Under its terms, Chiang and Mao each acquired a geographical sphere of influence which the other agreed to respect. The two enemies also agreed that they would cease their combat against one another and join forces to fight against the Japanese. The original Xi'an Agreement was among the historic treasures stolen by the burglars from the Georgetown gallery.

Jade skimmed the balance of the article, then refolded the newspaper and put it aside.

She looked up at Bing-wu, briefly hesitated, then said, "Eldest Brother, please use your exalted position and your prestige within our family, and talk to our father for me."

She lowered her head politely, offering respect and supplication to her older brother, and joined her hands together, interlacing her fingers on the table in front of her.

"I do not want to remain a pariah, exiled from my brothers and father I love so dearly."

Eldest Brother frowned and squeezed his hands into fists. "I will not speak of this matter to our father, Little Sister. Not until you cease ignoring our traditions and obey our father's command to rid yourself of your barbarian. Immediately end all contact with your *low faan* or continue to suffer the consequences of your actions."

Chapter 6

SOCRATES AND BING-FA settled into Queen Anne style wingback chairs located in a corner of Socrates' store farthest from the entrance. They sat so close facing one another, their knees almost touched. Bing-fa's sons watched them from across the showroom.

Socrates opened his mouth to speak, but Bing-fa raised his palm and stopped him. "You are wasting too much precious time pretending you must make some decision about fulfilling your obligation to your heritage," he said. "This is not discretionary."

Socrates' stomach tightened. He could feel his neck and face grow hot. He forced himself to breathe slowly and to hold his tongue. He didn't want to say something he might later regret if Jade learned about it. He crossed his legs, then immediately uncrossed them.

Bing-fa's clever, he thought. *He's using a classic bullying technique of persuasion, forcing the other person on the defensive by assuming the result the bully wanted, then aggressively pursuing that result as if it had already been agreed to, forcing the other person to bid against himself.*

Socrates weighed his next words carefully. Although he didn't want to be pulled into the investigation by dint of Bing-fa's aggressive attitude or because Bing-fa blatantly assumed

Socrates would help him, he also was mindful that he did want Bing-fa to accept him one day as Jade's lover and partner. He decided to buy some time.

"Explain what you have in mind," he said.

Bing-fa frowned and stared at Socrates for a few seconds.

"I expect you to use your knowledge of our customs to discreetly locate and retrieve the Mandarin Yellow writing instrument and the other stolen treasures. You will be well rewarded if you succeed in returning the treasures in time to include them in the rescheduled opening of the Embassy's glorious cultural exhibit."

"Why me?" Socrates said. "Why not the police? They're the professionals. If the cops aren't pursuing this, there must be a reason. What makes you think I can do any better?"

"We require your expertise with writing instruments," Bing-fa said, "to verify that the Mandarin Yellow you recover is our national treasure, not some substitute." He tapped his foot rapidly under his silk gown. "Now that I also am aware of your Mandarin language skills, you also will be useful in verifying the authenticity of the stolen documents when you have recovered them."

Socrates shook his head. *Time to bite the bullet before this goes too far, tell him my decision.*

"This isn't realistic," Socrates said. "I'm not a detective. You're asking me to do something totally outside my experience. I wouldn't know where to begin, let alone how to proceed." He shook his head again. "You'll have to find someone else to do your bidding."

Socrates stood up from his chair and walked to the other side of the store. He briefly faced the wall, his back deliberately to Bing-fa. Then he slowly turned around and, from the safety of his distance, folded his arms across his chest and waited.

Bing-fa rose from his seat and locked eyes with Socrates from across the room.

"People who assist me when I ask never regret it," Bing-fa said.

And, Socrates thought, *I'll bet people who don't assist you when asked, always regret it.*

———

SOCRATES DID NOT react well to threats. Not to those that were explicit and obvious, and not to those that were subtle and implicit. When confronted with a threat, Socrates typically shut down and emotionally *circled the wagon*s. But not this time. He and Jade had too much at stake. Socrates did not have the luxury now of pulling his head deep into the solid protection of his shell and waiting in the dark until the source of the threat left him.

Socrates faced Bing-fa from across the room, cleared his throat, and said, "You don't need me for the investigation. Have someone else find the Mandarin Yellow, then bring it to me to examine."

Without warning, Bing-fa crossed the room. He stopped less than one foot from Socrates, facing him. When Bing-fa spoke now, he spoke so softly that Socrates felt threatened by the simulated gentleness of Bing-fa's modulated tone.

"The country of your father and ancestors calls on you in its time of need, Socrates Cheng." He looked hard at Socrates. "We expect more from you than you have given. I warn you, do not make a decision you will later regret."

Socrates tensed. Anger slowly wormed its way into his spine. Beads of perspiration formed on his neck.

"You have a responsibility to your heritage," Bing-fa said. He kept his eyes fixed on Socrates' eyes.

Socrates shook his head. "China's not my heritage," he said. "I told you before, I'm American, and as much Greek as Chinese."

The irony of Bing-fa's position wasn't lost on Socrates. He was imploring Socrates to search for the Mandarin Yellow as his obligatory service to his Chinese heritage, the implication being that *for this purpose,* Bing-fa viewed Socrates as Chinese. Socrates decided not to point out Bing-fa's self-serving contradiction.

Socrates walked back to the Queen Anne chair, and lowered himself into it. He waited until Bing-fa had done the same and again faced him.

Socrates slowly shook his head. "The more I think about it," he said, "the more I realize I shouldn't become involved at all, not even as a consultant after the Mandarin Yellow is found."

Bing-fa sat impassively, his fingers interlaced on his lap. He stared silently at Socrates as if there was no more to be said.

It seemed to Socrates that Bing-fa now was mocking him with his silence, amusing himself by letting Socrates prattle on, making Socrates feel he was arguing more with himself than with Bing-fa. Bidding against himself.

"Now you listen to me, Bing-fa." Socrates, too, now spoke softly as he carefully formulated his statement. "Even if you ignore all the other reasons I've given you, I still have to run my store. I can't just shut it down. I have bills to pay."

"My eldest son, Bing-wu, will attend to this business while you are absent."

"Oh, really?" Socrates said, allowing his sarcastic tone to hang in the air. "What's he know about vintage fountain pens?"

"You seem to have no customers," Bing-fa said. He turned his head and glanced around the store, then turned back to face Socrates. "Bing-wu's lack of knowledge concerning writing instruments should not matter over several weeks."

"Cute," Socrates said, but he didn't smile. "Consider this then. I'm not licensed as a private investigator. That means I can't be paid for my efforts, and I'm not about to give up my time at the store for free."

Socrates mentally rested his case on that legal and practical note, and stopped speaking. He'd said all he could think of for now. He had almost convinced himself.

After a long thirty seconds of silence, Bing-fa said, "I understand your concern. If you assist me, I am prepared to arrange for a gift to you sufficient to justify your time away from your business."

Socrates frowned, bothered that Bing-fa obviously wasn't listening to him. "I just told you, I'm not licensed. I can't accept compensation, no matter what name you give it."

"We would structure our arrangement to conform with your concerns," Bing-fa said. "You will perform your services for me, free of charge, as a concerned citizen who wants to foster goodwill between the people of the United States and the citizens of the People's Republic of China. Afterward, a grateful People's Republic government will give you a gift to show its appreciation for your efforts. Surely, a gift from the country of your heritage would be acceptable, would it not?"

Socrates had had enough. He was frustrated by Bing-fa's intransigence. He held up both palms and said, "Hold it. That's enough. You're moving too fast and not listening to me."

Socrates abruptly stood up, then immediately sat again. He took a deep breath, held it briefly, then exhaled. He realized he'd lost all control of the discussion.

"Here's the deal, Bing-fa," Socrates said. "I need time to think about this. I'll give you my answer tomorrow. That's all I'll do right now. Take it or leave it."

Bing-fa, obviously unhappy with the added day's delay, frowned, then recovered his composure and stood up from his chair. He bowed slightly from his waist and said as he straightened up, "Do not delay beyond tomorrow, Socrates Cheng. Too much time has already been lost while you avoid your duty."

Socrates said no more. He wanted Bing-fa gone from his store.

Bing-fa started for the door, then abruptly stopped and turned back to face Socrates.

"I suggest you consult with Bing-jade," he said. "She will guide you correctly."

Then he left the store without any explanation.

Chapter 7

BING-FA'S PARTING REMARK shocked Socrates.

What could he have been thinking? Socrates wondered. *Consult with Jade? The daughter whose very existence Bing-fa denied? The daughter he had banished from her family because she insisted on dating Socrates?*

Socrates dialed Jade's cell number and let it ring five times before he ended the call. He wanted to talk to her, but it would have to wait since she wasn't picking up her calls. In the meantime, he had something else to attend to. His parents were arriving in town for a week's visit. He had to leave to pick them up at the airport.

Thirty minutes later, Socrates stood by the open trunk of his rental car and watched his mother and father maneuver their aging bodies into the front and back passenger seats, his mother in the front, as usual, and his father in the back.

Socrates smiled and turned his attention to their luggage. He lowered himself into a weightlifter's squat and wrapped his arms around their only suitcase. He closed his eyes and visualized himself as a four hundred pound Japanese Sumo wrestler, naked except for a loincloth. He took a deep breath, held it briefly, and, with a prodigious grunt, wrestled the suitcase up from the macadam and dropped it into the trunk, rocking the car from side-to-side.

Socrates climbed into the driver's seat of the rental, keyed the ignition, and checked to see that his parents were belted in before he drove off. Satisfied, he started the twenty-five minutes drive from Ronald Reagan National Airport in Arlington, Virginia to his parents' hotel, the Westin Grand, on M Street in the District, not far from his Dupont Circle condominium apartment.

"So," his mother said, "when did you buy this tiny car? And what's with the writing on the side? I liked your other car. It seemed fine to me."

"It's a rental, Mom, called a ZIPCAR. I rented it for a few hours so I could pick up you and dad. I sold my car a while ago. I didn't use it often enough, living in the city, to justify the cost and trouble of owning it."

His mother shook her head and made a *tsk, tsk, tsk* sound. "You should've stayed a lawyer, Socrates, so you could afford to keep your other car," she said, "even if you didn't use it much. It was better for grownups than this little thing."

Socrates decided to ignore this hot-button topic his mother had skillfully cast at him — his past foray into law practice. He changed the subject.

"I'd really feel better if you and pop would stay with me," he said. "It's silly for you to go to a hotel. You know I have plenty of room for you at my condo."

"It's better this way," his mother said. "You have your privacy and we have ours." She turned toward the back seat, looked at her husband, and raised one eyebrow.

His father shrugged and chuckled. When he caught Socrates watching him in the rear view mirror, he stopped laughing, turned his head and looked out the window.

I wonder what that's all about? Socrates thought.

"Anyway," his mother said, "you really need your privacy now that you're back seeing your cute Chinese girlfriend from college. Tell me her name again?"

"Jade, Mom, Li Bing-jade." *Why do I always feel guilty when they insist on staying at a hotel? It's obviously what they prefer.* "She wanted to come with me to pick you up, but she had a class to teach."

"I'm more comfortable at a hotel, Sonny," his father said.

"I can walk around in my underwear if I want and not scare your neighbors if they see me through your window."

"Your father's more comfortable, all right," Socrates' mother said, "because he doesn't want anybody hearing him snore like a train coming through a tunnel. Anybody but me, he doesn't."

She turned her head and briefly looked back at her husband. She punctuated her statement with a single, sharp nod directed at him.

"You'd think he'd do something about it, his snoring, with me begging for relief all these years. But, no, your father doesn't think he has a snoring problem."

"I don't have no snoring problem, Sophia. You have the snoring problem because you say it keeps you awake. I don't hear me. I don't even know if I really snore. I only know you tell me I do. Me, I sleep like a baby." He grinned, his Chinese eyes narrowing even more than usual.

No one said anything for the next five minutes. They drove north from Virginia along the George Washington Parkway, heading toward downtown Washington. The trees lining the parkway were beginning to sprout light green buds, infusing the late April afternoon with the soft ambiance of a French Impressionist landscape painting.

"You're both awfully quiet," Socrates said. "Is there something wrong? Something you want to tell me?" The anomalous silence unsettled him. His parents rarely were quiet when they had a captive audience. Especially when he was that audience.

"Everything's fine," his mother said. "We're tired from our trip, that's all."

Socrates glanced in the rear view mirror at his father, saw him look at his wife, shrug his shoulders, and quickly shake his head *No*.

"Is there something I should know?" Socrates asked again.

"No, not yet," his mother said. "We'll talk later. You and your father will."

They continued their journey, shrouded in silence until they were a few blocks from the hotel. Then Socrates' mother said, "So, Socrates, tell me, your pencil and pen store, it's better for you than being a lawyer? You don't mind not having your car anymore or dressing up for work or being important?"

Oh, boy, here we go, Socrates thought. *I came so close to dropping them off and making my escape without rehashing this.*

"Not pencils, Mom, and not ballpoint pens either. I sell collectible vintage fountain pens. Valuable pens. Expensive fountain pens. But you already know that."

"So I forgot, Socrates. So sue me, Mr. Big Shot Lawyer. Oh, excuse me. I mean, so sue me, Mr. Big Shot *ex*-Lawyer."

Socrates sighed. "The store's fine, Mom. Getting better every day. I'm happier doing this than I ever was practicing law. How many people do you know lucky enough to turn their hobby into their business?"

"I didn't like the way those lawyers treated you," his mother said, "but at least you made good money. It bothered your father, too, right, Phillip?" she said, as she turned toward the back of the car.

Socrates let the comment pass, but he could feel his sleeping anger toward his former law partners creeping back at the mention of his previous work life.

"So, Sonny," his father, always the Confucian conciliator, said, "your mother and me, we liked that Jade girl when we met her at your college." He paused as if collecting his thoughts. "You going out with her again after all those years apart, is that a good thing for you? Does she make you happy?"

Grateful his father had changed the subject, Socrates said, "Yes, Pop, dating Jade again is good for me. She makes me very happy."

"You should think about marrying her then, settle down," his mother said, "give us grandbabies to spoil."

Socrates raised an eyebrow. *So that's it. They must have been talking during their flight about marrying me off and couldn't wait to raise the subject with me.* Socrates didn't take the bait. He said nothing.

"Just think about it," his mother said, "that's all we ask. It's your life. You can do what you want, but it won't kill you to think about it, will it?"

Socrates did just that. He briefly thought about it, then quickly dismissed the thought as impractical and premature, and wisely said nothing. When enough dead air time had passed to make it clear he would not take his mother's bait and defend himself, Socrates' father broke the silence and said, "You know, Sonny, your mother liked that Jade girl even though she's not Greek." He paused and smiled. "Can you imagine that, your mother liking a girl for you who's not . . . ."

He interrupted himself to laugh and didn't finish his statement. He reached over the front seat and affectionately patted his wife's shoulder. She turned partly around to face him. "You can tease me all you want, Mr. Phillip Cheng, but being Greek's a great blessing. You should only be so blessed."

"Unless you're Chinese, born of the illustrious Middle Kingdom," Socrates' father responded, a wide grin on his face. "That's a greater blessing."

Socrates' mother turned in her seat again to face her husband. "Phillip Cheng," she said, casting a faux Evil Eye at him, "if you keep cracking wise, this Pythian daughter, this descendent of the Oracle at Delphi, predicts there will be unpleasant things in store for you when we return home."

When his father feigned fright and raised his palms to shield himself and ward off his wife's Delphic warning, first Socrates' mother, then his father, and, finally, Socrates, too, broke into large smiles, followed by much shared laughter.

Socrates dropped his parents at the Westin Grand and stayed with them while they registered and settled themselves in their room. Then he returned the rental car. He was walking back from the ZIPCAR agency at Dupont Circle, heading to Georgetown to his store when his cell phone rang. He looked at the digital readout to identify the caller.

"Hi, Mom. Longtime no see." He paused to let his mother tell him why she was calling him so soon after they'd just parted, but she said nothing.

"Did you forget something in the car?" Socrates asked. "I can walk back to the rental agency and . . . ."

"Socrates, did you notice anything unusual about your father?"

Socrates stopped walking. "What do you mean *unusual*? He seemed the same to me, basically quiet and reserved, like always. Why?"

"Your father's taking a shower right now so I don't have much time to talk. It's his memory. He's forgetting things and getting confused doing things he used to do easy."

"I didn't notice it when we were riding, Mom." Socrates could feel his stomach roil. He didn't like where this might be going.

"He seemed just the same to me," Socrates said. "How bad is it? Should I be worried?"

"It's bad. A little worse each week," his mother said. "And I feel awful because your father gets so hurt when I remind him we just talked about something he's already forgotten. Like I was making it up to pick on him . . . . I don't know what to do."

Chapter 8

THREE HOURS AFTER she weathered her regular morning dressing down by Director Hua, Linda Fong stood alone in front of her desk with her back to the alcove's entrance. She held a telephone handset against her right ear and quietly spoke into the mouthpiece. With her left hand, she tapped an impatient, rapid drum roll against her desktop blotter using the point of a No. 2 wooden pencil. Fong did not hear Director Hua enter the alcove behind her and quietly sit down at her desk to watch and listen to the assistant director.

"I'm saying it is possible, that is all," Linda Fong said, speaking in Mandarin, "but we must make our own opportunities. Yes, I know. I will be patient, but only for so long. That, too, will one day come to an end. Yes, I know. Thank you for reminding me."

Fong placed the handset back in its cradle on her desk, ending the call. She turned around, saw Director Hua frowning at her, and stiffened and blushed. She realized the director had likely heard the ending of the conversation, if not more.

"Oh, Honorable Director," Fong said, "I did not realize you were here. I am so sorry." Fong bowed her head and maintained her submissive posture.

"I know you do not approve of personal telephone calls at work, but this conversation could not be avoided. It will not happen again, Honorable Director, I assure you."

Fong raised her head, but avoided making eye contact with Hua. She immediately excused herself and began walking toward the gallery's entrance door, saying, as she resolutely fled, that she had a lunch appointment to keep.

Fong hurried away before Director Hua could tell her to cancel the appointment or before the director could engage her in a lecture intended to advise her just how unworthy an employee she was.

Chapter 9

SOCRATES WAS IN the stockroom rearranging supplies and killing time when he heard the entrance door's overhead bell. He put down the carton of empty pen boxes he was shelving and headed out front.

"Hello, Socrates."

Socrates stopped walking, put his hands into his trouser pockets, and said, "Hello, Todd. What brings you here?"

"I came to apologize. I hope you don't mind I didn't call first. I figured you might tell me to go to Hell and end the call before I could say anything."

You got that right, Socrates thought, but he didn't say it. He watched Todd with wary eyes.

"I know I should've done this sooner," Todd said, "but . . . well, I needed to let some time pass. Anyway, I'm here now. How've you been?"

"I didn't deserve what you all did to me," Socrates said. "We were all supposed to be friends, not just law partners."

Todd glanced briefly at his feet, then looked up and nodded. "You're right. I was a shit, I know that. We all were." He paused and wagged his head. "We'd like to make it up to you." He smiled feebly and raised both eyebrows.

Socrates could feel his anger bubbling up again. He had worked long and hard to paste over his hurt feelings and resentment, and now, with no more than his sudden appearance at the store, Todd had ripped away Socrates' protective scab.

"Don't bother," Socrates said. "I don't need you to make up anything for me. I'm doing fine without you and your partners."

Todd took a deep breath. "You were right to vote against the merger. It was a colossal mistake, just like you said it would be. Turns out we were no different than high-paid employees working at the beck and call of the New York attorneys, sometimes even their secretaries and first year law associates. So much for being partners in the combined firm."

Socrates slowly breathed in and savored the redolence of this sweet admission. He strained not to smile.

"We're pulling out," Todd said, "the four of us. We're taking six associates, some paralegals, a few secretaries, and setting up our own firm in a few weeks."

"Why tell me?" Socrates said. "I assume you're not here to watch me gloat."

"We'd like you to join us, work with us again as our partner, and get back into law practice, not do this." He canted his head toward the display case.

Socrates rubbed his chin and shook his head. "I don't think so. I've got a new life now." He swept his arm to corral his store. "Law practice is a closed chapter for me. I intend it to stay that way."

"That's what we thought you'd say," Todd said, "but I had to ask." Todd reached into his suit jacket pocket and fished out a business card. "If you change your mind, call me. That's the contact information for the new firm."

Socrates took the card and pocketed it. He never glanced at it.

Chapter 10

AS SOON AS Todd left, Socrates tried Jade's cell phone again. She still didn't answer. He didn't know which annoyed him more, that Jade almost never kept her cell phone turned on or that she almost never picked-up her voice mail messages.

He decided to call his friend, Brandon Hill, and talk over Bing-fa's demand with him. Socrates trusted Brandon's judgment and his pragmatic approach to issues. Socrates punched Brandon's speed dial number into his cell phone.

They agreed to meet as soon as Socrates could walk from Georgetown to Dupont Circle.

AS HE WALKED along M Street, heading from Georgetown to Starbucks on 19th, Socrates thought about his long-enduring friendship with Brandon.

They had met at Penn State, had roomed together for four years, and in that time forged a close friendship. Yet when they first met, had either of them been asked, Socrates and Brandon would have admitted there could not have been two college roommates who, having been randomly thrown together by the university's housing assignment computer, would have been less likely to become friends than Socrates, the Greek/Chinese American from a Levittown, Long Island blue collar background, and W. Brandon Trowbridge Hill, IV,

the white-shoe, Anglo-Saxon Protestant from Mainline Philadelphia, with his heritage deeply steeped in colonial America
and his vast wealth rooted in generations of old money.

To the casual eye, Socrates and Brandon were polar op-
posites in every discernible aspect, yet they gradually became
the Yin and Yang of college roommates, each seemingly different from the other, but each also seamlessly complementing
the other.

Brandon had straight blond hair, fair skin, large blue
eyes, thin lips, and a flawless, chiseled straight nose. Socrates
sported curly pitch-black hair, slitted dark eyes, jaundice-like
skin, full lips, and a broad, slightly hooked nose. All they had
in common physically was their height. Both Brandon and
Socrates stood 5'10" tall. Yet, as it turned out, both Socrates
and Brandon were comfortable in their respective skins.

Brandon was already seated at Starbucks when Socrates
arrived.

"Good day, Brother Hill," Socrates said, as he walked
across the outdoor patio to Brandon's table.

Brandon smiled and nodded. "You look uncommonly serious today, my friend, even for you. Had an argument with
what's-her-name? Or was it something else equally trivial?"

Socrates let Brandon's dig pass. He had more important
things on his mind right now than Brandon's and Jade's long-
standing antipathy for one another.

"I need to make a decision," Socrates said, "and I'd like
your input."

"Sit, then," Brandon said, gesturing toward an empty
chair. "The doctor is in."

Socrates described the visits from Bing-fa. Then he recited all the reasons why he thought he should not help Jade's
father, focusing more on his reluctance to temporarily close
down his store than on his inexperience as a private investigator. When he finished, he hadn't mentioned even one reason
why he should help Bing-fa.

When Brandon responded by saying, "Okay, with all
those reasons not to help him, don't help him," Socrates immediately switched gears. Now he recited his short list of reasons
why he thought he should help Bing-fa, emphasizing the most
important to him — his desire to ingratiate himself with Jade's

father and have Bing-fa accept him as Jade's lover even though he was not full-blooded Chinese.

When he finished, and Brandon said nothing, Socrates said, "So, what do you think?"

Brandon lifted his cup of tea, sipped it, then looked at Socrates. "What did Jade say when you asked her?"

Socrates blushed. "I haven't asked her yet. I wanted to get my own thinking straight before I raised it with her. That's why I'm here."

Brandon nodded. "You need to consider this in its proper context," he said. "How much do you care about Jade?"

"I love her. You know that. Why even ask?"

"That's my point," Brandon said. "Jade's the correct context. Talk to her. Otherwise you'll be saying she's not that important to you even if that's not what you mean. Then help her father if she wants you to or, if she doesn't want you to, don't help him. Take your cue from Jade and act accordingly."

Socrates looked away as he considered another obstacle he'd have to overcome. "It's not that simple. I'm not licensed as a PI."

"Christ, Socrates, so what? Who will ever know? Unlicensed people probably investigate things all the time. There must be some loophole in the licensing law you can use." He paused and shook his head. "You were a lawyer, figure it out."

Brandon paused, waiting for a response that didn't come. Then he said, "If you can't find a loophole, what's the worst can happen if you're caught? Probably a slap on the wrist, is all."

"What about my store? I can't just close it up. It's finally beginning to pay for itself."

Brandon shook his head and frowned as if he was growing impatient with Socrates' excuses. "I'll watch it for you. I can fake pen talk enough to keep from driving away customers. Besides, everything you have for sale is tagged with prices, so how hard can it be to be a sales clerk?"

Socrates groaned, bringing a big smile to Brandon's face.

"I don't know anything about investigating crimes," Socrates said. "This is serious, not one of our college games. A felony was committed, a burglary."

Brandon shook his head again. "Stop making excuses and

looking for reasons not to do it, Socrates. Just use your common sense and try to remember what you learned from all those *Law & Order* reruns we watched. Most important, don't get in the cops' way." He paused, and when Socrates didn't say anything, Brandon said, "What it all comes down to is, you have to decide how important your relationship with Jade is. That's really all we're talking about here."

AS SOCRATES WALKED back to his store after leaving Brandon, he used his cell phone again to call Jade. He not only wanted to talk to her about her father's insistence that Socrates help him, but he was anxious to tell her about Bing-fa's cryptic remark as he left Socrates' store. Once again, he didn't get her.

Socrates passed the balance of the afternoon at his store paying bills, re-shelving inventory and supplies, and waiting on three customers, one of whom bought a pricey Pelikan pen, *cir. 1942*, as an anniversary gift for her husband, and the other who purchased an expensive nineteenth century desktop crystal inkwell. The third customer, an elderly man, did not purchase anything, but he asked Socrates many questions about fountain pens and their collectability. Socrates enjoyed answering the man's questions and showing him examples of collectible pens, as much as he had enjoyed the two sales he made.

At 5:00 p.m., Socrates closed his store and walked home.

As he approached his building, Socrates paused on the sidewalk and thought briefly about his lack of plans for the evening. He decided to continue walking and go to Jade's condominium at 3400 Connecticut Avenue, just north of the National Zoo. He hoped she'd be home by the time he arrived there. If she wasn't, he'd use his key and wait inside for her.

Fifteen minutes later, Socrates took his key ring from his packet and knocked on Jade's door to make sure she wasn't home before he let himself in.

Jade opened the door almost immediately as if she'd been waiting for him. She glared at Socrates and said, "How dare you meet with my father without checking with me first. Who do you think you are going behind my back?"

Chapter 11

SOCRATES RECOILED IN response to Jade's hostility, and reflexively stepped back. He felt as if he'd been slapped. He managed a nervous smile, followed immediately by a frown. He hesitated, then moved in again toward the doorway and leaned in to kiss Jade's cheek. She pulled away.

"Wait a minute," Socrates said, his anger rising. "What's going on here? I haven't done anything to justify this."

"I asked you something, Socrates." Jade stretched her arms out horizontally and gripped the door frames on each side of the threshold, blocking Socrates' access.

"Why didn't you check with me before you met with my father? You know what's going on with him and me."

Socrates sighed and shook his head. He tried to view Jade's unexpected response in perspective. She was, after all, living with the continued stress of having been banished from her family by her father.

Socrates softened his voice. "I'll tell you why, Jade," he said, "but before I do, you need to let me come in, then we'll talk? Not out here."

Jade hesitated, then stepped aside, and then followed Socrates into the living room.

"Not here," she said. She walked through the living room

to the kitchen, and lowered herself onto a chair at the breakfast table. Socrates took the chair across from her.

Jade wiped her eyes with a tissue. "You know my father and I don't speak because of you. What did you think you were doing meeting with him without talking to me first?"

"Look, Jade," Socrates said, his hurt feelings and tamped-down anger bubbling up again and blending so they now were indistinguishable to him, "let's get one thing straight. It wasn't what you think. Start by accepting that much." He worked at keeping his tone soft, and waited until she nodded.

"I know everything with your family and us is hard on you, but you need to give me the benefit of the doubt and trust me, not assume the worst." He reached over and stroked her cheek with his finger. "I didn't go behind your back. I wouldn't do that. I didn't even initiate anything with your father. He came to me. I had no idea he was going to show up at my store."

Socrates watched Jade's eyes mist over. He took her hand. "You know me better than that, Jade. I wouldn't do anything to hurt you, especially not anything involving your family."

He watched as Jade's overt emotions ineluctably changed as she gradually let go of her anger and slipped into a state of bewilderment. Her face softened and her natural color replaced its previous flush. Her posture loosened and her normally narrowed eyes widened as she waited for Socrates' explanation. She offered him a weak smile.

"First off," Socrates said, "I called you several times to tell you, but I couldn't get hold of you." He opened his cell phone to the DIALED menu and reached out to hand the cell to Jade so she could see the listing of his dialed, but unconnected, call attempts. She didn't take the cell from him to look at.

"I know you wouldn't set up the meeting with my father," Jade said, "but once he was there, why'd you meet with him? You should have refused. You should have known I'd be upset."

"It wasn't that simple, Jade. I had no choice, it just happened. He showed up at my store and we spoke. What was I supposed to do, throw him and your brothers out?" He paused to take a deep breath, then said, "That's why I'm here, to tell you about it . . . . By the way, how'd you find out?"

"Youngest Brother left me a voice mail, but it was vague. He said he finally saw my barbarian when he went with our father and brothers to a meeting at your store. Then he hung up." She sighed. "What's going on, Socrates?"

Before he could respond, Jade said, "Did my father threaten you, tell you to stay away from me or something?" She didn't wait for Socrates' answer. "He had no right to do that or . . . ." She sniffed twice and let her voice trail off.

Jade picked up a napkin from the plastic holder on the table and methodically tore the paper into long, narrow strips. Then she balled up the strips, dropped the ball onto the table, and reached for another napkin.

"He shouldn't have bothered you. You haven't done anything to him." Jade finished shredding the second napkin, and reached for another. This time Socrates took her hand and held it in his. She was making him nervous.

Socrates held up his other hand, signaling Jade to stop. Then he walked her through his meetings with her father, but did not say anything about Bing-fa's implied threats.

When Socrates finished, Jade said, "Did he know who you were when he came to see you, that you were my Socrates, not some other one?"

Socrates couldn't help smiling. *Some other Socrates?* he thought. *Not likely. We're in Washington, not Athens.*

"He knew," Socrates said. "He even suggested I talk to you before I make a decision. Probably because you told him I'm a pen collector. Right?" When Jade didn't say anything, Socrates said, "You did tell him when you two were still talking, didn't you?"

Jade shook her head. "Of course not. I would have told you if I'd done that." She paused as if considering another thought, then said, "I'm surprised he didn't ask one of my brothers or one of his Triad flunkies to help him, instead of you. They'd do anything he asked just to please him."

Jade looked into Socrates' eyes. "What are you going to do?" she asked. Her question was delivered in a pitch nearly an octave higher than normal.

"That depends on you. If you want me to help your father, I will. If you don't want me to, I won't." He paused to gather his thoughts. "My only concern is I might make things worse with him if I screw up or if I don't recover the Mandarin Yellow and other stolen items."

Jade looked away, then turned back. "I think I know how this might have happened," she said. "Sometimes my stepmother calls me when my father's out. I've told her about you, including about your pen business. I'm sure she told my father. Otherwise, how would he know?"

Socrates shrugged, but said nothing. He didn't really care how Bing-fa knew.

"He probably came to you for other reasons, too," Jade said.

This should be interesting, Socrates thought.

"Maybe it's because you look Chinese," she said. "Your physical appearance won't raise awkward questions if people associate you with him."

"I am Chinese," Socrates said. "Half." He felt his barely suppressed anger well up at this all too familiar slight.

"You also read Mandarin," Jade said, "at least you used to. That indicates to him you're highly educated, something he values."

Socrates tried to decrease the tension he was beginning to feel again.

"Don't ever tell my mother you think I look Chinese," he said. "You'll break her heart. She thinks I look Greek, but with defective eyes and jaundiced skin."

Jade didn't even crack a tiny smile. She raised her eyebrows in what Socrates took to be her silent rebuke for his levity. She had completely missed the point of his attempt — that he, too, was nervous.

I'll drop the wisecracks, he decided.

Socrates cleared his throat and said in a serious tone, picking up on Jade's earlier comment, "I still read Mandarin occasionally, but your father didn't know that when he came to see me. It couldn't be that."

"There might be another reason," Jade said. She smiled, reached out, and took Socrates' hand. "I'm sure my stepmother figured out how much I love you even though I never came right out and said it to her. I'm sure she could tell from what I did say about you and how I said it."

Socrates smiled and squeezed Jade's hand.

"She must have told my father how I feel. That's why he came to you, that and your knowledge of pens," she said. She looked across the room, then added, "At least I hope that's why." Jade held onto Socrates' hand, leaned across the table and pulled him closer to her. Then she kissed him.

Socrates released their kiss after a few seconds, let go of Jade's hand, and straightened up in his seat.

"There's something else you should know," he said. "I met with Brandon about this. I wanted his input."

Jade noticeably tightened up.

"Come on, Jade, it's time you get over your problem with him, for your good and mine." He sighed at the known futility of his statement. They'd been through this many times before. "I intend to keep both of you in my life."

"Whatever," Jade said, as she shrugged. She looked up and stared at the wall behind Socrates, and tapped her fingers on the table as if now impatient to bring their conversation to an end.

"So," Socrates said, "you never answered my question. What do you want me to do? Help your father or not?"

Jade nodded. "Help him." She nodded several more times, then frowned. "But be careful. He and my brothers can be dangerous. Don't ever let your guard down, and never — never, never, ever — make the mistake of thinking they are your friends or care at all about your interests."

Chapter 12

JADE.
LI BING-JADE. Her name in vernacular Chinese.
JADE LI. Her name in western English.
By whatever name she was called, Jade was the love of Socrates' life.

SOCRATES *OFFICIALLY* MET Jade when she broke his arm.

HE HAD FIRST noticed her in 1987 during orientation week of their freshman year at Penn State. They each were seventeen years old. Socrates thought Jade was the most exquisite woman he'd ever seen.

She was almost his height — tall for a Chinese woman at slightly over 5'9" — and fit like a conditioned long-distance runner. She had burnished Mandarin skin, a smile that could melt the coldest heart, and long blue-black hair she wore tied in a fist-sized bun at the back of her head in the severe style made popular in the 1950s by Madam Chiang Kai-shek.

Because they both were China Studies majors, Socrates and Jade found themselves thrown together in several classes. Socrates saw this as his opportunity to meet, date and court Jade, but he was sadly mistaken. Try as he might to engage her in conversation, Jade would not give him the time of day. She was always polite, but aloof, conducting herself in that situation like the well-bred Confucian daughter Bing-fa had brought her up to be after her mother died. All of Socrates' attempts to break through Jade's reserve met with the same cool response. Eventually, for the balance of his freshman year, Socrates stopped trying to engage Jade in conversation and contented himself with watching her from across the classroom.

A FEW WEEKS after the start of their sophomore year, when Socrates signed up to take Saturday classes studying three related Chinese martial arts — *T'ai Ch'i Chuan*, *T'ai Ch'i sword*, and *Kobudo* — he discovered that Jade also had enrolled in the classes. But this happenstance did not change Jade's outward response to him. She rebuffed Socrates' renewed attempts at being friendly, and merely acknowledged his presence at the beginning of each class with a brief nod and a contained smile, before she turned away.

Yet Socrates believed he was making some progress with her. Several times during instruction when he suddenly looked over at Jade, he caught her staring at him. She immediately looked away each time, and sometimes also blushed, confirming Socrates' belief that Jade had been deliberately staring at him, as he'd hoped, and not merely daydreaming.

Socrates' first opportunity to breach Jade's cultural rampart occurred early in their second year at school during a Saturday *T'ai Ch'i Chuan* practice session when their instructor coupled Socrates and Jade as sparring partners for a weight-shifting and balancing exercise known in Chinese as *Taolu*, and in English as Push Hands.

Socrates and Jade performed this slow moving drill well together that first time, and although they went their separate ways without any conversation immediately after class, they voluntarily paired-up the following Saturday for a leg-kick and hand-to-hand combat sparring match known as *Shanshou*.

Within minutes after they began *Shanshou*, Jade caught Socrates with his attention wandering and dropped him to the mat with a cross-leg kick, sweeping both his feet out from under him. Socrates fell hard, his body fully rigid in his astonishment, and snapped the bone in his left arm just below the elbow. This, as Socrates liked to say from then on, was his lucky break.

As a result of this injury, Jade now paid attention to Socrates. She sat with him during classes and shared her lecture notes with him because left-handed Socrates could not now take his own notes. She also studied with him each evening at the school's Pattee Library, although Socrates, who welcomed her company, did not see why his broken arm compelled Jade to sit with him while he read assigned materials.

Over the remainder of the second half of that sophomore school year, Jade and Socrates progressed to spending time together socially, but only as friends, not as a dating couple. In due course, as they passed more time together and shared more and more personal thoughts, they discovered that in addition to common interests such as Chinese martial arts, China's history and culture, listening to jazz, and attending art exhibits, they also shared important core values, especially the veneration of their respective families and their high regard for education. By the end of their sophomore year, Socrates and Jade were dating. The two friends had become college lovers.

The only demonstrable flaw in their relationship was Jade's open hostility to Brandon. When Socrates occasionally questioned Jade about her hostility, she invariably answered with something to the effect that Brandon was too trendy, too full of himself, and much too rich for his own good. She often ended her recitation by saying, 'In short, he's a complete ass'. Socrates decided, although he never discussed it with her, that Jade was jealous of the considerable amount of time he and Brandon spent together. Socrates concluded that from Jade's point of view, he should have been spending much of that time with her.

When Socrates and Jade graduated from Penn State, they decided to end their dating relationship and go their separate ways unencumbered by the challenges of maintaining a long-distance romantic relationship. They both believed they needed to focus their full attention on their upcoming graduate-level studies. They parted as friends.

After Penn State, Socrates enrolled at Columbia Law School in New York. He eventually became one of five partners — including Todd — in a small Washington, DC law firm.

When Jade graduated from Penn State, she enrolled at Wellesley College where she earned her Master's Degree and then her Doctorate of Philosophy Degree, both in Chinese Thought. After finishing these studies, Jade moved to Washington to teach undergraduates in the Department of Philosophy at Georgetown University.

Almost fifteen years after they'd embarked on their divergent paths, Socrates and Jade found one another on a sunny, crisp Sunday fall morning while shopping at Eastern Market on Capitol Hill. They were overjoyed to find one another. Within two weeks of their fortuitous reunion, and after several late night lengthy telephone conversations, they resumed dating.

Chapter 13

SOCRATES SPENT THE night at Jade's condo. In the morning, after Jade left for work and he arrived home, Socrates called Bing-fa.

"I'll help you," he said. *But only because Jade wants me to,* he thought.

He and Bing-fa agreed to meet at 4:30 that afternoon at Socrates' store to go over what Socrates would need to get started.

After his call to Bing-fa, Socrates walked to the West End Branch of the District of Columbia public library at 23rd and L Streets. He borrowed three books that described how to conduct a criminal investigation. From the library, he walked to Georgetown and spent the balance of the morning at his store preparing to close it down until he finished with Bing-fa's investigation. He wasn't thrilled about interrupting his business this way, but it made more sense than having the business limp along using either Eldest Brother or Brandon to fill-in for him.

When he finished at his store, Socrates walked to Jade's office at Georgetown University to meet her. They had agreed they would meet at 11:30 a.m. to eat sandwiches and discuss Bing-fa's investigation so Socrates could benefit from Jade's perspective. He also brought along a surprise to show her.

They settled down on a picnic blanket outside Jade's office window. Jade immediately said, "What's your surprise for me? I've been dying to know all morning since you mentioned it."

"Not yet," Socrates said. "First, let's talk about your father's problem."

Jade nodded, but Socrates thought she looked disappointed.

Socrates bit into a tuna salad sandwich, swallowed his mouthful, and said, "Can I count on your brothers to help me if I need them?"

Jade raised her eyebrows and shook her head. "Probably not." She looked off in the distance as if contemplating her answer, then turned back to Socrates and said, "It depends on which ones you mean. The problem is, they all consider you to be *low faan* because your mother's not Chinese. In their view, that makes you a barbarian."

Socrates knitted his eyebrows together and frowned. *Even Jade*, he thought, *falls prey to her family's parochial attitude. She knows I know the meaning of low faan, yet she's defined it for me as if I am a barbarian who needs her explanation.* He sighed.

Jade reached out and sandwiched Socrates' hand between both hers. She lifted his hand to her mouth and lightly kissed his fingers, one at a time. Then she leaned her cheek against the back of his hand and said, "Eldest Brother won't help you because he blames you for my failure to demonstrate appropriate filial piety."

Socrates shook his head. "I don't get his attitude, Jade, all this filial piety crap. This is the 21st Century in America, after all, not in Shanghai. You know I respect my father, I always show him I do, but I don't carry on like Eldest . . . ."

"Our families are different, Socrates," Jade interrupted, "you know that. We're Chinese, very traditional in our beliefs and practices. Your family's not. You were raised like an Occidental, as much like a Greek as like a Chinese person. You can't possibly understand our orthodox world."

"We're Chinese, too," Socrates said, "at least my Shanghainese father believes we are, and I agree with him."

Jade fanned out her palms. "You must admit, Socrates, our families are different. I remember once when you and I were in college, and I visited you at your parents' home over Christmas vacation. It was a real eye opener for me, almost cultural shock at the time. You and your parents were very casual with one another. You even addressed your father using the salutation, *You*, rather than *Father* or *Honorable Father*, as we always did at home."

Socrates couldn't resist smiling at this. He tried to imagine his father rolling around on the floor laughing, with tears streaming down his cheeks, if Socrates had ever dared address him as *Honorable Father*. And he shuddered to think how such a salutation directed to his father might have disabled his mother's otherwise impenetrable self-control.

"As children," Jade said, "we were not permitted to speak in our father's presence unless he spoke to us first. I bet it wasn't like that in your household."

"You better believe it wasn't," Socrates said, smiling big.

"What most struck me when I visited your family," Jade said, continuing as if Socrates had not responded to her rhetorical question, "was that you and your parents laughed with one another, even teased one another. It was never that way in my father's household."

Jade looked off into the distance again, and said, "When we were growing up, my father's word was law. That's the way it is in a traditional Confucian and Taoist home."

Socrates rolled his eyes, but only in his imagination, not so Jade could see him do it. *He was many things*, he thought, *but he wasn't a fool. No point stirring the pot with an actual eye roll.*

Jade continued. "Respect, order and tradition were always the rules in our family, especially for Eldest Brother as the first born male." She nodded to underscore her point.

"My father imposed great demands on Bing-wu so he would present the correct example for us younger siblings," Jade said, again looking off in the distance as she spoke.

"Eldest Brother is so wrapped up in tradition," she said, "I don't think he'd help you even as a way of helping our father." She paused as if collecting her thoughts, then turned back and looked into Socrates' eyes. She took his hand again.

"Socrates, darling, listen to me. You must be wary of Eldest Brother. Don't underestimate Bing-wu's inclination to act against his own, and against our family's, best interests when his emotions take hold." Jade again kissed Socrates' fingers.

Socrates assumed an appropriately solemn expression to match Jade's message, and nodded.

"Eldest Brother is very reactionary. He hates Westerners. Bing-wu is so out-of-date in his beliefs, he's convinced Chiang Kai-shek was China's savior until the United States betrayed him, enabling Mao and the Communists to take over the country." She smiled, then said, "Believe it or not, Eldest Brother would live in Formosa, I mean Taiwan, if our father would permit it."

"That's very enlightened," Socrates said. He smiled at his attempt at levity, but it fell flat with Jade.

"My middle brothers, the Twins, won't help you either, but not because of you. They're just spoiled adolescents, in their own world, totally wrapped up with themselves and each other. I've been telling you that for years, and nothing has changed with them. Even our father has trouble getting the Twins to do anything for him. They say *yes* to father, then don't follow through. They give new meaning to the phrase, passive-aggressive." She smiled and shrugged. "What can I say?"

"Well, you're right about the Twins," Socrates said. "I've heard that song before."

"Youngest Brother will help you, if I ask," Jade said, "if for no other reason than to please me. I'll ask him if you want, but you should use Youngest Brother sparingly so he does not feel conflicted in his loyalty."

"I've got the picture," Socrates said. "I won't count on your brothers for help, including Youngest Brother."

That's probably best," Jade said. "Now, show me my surprise." She smiled, sat up taller, and wiggled her slim hips and flat butt into a comfortable sitting position.

Chapter 14

JADE WATCHED INTENTLY as she anticipated the surprise Socrates had brought for her.

Socrates reached into his sports jacket's inside pocket and withdrew a narrow, six inch long white cardboard box. He removed the lid and placed the box on the blanket, halfway between himself and Jade. He looked up at Jade, ready to bask in the joy she would experience once she saw the box's contents.

"That's it," Socrates said, pointing at the box. "A Parker Duofold Mandarin Yellow pen. This one's from my collection. It's similar to the one stolen from the exhibit, but without the historic attributes and without George Parker's inscription dedicating the first model of this pen to Chiang. Isn't it wonderful?"

Jade nodded slowly, almost warily, then leaned in and brought her face down close to Socrates' Mandarin Yellow. She squinted, then looked over at Socrates.

"So . . . that's it?" she said. "That's what all this fuss is about with my father? This yellow pen?"

Socrates felt like a suddenly deflated balloon. "It's the pride of my collection, Jade," he said. "It's not just a yellow pen." He strained to keep his voice from revealing his disappointment.

Jade looked down at the Mandarin Yellow, and said, "Okay, Darling, I'll buy that. Tell me what's so special about it other than its color? I mean, compared to other old pens?"

Socrates smiled again, inspired now as only someone can be who has been stricken all his life with the collecting gene. He picked up the box and carefully cradled it in both hands.

"Besides its historical connotations," he said, "the Mandarin Yellow is a beautiful writing instrument, wonderful to look at, wonderful to hold in your hand because of its fine balance, and a joy to write with because of its fine nib and smooth ink flow.

"As you can see, the outer surfaces of its cap and barrel are tinted with a beautiful yellow dye that was intended by George Parker to emulate China's Imperial Yellow, the color traditionally forbidden to everyone but the royal family. Part of the pen's visual attraction results from this yellow hue which becomes warmer over time, a rich, lustrous patina." He paused to see if he had Jade's attention. He did. She smiled, raised both eyebrows, and nodded him on.

"But its outer beauty was deceptive," Socrates added. "The Mandarin Yellow carried its own death wound with it because its outer skin was exceedingly fragile. The pen literally could crack if you looked at it wrong."

Socrates paused to gather his thoughts. Jade waited half a minute, then said, rolling her finger in a film director's *lights, cameras, action* motion, "And . . .?"

"Oh, sorry," Socrates said, as he blushed. "I was lost in thought."

He continued. "This means that even though all Mandarin Yellows look alike to the untrained eye, they weren't alike, especially underneath their beautiful yellow skins. That's because the Mandarin Yellow's outer beauty often masked hidden problems."

"Such as?" Jade said.

"Such as internal hairline cracks that would not become known for a long while until significant, irreparable damage had occurred from within. That's the irony and the curse of this wondrous writing instrument," he said, nodding toward the box.

"Okay, I get that," Jade said, "but how did you avoid that problem with your pen?" she asked. She pointed to Socrates' Mandarin Yellow sitting in its box between them. "Or, didn't you?"

"Truth is, I don't know," Socrates said. He reached out and lightly touched the box with one finger, then withdrew his hand.

"When I bought this pen, I didn't see any external cracks or dents or any signs that former cracks had been filled-in and repaired. On the surface, everything looked fine. But I really couldn't know at the time I bought it about possible hidden defects," he said. "In fact, I still don't know. I'll have to wait another dozen years or so to see if any show up." He cleared his throat.

"I bought this Mandarin Yellow on faith, hoping there were no concealed problems. That's really all you can do if you want to own one. You never really know if there are flaws lurking beneath the beautiful yellow skin until it's too late to do anything about them." He paused, shrugged, and smiled warily.

"That's the way it is with the Mandarin Yellow," he said. "Some things just have to be taken on faith, with a willingness to risk a mistake and the willingness to live with the consequences if you're wrong."

WHEN SOCRATES AND Jade finished lunch, Socrates headed back to his store. He spent the next half hour finishing the chores he'd started earlier to prepare the store to temporarily go dark. Then, still having a little time to spare before his 4:30 meeting with Bing-fa, he booted up his computer and went online to see what had been posted on the Internet about the burglary at the gallery.

Socrates assumed, based on what he'd read in art magazines over the years, that Interpol's General Secretariat and the FBI's Art Crime Team — perhaps even the London-based Art Loss Register — had posted news of the burglary on their web sites and had entered descriptions and photographs of the Mandarin Yellow and other stolen objects into their public online databases for anyone to view.

Socrates pulled up the web sites, but didn't find any references to the theft. *That doesn't make any sense,* he thought. *You'd think the Embassy or the gallery would want to have this information circulated as widely as possible. Why haven't they reported it?* he wondered, *or, if it was reported, why hasn't that information been posted online?*

Chapter 15

AFTER HE FINISHED his futile search for online information about the burglary, Socrates still had time to kill before Bing-fa was due to arrive for their meeting. He shelved the last of the supplies, ordered others he would need when he reopened the store, locked his most valuable pens in the store safe, and dusted the framed historic documents hanging on three walls. Then he paid bills and wrote a check for next month's rent just in case.

When he finished these chores, Socrates checked his watch. It was 4:00.

Socrates retrieved a bottle of Merlot from the stockroom and poured himself a generous glassful. He settled into a chair in the corner of the store, sipped his wine, and thought about Bing-fa. Specifically, he thought about the stories Jade had told him from time-to-time about her father's early years as an immigrant to America

ACCORDING TO JADE, Bing-fa, like many of the privileged eldest sons of upper-middle class Chinese families, had arrived in Washington from Shanghai in 1946 under a scholarship program established by Chiang Kai-shek to enable these favored eldest male children to study at American universities.

In return for the payment of all their living and college expenses, these young men were expected to complete their studies and then return to China where they would pursue the traditional Confucian path to a civil service post and would provide China with a lifetime of needed skills and services. Chiang's government also anticipated that these grateful young men would also offer Chiang Kai-shek their everlasting gratitude and personal loyalty.

This seemingly simple concept collapsed under the weight of China's wartime and post-World War II hyper-inflation, a calamitous condition widely believed in China to have been brought about by Chiang's voracious looting of the state's treasury and by his unfettered printing of currency to feed his insatiable appetite for wealth.

By the late 1940s, China's crippled economy and bankrupt state treasury had destroyed China's middle class and rendered Chiang's government unable to sustain the thousands of overseas scholarships it had sponsored.

In 1947, Chiang yielded to economic reality and pulled the plug on the scholarships. As a result, approximately four thousand Chinese students in the United States suddenly found themselves abandoned by their government and cut off from all financial support from home. Most of these students returned to China to face uncertain lives of unimagined poverty, hardship and political upheaval.

Nineteen year old Bing-fa did not escape this nightmare.

With his scholarship lost, Bing-fa dropped out of George Washington University, but did not return to Shanghai. Instead, he wrote to his father seeking instructions telling him what to do.

The return letter arrived four months later, but the reply came from Bing-fa's mother, not his father.

Honorable son, Li Bing-fa:

Do not return home. There is nothing here for you to return to. No work at all. You cannot help yourself or our family by returning to Shanghai. All our property is lost to government bandits and banks, swallowed by high prices, increasing taxes, and unpayable debts.

Your loving, venerable father, overwhelmed by his loss of face, has shamed himself by eating the fruit of the hemlock plant in the flowering season.

Three weeks ago, several soldiers from Generalissimo Chiang's army came in the late night to our temporary dwelling and took both your younger brothers with them to fight the Communists. Your brothers are forever lost to us. We will never see them again.

Your beloved youngest sister and your cherished middle sister also are lost to us. They now work as Sing-Song girls at the Garden of the Perfumed Flowers on Foochow Road.

I cannot bear the disgrace that has visited itself upon our family. I will join your father with our ancestors before you receive this letter.

With his family destroyed by Chiang's economic policies and greed, and with no property or family left to return to in Shanghai, Bing-fa remained in Washington. For the next three years he worked as a dishwasher at a restaurant in Chinatown. He later became a waiter at the same restaurant, then a cashier. Six years later, he left the restaurant and became a messenger for a local Chinatown Triad known as *The Lotus Leaf Brotherhood*. Eventually, Bing-fa became a salaried officer in the Triad. His life immediately began to improve.

In 1967, Bing-fa left *The Lotus Leaf Brotherhood* and organized his own Triad, the *Jiao tu san ku* — the *Cunning Rabbit With Three Warrens Society*. This Triad associated itself with a similar organization in Shanghai run by Big Eared Tu, who also headed Shanghai's notorious criminal enterprise known worldwide as the Green Gang.

The *Cunning Rabbit With Three Warrens Society* operated as a secret charitable and fraternal organization. Within two years of its founding, the Triad ruled Washington's Chinatown community. Bing-fa ruled the Triad.

Its members received many benefits. In return for a small weekly dues payment, the Triad's members received many services such as traditional medical care, life and burial insurance, legal advice, day care services, and personal, business and real property protection. The Triad also provided translation services, low-cost prostitution services, daily card games, cricket fighting matches, and other popular forms of gambling such as thirteen-card *fan tan*, *tien gow*, and the popular thirty-two dominoes game of chance, *pai gow*. In hard financial times, the Triad paid the costs of educating members' children, found or created jobs for the unemployed, and otherwise subsidized members' families who were in financial crises.

As the years passed, Bing-fa continued to prosper. By 2001, he openly owned a popular Chinatown restaurant (called the Golden Dragon), a successful hand laundry, a grocery store, a walk-in medical clinic, an herbal pharmacy, a furniture emporium, and a fully occupied luxury rental apartment building on H Street, known as the White Plum Blossoms Apartments, where Bing-fa, his second wife, and Bing-fa's sons lived.

Bing-fa also silently controlled, in a secret pact with the Green Gang, three Washington, DC gambling parlors, two local Chinatown banks, a Chinatown-based savings & loan association, a mahjong hall, four massage parlors/places of prostitution, a neighborhood barber shop, a small-loan finance company (located in the central business district of Washington, not in Chinatown) and two pawn shops located in the Dupont Circle area.

In 2004, Washington's Mayor Anthony Williams and the Greater Washington Area Board of Trade designated Bing-fa as Washington's Man-of-the-Year to honor him for his many years of community service and perceived rectitude.

SOCRATES REALIZED AS he recalled Jade's stories, Bing-fa was a well-connected, somewhat unsavory, and very powerful man. He definitely was not a man to be taken lightly.

As Socrates dwelled on this last thought, his attention was caught by the ringing of the entrance door's overhead bell. Bing-fa had arrived for their meeting.

Chapter 16

THE MEETING WITH Bing-fa went well. Socrates described the information he would need to begin his investigation, and Bing-fa promised to deliver it to him the next afternoon.

The next day, within minutes before Socrates closed his store for what he expected to be the last time for several weeks, the Twins barged in as if they were being chased. They brought a package for Socrates from their father.

"So," Bing-luc said, as he strutted up to Socrates, "you are the *low faan* causing the troubles between Elder Sister and our father."

There was no levity nor any goodwill intimated by Bing-luc's statement. Neither he nor his Twin brother smiled as Bing-luc said this.

"You should be more respectful of tradition and the obligations of familial piety owed by a daughter to her father and brothers," Bing-luc said.

Bing-luc's statement surprised Socrates, not because of its overt hostility and implicit menace, but because the Twins had even bothered to say it at all. Socrates hadn't expected the Twins to depart from their reputed lassitude when it came to Li family matters.

Socrates didn't reply. Instead, he reached out to Bing-luc's hand, snatched away the folder Bing-fa had sent over, and quickly skimmed its contents to make sure, at the very least, that the inventory and photographs of stolen items he'd asked for were there.

When he finished looking through the materials, Socrates said, "Tell your father I'll call him when I'm ready to meet again." He turned away and walked back behind the glass display case.

Bing-luc stared at him with an expression Socrates could only interpret as the mental equivalent of rage.

"You have been warned, *low faan,*" he said to Socrates. Then he and his brother turned away and left the store.

AFTER THE TWINS left, Socrates cleared off an accumulation of *Pen World* magazines he kept on a small library table for customers to read, and made a work space for himself. He pulled up a chair, took the materials Bing-fa had sent over, and sorted through them.

He created three piles, stacking index cards and pages according to their general subject matter: people involved with the exhibit; written descriptions of the stolen items; and, photographs of the stolen objects. He later would look for some unifying thread or other relationship among the items described in the piles.

He next looked through the information on the 3" x 5" index cards. Each card named one person, and stated that person's role with respect to the exhibit. The card also gave the person's title, if any, the work address, and the person's work telephone number. Only a few cards also showed e-mail addresses or Twitter, Facebook or other social media contact information.

From Bing-fa's card Socrates learned that Bing-fa had originally conceived of the idea for the exhibit and then had convinced the People's Republic government to approve it, to ship the objects from Mao's secret archives to its Embassy in Washington, and to underwrite all costs. This, Socrates realized, explained Bing-fa's belief that the burglary and postponement of the exhibit's opening had caused him to lose face in the Chinese community.

Socrates learned from another card that Iris Hua, the gallery's director, had supervised Bing-fa's sons in performing heavy lifting for the exhibit, tasks such as transporting the objects to be exhibited from the Embassy to the gallery, hanging the wall art, and setting up glass-enclosed exhibit cases and pedestals for the porcelain ware and sculpture. Iris Hua had also assisted the Embassy's cultural attaché in selecting the photographs for the exhibit's full-color catalog and in writing the catalog's descriptions for the objects to be exhibited.

Other people, whose names or job descriptions Socrates didn't recognize, also were described on the index cards. Some were temporary gallery employees and some were student volunteers and interns brought in to work on various aspects of the exhibit.

Socrates planned to conduct face-to-face interviews with the principal players named on the index cards, specifically, the gallery's director, the assistant director, and any other gallery employees. His goal would be to gather as much general information as possible in each interview to determine who stood to gain and who stood to lose the most by the postponement or cancellation of the exhibit. That information might provide him with the motive for the burglary which, in turn, might point the way to the identification of the criminals and to the recovery of the Mandarin Yellow and other stolen artifacts.

Socrates opened a yellow legal pad to a blank page, and made a list of the tasks he thought he'd have to perform in addition to the interviews at the gallery: study the inventory of stolen items to identify a common theme among the objects taken; visit the scene of the crime; study the exhibit catalog looking for one or more themes among the objects *not* taken by the burglars; and, review the police file to obtain the benefit of the lab reports and the crime scene reports. He thought a moment, then added to his list, 'talk to Embassy personnel'.

Another thought occurred to him. Before he conducted the interviews at the gallery, he would visit the gallery without identifying himself, in the guise of an art lover, to acquire the feel of the crime scene. Then, after he'd had a chance to review the police file and was more knowledgeable about the case, he would go back to the gallery, but this time he would identify himself as an investigator working for Bing-fa. He would then ask the hard questions.

Chapter 17

SOCRATES CHECKED HIS watch. He and Jade had agreed to meet for dinner that evening. Socrates had just enough time to hurry home, shower and change into fresh clothes, then get over to Jade's condo to meet her when she arrived home from the university. They planned to talk during dinner about Socrates' planned approach to the investigation. Socrates hoped Jade might give him some helpful insights from her father's perspective.

Ninety minutes later, Socrates stood in Jade's living room sipping from a glass of *Baijiu* — a white liquor distilled from sorghum, popular in China — while Jade showered and dressed for dinner. He looked around the living room, the dining room and the connecting foyer from his vantage point in the living room over by the dry sink.

Nothing about the tasteful decor of Jade's condo surprised him. Not the traditional *feng shui* interior north to south flow, not the high quality of the Chinese art and ceramics Jade displayed, and not the clusters of photographs she had placed on several walls and on one table in a very un-Chinese-like manner of decorating. In many ways, Socrates realized, Jade's style of furnishing and appointing her condo was merely an upscale extension of the way she had set up her dorm room at Penn State.

The condo's furnishings consisted of several examples of country furniture that had been constructed in various North China provinces from the late 1800s through the mid-1930s. There were tables of differing sizes and shapes, yoke-back and horseshoe-back chairs, and five decorated wooden Revolution Chests scattered among the three rooms. Jade also had distributed brush pots, ink sticks, ink stones and other traditional scholars' studio objects throughout the rooms, subtly mingling these objects among the vernacular furniture.

Socrates checked his watch. He was hungry, and Jade, as usual, was running late. He walked over to the foyer to look at Jade's display of black and white photographs.

Jade had covered one wall with images of her family members taken during various stages of their lives. There were images of Bing-fa as an adolescent in China, and others of him as a young man in America. Socrates particularly liked Bing-fa's wedding photograph, taken of him and Jade's deceased mother in Washington's Chinatown sometime in the early 1950s. When Socrates first saw this photo in Jade's dorm room, he thought he was looking at a picture of Jade, she so resembled her deceased mother at approximately the same age.

Jade's display also included photographs of Jade and her brothers at various ages. Socrates couldn't help smiling as he traced Jade's development, as depicted in nine images, from a prepubescent girl into her teenage years and then into young womanhood.

There also were several photographs of Eldest Brother. He appeared sullen in all of them, even as a child. *No big surprise there*, Socrates thought.

Socrates moved over to the photographs of Bing-enlai — Youngest Brother — Jade's special sibling for whom she had acted as surrogate mother after their natural mother died. He appeared friendly, but befuddled, in his few photographs.

Socrates walked over to another wall. He examined, with some amusement, the photographs of the Twins. These boys puzzled him. He barely knew them except for what he'd learned years ago from Jade when they were students at Penn State, and what he occasionally now gleaned from comments she sometimes dropped about them.

Socrates counted twelve photos of the Twins on this wall.

The boys always appeared together, even in photos taken of them with their father, their stepmother, or with Jade or with their other male siblings. It was as if, like many Twins, Bing-hao and Bing-luc had no separate identities, one from the other.

Socrates eyeballed the Twins' photographs. Among the twelve was a large black and white image which portrayed the boys when they were seven or eight years old and, according to the caption, had been costumed for a school play. In this photo, young Bing-hao wore a tuxedo with tails, a top hat, a fake handlebar mustache, and a pince-nez. He held a long black Franklin Delano Roosevelt-type cigarette holder in his left hand and stood posed in the lackadaisical manner of a Kurt Weill noir character in a post-World War I Berlin operetta, with one hand on his hip and the other balancing the cigarette holder at his lips. His twin, Bing-luc, was costumed in this same photograph as a young woman, replete with a pillbox hat, a mesh veil that covered his eyes and nose, and an ankle-length ostrich feather boa draped around his neck and over his shoulders.

Socrates looked at his watch again, shook his head and smiled, then walked into the dining room where Jade had set aside a corner table and two converging walls to display photographs and other memorabilia relating to Soong Mai-ling, aka Madam Chiang Kai-shek.

The walls' array of Madam Chiang photographs consisted of three framed black and white portraits of her: one as a young student at Wellesley College; another of her as a middle aged woman; and, a third as a dowager living near Gracie Square in New York City just before her death in 2003. There also was an 11" x 14" color portrait which Madam Chiang had autographed and given to Jade when Madam Chiang delivered the keynote speech at a Wellesley College Alumni weekend Jade had specifically attended in anticipation of Madam Chiang's presence. The last photograph in the arrangement consisted of Soong Mai-ling's wedding portrait taken with her groom, Generalissimo Chiang Kai-shek. This photograph had captured Socrates' imagination when he first saw it in Jade's dorm room because Jade, using scissors, had carefully cut away Chiang Kai-shek's image, leaving only his young bride in the slimmed-down, expurgated wedding portrait.

In addition to photos, Jade's corner display consisted of several framed mementos set up on a small, three-sided box-wood corner table. These consisted of laminated copies of Madam Chiang's speech to the United States Congress in February 1943, her speech that same week to the students and faculty at Wellesley College, and her speech years later at Wellesley during the Alumni Weekend Jade had attended. Jade also had placed on this table a framed laminated copy of the *New York Times* obituary published when Madam Chiang died in Manhattan at the age of 105 or 106.

Socrates looked at his watch once more, then looked wistfully at the hall leading to Jade's bedroom as if his glance over there could draw her out to him. He shrugged and moved on to the last group of photographs, those hanging in the living room.

These pictures depicted Jade with her brothers, others with her father, one with her stepmother, one of Jade alone wearing her cap and gown at Wellesley as she accepted her Master's degree, and another at Wellesley of Jade accepting her Doctorate degree.

Interesting wall, Socrates thought. *I wonder if . . . .*

Jade interrupted Socrates' thoughts by quietly coming up behind him, putting her hands on his hips, and slowly rotating him until he faced her. Then she moved in close and kissed him, running her tongue around the inner border of his lips, holding the kiss as they slowly melded their bodies.

"Ummm," she said, when they finally broke contact. "How nice that is! You're definitely a keeper, Socrates Cheng. Let's put off dinner a while." She smiled, winked, and led Socrates by his hand to her bedroom.

ACROSS CONNECTICUT AVENUE, squatting on his haunches deep in the shadows of the entryway to Cathedral Park Dry Cleaner, Youngest Brother stared up at the bank of Jade's five living room windows until, almost one hour later, Jade and Socrates emerged from the building holding hands. They walked south along Connecticut Avenue to Calvert Street, then headed east to Adams' Morgan, a popular ethnic neighborhood in Washington.

Youngest Brother followed them to Julia's Empanadas, a Latin American cafe, and again waited in hiding across the street from the restaurant. Two hours later, Youngest Brother followed Jade and Socrates back to Jade's condo. He again squatted across Connecticut Avenue, shielded now by the cover of night.

Youngest Brother stared up at Jade's lighted windows for forty-five minutes until the windows went dark. Then he muttered something unintelligible and left.

Chapter 18

THE NEXT MORNING on his way home from Jade's condo Socrates stopped at Trader Joe's on 25th Street and picked up his week's groceries. Thirty minutes later he stood by his front door and sorted through his key ring looking for the key to the condo's standard-issue door lock the apartment had come equipped with and for the other key that opened the heavy duty, pick-proof STRASBURG lock he'd had installed when he moved in.

Socrates unlocked the door and turned the knob with his free hand, nudged the door open with his knee, and headed directly to the kitchen to put away his groceries. When he finished, he walked to his bedroom to undress and shower, unbuttoning his shirt as he moved toward his bedroom.

Socrates stepped into his bedroom, but pulled up short, unwilling to move any farther into the room. He slowly turned his head to confirm what he'd sighted from the corner of his eye.

He found himself staring at a sheet of white letter-size paper that was propped up against the pillows at the base of his bed's headboard.

He began to sweat. He caught his breath, then began to breathe quickly, too quickly. He was almost panting.

Someone had made it past the doorman downstairs, past his STRASBURG security lock, and into his home.

Chapter 19

SOCRATES WAS SHAKEN and angry.

He rushed over to his bed and picked up the paper, but could not read it at first because his hand shook so violently. He inhaled deeply, held his breath briefly, then slowly hissed it out, centering himself.

When he'd calmed, Socrates grasped the note in both hands to steady it, and read the message:

> We can get to you and the people you love anytime, anywhere, on the street or behind double-locked doors. You are never safe from us. Do not be where you do not belong. Do not do what you have no business doing.

Socrates crumbled the note into a tight ball and squeezed his fist around it. He was furious. He'd been defiled in his own home, rendered vulnerable by the intruder's entry into his bedroom, by someone who profaned his peace of mind. Socrates again took shallow, but now uncontrolled breaths, rendering him light-headed.

He forced himself to breathe slowly, to pull himself together.

He uncrumbled the note, placed it on his dresser, and ran his palm over its wrinkles, smoothing out the page. He would hold onto the note for now, not toss it into the wastebasket as he almost had.

Whoever had left the note had either bypassed the doorman and electronic security system downstairs or had made it past the entrance door by following an occupant into the building by tailgating.

Socrates hurried downstairs to the building's front entrance, bypassing the slow-paced elevator by taking the interior fire stairs two steps at a time. He quick-stepped over to the doorman, and said, "George, did you let anyone in this morning or yesterday who might have gone up to my apartment while I was out?"

"No, Sir, no one. Not me. I wouldn't do that, not without checking with you first."

"Well somebody got in the building and broke into my apartment," Socrates said. He could feel his neck growing warm with impatience. He'd never liked this doorman with his pretentious attitude.

"I'd remember if anybody went up to your place, Mr. Cheng. That's my job. No people from outside gets by here without me knowing who they are and what's their business."

"So you say, George, but someone got by you and I need to know who." He waited for some response, then said, "It's important, George."

"I'm sure it is, Mr. Cheng, to you, Sir." He touched the bill of his cap with two fingers in a mock salute. "I don't know nothing else to tell you." He turned away and headed for the front door.

"Wait a minute, you. Come back here," Socrates said. "I haven't finished."

The doorman turned back toward Socrates and shrugged. "Yes, Sir, Mr. Cheng. Anything you say. No disrespect intended." He reached into his uniform's jacket pocket, pulled out a toothpick, and slipped it into the corner of his mouth. He stared hard into Socrates' eyes.

"I want to see your sign-in log and yesterday's and to-day's security videos for both entrances," Socrates said. He pointed to the camera mounted above the entrance.

"You'll have to take the videos up with the management people. I don't have no authority to give the tapes to nobody, not even condo owners." He smiled. "You can look at my log book if you want, it's at the desk." He smiled again. "Now, Sir, if there's nothing else, I have doors to hold open."

SOCRATES SPENT THE next twenty-five minutes on the tele-phone with the management company, imploring the build-ing's agent to release the security videos to him in return for his goodwill. When this appeal fell flat, he threatened to call in the police. This carried sufficient inducement. The build-ing's management agent authorized the doorman to turn over the security tapes.

Socrates called Jade and read the note to her. He described how jolted he'd been when he first noticed it in his bedroom and then again when he actually read it. He invited her over to watch the security tapes with him.

JADE ARRIVED AS Socrates was inserting the first cassette into the VCR. He showed her the note. They went into the bed-room so Jade could see the pillow and bed she already knew so well. She also inspected the condo's windows, all of which were locked from the inside. They returned to the VCR.

"I called Youngest Brother before I came here," Jade said, "even though I knew what answer to expect to my question. Bing-enlai was upset that I was so bold in my direct approach to him, afraid our father might find out we were in contact.

"I wanted to know where my brothers were yesterday and this morning, if they were where I expected them to be. I didn't say anything to him about you."

Socrates remained silent, but nodded.

"As I anticipated, my brothers were with our father at the Golden Dragon, all day and evening, both days," she said.

"They were occupied with our family's annual homage to our deceased mother on the anniversary week of her death."

Socrates listened and held his skepticism in check.

"We conduct Taoist ceremonies all week long every year, and stay together for the week." Jade looked away briefly, then turned back to face Socrates. "I should have been there, too," she said. "None of my brothers invaded your home and left the message on your bed, in case you thought that."

Socrates wasn't quite as confident as Jade concerning the innocence of her brothers in this matter, but he said nothing. As always, he allowed Jade leeway with her family. He'd get to the bottom of this in his own time and in his own way. Either Jade's brothers were responsible or they weren't. In the meantime, he'd assume they were involved.

Socrates and Jade sat in silence and watched the two videos documenting the comings and goings of people at the building's two entrances. After much fast-forwarding, Socrates rewound the second cassette, ejected it, and turned off the VCR.

"That was a total bust," he said. "Any one of the three pizza delivery men, the STAPLES office supply guy, the florist's delivery woman, or the four dry cleaners' delivery people could have been the intruder. There's no way to tell from these tapes."

Jade leaned over and put her arms around him. She pulled him in close, hugged him tightly, then kissed him on his cheek.

"You don't have to do this, you know. If you pull out now we won't be any worse off with my father than before you became involved. We'll still have each other."

Socrates shook his head. "It's too late for that. I might be worse off with your father if I pull out after telling him I'd go forward. Besides. I want to know who broke in to my home and is threatening me and the people I care about — meaning my parents and you. I can't just ignore that."

Socrates paused and let his eyes stray across the room. Then he looked back at Jade. He dipped the tip of his finger into his glass of iced tea and slowly swirled the cubes.

"The problem is," he said, "I don't know if I'm being warned to stop helping your father with the recovery of the Mandarin Yellow and other stolen objects or to stop seeing you."

Jade shrugged. "Probably both," she said.

- Part Two -

Chapter 20

AFTER JADE LEFT him to go back to the university and Socrates had redelivered the security tapes to the doorman, he returned to his apartment and reread the intruder's note. He was convinced that Jade had been correct and that the note's subtext carried a threat against his parents and Jade if he went forward with the investigation as well as a warning to stop dating Jade. After all, if the message was only for him to stop seeing Jade, he should have received this note months ago.

He considered telling Bing-fa he'd changed his mind and would not help him, but it wasn't that easy and clear cut. He had to consider what Jade wanted him to do. He was sure that Jade's unstated desire was to use Socrates' assistance to her father to generate enough goodwill that Bing-fa would not only repatriate Jade with respect to her family, but would also accept Socrates as her lover. Since Socrates wanted these things, too, there was no reason for him not to help Bing-fa, at least as long as there was no immediate clear danger to his parents or Jade.

Socrates left his condo and walked the half mile into Georgetown to the THREE PROSPERITIES CHINA ARTS GALLERY. He paused just inside the entrance door and studied the large rectangular exhibit room.

The exhibit room was typical of other exhibit areas in other galleries he'd visited over the years — open and airy with soft, indirect lighting whose illumination evenly over-spread the room. The gallery's oak floors were bleached blond; its ample display walls were painted oyster shell white.

Socrates' observations were cut short by Assistant Director Fong's arrival directly in front of him.

"May I help you, Sir?" she said. Fong barely looked at Socrates as she spoke. Instead, she fixed her eyes on her eyeglasses which she held in one hand and vigorously polished.

Before Socrates could respond, Fong explained that the paintings currently on exhibit had been hastily assembled because of the recent burglary at the gallery.

"This show," she said, waving her arm at the walls, "is a short-term display of present-day Celestials' art available in inventory. We expect to open the postponed cultural exhibit in two or three weeks."

Fong offered to assist Socrates and to answer his questions about the works on display or about the artists. "Everything up on the walls," she said, gesturing again with her hand at a group of paintings, "is for sale."

There's a shock, Socrates thought.

Socrates strolled around the gallery, stopping occasionally to examine a painting, slowly walking his way through his charade, pretending to be interested in the substitute exhibit. After fifteen minutes of this, he yielded to boredom and dropped all pretense of being interested in the display. He walked over to the alcove where Ms. Fong sat at a desk. She got up out of her seat and smiled warmly as he approached.

"Did you see something that interested you, Honorable Sir?" she said. "I can consult with my superior to offer you reasonable payment terms."

Socrates shook his head. "I don't think I'll make a purchase today." He thanked Fong and assured her the gallery would be in his thoughts.

WHEN SOCRATES LEFT the gallery, he headed to the Second District police station (known among precinct cops and local newspaper reporters who covered the police beat as the 2D) to look at the official burglary crime file compiled by the investigating officers and by the police laboratory. He walked the mile and one half to the 2D from Georgetown, walking north along Wisconsin Avenue to the outer border of the Second District at Idaho.

The 2D station house was a two story, bland, oatmeal-colored brick cereal box resting on one long side. The front lawn that bracketed the entrance had lost most of its vegetation and now resembled a Hollywood version of the Moon. Most of the windows visible to Socrates from the front sidewalk were covered over and dark. The building had been constructed in the late 1960s or early 1970s, and would have been totally nondescript and fully forgettable if it weren't so ordinary and homely and, therefore, conspicuous in this otherwise attractive, mixed-use commercial and residential neighborhood. The building was, Socrates thought, a great argument against reflexive historic preservation. He fully expected that someday someone would argue that the 2D structure should be preserved, not demolished and replaced, as the singular historic example in Washington of its type of ugly municipal building.

SOCRATES ENTERED THE 2D, walked up five steps into a small, dimly lighted vestibule, and passed through a metal detector under the watchful eyes of an elderly man who wore a policeman's uniform. He found himself facing a raised counter enclosed in thick, yellowed Plexiglas. A police sergeant sat behind the protective shield. He looked up as Socrates approached and eyeballed him from head to toe as if taking the measure of any threat this visitor might present.

"May I help you, Sir?" The officer spoke through an amplification system that caused his voice to seem computer generated, but which permitted him to keep the bullet-proof shield closed.

It seemed to Socrates, based on the sergeant's furrowed forehead and barely visible scowl, that he was neither happy to see Socrates nor really interested in helping him.

Socrates played the role of the submissive civilian expected of him in this situation.

"Yes, Sir, I hope so," he said, feigning enthusiasm. "I'm looking into the burglary at the THREE PROSPERITIES CHINA ARTS GALLERY in Georgetown."

Socrates consciously modulated his voice, softening it. He maintained eye contact with the sergeant to the extent the cataract-like Plexiglas permitted eye contact. He nodded several times as he talked. His entire persona spoke by-the-book positive body language.

"I'd like to look through your file on the burglary, if you don't mind," he said.

The duty sergeant returned Socrates' nod, but not his smile. "Who are you and what's your connection to the case? Are you with the prosecutor's office?"

"My name's Socrates Cheng, Officer. No, I'm not an assistant DA."

Socrates pushed his driver's license through the small opening at the bottom of the Plexiglas shield. He felt as if he'd slipped his money through the slot of the cashier's office to buy a ticket for a movie that was already sold out.

"I'm looking into the burglary on behalf of a concerned citizen," he said.

The officer picked up Socrates' license, looked at it, then pushed it back through the opening. He studied Socrates' face through the opaque shield.

"So you're investigating the burglary, are you? Well now, that certainly makes all the difference in the world, doesn't it? It's a relief knowing the case will now be in capable hands."

This time the sergeant did smile, at least Socrates assumed it was a smile he saw undulate above the policeman's jaw. "Why don't I arrange for someone to gather up the files for you. I'll also bring in the investigating officers so you can interview them during their leisure time."

Socrates briefly considered responding in kind to the sergeant's sarcasm, but decided to let the man's mocking attitude pass. He reminded himself his mission at the 2D wasn't about accruing personal debating points. It was about gathering information already known to the police so he might find new leads to follow and also about avoiding leads the authorities had already determined to be dead ends.

"Sir," Socrates said, again consciously modulating his voice, "I'm just trying to assist some concerned DC citizens. I'm not trying to get in the way of the investigating officers or interfere with the official investigation. I don't mean to be a

problem, but I'd appreciate it if I could get some help by looking at the case file."

"Are you licensed?"

"No, Sir, I'm not, but I don't need to be. I'm not acting
as a paid private investigator. I'm just making some informal
inquiries as a private citizen, as a DC taxpayer helping someone."

"Oh, I see . . . . A *private* private investigator." He smiled
again, but this time his smile seemed twisted to Socrates.

"Well, Mr. *private* Private Eye, you can't see the file. The
investigation's still going on. You'll have to wait like anybody
else and look at the PD 251 Report when the case closes." He
paused briefly, smiled again, then added, "The operative term
being *when the case closes*. In the meantime, Sir, have a nice
day."

Chapter 21

SOCRATES CHECKED HIS watch as he left the 2D. He pushed
all thoughts of the investigation out of his mind for the time
being because he had something more immediate to contend
with. He and his father had agreed to meet for lunch.

This, in and of itself, was not unusual except that his
father wanted them to have lunch without Socrates' mother
coming along. His father had emphasized this point at the beginning and, again, at the end of the conversation when he'd
called to set up the meal.

Socrates couldn't remember the last time they'd gone out
to a meal without his mother coming along. So when his father
asked that they do so today, it set off alarm bells. Socrates had
responded, first, with a declaration of pleasure at the invitation, then, with a mild statement of surprise. His final reaction, one he left unstated, was a strongly felt sense of appre-
hension.

"SO, POP," SOCRATES said, as they settled into a booth at the
Full Kee Po restaurant located at 7th and H Streets in Chinatown, "I'm glad we're having lunch together, a guys' day out.
I must admit though, I was surprised you didn't go to the zoo
with mom or bring her along for lunch."

"I told your mother I was too tired to walk around just

to see a baby elephant. I wasn't though, not too tired, I mean. Anyway, I wanted time alone with you so we could talk. There's something you need to know."

Socrates nodded thoughtfully, but he felt his stomach tighten. He didn't like this preface to their talk. Not at all.

"That's fine, Pop," he said. "What's going on?"

"We talked it over, your mother and me. It's time for me to retire from the plant."

Socrates sighed softly and smiled. He realized he'd been holding his breath. "Is that all?" he said, relieved. "That's what you had to tell me?" *I was worried for nothing,* he thought.

But then it dawned on him that this innocuous piece of information could not be the reason his father wanted to have a private lunch with him. After all, his mother already knew about the retirement decision; his father had just said so. Something else was in play here. He'd just have be patient and go along with his father's script to find out what it was. So instead of pursuing his concerns, Socrates recited his expected responsive lines. But his sense of relief was gone.

"That's great, Pop." Socrates contrived a big grin. "You've earned it, that's for sure. Now you and mom can really start enjoying life, begin traveling and all, doing the things you never had time for when you were running the plant."

"There's more, Sonny. We're going to sell the house and move into a small condo."

"Smart decision," Socrates interrupted. "You don't need to be taking care of a big house anymore, especially since I'm in DC and rarely get back home."

"You know, somewhere here in Washington or nearby," his father continued, as if Socrates hadn't interrupted him. "Maybe in Maryland so we can be closer to you."

"Oh . . . ," Socrates said. He paused, then added, "That's nice. But are you sure this is the right move? Aren't you too young to retire? What'll you and mom do with yourselves? You'll drive each other nuts with all that time on your hands."

Socrates stared across the restaurant, unaware now he wasn't looking at his father as he spoke to him.

"Are you sure it's smart to pull up roots and leave your friends? I mean, does it make sense at your age and mom's to start over in a new city?"

"We want to be near you, Socrates, but it sounds like you don't like the idea," his father said.

"Of course I do, Pop. It's just . . . well, you know . . . ."

"No, I don't know," his father interrupted. "What's your problem with it?"

Socrates watched his father look away as he finished his question, and saw the corners of his mouth turn down, both time-tested indicators that his father's feelings had been hurt and he was fighting back tears.

Socrates had done it again. He had fallen prey to that old rule that had dogged him ever since he was a teenager whenever he had serious talks with his father *open mouth and insert foot*. His instinct now was to dissemble, to assuage his father's hurt feelings by saying he didn't mean his statement to sound the way it had come across. But his father knew him too well to be fooled by such a craven attempt at misdirection. When it came to seeing through Socrates, his father was as clear-sighted as any son could possibly dread. He always had been.

"Well, then," his father said, recovering his composure and sounding as he did when Socrates was a child and his father had disciplined him, "tell me what's your problem with me retiring and us moving here?"

Socrates balked at answering, at responding candidly. There were some things you just didn't say to your parents. He couldn't tell his father he feared he would inevitably slip into the role of being the parent of his parents if they moved nearby, or say that he'd prefer to handle their needs as they aged by proxy, using surrogates he would hire if they continued to live a few hundred miles north in Levittown.

As quickly as these thoughts romped through his mind, they evaporated. *It's time to stop feeling sorry for myself*, Socrates thought.

He looked at his father, nodded once, and said, "Actually, Pop, I think it's a great idea, both you retiring soon and you moving here. I'm all for it. You just caught me by surprise, is all. Sorry if I came across the wrong way." He reached across the table and patted his father's arm.

"There's one thing I don't understand, though," Socrates said. "Why couldn't mom come to lunch with us if retiring and moving here's what you wanted to tell me since she already knows?"

His father slightly lowered his chin and looked at Socrates over the top of his eyeglass frame. "Because there was something else I was going to bring up, something I haven't told your mother yet. I was going to tell you today, but I don't want to talk about it right now. Some other time, maybe."

Socrates didn't like the sound of that. Not at all.

SOCRATES WALKED HIS father back to the Westin Grand and chatted briefly with his mother who had already returned from the zoo. Afterward, Socrates walked home. As he neared his condo, his cell phone rang. It was his mother.

"Did I forget to kiss you goodbye or something, Mom?" Socrates said, smiling into his Droid smartphone.

"I want to know what you think about your father's condition. Did he have trouble remembering things?"

"Not at all. In fact, I was surprised because of what you said. Maybe he was just tired those other times."

"I didn't imagine it, Socrates," his mother said, speaking slowly and deliberately. "He's getting worse all the time. Did he tell you about the problem with the IRS he thinks I don't know about?"

"What IRS problem?" Socrates felt his spine reflexively shudder at the thought of a problem involving the tax authorities. "What're you talking about?"

"I'm not sure. He hasn't said anything to me, but the morning we left to come to DC someone from the IRS called to talk to him while he was in the shower. I tried to get the caller to tell me what it was about, but she wouldn't. She would only speak with your father because it concerned the plant, not our personal taxes."

"What did pop say when you asked him?"

"He said it was nothing, a misunderstanding." She paused, then added, "But I know that look he gets on his face when he's hiding something from me. I can't get anything out of him right now, but I wanted you to know something's going on with your father and his work. Something bad, or he'd tell me."

Chapter 22

AFTER HE LEFT his father and mother, Socrates, back home now, turned his attention to his investigation of the burglary.

He wanted some white noise in the background because he was about to undertake some mindless, but necessary, preliminary work. The white noise, he hoped, would take his mind off his father's problem and enable him to concentrate on the task at hand.

First, Socrates inserted a Thelonious Monk CD disc, *After Hours at Minton's,* into the CD player. Next, he fired up his computer. Once it booted, he entered the information from Bing-fa's listing of stolen objects into the computer, using a software program and an inventory database structure he had used the previous winter to keep track of his pen shop stock.

By using the database to catalog the stolen items, he'd later be able to sort through the records he had entered, using various combinations of search criteria (type of stolen object, value of each, age of object, and so forth). If he was lucky, the computer searches would reveal some pattern or theme among the stolen items where his own eyes saw none.

Once he obtained a copy of the exhibit catalog, he would enter the descriptions of all the exhibit's objects into his database — those stolen and those left behind by the burglars. He then would rerun the software to look for a theme that was common only among the stolen objects, another that was common only among the objects left behind by the burglars, and, another that was common to both groups of objects.

It took Socrates almost three hours of non-stop typing to fully populate the database. When he finished, he sorted the individual data records into seven general categories of Chinese cultural objects: WATERCOLORS AND CALLIGRAPHY SCROLLS, BRONZE VESSELS, JADE CARVINGS, IMPERIAL WARE PORCELAIN, BLUE & WHITE EXPORT CERAMICS, HISTORIC DOCUMENTS, and, the MANDARIN YELLOW fountain pen.

Socrates opened the database and scrolled to the category he'd labeled, IMPERIAL WARE PORCELAIN.

Imperial Ware was the finest porcelain produced in China, specifically created for the ruling emperor or empress by the most highly skilled potters and ware painters in the empire.

Each item of Imperial Ware underwent rigorous inspection during its creation to uncover any imperfections before its fate was settled. Three inspectors, each acting independently of the other two, scrutinized each object at every stage of its production. Only those few pieces without any imperfections were moved along to the next step; the others were smashed into unusable shards. The few finished artifacts that made it through this rigorous process would thereafter grace the tables of the Imperial Court for a one-time-only use, after which they were unceremoniously destroyed.

In undertaking this honorific duty, each inspector put his life on the line. If he missed a flaw and permitted an imperfect object to pass to the next stage of production, he would be summarily executed.

Imperial Ware was never lawfully exported from China. All Imperial Ware found outside China, whether in private collections or in museums, had been stolen and smuggled out of the country.

SOCRATES READ THROUGH the records he had entered into his database describing the Imperial Ware stolen from the gallery.

```
Small female rider on horse.
Polychrome glazed pottery.
Appropriate reign mark on bottom
Tang Dynasty [618-907 CE]

Green over white underglaze plate in
the shape of Lotus Petals. Yuan
Dynasty [1271-1368 CE]

Yellow glass bowl. Carved with
large dragon around sides amid
clouds. Qianlong reign mark on
bottom. No date.

Celadon vase. Southern Sun Dynasty.
Bluish green glaze with areas of
crackling. Flat base with six spur
marks. Appropriate reign mark on foot.
No date.

Ming yellow and white glaze warming bowl.
Circa. first half 16th Century CE.
Painted in the Cheng-hua palace bowl
style.

White glaze jar with dragon design on
interior. Ch'ing mark and period
[1644-1912]. Thick, creamy overall warm
glaze.
```

Socrates leaned back away from the monitor, closed his eyes and sighed a long, shuddering sound. He realized he was out-of-touch with recent Imperial Ware scholarship and discoveries. His knowledge of the subject dated back almost two decades to his course studies in college. Some important finds likely had been made since he stopped following China's archeological discoveries. He would have to engage in some intense reading to come up to speed.

He turned his attention back to the computer and opened the database category he had designated WATERCOLORS AND CALLIGRAPHY SCROLLS. He read through the descriptions of the stolen scrolls:

```
Portrait of Zhao Shi'e by Zeng Jing. Ming
Dynasty. Dated 1624 CE. Hanging scroll
painted on silk. With artist's chop and
three collector's chops.

Anonymous. 19th Century CE. Three
unframed portraits. Ink on silk.

Dong Qichang. Calligraphy in running
script. Hand scroll. Ink on silk. No
date.
```

He did not see anything helpful there.

Next, he considered the description of the only bronze vessel taken in the burglary:

```
Shang Dynasty. Wine cup. T'ao Tieih
design. Inscribed Shou-wui. No date.
```

It, too, appeared to be a dead end.

Socrates passed by the category BLUE & WHITE EXPORT CERAMICS stolen in the burglary because under this class he had entered the word: None.

He next turned his attention to the stolen historic documents. He was particularly interested in these artifacts because of his brief venture into collecting and selling Shanghainese commercial ephemera. He assumed the database descriptions would be meaningful to him because of his general knowledge of the Mandarin language and commercial documents, although all of the documents stolen would have been Imperial instruments, not commercial documents.

He looked over the five records:

Ch'ing Dynasty. Imperial mandate by Emperor
Kuang-hsti concerning trade with barbarians.
Dated 1874 CE.

Northern Sung Dynasty edict relating to Middle
Kingdom relationship with invaders from the
East. Dated 577 CE.

Xi'an Province. Primary Agreement, with
ancillary Secret Protocol. Both documents
signed by Chiang Kai-shek and Mao Tse-tung.
Both dated December 24, 1936.

Ch'ing Dynasty statement concerning condition of
navy and repairs of the northern wall along the
barbarian border. Dated 1851 CE.

Ming Dynasty. Record of important political
events during the reign of Emperor Cheng-hua.
Dated 1745 CE.

Socrates leaned his chair back on its hind legs, away from the monitor, and laughed. So much for his assumption he would have a leg up on this category. He didn't understand the import of these five documents, in terms of uncovering some theme, any more than he understood the significance of the other objects he'd just reviewed. He decided he probably needed to work with a larger sampling if a theme was to reveal itself to him. This, of course, assumed there was a theme and he wasn't drilling down a dry hole.

He next turned his attention to the stolen jade carvings. He thought about his father's deeply felt reverence for this mineral, a trait shared by many Chinese for whom the gem stone signified the five cardinal virtues of Confucianism: charity, modesty, courage, justice, and wisdom. His father and mother kept several small, modern jade objects prominently displayed in their home.

Socrates read through the descriptions of the stolen jade:

```
White jade bowl. Qianlong Period. Steep
sides. Beveled foot ring. Underside
inscribed with correct reign mark. No date.

Carved jade figure of a horse. Ming
Dynasty. Undated.

Jade Chrysanthemum dish. Thinly carved on
interior with overlapping petals. 17th
Century CE.
```

Socrates actually preferred carved ivory or wrought gold to jade. *Perhaps Bing-fa was correct about him after all,* he thought. *Maybe he didn't venerate jade like the typical Chinese person because he wasn't as Chinese as he liked to think he was.* He smiled, both at his little joke on himself and because he'd finally arrived at the description of the object he'd been savoring and saving for last, the historic Mandarin Yellow fountain pen.

The inventory's description of the pen was exactly what Socrates would expect to find in an exhibit catalog where the purpose of the description was to assist people in appreciating the displayed object, not to promote the sale of the item, as in an auction sale catalog.

The entry read:

```
Parker Pen Company Duofold model Mandarin
Yellow. First manufactured 1927. "Lucky
Curve" imprint on barrel with single,
narrow gold band on cap. This pen was
Production Copy No. 1. Inscribed by Parker
on barrel to Chiang Kai-shek.
```

Socrates finished reviewing the database records and looked at his watch. It was almost 10:30 p.m. His head ached and his bloodshot eyes burned and watered. He was bone tired, brain dead, and slightly buzzed from a scotch he'd been sipping. He was ready to quit for the night, too tired even to call Jade to say goodnight. He had only one more thing he needed to do before he logged off the computer and closed down.

Socrates opened the Firefox web browser, went online to the Google search engine, and looked for English translations of each of the five stolen documents. Having English language translations, he reasoned, would make his life much simpler. He wouldn't have to spend time brushing up on his Mandarin pictographic vocabulary in order to follow the texts.

His search for translations took him a little more than twenty minutes to complete. He found English language versions of all the documents except the Secret Protocol. He decided he would look for a translation of that document later in the week when he was less tired. He printed copies of the translations he'd found, and put them aside for the night.

Socrates logged off the computer, washed up and then climbed into bed. He was sorry now he hadn't taken a break earlier and called Jade to say 'hello' and then 'goodnight'. It would have been nice to hear her voice.

He laid in the dark with his eyes shut, hoping to trick his body and brain into shutting down, but he was unable to switch off his racing mind. Bing-fa's inventory kept scrolling by behind his closed eyelids as if he was still looking at the computer's monitor. The harder he tried to stop the parade of rolling images, the more insistent they seemed to be. He decided it was a losing battle.

He gave up after forty minutes and walked out to the living room. He poured himself a single malt scotch and put on a remastered CD of operatic arias, including one of his favorites by the composer Cilea, originally recorded in 1954 by Maria Callas. Then he stretched out on the couch with a Lawrence Block *Bernie Rhodenbarr* mystery.

Socrates always enjoyed Block's well-written and well-plotted Rhodenbarr novels featuring a main character who was a good natured, often humorous, seller of secondhand books in New York City, but who also happened to be a part time burglar specializing in stealing rare books, art and scarce collectibles. Invariably, while engaged in a burglary, Rhodenbarr would come across a dead body at the burgled premises, and, to avoid becoming the prime suspect in the homicide, would have to solve the murder himself before the cops found out about him and his role as burglar at the homicide crime scene.

Socrates decided he would read himself to sleep even if it meant falling asleep on the couch and spending the night there.

He had just started reading when his telephone rang.

Chapter 23

"HI, SOCRATES. IT'S me," Jade said. "Hope I'm not calling too late."

Socrates bolted up into a sitting position, dropping his feet to the floor and launching Bernie Rhodenbarr from his chest, where the book had been perched, far away from the couch, out onto the carpet. Socrates' smile split his face.

"Are you kidding? Not at all. I'm glad you called. It's never too late to talk to you." Socrates could feel his fatigue leach from his body as his adrenalin kicked in and he came awake.

"I'm starving," Jade said. "I'm at my office. I've been grading papers all day and night, and I'm going blind. Want to meet me in Georgetown for something to eat, then we can go home together?"

Socrates glanced at his watch. It was 11:40 p.m. Why not, he thought, he'd eaten later than that many times. "I need about twenty minutes to freshen up," he said. "I'll meet you at Billy Martin's, if that's all right."

Jade had arrived first. When Socrates walked in he saw her sitting at the bar facing the entrance. They exchanged waves from across the tavern floor as Socrates headed across the room to her.

Socrates leaned in and kissed Jade, holding the kiss.

When he moved to pull away, Jade held his lips to hers with a quick shake of her head, signaling him to keep going. The kiss lingered on.

Socrates heard a woman, who was sitting not far from them, say to someone, "You'd think they'd stop and come up for air."

Socrates glanced over and watched the woman shake her head in disapproval. He also saw the woman's companion, a middle aged man, slowly examine Jade from head to toe, and heard the man say, "Why? I wouldn't stop if I was him."

THEY DIDN'T WANT a full blown, multi-course meal, not at that late hour, so Socrates paid for Jade's drink and they left Billy Martin's. They walked north on Wisconsin Avenue to Five Guys to get two small hamburgers and Cokes.

Socrates and Jade threaded their way through the Five Guys' crowd of college-aged customers who were milling around the counter area waiting to pick up orders. They found a small table back in a corner of the enclosed patio. As they waited for their check-receipt number to be called, indicating they should pick up their order, Jade said, "So tell me, how's the aspiring private eye doing on his first case?" She smiled warmly, than pursed her lips and blew him a kiss.

"I'm making progress," Socrates said. "I'm figuring out what to do and how to do it by reading books about conducting criminal investigations, and by working with a database to query your father's inventory list. I'm still in the *taking baby steps* stage, trying to recognize the so-called proverbial *rope* so I can, as they say, *learn the ropes.*"

"Rrrrright," Jade said, stretching out the word for all the dramatic effect she could milk from it. "I know you, Socrates Cheng, better than you think. You're being too modest, as usual. What you call learning the ropes and taking baby steps, anybody else would describe as serious study and meaningful progress."

She waited a few seconds, giving Socrates time to demur. When he shrugged, blushed and remained silent, Jade said, "Come clean with me, Sherlock. My curiosity's killing me. What have you learned so far?"

Socrates grinned. He was pleased Jade was curious. "I've

developed questions and processes to think about," he said, "but I'm really still in the fact gathering stage, is all." He paused, waiting for Jade to respond.

When she remained silent and rolled her eyes, he said, "Really, Jade, that's all so far. And my attempts to find some theme or pattern among the stolen objects and non-stolen objects are on hold until I can get my hands on the exhibit catalog."

"Oh, dear," Jade said. "I wish I'd known. Youngest Brother brought me a catalog to look at, but I returned it to him after I finished with it, before our father could find out what Youngest Brother had done. I would have kept it for you if I'd known."

"Not to worry," Socrates said. "I'll get one from the gallery."

Jade nodded. "Good. But Socrates, my love, you're not off the hook. Give me a *for instance*, one question you came up with you can't answer until you have the catalog."

Socrates thought about the open issues he had mentally filed away to address at a later time.

"All right, here's one. I wonder why photographs and written descriptions of the Mandarin Yellow and other stolen objects haven't been posted on the Internet by the FBI or by Interpol. Such postings are standard art theft protocol."

"What's the answer?" Jade said.

"What do you mean?"

"What do *you* mean?" Jade said. "I asked first. What's the answer?"

Socrates slowly shook his head and smiled. "Come on, Jade. If I knew the answer, I wouldn't have described this as an open question, would I?"

Jade's face and neck reddened. "Point taken," she said. She smiled again. "Tell me another question you're actually struggling with, one more. I won't make a stupid remark afterward. Well, hopefully not."

Socrates looked at his watch. "Last one. Our order should be ready soon." He briefly closed his eyes and considered the open question. "Here's one that puzzles me." He paused for dramatic effect.

"Each of the cultural categories in the exhibit suffered the loss of at least one object in the burglary. All except the category Blue & White Export Ceramics. It makes me wonder why not that category? There certainly was a large enough selection of this ware for the burglars to choose from. What was it about the Blue & White Export ware that made the burglars leave it all behind?"

Socrates paused again for effect, then elaborated on his question. "Specifically, what does it say about the burglars?" He stared at Jade, then said, "Any thoughts?"

Jade split her face with a large grin and uttered a *tsk, tsk, tsk* sound as she held up her hand and wagged her index finger from side-to-side, as if she was gently reprimanding a small child.

"That's a no brainer, Socrates. I'm surprised you haven't figured it out. Maybe you're not as good a detective as my father thinks."

Socrates' face flushed. He was embarrassed and also annoyed by Jade's remark. "Cut the bull, Jade. What's the answer?"

Jade's smile grew larger, inspired by Socrates' reaction to her teasing. She looked lovingly at him and took his hand. Then she said, driving the knife in a little deeper, "I guess my father and Eldest Brother were right about you. You're not really Chinese after all. If you were, you would know the answer without me telling you."

Socrates frowned. "I *am* Chinese," he said, "but I don't know the answer. Either tell me or let's change the subject. I'm not in the mood for guessing games." He looked at his watch again. "Where's our food. It's taking too long."

Jade uttered *tsk, tsk, tsk* again and, undeterred by Socrates' self-conscious grim mood, grinned while she stared into his eyes. She patted his hand lovingly.

"The answer is simple, Darling. No knowledgeable Chinese man or woman considers Blue & White Export ware to be something worth owning. It's junk and everybody knows it."

She threw Socrates a kiss. "Everyone who's Chinese knows that Blue & White Export ware was inferior pottery that was mass produced by low-skilled potters, specifically for sale to the unsophisticated West. It was intended to satisfy the West's limitless desire for all things Oriental."

Socrates felt the warmth of a slow blush overspread his face, like a window shade slowly being drawn down.

"So," Jade said, "the answer to your question is obvious, isn't it?"

Socrates did not take the bait. He stared at Jade, waiting for her answer while he impatiently tapped his foot under the table.

"The answer is," Jade said, not yet letting go of the bone she'd clamped her teeth onto, "the burglars were Chinese, not Occidental. I know that because no self-respecting Chinese burglar would be caught dead stealing Blue & White Export ware."

In spite of himself, Socrates laughed, then pointed his finger at Jade, and said, "Touché."

But then he considered what Jade had said. *That makes sense*, he thought. *But given what Jade just described, why was the Blue & White even included as part of an exhibit intended to demonstrate the beauty and majesty of China's cultural heritage? Did its presence have some subtle purpose as yet unknown to him?*

Chapter 24

SOCRATES AND JADE spent the night at Socrates' condo. The following morning after Jade had left, Socrates called Bing-fa and asked for a meeting. They agreed to get together at the Golden Dragon.

Youngest Brother and the Twins met Socrates just inside the restaurant's entrance. They seemed to be waiting for him. Socrates nodded to them as he entered, but said nothing. He eyed them warily.

The three brothers darted their eyes back and forth among themselves as if they were silently conveying messages only they could understand. Latent hostility imbued the air. Youngest Brother turned to Socrates and said, without otherwise acknowledging his arrival, "Come with us."

Bing-fa sat at the head of a long, rectangular rosewood table in a small, private dining room located at the back of the restaurant. He rose from his chair as Socrates entered. Bing-fa, speaking Mandarin, ordered his sons to leave him alone with Socrates and to close the door on their way out. Socrates was pleased he was able to understand Bing-fa's vernacular, non-Shanghainese instructions to his sons.

After they concluded the ritualistic greetings and small talk expected for these occasions, Socrates gave Bing-fa a full status report concerning the investigation. He emphasized his unsuccessful attempt to look at the police files.

"Without access to these files," he said, "I won't have the benefit of the lab's work with the physical evidence or know the identities of potential witnesses. I'll have to cover the same ground the cops did, costing us valuable time. Not only that, it's also possible I'll miss something or someone that they, as seasoned pros, think relevant."

Bing-fa shrugged and fanned out his palms and fingers in gestures Socrates interpreted as Bing-fa's tacit message: That's your problem, not mine. Deal with it.

"I am confident," Bing-fa said, "you will locate the precious objects within the required time without needing the crutches local authorities rely on. Ineffectual, dependent bureaucracies are the same everywhere."

Socrates said nothing. Bing-fa's attitude left him with mixed feelings. Should he be flattered by Bing-fa's blind faith in him or annoyed that Bing-fa had just flippantly brushed aside his legitimate concern?

Socrates forced himself to refocus his attention on the reason he'd wanted this meeting. He had come to Bing-fa with a full tray of questions to serve on him.

Socrates led off by stating he was surprised photographs and descriptions of the stolen objects had not been posted on the usual art theft web sites for the world to see. Such postings, he said, would limit the ability of the burglars to dispose of their contraband and make it more likely the stolen objects would be recovered.

"Were you aware of this, Bing-fa?" Socrates said.

"I was."

Bing-fa's response blindsided Socrates. He hesitated, regrouped, and asked, "Then why wasn't that done?"

"The Embassy and I believe such an action might unduly involve the authorities and the public in matters better left private. We prefer that the stolen articles be discreetly recovered by you."

Bing-fa's answer struck Socrates as odd if Bing-fa's true objective was to recover the stolen objects. This seemed especially true given the compressed timetable they were operating under. He let the issue pass for the time being.

"There's something else I need to know," Socrates said. "How did you and the cultural attaché select the items to exhibit? You must have had many treasures in Mao's secret archives to choose from."

Once again Bing-fa remained silent.

After a long pause weighted with unstated ambiguity, Socrates said, "Bing-fa, if I'm going to be able to help you, I need to know . . . ."

"You do not need to know this to perform your duties," Bing-fa said. "Our reasons are not relevant to your investigation . . . . Now, what else do you want?" Bing-fa tapped his foot under the table.

Socrates thought about his mounting frustration. He needed answers to his questions. Bing-fa's responses might hold the key to the reason the burglars chose certain objects to steal and opted to leave others behind. That information, in turn, might point the way to understanding the burglars' overarching motive for the theft. And knowing the burglars' motive might point the way to the identity of the burglars and the recovery of the Mandarin Yellow and other stolen objects.

Socrates refused to acquiesce in Bing-fa's unwillingness to answer his questions. He pressed on, feeling he had nothing to lose at this point, crafting his questions so they were more specific.

"Why'd you select the Ming Dynasty yellow and white glaze warming bowl rather than choose some other Ming ware or some other dynastic porcelain ware of equal or greater aesthetic value or historic importance?"

Again, Bing-fa did not answer. He slightly shrugged his shoulders, then continued to sit passively with his fingers interlaced on his lap. He stared into Socrates' eyes.

Socrates sighed. He would give it one more try. If Bing-fa remained uncooperative, he'd call it a day.

"All right, Bing-fa, let's try it this way. Why'd you pick the Xi'an Agreement and its Secret Protocol to exhibit rather than some other historical document equally important in China's history? You must have had some reason for your choice. Or, was your decision merely capricious?"

This time Bing-fa surprised Socrates by responding.

"We did not act whimsically, but you do not need to know why we acted as we did."

This response did not sit well with Socrates. *That arrogant son-of-a-bitch,* he thought. *Intentionally blindfolding me, then sending me out under a tight deadline. Lots of luck resolving this in time for the rescheduled opening.*

Socrates consciously relaxed his body to release the tension in his shoulders and neck. He recited, sotto voce, the Taoist phrase he had learned from his father and had put to good use many times in his lifetime — *wei wu wei* — the Taoist mantra meaning *do not get in your own way.* Act without forcing results. Let matters take their own course.

Socrates looked closely at Bing-fa and nodded grudgingly. "We have to get something straight, Bing-fa, if I'm going to be able to help you. I need your full cooperation. Otherwise, we're just wasting our time. Time, I might add, we don't have the luxury of wasting if you really want the exhibit's rescheduled opening date to be your deadline for me."

Bing-fa nodded thoughtfully. Socrates welcomed this as his indication of agreement.

"Okay, then," Socrates said, "this is what I want you to tell me. Was there anything common among the stolen objects that was absent from the items not taken? Some theme, maybe, or some pattern I should be aware of?"

Bing-fa responded by delivering a brief lecture. He acted as if Socrates knew little or nothing about China's art, history and culture, as if Socrates had not studied the subjects as his college major, as if Socrates had not grown up in the home of a Shanghainese father and Shanghainese grandparents.

Bing-fa concluded his lecture by saying that he and the Embassy's recently deceased cultural attaché had designed the exhibit to display the splendor and majesty of cultural and historic China for the West as reflected in objects hidden from public view in the Chairman's secret archives. He also said that the objects selected, when taken together, conveyed an accurate representation of the aesthetic achievements of the Middle Kingdom over several hundred years.

Then Bing-fa laughed softly, and added that China's cultural achievement included the Middle Kingdom's success in deceiving the West into believing that inferior Blue & White Export Ware was worth acquiring from China.

"Our decision to include Blue & White Export ware among the many priceless treasures was our little joke on barbaric Occidentals who would come to see the presentation." He chuckled again.

Then Bing-fa's face changed and lost its mischievous look. "In making the other selections," he said, "we did not intentionally seek any common aspect among the objects to be displayed. That never occurred to us. But reflecting now upon your question, I see that such commonality might have existed."

Socrates perked up and listened attentively. This was what he'd been waiting for.

"All the objects to be displayed, other than the Blue & White Export ware, were discovered in the Chairman's secret archives within the past eight years. None has ever been seen by the public before, East or West. The opening of the exhibit will be their public unveiling."

Bing-fa stopped and adjusted the knot on the belt around his waist. Then he continued. "Several of the stolen objects — the female rider on a horse, the Xi'an Agreement's Secret Protocol, the Shang Dynasty wine cup, the Northern Sung Edict, and the Ch'ing Dynasty Imperial Mandate — were not even known to exist before the planning for the exhibit, not even as rumors, until recently."

Chapter 25

THE NEXT MORNING when the THREE PROSPERITIES CHINA ARTS GALLERY opened for business, Socrates was out front on the sidewalk staring at the CLOSED sign hanging behind the glass door. He watched as a disembodied wrist and hand suddenly materialized from the darkness behind the glass, gripped the small sign, and turned it over. The sign now indicated OPEN.

Socrates waited a few seconds to compose his thoughts, then stepped into the gallery and looked around. At the same time, Linda Fong looked up at him from where she stood alongside her desk. Socrates quick-stepped across the showroom over to the alcove.

Fong fixed her gaze on Socrates as he approached. She perched her left hand on one hip and cocked that hip and her head to the side.

Socrates suppressed a smile. *All she needs is an accordion playing in the background,* he thought, *a navy blue beret on her head, and a cigarette dangling from the corner of her mouth to make the Parisian noir image complete.*

"Good morning," Fong said. She smiled broadly. "Welcome back. Are you here to buy one of the watercolors or, perhaps, to see the exhibit again? She gestured with her hand toward some paintings on one wall.

"Not today," Socrates said. "I'm here to see the director. My name's Socrates Cheng. Tell her I'd like to talk with her for a few minutes."

Fong's bearing noticeably stiffened. She dropped her left hand from her hip and narrowed her eyes. "The honorable director is not here." Fong turned away from Socrates and walked around behind her desk. Then she turned back to face him.

Fong's sudden hostility puzzled Socrates. He consciously softened his voice. "When do you expect her?"

Fong shrugged. "In the early afternoon, perhaps. Or possibly later. It is hard to say." There was no warmth in her voice.

"In that case," Socrates said, "so my trip here's not wasted, I'd like to buy an exhibit catalog. The one for the postponed cultural exhibit, not for the show up now," he said, tilting his head toward the paintings on display.

Fong shook her head. "The catalogs are not for sale, not until the replacement catalogs have come back from the printer. Is there anything else I can do for you?"

The irony and sarcasm of Fong's last statement were not lost on Socrates. He took a step closer to her, moving around to the side of the desk. He glared at her as he spoke.

"That's not good enough, Ms. Fong. I'm investigating the burglary at the request of Master Li Bing-fa. I need the catalog for my investigation for him." He pointed to the stack of perfect bound catalogs piled on a chair across from the alcove.

Fong followed Socrates' finger with her eyes, then looked back at him and shrugged her indifference. "I just told you, they are not for sale. The color is wrong. The books are going back to the printer to be pulped and reprinted. You cannot have one."

Socrates stepped back, away from the desk, and deliberately raised the tone of his voice half an octave to moderate it. He cocked his head slightly to one side in a subtle attempt at classic subservient body language.

"Please, Ms. Fong," he said, speaking gently. "I really need your help. Just let me buy one of the defective catalogs. I don't care about the print color. I just need to see the images and read their descriptive captions for my investigation."

Fong's eyes hardened. "I just told you, they are not for sale. Now, if you don't mind, you are keeping me from my work."

Socrates knew he was beaten for now. "What's the best time for me to come back today to talk with Director Hua?" he asked.

"After 1:00, maybe later, but you will be wasting your time. The director won't permit you to have a catalog either."

Chapter 26

SOCRATES RETURNED TO the gallery a little after 3:00 o'clock to meet with the director. He hoped Fong would not be there.

He'd intentionally delayed his return to the gallery to a time later than the 1:00 hour when, according to Fong, Iris Hua was due to arrive back. He wanted to give Director Hua breathing room after she returned to work, time to respond to phone messages and time to catch up with anything else that demanded her immediate attention. He hoped his unstated thoughtfulness would reflect itself in her good mood and make her more amenable to talking with him.

Socrates entered the gallery, removed his sunglasses, and waited for his eyes to adjust to the artificial light. He could barely make out the silhouette of a woman standing next to a desk in the alcove. She had her back to him. Because she was not the assistant director, he assumed she was Iris Hua.

Hua turned toward the entrance door as Socrates closed it. She hurried across the exhibit room, taking short, quick steps toward him. An effusive smile overspread her face.

While still a dozen feet away from Socrates, but closing fast, Hua abruptly shut down her smile and stopped walking. The director had just recognized Socrates, although they had never met.

The word's out about me, Socrates thought. Hua's assistant obviously had warned her that Socrates would be coming back this afternoon.

"I'll be with you in a minute," Hua said. There was no vendor's warmth in her voice. She clearly knew who he was and why he was there, and she wasn't pleased.

Hua turned and walked back across the exhibit room to her desk. She gathered up some papers and put them in a drawer. Then she turned to face Socrates again, but this time from across the showroom. She stared at Socrates and remained silent.

Socrates walked over to the alcove. "I'm Socrates Cheng," he said. He extended his arm to shake hands as he stepped into the alcove. "I came by this morning to see you. I spoke with your assistant."

"She told me." Iris Hua did not accept his proffer to shake hands. "What is it you want, Mr. Cheng? I doubt I can help you."

"I'm investigating the burglary," Socrates said. He paused a few seconds, waited for some reaction, then resumed when none was forthcoming.

"I'm acting on behalf of interested parties," he said. "I represent powerful people in your community." He paused and again waited futilely for some response, then said, "I have some questions, only a few, then I'll get out of here and leave you alone."

The director shook her head, but didn't say anything.

"There's one other thing," Socrates said, "besides my questions. I need an exhibit catalog. I don't care about the color. I need the information written about each object and the 1:1 scale photographs. I'll pay for the catalog. How much is it?" He slid his hand into his right pants pocket and pulled out a folded stack of currency held together by a silver money clip.

"I won't answer your questions," Hua said, "and the catalogs are not for sale. Now, unless you have something else to say, I would appreciate it if you will please leave. I am very busy."

She did not apologize for her unaccommodating attitude or offer Socrates any off-the-shelf excuses. She simply nodded sharply once as if to underscore the rightness and non-negotiable character of her position, then turned away and walked around behind her desk. She started rearranging a stack of mail.

"Anything you say to me will stay between us," Socrates said. "I won't make things awkward for you. I promise. I'm just here trying to help Honorable Li Bing-fa, is all."

The director looked up. She raised her head and eyes to Socrates' level and moved her head with what Socrates thought was contrived languor, as if she was emerging in slow motion from a trance.

"Mr. Cheng," she said, her voice taking on a patronizing sing-song tone, "I already know you represent the Honorable Li Bing-fa so I am not influenced by your statement and its implied coercion. But I am curious about one thing. Please tell me, if you will: Which part of what I just said to you, do you not understand?" She locked gazes with Socrates. Then she said again, speaking very purposely, "I have nothing at all to say to you, except, this: I will not talk with you about the burglary or permit you to have a catalog. That is final." She let this sink in briefly, then said, "Now, leave before I call the police."

Socrates' neck and face burned. "Wait a minute," he said, his nascent irritation now maturing into anger and percolating to the surface. "I don't appreciate being brushed off. I don't know who you think you are. I told you, I'm here on behalf of . . . ."

He let his statement fizzle into silence in the face of Director Hua's almost imperceptible shrug and briefly raised left eyebrow, which together silently screamed her indifference. Socrates saw the picture. The woman was neither impressed with his fervor nor daunted by his assertion of putative authority.

Iris Hua slowly wagged her head. She spoke very softly, but deliberately now, emphasizing each word, using a condescending tone that offended Socrates. "Mr. Cheng, I do not care who you are, why you are here, or who you represent. I want you to leave. Now." She crossed her arms over her chest.

Socrates was about to respond in kind when he heard the

unmistakable clicking sound of wooden doorway beads banging together as someone walked through the hanging strands
into the exhibit room. He turned in time to see Linda Fong
emerge from the beaded doorway.

"Is there a problem, Director Hua?" Fong said. She rushed
over to the alcove. "I heard angry voices."

Oh, right, thought Socrates. *You obviously were eavesdrop-
ping on us. We weren't loud and we weren't angry, just determined,
was all.*

The assistant director stopped walking when she came
near Socrates. "Oh, it's you," she said. She turned her head
toward the director. "I am sorry, Honorable Director Hua. I
did not mean to interrupt. I is just I thought I heard someone
arguing."

"Everything is fine, Assistant Director. Go back to your
work. This person is just leaving." She flicked the back of her
hand at Fong, motioning her away.

Assistant Director Fong bowed her head once, looked at
Socrates from the corner of her eye, and turned and headed
back through the wooden beads.

Socrates waited until she'd left, then said to the director,
"Ms. Hua, what's the problem selling me a catalog? I don't
plan on passing it around. I just want to use it as a reference
tool for my investigation. I'll even bring it back to you when
I'm finished, if you want."

Iris Hua drilled her eyes into Socrates' eyes, and said
again, speaking as slowly and deliberately as one might talk
to a recalcitrant child, "Please listen to me, Mr. Cheng." She
paused until Socrates nodded. "I told you, I will not answer
your questions and I will not sell you a catalog. Is that clear?"
She waited a beat, then said, "Now, please go and stop wasting
my time. I have no more to say to you."

Socrates said. "Fine. Have it your way. For now."

He turned to leave and noticed Linda Fong standing
across the room in the doorway behind the beads, listening.
He winked at her as he walked past.

Socrates left the gallery and walked around the corner.
Once out of sight of the gallery, he took out his cell phone and

called Bing-fa. Socrates recounted his experiences that morning with the assistant director and this afternoon with the director.

Bing-fa said he would remedy the situation, that he would arrange for Socrates to have productive meetings with both women, and would see to it that Socrates received a catalog. He told Socrates that he or one of his sons would soon get back to him.

Chapter 27

THE NEXT MORNING Socrates awoke early and went for a run in Rock Creek Park. He ran three miles out and three in. The run worked. Socrates no longer felt stressed.

His plan for the day was to shower, then call Jade to see if she could meet him for lunch, and then turn back to the investigation.

As he approached his front door, Socrates pulled out his key ring, but stopped abruptly, his key poised inches from the STRASBURG dead bolt security lock.

The door was open nearly two inches.

Socrates stood motionless, held his breath, and listened for the sound of movement inside. He heard nothing.

Adrenalin kicked in and lubricated his judgment. His eyes narrowed; his nostrils flared. One part of his conscious mind, fueled by his flowing hormones, hoped he would find the intruder present. The resistant, rational part of his conscious mind hoped the intruder had already left.

He placed his knee against the door and slowly pushed it open until he could ease himself inside. He was feline alert, listening for the faintest sound as he tried to sense the presence and location of the intruder. He tiptoed into the foyer and looked around. Nothing seemed out of the ordinary.

He stepped over to the living room and looked in. Nothing.

He quietly walked to the kitchen. It, too, was clear. He looked in the guest bedroom and bathroom. Still nothing.

Just a few areas left to clear, he thought. *The master bedroom, its bathroom, and all the closets.*

He edged up to the wall alongside his bedroom doorway and listened. The room seemed preternaturally still. In fact, the whole apartment seemed unnaturally quiet. No street noises seeped in through the bank of windows fronting the street, and no neighbors along the hallway slammed doors as they entered or left their condo apartments.

He waited, taking shallow breaths so he could hear the slightest movement inside.

Nothing.

He stepped into his bedroom and looked around.

Everything seemed to be in order. Everything, that is, except for the one thing on his bed, and that thing left him breathless.

Chapter 28

IT HAD HAPPENED again. Someone had bypassed his two locks and the building's security and had entered his home.

This time the intruder hadn't left a threatening note. Instead, this time the intruder left a copy of the exhibit catalog, a copy with its front cover torn off, sitting on Socrates' bed, leaning up against the pillows where the note had been left.

Socrates broke out in a heavy sweat. He wiped the perspiration from his forehead with the back of his hand and gradually took control of his emotions. He forgot all about checking the closets to see if the intruder, surprised by Socrates' return before he could exit, still lurked in the apartment.

Socrates picked up the catalog, using his handkerchief to hold it by its corner, careful to preserve any latent finger or palm prints or DNA the intruder might have left on the defaced book. He placed the catalog in a large, clear plastic Baggie, left his apartment, and taxied over to the 2D. He reported the break-in to the police, completed several forms reporting the crime, and left the bagged evidence with the cops. Then he walked home.

He was stressed. More than he'd been in a long time. He decided not to shower yet, not to change into fresh cloths just now. He needed to run again. So he donned his running gear and headed back to Rock Creek Park.

AS SOCRATES REACHED mile two in his run, he smoothed his pace, instinctively lengthened his stride, and, ever aware that time was slipping away before the date of the exhibit's rescheduled opening, thought about his progress so far in understanding the burglary.

He tried to put himself in the frame of mind of the gallery's burglars, and considered possible reasons they might have selected one object to steal over another. *Why would they take nineteen objects and leave behind several hundred others?* he wondered. *What would I have been thinking had I been the burglar?*

Socrates comfortably passed the three mile mark in his run.

In considering the burglars' rationale, Socrates first eliminated the size and weight of the objects left behind as criteria because Bing-fa had told him that all the objects in the exhibit were small, easily hidden, and could be easily carried away. Even the large calligraphy scrolls could be rolled and readily transported.

Socrates' fundamental dilemma was that he didn't understand why someone would bother to steal any of the objects, let alone the specific works they'd selected. *After all*, he thought, *it wasn't as if there was a ready-made secondary market for them. At least there wouldn't be if the Embassy and Bing-fa would change their approach and report the crime to the FBI and Interpol.*

Yet the burglars could not have known that the theft wouldn't be posted when they planned it. They would have assumed — rightfully, he thought — that the usual protocols would be followed, information about the burglary would be posted online, and that, as a result, it would be difficult for them to dispose of the stolen objects. Socrates doubted, therefore, that the primary reason for the burglary was to dispose of the articles in an aftermarket. There had to be some other reason.

Socrates quickened his pace, passed the four-mile mark, and thought about the usual reasons professional thieves stole art.

The typical reason for art theft was no different than the usual reason for most thefts — the thief's desire either to possess the contraband for himself or to convert the loot into cold cash. Socrates discounted the first reason as unlikely. Professional burglars rarely were motivated to commit a theft so they could own the stolen property, *professional* being the key term here.

The second reason—the 'convert to cash' motivation—made good sense if the objects taken were not well known and would not raise an instant alarm in the art community if they were offered for sale. But this motive would not serve the thief well if the stolen objects were the subject of an exhibit catalog or were illustrated in books, magazines or journals, or were otherwise so much a part of the cultural landscape that they could be readily identified. In this instance, Socrates decided, the burglars would have anticipated that the stolen objects would be the subject of an illustrated catalog as part of the exhibit. The items, therefore, from that point of view would not be readily convertible into cash in the usual black market outlets.

Socrates thought about this in light of what he'd learned from Bing-fa at their meeting. The only common thread running through the stolen objects was that they all had been recently discovered, at most, within the past eight years and some as recently as six months ago, and none had ever been displayed to the public. This suggested that resale could have been the burglars' motive after all, even though the objects were illustrated in the exhibit catalog, because it would have been unlikely that any of the articles would be recognized if surreptitiously offered in the black market in some city other than Washington.

Yet, as logical as this was, it seemed to Socrates that the burglars might still have difficulty selling the objects to third parties. The problem might result from the current trend among governments to criminally prosecute art and antiquities dealers, collectors, and museum curators by assuming that any artifacts they possessed over a certain age had been stolen or plundered. This put the burden of rebutting the presumption on the person arrested and charged with unlawful trafficking, including buyers of the antiquities who often knew no more about their purchases than the sellers were willing to tell them.. Consequently, most prospective buyers had become very demanding in their requirement for legitimate, defensible paperwork that authenticated the age, lineage and purchase history of offered items.

Socrates thought about this. This negative climate militated against the so-called resale theory, and led to another common motive for art theft, in particular — the desire of the thief to obtain the stolen goods to meet the specific request of a specific client.

Socrates had once read in *Connoisseur* magazine that there existed a netherworld of super-wealthy collectors scattered around the planet who paid large sums of money to acquire well known, but stolen works of art or historic documents. In certain instances, the magazine article indicated, the thieves stole objects to order, targeting specific artifacts to satisfy a collector's particular request.

These collectors never displayed their purloined art or documents for others to see. They took their pleasure in the very possession and private viewing of such well known, high profile stolen works, deriving perverse gratification from knowing that they alone possessed, and that they alone could gaze upon, the stolen object.

That, Socrates thought, *might explain the burglary at the gallery.* At least it would explain it as much as anything else he'd thought about it so far.

SOCRATES FINISHED HIS run, showered and dressed, and made himself a peanut butter sandwich. After he finished eating, he inserted another Maria Callas disc — her June 1955 Rome performance of *Norma* — into the CD player, and laid down on the living room carpet in front of one of his speakers. He thought about his two prime motivations for pursuing the investigation for Bing-fa: to please Jade by pleasing her father; and, his desire to win Bing-fa's approval of his relationship with Jade. As he thought about this, three loud, rapid knocks on his door jarred Socrates from his reverie.

That's strange, he thought. *No one's supposed to get up here without first being announced over the intercom. This won't do at all. I'll have to talk to George again.*

But then he thought, *A lot good that'll do. Whoever left the note during the first break-in and dropped off the catalog on my pillow during the next one, obviously had bypassed George.*

Socrates walked to the door and looked through the security peep hole. He smiled and opened the door.

"Hello, Youngest Brother. Nice surprise. Come in."

Youngest Brother didn't move. "I have come with a message from my venerable father. He has instructed me to tell you that Director Hua will meet with you tomorrow morning at 10:00 at the art gallery, and that she will be most pleased to cooperate with you in all respects."

Socrates nodded and smiled. *Good,* he thought, *Bing-fa came through after all.* "Please thank your honorable father for me," he said.

Youngest Brother bowed his head, then looked up and said, "I have a second message. My venerable father would be most grateful if you will meet with him at the Golden Dragon. He suggests a meeting within the hour would be suitable."

This stoked Socrates' curiousity. What might be so pressing that Bing-fa gave him less than an hour's notice to meet. He knew it would be futile to press Youngest Brother for more information. Bing-enlai probably didn't know what his father had in mind, and surely wouldn't tell Socrates even if he did know.

Socrates said, "Tell Honorable Bing-fa I will be happy to meet with him within an hour."

When he was alone again, Socrates ran through a mental checklist of possible reasons for the unplanned meeting. He came up empty.

Chapter 29

WHEN SOCRATES ARRIVED at the Golden Dragon forty-five minutes later, Eldest Brother met him at the front door. True to form, he said nothing to welcome Socrates. He merely glared at him and said, "Come." Eldest Brother turned away and walked toward the back of the restaurant. He led Socrates to a room where Bing-fa sat alone at a rectangular table.

Bing-fa remained impassive until his son had left the room and closed the door. He turned toward Socrates, smiled, and gestured toward a chair.

"Excuse my intrusion today into your affairs, but we have encountered a new circumstance."

This should be interesting, Socrates thought, *else why'd he get me over here in such a hurry?*

"This morning," Bing-fa said, "I received a communication from someone who offered to deliver the precious writing instrument to me in return for my payment of $8,000 and my pledge of silence. I intend to conform to the caller's requirements."

Socrates raised an eyebrow. He didn't like this turn of events. It suggested too many possibilities, most of them negative. He decided, however, that he should be circumspect and, at the very least, explore the matter with Bing-fa before he threw a wet blanket over it.

"Did you recognize the caller's voice, Bing-fa? Was it a male or a woman?"

Bing-fa shook his head. "A man. A Celestial person. He spoke Shanghainese."

Socrates nodded thoughtfully. "Did he say anything about the stolen art and documents? Are they included in the $8,000 ransom?"

"We spoke only of the cherished Mandarin Yellow."

"Have you called the police?"

"Of course not. I will not involve the authorities."

Socrates pushed back his chair. He stood and walked to the far side of the room, keeping his back to Bing-fa. He thought about what he'd just been told.

He slowly turned back to face Bing-fa. "I don't think you should do this," he said, "not until we know more. It might be a scam."

Socrates watched Bing-fa's eyes narrow. He wrinkled his forehead and glared at Socrates. *He clearly wasn't pleased with that response*, Socrates thought.

"Explain yourself," Bing-fa said. He voice had acquired an edge.

"You don't know if this person actually has the Mandarin Yellow," Socrates said, "your Mandarin Yellow. You only know he said he does. Keep in mind that the pen was the only stolen object specifically mentioned in the *Washington Post*'s article. The caller could have learned about it from the newspaper. He might not actually have your pen." Socrates paused to let Bing-fa respond.

"Go on," Bing-fa said.

"If you want to assume this isn't a con, and you pay over the money and actually get back your Mandarin Yellow, that's good. It's your money. You can risk it if you want. But I have to ask, what's next? Do you keep on paying, over and over, until you buy back everything, probably one at a time?"

Bing-fa shrugged. "That would not be important. What matters is that we rescue our country's stolen patrimony and return it to the gallery in time for the opening of the Embassy's glorious exhibit."

"It's blackmail," Socrates said, "extortion. You'll have a

fortune squeezed from you, one artifact at a time, if you give in now."

Bing-fa shrugged again as if to say, *What part of 'That would not be important'* did you not understand?

Socrates realized he was beating the proverbial dead horse, but he was frustrated by the ease with which Bing-fa seemed to be willing to dismiss his efforts and surrender to the burglar's demands.

Well, Socrates thought, *if that horse is dead, so be it.* He'd let it lie there. "It's your money, Bing-fa. You can spend it any way you want."

When Bing-fa remained silent, Socrates realized he couldn't leave well enough alone. Bing-fa's cavalier attitude gnawed at him. "It doesn't seem very smart to me, however, to give in without at least trying to negotiate a better arrangement for yourself."

Socrates walked back and again sat across from Bing-fa. He put his hand on the table and rolled quiet drumbeats with his fingers.

"Paying $8,000 for a $2,200 pen, even one with great historic associations like your Mandarin Yellow, isn't a good way to bargain for the other stolen art and documents, *bargaining* being the operative term here," Socrates said. "Whoever broke into the gallery probably won't be able to sell the art and other objects except to you. You're undoubtedly his best customer, maybe the only one. You should take advantage of that and negotiate a more realistic price." He paused to let Bing-fa respond.

Bing-fa still said nothing. Socrates didn't know how to read Bing-fa's persistent silence.

"If you insist on going ahead," Socrates said, "in spite of my advice, I'll handle the negotiation for you. It's what I do. I mean, it's what I did, as a lawyer. I assume that's why you wanted me here today."

Bing-fa shook his head. "No. I will do this myself," he said. "I must recover the beloved Mandarin Yellow in just the manner the caller specified. I won't jeopardize our national treasure to preserve money or to win an inconsequential financial advantage. The price is of no consequence to me."

Socrates wasn't surprised by Bing-fa's response.

"I have told you this because I thought you should know," Bing-fa said, "not to obtain your approval."

Socrates wasn't quite ready yet to let go of his point. "Don't you find it strange the caller didn't also offer you the other stolen items, even for an additional payment?"

Socrates waited for Bing-fa response. When none came, he continued. "Wouldn't it make sense to sell you everything at once rather than risk being caught each time he arranges another sale?"

"I only know what the caller told me and what he has offered and demanded," Bing-fa said. "Nothing else." He paused, then said, "Now I must leave to gather the payment in the required small denomination Yuan. The caller will contact me again to make arrangements to meet."

Socrates fanned out his hands, palms up, and said, "So be it."

As he left the Golden Dragon, an ominous thought crossed Socrates' mind. If Bing-fa successfully ransomed the Mandarin Yellow and if he later made arrangements to buy back everything else, he'd no longer need Socrates' help. Socrates' role would be over and he'd never be able to earn his way into Bing-fa's good graces. And that would mean, as far as Socrates winning Bing-fa's approval of him and Jade remaining together, that this possibility, too, would come to a premature and infelicitous end.

Chapter 30

THE FOLLOWING MORNING Socrates walked to the gallery to keep the 10:00 appointment he'd made with the director thanks to Bing-fa's intervention. He arrived ten minutes before opening time, but hesitated at the front door, surprised to find it slightly ajar. He checked his watch. Not quite 10:00 yet. The CLOSED sign still showed through the door's glass pane.

Socrates stepped inside and was immediately enfolded in a mantle of ice cold air. Neither Iris Hua nor Linda Fong was anywhere in sight.

The first thing Socrates noticed, aside from the frigid temperature and the conspicuous absence of the gallery's only two employees, was a pervasive copper-like odor. He sniffed, and scrunched up his nose. The aroma was sweet, too sweet, not at all pleasurable.

The exhibit room was as dim as at dusk, neither lighted up nor dark, but sharing ghostly elements of both. The only illumination came from the indirect morning light that filtered in through two plate glass windows at the front of the gallery.

Socrates checked his watch. It was five minutes before the designated opening time. *Someone should be here*, he thought, *especially since the door was open.*

"Hello, is anyone here?" he called, but not too loudly. He had mixed feelings about bringing attention to himself before the designated opening hour. He felt as if he was trespassing, that the open door might not have been the invitation to step inside he'd taken it to be.

"Ms. Hua," he called, "Ms. Fong. Anybody? It's Socrates Cheng." He listened for some response and waited.

Dead silence.

Socrates closed the entrance door and turned back to face the exhibit room. "Hello," he said again, louder this time, but still feeling out-of-place. "Is anyone here?" He listened to the pervasive silence. "It's Socrates Cheng. Honorable Li Bing-fa told you I'd be coming today. I have a 10:00 appointment with Director Hua."

He listened for the slightest sound, any intimation someone was somewhere in the gallery and hadn't heard him.

But there was nothing. Only dead air.

He wiped his forehead and neck with his handkerchief. He looked to his left, over at the doorway defined by the hanging beads, and considered going through to look for someone, but decided not to. He'd never been back there and had no idea what to expect. For all he knew, the back area might be the director's private living quarters.

Socrates was puzzled and rapidly becoming irritated. He didn't understand what was going on, why the front door had been left partly open with the air conditioning blasting, and yet no one seemed to be there. *So much for Bing-fa's influence with the director*, he thought.

He decided to leave, not waste any more time at the gallery today. He'd try again tomorrow. In the meantime, he'd leave a note for the director, a note which would suggest in a few curt words his annoyance at being stood up and would remind the woman that Bing-fa was now directly involved, yet would not emphasize his annoyance. *After all*, he thought, *he didn't want to discourage the woman from meeting with him some other time or cause her to be so resentful that she would meet with him, but would render the meeting meaningless. The last thing he wanted to do was provoke a passive-aggressive response from the director.*

Socrates wrote out the note, then walked across the exhibit room to the alcove to leave it in a conspicuous place for the director to find.

That's when he saw Iris Hua.

She lay on the carpet on the far side of her desk, partly blocked from view.

At first, as he approached the alcove, all Socrates could see were her calves and ankles which extended out beyond the desk. He hurried over to her. Iris Hua lay sprawled on her back, her legs and one arm akimbo.

"Sweet Jesus!" Socrates said. He sucked in a deep breath.

Socrates lurched away from the director's body as if he'd touched a hot stove. He kept his eyes fixed on Hua until he bumped up against Linda Fong's desk behind him. He sucked in air in erratic, large gulps, then let his breath whoosh out between his clenched teeth. He leaned back against the edge of Fong's desk and stared at the director.

After a minute, he walked back to the director 's body and stood above her, looking straight down at Hua. He placed his palm against his churning stomach and pressed hard to suppress its waves. He flattened his other palm against the top of the director's desk and briefly leaned his weight into his arm to steady himself.

The director's half open, dead eyes glared up at Socrates, berating him for arriving too late to help her. Her mouth had frozen wide open in a soundless scream. Hua's right arm and hand were locked in a cadaveric spasm as if she'd been trying to protect herself from her assailant. A dried, thin strip of dark blood banded her throat from one side to the other. Hua's silk blouse was stained coppery red along the neckline and down over her chest.

"Oh, shit!" Socrates said. He shook his head and again pressed his hand against his stomach. He licked his lips and wiped them with his sleeve. The malodorous scent of his own stomach filled his nose and painted his mouth.

Socrates abruptly turned away and grabbed a nearby waste basket, lifted it to his face, and exploded the remains of his breakfast and stomach bile into the basket, not stopping until long after his retching had turned painfully dry. He slumped against Hua's desk. His shirt reeked with perspiration, redolent of someone very aged and very ill.

Socrates pulled out his handkerchief and wiped his face,

neck and forehead. That was when he noticed the director's left hand. It was closed in a fist clutching something.

Socrates took a deep breath and held it while he leaned on one knee and lowered his face close to the director's hand. Her fingers held a tuft of reddish-brown hair.

"Terrific," Socrates said to no one. "Just what I need. A clue."

He placed two fingers against the director's carotid artery and felt for a pulse, but there was none. The director was dead, just as he'd known she was as soon as he found her. He stood up and moved over to the edge of the alcove, away from the corpse.

That's it, he thought, *I'm out of here.* He wanted to be away from the director and away from Death's pernicious presence. He wanted to draw fresh air into his lungs, regain a clear head, and figure out his next play. He had to make some decisions while he still had the opportunity to do so, before some other gallery patron or Linda Fong wandered in from the street and found him with the body.

Socrates considered his possible courses of action. There was, he realized, the right thing to do. He could touch nothing else, stop showering the director's body with his skin flakes and hair, his DNA, and God-only-knows what other forensic evidence, and promptly go outside, call 911, and wait for the police to arrive.

But what he'd rather do would be to leave the gallery without being seen, act as if he hadn't been there today, not call in the crime, and hopefully be uninvolved in whatever happened next. In that event, he could claim, if it ever became necessary to explain the presence of his DNA, that he had visited the gallery on other occasions and had spoken with the director on one other occasion.

It was too late for that approach, he realized. He *was* involved, no matter how he tried to rationalize it away. If he tried to avoid his responsibility and his presence today at the gallery was later discovered, he'd risk having his intentions and his role in the crime misinterpreted. They would call it 'consciousness of guilt', leaving the crime scene and not calling the cops.

Socrates walked out of the gallery and lowered himself onto the curb. He'd call 911.

Socrates opened his cell phone to place the call, then closed it. He had another thought.

There was one more thing for him to do before he called in the police. He would re-enter the gallery and retrieve a copy of the exhibit catalog from the pile in the alcove —a complete copy since he couldn't be sure the coverless one left on his bed was complete. After all, he rationalized, Bing-fa had said the director was going to fully cooperate with him, and this would have included having the director give him a catalog.

For the first time since he'd entered the gallery this morning, Socrates smiled. *I'm thinking like a defense lawyer at trial*, he thought, the irony of this not being lost on him since he had been a business transactions lawyer, not a trial attorney.

Socrates looked up and down the street to see if anyone was nearby. He seemed to be alone, so he reentered the gallery.

He walked across the exhibit room and headed right for the stack of auction catalogs he'd seen the day before. He took his handkerchief in his hand and lifted the corner of the pile to expose a catalog part way down in the pile. He didn't want to disturb the top catalog in case there were relevant fingerprints or a palm print on it.

Socrates teased out a catalog, then, clutching it in one hand, did an about-face and walked a straight line from the stack to the front door. As he stepped outside, he pulled his cell phone from his pocket and dialed 911. When the emergency call operator came on the line, Socrates said, "I'm calling to report a murder."

Chapter 31

SOCRATES HEARD THE approaching sirens long before he saw the red, white and blue striped Metropolitan Police Department vehicle career around the corner, fishtail toward the distant curb, and then, in authentic animated cartoon style, regain its traction and lurch up the street toward the gallery.

Two uniformed police officers exited the patrol car with their weapons drawn. One officer approached the gallery's front door and waited there. The other ascertained that Socrates was the civilian who had called in the crime, and that Socrates believed there was no one in the gallery other than the victim. The officer asked Socrates his name and entered the information into a spiral-bound notebook. He told Socrates to wait for him by the patrol car. The two officers then entered the gallery. They came out twenty minutes later.

One officer walked over to the patrol car, opened the trunk and pulled out a roll of yellow crime scene tape which he then stretched across the gallery's entrance. The other officer walked over to Socrates.

Socrates smiled sheepishly and moved away from the front fender he'd been leaning against.

The officer opened his notebook. "You called this in, Sir, right?"

Socrates nodded.

"I need to see your photo ID." He extended his palm toward Socrates.

Socrates handed over his driver's license. He shifted his weight from one foot to the other while the officer copied his ID information.

The officer returned the license, and said, nodding first toward the gallery, then back at Socrates, "Tell me how you came to be in there, Sir, and what you saw and heard. Start from the time you arrived until we got here."

Socrates described his account of events at the gallery. He did not mention his investigation for Bing-fa as his reason for being there or that he had left the gallery, reentered it, and removed a catalog before calling 911.

The officer wrote down Socrates' statement. He didn't ask any follow-up questions.

As Socrates finished giving his account of events, a second MPDC patrol car arrived, followed immediately by an unmarked white Chevy IMPALA sedan, an EMT bus carrying two emergency medical technicians, the evidence technician's van, and the medical examiner's crime scene laboratory vehicle.

The uniformed officer told Socrates to wait by the scout vehicle again. He left Socrates and walked over to the two plain clothes officers who had climbed out of the unmarked IMPALA. Socrates assumed they were the homicide detectives who would handle the investigation.

Socrates watched for almost ten minutes as the uniformed policeman, referring to his notebook from time-to-time, talked to the detectives. The officer and two detectives occasionally turned their heads and glanced over at Socrates, indicating by their collective action that he was the subject of their discussion at that moment.

Eventually, the patrolman nodded at the detectives, flipped his notebook closed, and rammed it into his back pocket. He left the detectives and joined his partner at the gallery's entrance, standing vigil while the forensic team and medical examiner worked inside the building.

The detectives walked over to Socrates. They looked him up and down as if they were mentally frisking him as they approached.

One detective reached inside his suit jacket — a faded grey garment that once had been married to a pair of matching trousers, but now was paired with pants that had been cannibalized from some other worn suit — and extracted a billfold from his inside pocket. As he came close to Socrates, he flipped the billfold open exposing a gold shield and an ID card, then closed the wallet with the same practiced motion before Socrates could read the badge or ID.

Socrates nodded, and said warily, "Detective . . . ."

One detective walked directly up to Socrates and stopped in front of him. The other detective moved off to Socrates' side, and took a position slightly behind, but facing him.

"I'm Detective Harte," the detective in front said. "That's Detective Thigpen." He indicated the detective behind Socrates by pointing his finger.

Detective Harte clicked open a ballpoint pen, wet the tip of his finger and used it to turn a page in his notebook. He looked back at Socrates. "Tell us what happened here," he said, cocking his head in the direction of the gallery. "What you saw, and anything else you know about it."

Socrates told the detectives the same story he'd told the uniformed officer, withholding the same information as before. When he finished, Harte asked some questions about his reason for coming to the gallery and his relationship with the victim.

Socrates didn't lie, not blatantly at least, but he told the detective only enough of the truth to satisfy him that Socrates wasn't holding back information, just enough to avoid teasing the detective's appetite to know more.

Harte listened to Socrates, asked a few more questions, wrote more notes, and said, "So you didn't see or hear anyone? Not when you arrived? Not after?"

"No one."

Harte looked off in the distance as if contemplating his next move, then looked back at Socrates. "Run through it again, Mr. Cheng. All of it." He paused and glanced briefly at his partner, then again at Socrates. "But this time start with why you came here today. The part you left out before."

The detective now listened to Socrates without taking notes or interrupting him with questions. He also didn't take his eyes from Socrates' eyes the entire time Socrates repeated, and slightly expanded, his original account of events.

"You say you came here to meet with the director? Be more specific about why," Harte said.

"To talk to her about something I'm working on, like I said."

"What would that be?"

"The Chinese cultural exhibit — the postponed exhibit — and the burglary at the gallery. I wanted to see what she could tell me about them."

Socrates noticed Harte furtively glance at Detective Thigpen. Something silent had just passed between them.

"Here's what I don't get, Mr. Cheng. I need you to help me out here," Harte said. "You say you came to the gallery to talk about a burglary and art show. Okay, I get that. But what you still haven't told us is *why*." He paused. "Are you an art critic or art dealer, something like that? Maybe a collector?"

"I'm trying to locate the stolen property, specifically, the historic Parker Company fountain pen called the Mandarin Yellow. And the stolen art and the historic documents, too, if I can, although my focus is on the missing pen. I wanted to ask the director some questions about gallery security."

"That's strange," Harte said. "I don't remember seeing you around the 2D. Where's your Gold Shield, Detective Cheng? I need to see it to make sure you're not impersonating an MPDC detective."

Socrates blushed. "I'm not a detective," Socrates said. "You already know that."

"A private dick, then?" Harte said. "Let me see your license card." He reached out to take the card.

"I'm not private either," Socrates said. "The point is, Detective, I don't need a license. I'm not breaking any law doing what I'm doing, helping an interested party, an acquaintance. Informally helping him. I'm within my rights as a citizen."

Harte suppressed a smile. "Don't be so sure you're right about that. You might be interfering with an ongoing investigation, maybe something worse. Who's the interested party?"

Socrates realized he'd deftly maneuvered himself into a tight corner. He and Bing-fa had never discussed whether Socrates could reveal his name if the need came up. Socrates assumed, based on what he'd learned over the years from his father concerning the overseas Chinese community's fervent insularity, that Bing-fa would want to remain anonymous. Bing-fa had as much as said this when he explained to Socrates why he had turned to him to recover the stolen objects rather than go to the police for help. Yet Socrates did not want to cast suspicion on himself merely to protect Bing-fa's identity. He thought about what he needed to do to extricate himself.

He said to Harte, "I'll be glad to tell you, Detective, but first I need permission. If you can wait a minute," he said as he pulled his cell phone from his pocket, "I'll call and get the okay."

Without waiting for a response, Socrates turned from the detectives and walked a few feet away. But he didn't call Bing-fa. Instead, he dialed his own home landline.

This way, he thought, *he'd protect Bing-fa's telephone number from possible discovery by the cops and disclosure later on.*

As Socrates punched in his own home number and listened to it ring, a taxi pulled up and stopped a few feet from the detectives and him. The backdoor of the taxi opened and Linda Fong stepped out. She stared across the sidewalk at the crime scene tape blocking the gallery's entrance.

Fong looked around and frowned, then crossed over to Socrates. She stopped in front of him, and said in heavily accented English, "What is the matter here? Where is Honorable Director Hua?"

Without waiting for Socrates to answer, she turned toward Detective Harte. "Please . . . what is going on here?"

Detective Thigpen quickly stepped from behind Socrates and inserted himself between Socrates and Fong. Thigpen flashed his ID and shield at her.

"Over here, Miss," Thigpen said, taking her by the elbow and guiding her to a place on the sidewalk several feet away from Socrates and Harte.

Socrates looked at Fong and said to her, "I came for my 10:00 o'clock appointment with the director. She was already dead when I got here."

"Dead? Oh, my God," Fong said. She turned and faced Harte. "I heard this man threaten Director Hua when he came here before." She pointed at Socrates. "The director said that after he argued with her, she was frightened of him."

Chapter 32

LINDA FONG'S ACCUSATION stunned Socrates. He wasn't able to respond except with the most feeble of protests. He turned to Detective Harte and blurted out, "It's not true, what she said. It didn't happen that way. I didn't threaten the director. We didn't even argue. You've got to believe me."

Even as he demurred, Socrates instinctively stepped backwards, away from Fong, and pushed out his palms as if to fend off her accusations. He looked at Harte and shook his head. "She was dead when I got there, just like I said. I didn't . . . ."

Harte held up his hand, signaling Socrates to stop talking. "Go over to the IMPALA, Mr. Cheng." He tilted his head toward the unmarked vehicle. "Wait there." He paused, then realizing Socrates hadn't moved, said, "Go, Mr. Cheng. Now."

Harte turned back to Fong. "Please go with Detective Thigpen. He'll take your statement."

Socrates waited by the unmarked IMPALA, shifting his weight from one foot to the other. He dug his hands deep into his pants pockets and gripped the exhibit catalog between his right arm and armpit. He kept his eyes on the detective as Harte now walked toward him.

As he neared Socrates, Harte said, "I'd like you to come with us to the station house, Mr. Cheng. We'll take your statement in writing." He paused, waiting for Socrates' assent. When Socrates failed to respond, he added, "You don't have a problem with that, do you?"

Socrates shook his head. "No, detective, not at all." *This is crazy*, he thought. *They can't really think I killed that woman.*

"IN HERE," HARTE said. He held the door open for Socrates, making Socrates enter the interview room first.

The room was just what Socrates expected based on his limited TV exposure to interview/interrogation rooms. Not warm and inviting, but not quite foreboding either. Private and isolated, to be sure, but not a place to expect to receive the so-called third degree.

A rectangular table, constructed from synthetic veneer imitating wood, and flanked by three chairs — one of which was bolted to the floor — occupied the center of the room. A beige commercial grade carpet covered the floor. *The kind of carpet that probably looked tired the day the installers put it down*, Socrates thought. He could feel the floor underneath the thin pile as he walked into the room.

Stock photographs of national monuments and well known federal government buildings were randomly splashed across three walls. The fourth wall contained a 5'x 7' mirror that Socrates assumed was a one-way looking glass masquerading as a normal mirror.

Socrates had learned the value of mirrors in interview rooms from a Bar Association course he and two of his former law partners attended years before. By the time the one week class ended, Socrates and his partners were so impressed with the benefits of mirrors as negotiating and interviewing tools, that they'd had one (although not a one-way looking mirror) installed in their conference room. From that time forward, they always made sure that their opposite-number-attorney sat facing the mirror so he could see himself in it.

This seating strategy reflected their understanding that a mirror's utility extended beyond its possible one-way looking capacity, which enabled the people on its other side to observe the room's occupants. If this had been their goal, Socrates and his partners could have achieved this by using cameras, microphones and other technology surreptitiously placed around the room. Instead, as business transactions lawyers, their goal was to use the presence of the mirror to deter the attorney they were negotiating with from lying, bluffing or otherwise misleading them. The presence of the mirror would achieve this, they learned in their course, because people who could see themselves as they spoke were less likely to tell lies. The MPDC subscribed to this same belief.

Harte pointed to the bolted-down chair which faced the mirror. "Sit there," he said. The detective eased himself into a chair at the head of the table so he would not block Socrates' view of himself in the mirror.

Harte stared at Socrates, but now said nothing. He used his hard gaze, his silence, and his dominant position at the head of the table as his manipulation props to establish his authority in the room.

The detective's silence continued for so long Socrates was tempted to say something just to break the accumulating tension. But he knew better than to do this and thereby surrender his will to Harte, so he remained quiet, softly tapping his foot under the table, waiting, and staring back at the detective.

Socrates knew Harte was testing him to see how easily he could be manipulated. The technique was right out of INTRO-DUCTORY INTERROGATIONS 101. Once Harte established himself as the alpha dog in the room, he would next define a truth-response baseline by asking Socrates innocuous questions to which Harte already knew the answers. As he did this, he would watch Socrates' physical tics and other body language clues to see how Socrates behaved when he responded truthfully or when he lied. Harte would carefully note any anomalies, watching for visual and verbal tells that demonstrated nervousness or dissembling, looking for indicators the person usually had no idea he was expressing, but that were apparent to a trained observer.

Socrates also knew he'd have to be careful not only with the truthfulness of his answers, but also how he phrased his responses. Vague answers, particularly to questions that called for a *yes* or *no*, would scream deceit even if he did not intend to be deceitful. It would not do to respond, *I guess, I think,* or *not really* when a question called for an unequivocal reply. It also wouldn't do to use such phrases as *You've got to believe me* or *You have to understand* and the like when answering questions. Such phrases shouted out deception.

Harte's silence continued for another few minutes at which point he said, "I appreciate your cooperation in coming in, Mr. Cheng." Harte was now established as the alpha dog.

"I'm happy to help, Detective." Socrates was relieved the silence had ended. "That Fong woman was wrong. I didn't threaten anyone or kill Director Hua. I found her dead on the floor, like I said."

"Can I get you something to drink?" Harte asked. "A Coke, coffee, some tap water?" Harte now eased himself into phase two of his interrogation technique, establishing rapport with Socrates.

A few minutes later Harte returned carrying two Cokes. This time he ignored the chair at the head of the table and headed for the third one. He lifted the chair and carried it toward Socrates, setting it down backwards about three feet away facing Socrates. Then he straddled the chair and draped his weight lifter's forearms over the chair's back, leaning in toward Socrates.

Harte smiled. The entire stage set, including the detective's relaxed body language and his inanimate props, now whispered to Socrates, *Trust me.*

Harte led Socrates through several questions to establish the baseline. He never took his eyes from Socrates as he mentally cataloged Socrates' tells and tics. Meanwhile, behind the mirror, Thigpen, too, made mental notes about Socrates' physical and oral responses. Alongside Thigpen, a video camera and audio recorder memorialized the entire session for later review by the detectives.

When Harte satisfied himself he knew Socrates' baseline body language, he said, "You're not required to be here, Mr. Cheng. You don't have to answer any questions. You're not a suspect or person of interest, just a witness. You're free to leave at any time."

Socrates told the detective he understood, and acknowledged he had come to the station house voluntarily. With that oral understanding out of the way, Harte handed Socrates a printed form and asked him to read and sign it to indicate he understood the consensual nature of the interview. Socrates signed the document without reading it.

"Why don't you go through your story again," Harte said. "I'll take notes so I can prepare a written statement for you to review and sign."

Socrates nodded.

"But this time, Mr. Cheng, I want the whole story from you. No more bullshit. Understand?" He paused a beat. "I want everything. The exhibit catalog you lifted and have been carrying around, the name and location of the person you say you're working for, the fact you up-chucked into a waste basket, but didn't tell us, and anything else you left out before. Got it?"

Socrates told it all, including Bing-fa's name and role.

The detective had Socrates repeat his story twice more. During Socrates' second and third times through, Harte peppered him with questions, interrupting his narrative, testing his consistency.

When Socrates finished his third recounting of events, Harte said, "You should've told us everything right off, without us asking. It doesn't look good when we have to drag it out of you."

Socrates blushed. "I know, Detective. Sorry. Am I a suspect now?"

"You're a person of interest now . . . . and a witness, too."

"Should I get a lawyer?"

"Think you need one?"

"Well, I suppose . . . ."

"We won't be able to be this informal if you lawyer-up," Harte said. "Once you bring in your shark, it's a whole different ball game." Harte paused to gauge Socrates' reaction, then added, "But you already know this seeing as how you used to be a lawyer yourself. Right?"

Socrates shook his head and sighed. "My practice wasn't criminal law," he said, "but I didn't do anything wrong. I'll hold off on getting one for now."

Harte nodded his agreement, and said, "I'm finished for now, Mr. Cheng. Keep yourself available." He reached into his jacket pocket, fished out a business card and handed it over to Socrates.

Socrates took the card, glanced at it, then nodded as if to say, I understand your unstated message, Detective: call if I remember something I left out or want to change my story. He put the detective's card in his wallet as he left the 2D.

Chapter 33

AFTER IRIS HUA'S death, Linda Fong settled with seamless ease into her new role as acting director of the gallery.

The first thing she did was change the siting of her desk in the alcove so that now when she sat behind it, she faced south as ordained by *feng shui* liturgy.

Fong also added personal, previously forbidden, touches to the work area. Where before she had been required by the director to discard all exhibit catalogs received in the mail from other galleries, Fong now stacked the catalogs on the former director's desk and chair, sometimes even when she hadn't bothered opening their mailing envelopes.

Beyond these two acts of belated rebellion, Acting Director Fong also impressed her imprimatur upon the gallery itself by bringing to her office her modest collection of art reference books which, under her predecessor's rules, she had been required to keep at home. Now, Fong randomly scattered the art volumes across the surface of the former director's desk, strewing them among the exhibit catalogs, exactly in the manner the former director would have forbidden her to do if she were still alive and in charge.

FONG LOOKED UP at the sound of the entrance door opening and closing. Recognizing the visitor, she smiled and hurried out to the exhibit room.

"Hello, Jade," she said, speaking Mandarin. "Welcome to my gallery. I am most pleased you have honored me with your presence."

Fong did not bow her head in her usual servile, traditional manner or wait for some return acknowledgement from Jade before again speaking.

"I am sorry for this disorder," she said, still in dialect, sweeping her arm to corral the room. "I am trying to reorganize everything for the exhibit's postponed opening." She paused to let Jade respond.

Jade looked at Fong, but said nothing. She frowned and crossed her arms over her chest.

The acting director missed Jade's implicit message, and continued. "The gaps in the exhibit created by the stolen Mandarin Yellow and other treasures have destroyed the natural flow of the display. I am trying to shift objects around to make the breaks less noticeable." She looked over at the paintings and framed documents sitting on the floor, each one leaning against the base of the wall where, presumably, it would soon hang for the reorganized exhibit. "Unfortunately, I am alone here, without any volunteers to assist me, and there is so much to do to prepare for the rescheduled opening." She canted her head in the direction of a group of discarded art packing boxes. "But that is my problem, not yours." She smiled. "To what do I owe the honor of your visit?"

Jade, also speaking Mandarin, said, "You no doubt are aware that my father has engaged the services of a non-Celestial to recover the stolen national treasures. His name is Socrates Cheng."

"I am aware of the barbarian," Fong said. She briefly lowered her head, then looked up.

"Mr. Cheng will soon come to see you," Jade said. "When he does, it is important that you cooperate with him."

The acting director narrowed her eyes. "This person is an outsider, Jade, *low faan*. We have the resources at the Embassy to adequately assist the venerable Li Bing-fa. Why must your father force the barbarian upon us?"

"That is not your concern," Jade said, her voice becoming strident. She looked hard at Fong. "I have asked you to assist my father by assisting Mr. Cheng. That should be sufficient reason for you to do so without questioning those with higher standing than you." Jade waited a few seconds, then said, "If not, then perhaps as a patriot it would be the prudent thing for you to do for your heritage and homeland."

The two women stared at one another. Jade looked directly into the acting director's eyes without once blinking or releasing contact. Linda Fong lowered her gaze and stared at the floor.

"Of course, Jade. I understand." Fong did not lift her eyes to look at Jade as she spoke. "I will be pleased to do as you suggest. In return, I would ask a favor from you, if I may be permitted to do so."

"Oh?"

"I would be most grateful if you would speak to the Honorable Li Bing-fa on my behalf. Please request that he intercede with the Embassy to assist me in becoming this gallery's permanent director."

"If you assist Mr. Cheng, I will see to it that my father learns you have cooperated in furthering his interests in this unfortunate matter. That will please him and might possibly inure to your benefit."

"Thank you. And if I do not cooperate?"

"In that event, Youngest Brother will carry a different message to our father."

Chapter 34

SOCRATES LEFT THE 2D station house as soon as Harte finished with him. He was glad to be free of the interview room and its tacit, unavoidable psychological coercion. He walked along Wisconsin Avenue heading to his store to check his mail. His stomach growled, reminding him he hadn't eaten all day.

He pulled out his cell phone as he walked.

He wanted to tell Bing-fa about the director's death and find out if Bing-fa had recovered the Mandarin Yellow from the mysterious caller. He also wanted to alert Bing-fa to the possibility that the police might contact him. He didn't look forward to delivering this last piece of news.

He was scrolling through his contact list to highlight Bing-fa's speed dial symbol when the cell phone burped its ring tone, startling him. He looked at the readout to identify the caller.

"Hello, Mom."

"Socrates. Is that you? It's your mother."

Socrates smiled. "It's me, Mom. And I know it's you. I have Caller ID." He picked up his pace. "Where are you calling from?"

"What do you mean, *where*? From your condo, from in your practically unused kitchen, that's where. I'm cooking for you and your Chinese girlfriend and your father. Remember?

We talked about it. Are you coming home soon? It's already after 6:00."

Uh, oh! Socrates thought. *Did I screw up which night we said?*

"Um, Mom, didn't we agree on tomorrow night for dinner? That's what I told Jade. Did I mess up?" He paused for a response that did not come, then said, "I thought we left the time open. I didn't realize I had a curfew. I thought I outgrew that when I went off to college."

He waited for his mother's predictable response: *Is that any way to speak to your mother? You put a knife in my heart, when all I did was ask you a simple question because I care about you.* She surprised him by not saying anything.

Socrates immediately regretted his wisecrack. "I'm sorry, Mom, I shouldn't have said that. I guess I messed the nights up. I have a few more things to do, then I'll be home. In about an hour or so. I'll try to get in touch with Jade and see if she can join us tonight instead of tomorrow. I'll call and let you know what she says."

"Where are you, anyway?" his mother said. "I called your pen store, but nobody answered. Nobody ever answers at your store. Don't you work anymore? No wonder you don't make a good living if you're never in your store when customers want to come in and shop?"

"It's a long story, Mom. I'll explain another time. I'm heading to my store now."

Socrates ended the call, walked quickly to his store, and looked through his unopened mail. Then he called Jade, reached her on his first try, and smiled when she agreed to come to dinner with his parents this evening.

After he and Jade finished talking, Socrates marked a carton of pen demonstrator samples that had come to him unsolicited, REFUSED. RETURN TO SENDER, and put the box outside the front door in the mall's covered walkway for the mail carrier to take back to the post office the next day. Then he went back inside and called Bing-fa. He reached him at the Golden Dragon.

"Bing-fa," Socrates said, intentionally speaking softly and in a somber tone, "Director Hua is dead. Murdered." He waited for Bing-fa's reaction.

Nothing. Stone cold silence.

He tried again. "I said I went to the gallery to talk to the director, like you arranged. I found her dead. Somebody had cut her throat."

"I have the cherished Mandarin Yellow in my possession," Bing-fa said. "You must come here immediately to examine it."

Socrates forced himself to speak quietly and slowly. "Bing-fa. Did you hear what I said? Director Hua's been murdered and the police think I might've done it." Socrates paced in front of the store's glass display case.

"I heard you the first time, Mr. Cheng. It is of no consequence unless you did take Director Hua's life. Since I assume you did not, and we can do nothing to change the woman's situation or alter what the police might currently think, we have other important matters to address today. Come to the Golden Dragon. From there we will proceed to my home where you will inspect the Mandarin Yellow. I am sure you will not regret the opportunity."

Socrates thought about this. Bing-fa was right, of course. But it embarrassed him to realize that seeing the historic Mandarin Yellow, and perhaps even holding it — a once in a lifetime opportunity for a collector — was so important to him that he was ready to drop the subject of the director's murder.

He would explain to his parents and Jade at dinner why he had to go out as soon as they all finished eating. Jade certainly would understand, but his parents would have mixed feelings and many questions, especially once they realized Jade was not joining him in visiting her father. He would leave it to Jade to explain to his parents what that was all about. He wished he could be there to hear her explanation.

BING-FA LED THE way to his private elevator and up into his eighteen room, three-floor penthouse suite at the White Plum Blossoms apartments. Once there, Bing-fa marched across the Great Room like a battlefield commander after a momentous victory.

Socrates trailed close behind, matching Bing-fa step-for-step as if they were tethered and had rehearsed their walk. Socrates smiled. He pictured a hunched-over Groucho Marx,

flicking his cigar and flashing his eyebrows as he trailed closely behind a clueless Margaret Dumont in *A Night at the Opera*.

Bing-fa led Socrates into his scholar's studio. He gestured
for Socrates to take a seat in front of the desk.

Socrates glanced around the room. Bing-fa's studio followed traditional principles of design, siting, furnishing and
use. It was Bing-fa's private sanctuary. If Confucian tradition,
as Socrates had learned it from his father, held sway here, no
one, not even Bing-fa's family, ever entered this room without
his permission.

Bing-fa had furnished the room with a simple Ching period desk, a single horseshoe back wooden chair made from
huanghuali wood, and with two yoke back wooden chairs,
also made from huanghuali wood. The desk consisted of a
plain rosewood top, no drawers, and tapered rosewood legs.

The only other furniture in the studio were a five-me-
ter high A-frame antique mahogany cabinet in which Bing-fa
stored his collection of calligraphy scrolls and landscape wa-
tercolor scrolls, and a low, eight-foot long table with claw feet
on which Bing-fa spread the scrolls when he opened them to
study from above.

Socrates inspected the desk's surface. It was the polar
opposite of disorder. There was no randomness at work here,
not like his own desk at home. Every object seemed to be in
its proper place, and nothing was there that didn't seem to
belong. Bing-fa had organized the desktop like a great sym-
phony or fine poem, with not one musical note, not one word
or, in the case of the desktop, not one object too many.

There were several ink stones, modern and antique calligraphy horsetail hair brushes, a dozen or so ink sticks, a brush
pot, and three Ming period ivory brush rests on the desktop,
all objects of the type and quality typically collected by Confucian and Taoist scholars for their utility, their specific histo-
ries, and their individual and collective beauty.

Socrates looked across the room toward the persistent
sound of chirping. Bing-fa's caged song birds and his lucky
crickets resided in hanging cages located, respectively, in the
far corners of the studio.

Socrates slowly lowered himself into the chair Bing-fa
had pointed to. He moved cautiously, wary of depositing his

157-pound body onto the antique horseshoe back chair which, in his judgment, was more wisely looked at and admired than actually sat in.

For his part, Bing-fa had settled himself in an antique chair behind his desk. He silently watched Socrates study the room. When it was clear Socrates had finished, Bing-fa reached within his silk gown and extracted a narrow box from a hidden fold. He placed the box on the desk between them, removed its lid, and used one finger to nudge the box across the desk to Socrates.

Socrates untied the thin teal ribbon that held the Mandarin Yellow against the box's foam-lined interior and carefully removed the pen. He slowly unscrewed its cap, taking care not to chip or crack the cap's delicate lip.

He examined the Parker Company factory imprint identifying the pen model and George Parker's laudatory dedication to Chiang Kai-shek inscribed on the barrel. Both seemed to him to be strongly struck, intact and undamaged. Neither had been burnished by gripping fingers.

Socrates examined the individual letters of each imprint. None of the letters in the two imprints was out of alignment, as they might have been if they had been reworked or hastily added. Socrates knew this wasn't conclusive evidence that the imprint and engraving were genuine, but at least this visual evidence did not eliminate the possibility.

He looked up at Bing-fa. "Very nice," he said, smiling and nodding enthusiastically.

He next brought the yellow barrel up close to his eyes and looked for hairline cracks in the delicate surface. He didn't see any. He removed a small 10x power magnifying glass from his pocket and again examined the barrel, the cap, its lip and the end cap, seeking subtle defects or hidden repairs not visible to the naked eye.

He next closed his eyes to avoid distractions and gently, being careful not to touch the pen with his fingernail or thumbnail, applied the all-important Braille test, running his index finger and thumb up and down the length of the barrel and cap, feeling for indentations or filled-in bite marks, dings or cracks.

Socrates looked up. Bing-fa was watching him with more concentration than he'd ever seen Bing-fa display toward him.

"Finished," Socrates said.

He gently screwed the cap back onto the barrel and returned the pen to its box. He carefully re-tied the ribbon and fastened the Mandarin Yellow in place. Then he nudged the open box back across the desk to Bing-fa.

"What did the person look like who returned this to you?" Socrates asked.

"I did not see him," Bing-fa said. "He required that I place the canvas bag with the payment on a table, turn away, and face the wall. I heard him walk up behind me, unzip the bag, and then walk back across the room and out the door." Bing-fa paused. "I waited for other instructions if he returned, but he did not.

"I soon turned to face the empty room and saw the pen box on the table where the money had been." He paused again as if gathering his thoughts. "I opened the box. It contained the glorious writing instrument," he said, nodding down at the boxed Mandarin Yellow. "Then I left, satisfied he had kept his part of our agreement, just as I had kept mine. That is all."

Socrates wrinkled his forehead, and said, "He didn't say anything about returning everything else?"

Bing-fa looked hard at Socrates. His patience was taxed. "As I said before, this transaction involved only the return of the treasured Mandarin Yellow. Nothing else. I will wait for the other objects to be offered to me at some later time. Perhaps now that I have shown my good faith in this first transaction, this person will again contact me so we can arrange my purchase of all the stolen treasures."

"Bing-fa," Socrates said, "I have to tell you something." He hesitated and took a deep breath as he gathered his thoughts.

"This Mandarin Yellow," Socrates said, pointing at the pen box sitting between them on the desk, "the pen you just ransomed. It's beautiful and it seems to be undamaged. Unfortunately, it's also a fake."

Chapter 35

SOCRATES' FIRST INCLINATION upon declaring the pen a fake had been to puff out his chest and silently say to himself, *I told you so,* to find some measure of gratification in his minor triumph over Bing-fa's continued disdain for his advice. After all, he didn't particularly like the man and he resented Bing-fa's unceasing haughtiness. Yet all that changed as Socrates watched Bing-fa react to his stark statement, when he saw Bing-fa's shoulders slump, his mouth turn down, and his chin droop toward his chest. Socrates immediately wanted to undo the anguish he'd just caused, to offer words that would prove to be an anodyne for his ill-chosen candor.

In an effort to salvage something from a bad situation, Socrates assumed a saddened facial expression appropriate for the circumstances. He reached across the desk, picked up the pen box, and looked closely at the Mandarin Yellow as if he just realized he might have missed something critical the first time. He stepped out of character now and ignored the so-called First Rule of Holes he usually prided himself on following — the rule that stated, *When you're in a hole, stop digging.*

"Honorable Bing-fa," he said, "perhaps *fake* was the wrong choice of word, was misleading. I think the pen is probably genuine, a vintage Parker Duofold Mandarin Yellow, but I'm afraid it's not your pen, not the historic writing instrument stolen from the gallery."

Bing-fa said, in a soft, flat tone, "Under the circumstances, Mr. Cheng, that seems to be a difference without a distinction."

Socrates nodded, and paused briefly to consider how he now wanted to approach this.

"For this to make sense to you, Bing-fa, I need to explain a little of the production history of the Mandarin Yellow, to put your pen and my statement in context."

"Proceed," Bing-fa said as he burrowed his arms up his wide sleeves.

Socrates briefly told Bing-fa the story of how George Parker had decided to create the Mandarin Yellow model in 1927, and said, nodding toward the box on the table, "So, what we first have to decide in evaluating this pen is whether it's the 1927 model or a later one. If we conclude it wasn't manufactured in 1927, then this Mandarin Yellow couldn't be Production Copy No.1, your pen."

He paused to let Bing-fa process this information.

"Continue," Bing-fa said. His impatience was palpable.

Socrates placed his fingers on the box, thought about his next words and, without lifting the box from the table, slowly rotated it clockwise like a slowly moving ceiling fan in a 1940s Grade B tropical-locale Hollywood movie.

"The 1927 Mandarin Yellow had two important stylistic characteristics," he said. "One was that its barrel was stamped with a banner containing the words, Lucky Curve." He pointed to the Lucky Curve inscription on the pen sitting between them.

"But George Parker used the phrase LUCKY CURVE on both the 1927 and the 1928 Mandarin Yellow models. Starting in 1929, you don't see it anymore. That means that this pen," he said, pointing at the box, "was manufactured in 1927 or 1928, not later. That narrows the inquiry for us. Now we have to decide if this pen is a 1927 Duofold or the 1928 model."

Socrates stared at the pen and box for a few seconds, then looked up.

"Another characteristic of the 1927 model was that it had a single gold band ringing the cap. Parker's customers seemed to approve of this style, and the pen sold fairly well, but Parker was a salesman at heart and always looking to increase sales. As such, he subscribed to the doctrine articulated by General Motors in 1923 called Dynamic Obsolescence which posited that to bring in new customers, you had to continuously offer new (or changed) products. Accordingly, Parker in 1928 created a new model Mandarin Yellow by replacing the single gold band with two narrow gold bands."

"That means, Bing-fa, that this pen here," he pointed again at the box sitting between them, "since it has both the LUCKY CURVE slogan and two narrow bands on the cap, was manufactured in 1928, not 1927." Socrates paused to give Bing-fa a chance to register the import of this information. Then he continued: This pen cannot be Production Copy No.1." He fanned out his palms as if surrendering to the inevitable. "It's not your Mandarin Yellow."

Socrates wondered why he still felt as if he should apologize to Bing-fa for bringing him this incontrovertible bad news.

Bing-fa spoke in a soft, unemotional voice. "So this writing instrument I paid ransom for," he said, "is not our national treasure even though it contains the inscription to Generalissimo Chiang?"

"I'm afraid not," Socrates said. "The pen's not a fake, strictly speaking. It is a genuine Mandarin Yellow." He paused, then added, "But it's not the pen George Parker presented to Chiang Kai-shek, not the Mandarin Yellow used by Chiang and Mao when they signed their temporary truce in 1937, and definitely not the vintage Duofold stolen from the gallery."

Chapter 36

ONCE SOCRATES COMPLETED his explanation of the pen's status and provenance, he and Bing-fa had nothing more to say to one another so Socrates left and walked home. He checked his watch as he approached his condo. It was too late to go over to his parents' hotel to visit them and root out Jade's earlier explanation to them why he had abandoned them and Jade after dinner. They'd be settled in for the night.

Socrates stepped through the doorway into his apartment, tossed his unopened mail and keys into a round wicker basket he kept for this purpose on a sideboard table in the foyer, and walked to the kitchen. He put water on the gas stove to fix himself a cup of green tea. While he waited for the water to heat, he called Jade, but didn't reach her. He left a message on her voice mail saying he would like to get together for dinner the next night, if she had time, to make up for abandoning her to his parents tonight. Then he changed clothes, sipped his tea, and afterward went out into the night for a short run.

He was dressing after his run and shower when the intercom buzzed. He looked over at his clock radio. It was a little after 10:40 p.m.

Socrates smiled and ran his palms over the sides of his head to smooth back his damp hair as he quickly walked across the living room to the intercom panel by his front door.

A surprise visit by Jade, he thought. *How nice.* He pushed the 'Talk' button and said, "Hello, Jade."

No one answered. Not even George, the doorman, who should have been monitoring the intercom until he went off duty at Midnight. Socrates pushed the 'Talk' button again. "Hello," he said.

Still no response.

She's probably on her way up, he thought.

It wouldn't be the first time, he realized, that someone who lived in the building, someone going in or coming out the front door, noticed an attractive woman standing at the intercom panel and gallantly held the door open for her without requiring that she be screened from upstairs or by the doorman as the condo's security rules required.

No big deal, he thought. *People probably recognized Jade by sight, she's been in and out of the building so often. Her beautiful Asian appearance was memorable.*

He decided he would greet Jade by waiting in the hallway so she would see him when she rounded the corner coming from the elevator.

Socrates stood in the hallway and smiled in anticipation as he listened to the elevator's door slide open and then slide closed.

He could not have been more wrong about the identity of his visitor.

"WHAT ARE YOU doing here?" Socrates said. He reflexively stepped back to the edge of his doorway and warily watched Eldest Brother approach him.

Bing-wu ignored Socrates' question. He glowered at him, then brushed past Socrates, striding through the open door into the condo. Socrates followed him in, but intentionally left the door open.

Eldest Brother turned to face Socrates. He answered Socrates' question without emotion, and spoke in a timbre so flat and subdued, so seemingly without menace that Socrates felt menaced by it. Eldest Brother's well-modulated, minatory tone exuded authority, restrained power and, above all else, latent peril.

"You were told by my Twin brothers to cease your interference in matters involving our family," Bing-wu said, "but you have chosen to ignore us. Because Bing-jade seems to care for you, even though you are *low faan*, I will warn you one more time. After this, you will regret it if you continue to disregard me."

Socrates instinctively clenched his fists, although he knew better than to physically challenge Eldest Brother or even to suggest with his body language that he might challenge him. Years ago, Jade had told Socrates that Eldest Brother was a student of various Chinese martial arts forms and had been such since he was five years old. Eldest Brother, according to Jade, still was a skilled and dangerous martial artist.

Socrates, long out of practice and these days entirely divorced from his martial arts studies, had no desire to find out for himself. He relaxed his hands and let his arms dangle by his sides, his open palms facing Eldest Brother in a classic, submissive posture. To further avoid provoking a confrontation, he also did not look directly into Eldest Brother's eyes. Instead, he looked at Bing-wu's feet while Eldest Brother spoke to him.

"You will stay away from Little Sister and you will no longer involve yourself with our father. Do you understand?"

Socrates said nothing, and deliberately gave nothing away about his mounting anger. He continued to stare at Eldest Brother's feet.

Eldest Brother said, pointing his finger at Socrates, "You have been told for the last time. There will be no other warnings."

He didn't wait for Socrates to acknowledge that he understood. Instead, having delivered his point once again, Eldest Brother strode past Socrates, bumping into him and knocking Socrates off-balance, as he stormed out of the condo.

Chapter 37

The next afternoon, Socrates sat in his living room thinking about his recent brush with Eldest Brother when his cell
phone rang.

"Hi, Pop," he said. "Nice surprise. What's up?"

An anomalous silence followed. Then his father coughed
once, cleared his throat, and said, "Your mother is taking a
bath."

Socrates wondered why his father answered his question
by telling him about his mother? It was not a promising sign.

"I need to talk to you, Son, as soon as possible. Today."

The urgency in his father's plea was unmistakable.
Socrates' stomach tightened. He held his breath, then slowly
let it out, and said, "What's wrong?"

"It's nothing. I'll tell you when I see you. Don't worry.
You'll help me work it out."

"When and where?" Socrates said.

"The sooner the better. I don't care where as long as I can
get a drink there. Something strong. For this, I need something with a kick to it."

That statement fueled Socrates' concern. All his life, on
those few occasions when his father said he wanted a strong
drink, that was his father's signal he had something very serious and problematic on his mind.

———

THEY SETTLED IN at a corner table at the M Street Bar & Grill located in the Hotel St. Gregory on the corner of 21st and M Streets, not far from Socrates' parents' hotel. They ordered drinks.

Socrates waited until the waitress left them before he broke the ice.

"I'm worried, Pop. You didn't sound like yourself on the phone."

His father looked down at the table as he spoke.

"When we had lunch the other day and you asked me how I was doing, I wasn't straight with you. I've done something I shouldn't have done, and I was ashamed to tell you."

Socrates took a deep breath and waited. He knew better than to rush his father at a time like this.

His father raised his eyes from the table. "It's the government, Sonny, the tax people. I screwed up and I'm in trouble. I put off dealing with a tax problem for the plant, and now it's caught up with me. I don't have no choice any more. It might even be too late." He slowly wagged his head and looked back down at the table.

Socrates reached over and put his hand on his father's forearm. "What's the problem, Pop? Tell me."

"I didn't pay my employees' payroll taxes," his father said. "I needed money to keep the plant open. I figured I could make it up later when things got better." He paused and shook his head. "It was either that or lay off workers who worked for me for years. I couldn't do that to them."

His father looked up at Socrates. "I haven't been honest with your mother either. I got a letter from the tax people, and hid it. I couldn't bring myself to tell her, I was so ashamed and scared. When I got a second one, I didn't say anything to her because I didn't know what I'd say if she asked me why I didn't show her the first one. After that, it got worse with each letter. I really messed up." He wiped his eyes with his sleeve.

"Mom already knows, Pop. Not the details and not about the letters, but she knows something's going on with the IRS. She answered the phone the morning you were coming to

Washington. You were in the shower. It was the IRS calling you. Mom said she told you, but you said it was nothing, just a mistake. Don't you remember?"

His father looked confused. He squinted, then slowly shook his head. "I didn't know," he said quietly.

Socrates watched his father's face morph from puzzlement to relief as the import of Socrates' words took hold. Socrates strained not to pepper him with questions. Instead, he kept quiet to let his father unburden himself at his own pace.

"I never answered even one letter or called the tax people like the letters said. But I didn't do any crime, Sonny, nothing like that. What I did was I didn't pay my share of payroll taxes, the owner's part. I only paid my worker's portion."

His father paused. Probably, Socrates thought, to give him a chance to say something, But Socrates remained quiet, processing what he'd just heard and thinking about its implications.

His father continued. "It all came to a head a few weeks ago. The tax people shut down the plant. They swooped in one morning, made everybody leave, and padlocked the doors." He shook his head and closed his eyes.

"Their printed sign on the door said they're going to sell everything. Then they'll come after our house and bank accounts if the sale isn't enough to pay what I owe." He again looked back down at the table.

Socrates didn't know what to say that wouldn't come across either as patronizing or as condemnatory. The fact was his father had screwed up big time. There was no doubt about that. The IRS does not like to be ignored and will come down with both feet on a taxpayer's throat if it is ignored. Especially when the issue involves an employer's failure to pay his or his employees' share of payroll taxes which the IRS considers to be a trust fund held by the employer for his employees.

Socrates reached out and put his hand on his father's shoulder. He squeezed gently.

His father looked up at him with rheumy eyes.

"I know this is hard for you, Pop, but we'll work it out somehow. We'll all get through it together. You're not ignoring the problem anymore." He squeezed his father's shoulder again. "I'll call the IRS and deal with them for you."

Chapter 38

SOCRATES' CELL PHONE rang as he and his father arrived back at the Westin Grand lobby. He looked at the readout screen, turned to his father, and said, "It's Jade. Should I take it or let it go to voice mail? It's up to you. Either way's okay."

"Take it," his father said as he stepped away.

The call surprised and pleased Socrates. Jade rarely called him during the work day.

Jade suggested that she take Socrates and his parents out to dinner that evening using her university department's *use it or lose it* junior-faculty goodwill expense-account to make up for their recent disjointed dinner together.

Socrates put Jade on hold and passed the dinner invitation on to his father who now was standing alongside him.

His father shook his head. "Thank that Jade for us," he said, "for your mother and me. That's sweet of her, but you young people should have some time alone, even when your mother and me are in town. Besides," he said, "I need to talk to your mother about my problem. We won't be hungry after that." Socrates didn't try to talk his father out of his position.

JADE AND SOCRATES decided they would go to their old standby, the Tastee Diner in Bethesda, Maryland, for a quiet, uncomplicated meal. Jade offered to drive to put some mileage on her car and so Socrates wouldn't have to rent one.

They drove north from the District through Rock Creek Park, then west along East-West Highway to Wisconsin Avenue. They turned north again on Wisconsin and immediately crossed into Maryland. They drove another half mile until they arrived at the diner on Woodmont Avenue.

They settled into an authentic 1940s-era high-back wooden booth and faced one another across a Formica top table that was edged with shiny stainless steel trim, and bolted to the wall. Their seats were rock hard, highly lacquered wooden benches covered with red vinyl masquerading as leather.

Socrates dug into his jeans pocket and pulled out a pile of quarters he'd brought with him specifically for this meal. They reviewed the familiar musical selections available on the tiny juke box mounted on the wall alongside their booth, then jointly selected ten Hit Parade songs from among the 1950s and 1960s-era 45 rpm records. That completed, they turned their attention to the tabloid-newspaper-size laminated menus sitting on the table between them.

They passed a few silent minutes as they intensely read the familiar offerings listed on the menus. Then they dropped the menus back onto the table between them and ordered the same food they always ordered at Tastee, two cheeseburgers with extra pickles, tomato, mustard, and raw onions, with one side of hash browned potatoes covered with brown gravy to share.

Jade reached across the table. She took Socrates' hand, and said, "Are you all right, Darling? You seem miles away."

"Sorry," Socrates said. "I'm fine. Just a little preoccupied with all that's going on."

Jade looked puzzled. "What's going on that I don't know about?"

Socrates walked Jade through the drink he'd had with his father and the state of his investigation so far for her father. He also told her about, but dismissed with a shrug and the flip of his hand, the second break-in at his condo. Then he described Eldest Brother's late night visit to him with his *final* warning.

Jade let out a soft whistle. "No wonder you're preoccupied. And you're upset, although you won't admit it."

"Okay," Socrates said. "I admit it. I'm a little upset."

Jade reached across the table and squeezed his hand. She lobbed a kiss across the table.

After dinner, they went back to Jade's condo.

While Jade showered, Socrates sat in front of the TV in the living room and sipped a glass of *mui kwe lu*, a potent Chinese brandy made from rose petals, as he watched the local Channel 5 10:00 p.m. news. This was the nightly news show he and Jade generally referred to, partly tongue in cheek, but partly not, as the *10 p.m. Murder News* because a good part of the broadcast usually was taken up with descriptions of that day's homicides in Washington and the surrounding Maryland and Virginia suburbs.

Approximately twenty minutes into the broadcast, Jade walked into the living room, furiously drying her hair with a big bath towel. Her white terry cloth bathrobe flowed behind her.

"Can I get you anything, Dear?" she said.

Socrates looked up and smiled. "I'm fine." He held up his bubble snifter to show her he had a drink. "How about you, can I do anything. . . ."

The buzzing of the intercom interrupted his question. They looked at each other, said nothing, then turned in tandem to face the intercom panel over by the entrance door.

Jade glanced at her watch. "Who can that be this late?"

Socrates shook his head. "Do you want me to see?"

"Don't bother," Jade said. "I'll take care of it, but come with me." They walked together to the intercom. Jade pressed the *talk* button.

"Who's there?"

"Little Sister, I must talk to you."

Jade frowned and looked at Socrates.

Socrates said, "It's okay. Let him come up." He felt the hair on the back of his neck bristle.

SOCRATES WAS TOO nervous to stand still while he waited for Eldest Brother to arrive. He paced the border of the living room, pausing each time he passed the archway to glance across the foyer at the front door.

Jade, while she waited for her brother to arrive, turned away from the foyer and looked over at Socrates. She smiled and walked up behind him, catching up with him as he completed a second lap around the living room's perimeter. She clucked her tongue, making sounds loud enough for Socrates to hear, and put one hand on his shoulder from behind, signaling him to stop pacing. She waited while Socrates turned to face her, then kissed his cheek. She wrapped her arms around his waist and pulled him in close.

"Don't lose sight of the fact I love you," she said. "No matter what Eldest Brother says to you or me. We'll get through this together."

Three heavy, fisted knocks on the door announced Eldest Brother's arrival.

"WHAT IS THE *low faan* doing here, Little Sister?" Bing-wu said, speaking Mandarin. He pointed at Socrates as he walked in. "I want to talk to you alone, not with this barbarian here." He glared at Socrates. "Order him to leave."

Jade's face reddened. "Speak English, Eldest Brother, for my guest. You are rude not to."

Eldest Brother frowned at Jade, but nodded.

"Socrates is here because I invited him," Jade said. "He is my guest. Have you forgotten your manners, Eldest Brother? You, too, are now a guest in my home, so act appropriately." She paused and inhaled deeply, then let her breath out slowly while she bought time to consider her next words. "Your behavior brings disgrace to me, Eldest Brother." She stepped closer to Socrates and took his hand. Her eyes never left Bing-wu's eyes.

Eldest Brother, moving his head slowly and with studied deliberation, looked over at Socrates, then turned back to Jade.

"Little Sister," he said in English, "I will not say to you what I should say, not in front of this person." He gestured with his chin toward Socrates.

"I will leave now," Eldest Brother said, as he turned away. He hesitated, and turned back to face Jade. "Know your place, Bing-jade, and know your responsibilities in that place," he said, speaking Mandarin again. "It is not proper or wise that you continue to defy our father's commands. There are consequences for doing so." He turned away and, without another word, left.

Socrates walked over to the open door, closed and double latched it, and then joined Jade in the living room.

Jade was sitting on the couch, staring at the wall on the other side of the room. She had crossed her arms over her chest, not in a defiant way, but in a self-protective manner, gripping each bicep with her opposite hand as if she was holding herself together.

"I think you were just threatened," Socrates said, as he walked into the room. "Sorry I brought that on you."

Jade shrugged. "He doesn't mean anything by it," she said. "At least not in terms of me, he doesn't."

Socrates wondered if Jade really believed that or was just saying it for his benefit or to convince herself.

"That's just Bing-wu's way. Besides," she said, smiling now and dropping her hands to her lap, "if I know Eldest Brother as well as I think I do, that was his oblique way of threatening you, not me. I'm perfectly safe with him. You, on the other hand, are another matter."

Chapter 39

THE NEXT MORNING, back home again, Socrates planned his day. He wanted to move the investigation along, to become more proactive than reactive, but his choices how to do this were restricted by his limited experience and by his unofficial status as an unlicensed private investigator.

Because he lacked actual experience with crime, criminals, and crime investigations, Socrates couldn't count on so-called *cop's hunch*, that ineffable intuition that evolves from years of investigating crimes, and which points police officers in the direction of the criminal and the crime's solution even when evidentiary signposts are absent along the way or are not readily apparent.

Because he wasn't an official law enforcement officer, Socrates also lacked the coercive authority inherent in carrying a policeman's badge. This meant that unlike MPDC detectives who could question witnesses and persons of interest using the implicit threat that the person's failure to cooperate might indicate culpability and lead to arrest, Socrates had to approach such people obliquely, never head on.

To compensate for the absence of these useful law enforcement tools, Socrates went forward as he usually did when confronted with something about which he knew little, but for which he needed to quickly develop some expertise. He immersed himself in books and ingested instant, vicarious experience and knowledge. He never reinvented the wheel if he could avoid doing so.

Socrates left his condo and walked to the West End Branch library on 23rd Street and borrowed several more books dealing with criminal investigations. He also checked out two books pertaining to China's history in the 20th century.

Afterward, back home again, over the balance of the day and early evening, Socrates skimmed through *The Private Investigator's Handbook* by Chambers, *The Complete Idiot's Guide to Private Investigating* by Brown, and four similar books. He also read portions of Jonathan Spence's scholarly *The Search For Modern China* and Reginald Hallard's *China Under the Republic [1912-1949]*.

Two of the books indicated that the FBI's favorite method of gathering information was to conduct a neighborhood canvass. The formula for this was simple: Pound the pavement and wear out shoe leather, knock on doors, and ask questions. The FBI's neighborhood canvass approach was a tried and true federal law enforcement investigative tool. Socrates decided that if the process was good enough for the FBI, it was good enough for him.

Having made this decision, now came the hard part: figuring out what questions to ask. Once again, the library books, although not geared to his specific problem, came to his aid. The books described some typical neighborhood canvassing scenarios for various categories of crimes. Socrates was confident he could extrapolate the requisite principles from the books' scenarios and apply the principles to his own investigation. *After all*, he thought, *that was basically what he'd done in his law practice every time he faced a new client or a new legal issue to resolve. He never discarded his prior experience and knowledge to seek out and apply entirely new methods and principles. Instead, he cherry-picked what he already knew and applied the harvested fruit to his new situation.*

That afternoon, Socrates set aside the books and hit the streets.

SOCRATES SPENT THE first twenty minutes walking around the gallery's neighborhood developing a general feel for the environment in which the crime occurred. After that, he began his systematic inspection of the area. He knocked on residential doors and talked to people who lived in the neighborhood. He visited stores and spoke with owners and employees.

An hour and forty-five minutes later, Socrates sipped the coffee he'd picked up at a nearby Starbucks, and knocked on the door of an old brownstone located on 30th Street, at the corner of P.

Silence. He knocked again and stepped closer, putting his ear to the door, listening for movement inside. He heard the footsteps of someone approaching. He stepped back and closed the screen door, being careful not to let it slam. Then more silence. He assumed he was being inspected through the door's security peephole. He waited. After what seemed like many minutes, a woman spoke to him through the closed door.

"What?" she said. Her voice was coarse from years of smoking.

"Hello," Socrates said. "I'm investigating a recent burglary at a neighborhood art gallery. I'd like to ask you some questions. It'll only take a few minutes."

No response.

"Please," Socrates said to the closed door, "I can really use your help."

After half a minute of dead air time, he heard the rasping scrape of metal on metal as a heavy bolt pulled back. The inner door crept open a foot.

A middle-aged woman looked at Socrates from behind the inner door. Only her face was visible. Socrates could barely make out her features through the thick wire mesh of the closed screen door. He soon was enveloped by the cloud of cigarette smoke that drifted through the screen door across the porch.

"Thank you," Socrates said. "I appreciate your time. I'll be quick."

"I don't know nothing to tell you. Only what I read in the paper."

"That's okay," Socrates said. "Maybe my questions will jog your memory. You might've seen or heard something without realizing its relation to the burglary."

"My memory's good. It don't need no joggin'. Besides, I don't have much time," she said. "My show's on the TV and the commercials are almost over soon. I have to get back."

"May I open the screen door while we talk?" Socrates said. He gripped the door's handle and slowly eased the screen door open.

"No, don't," the woman answered, looking at the moving screen door. Her eyes widened. "Stop," she said. She grabbed the inside handle and yanked the door from Socrates' grip, jerking the screen door closed and, in the process, knocking it's edge against Socrates' cup of coffee, splashing him. Then she slammed the interior door and rammed the security bolt back into place.

Over the course of the next three hours, Socrates interviewed several more home owners, a few store employees and the few neighborhood kids he came across as he walked around. Socrates especially sought out teenagers because they often saw more than adults did in the same situations or, if they saw the same things, saw them from a different perspective. Teenagers, he thought, could be a valuable resource and were not to be underestimated.

But all in all, Socrates' attempt to emulate the FBI's canvassing methodology was a colossal flop. At the end of the day, all he had to show for his efforts were sore arches and fresh coffee stains on his suit jacket caused when the 30th Street woman slammed the screen door on him.

Beyond that, one woman, when she answered the door and heard what Socrates wanted, turned up her eyeballs and showed him the whites of her eyes — a traditional, disdainful response the Chinese call *giving someone white eyes*. Although he didn't think it was funny at the time, Socrates later smiled when he thought about this. He couldn't wait to enjoy Jade's laughter when he told her about being given white eyes by a woman who wasn't Chinese. The absolute, the ultimate putdown, he decided.

Socrates was frustrated by his lack of success during his neighborhood canvass. He didn't yet know the fundamental lesson known to every seasoned police detective concerning witnesses: You cannot ignore them, but you also can't count on them. Most witnesses are reluctant to come forward and must be coaxed or coerced. When they do come forward, either under duress or voluntarily, they either lie, exaggerate or are honestly mistaken with respect to what they think they saw. Socrates would have to learn this lesson in his own time.

So much, he decided, for the FBI's favorite way of investigating a crime.

Chapter 40

AT ABOUT THE same time Socrates was walking around the gallery's neighborhood conducting his futile FBI-style canvass, Eldest Brother walked into the THREE PROSPERITIES CHINA ARTS GALLERY, just two blocks away from the house where Socrates had been given white eyes.

Acting Director Fong looked up at the sound of the overhead bell. She frowned when she saw Eldest Brother. Then, with a merchant's disciplined smile fixed firmly in place, she walked out to meet him.

"Hello, Bing-wu. How is Eldest Brother today? I am very pleased to see you."

Bing-wu wasted no time engaging in small talk. He went right to the point of his visit. "You might be visited by a *low faan*, the one called Socrates Cheng. He will claim he is helping my honorable father."

He paused briefly and pointed his finger at Fong. "You will not cooperate with him. Do I make myself clear?"

"Yes, Eldest Brother, quite clear. But you should know that Little Sister also visited me with regard to this matter." She waited, but seeing no reaction from Eldest Brother, continued. "Bing-jade instructed me to cooperate with this Socrates Cheng.

"I am caught between contrary instructions," she said, "between counterpointing directives from an honorable sister and an honorable brother, both of whom I respect and wish to accommodate. I am at a loss to know how to proceed."

Fong demurely lowered her eyes, bowed her head and rested her interlaced fingers on her chest. Then she said, without raising her head, "Little Sister said she would have Youngest Brother speak to venerable Bing-fa on my behalf, to ask your honorable father to use his influence with the Embassy to help me become the replacement director for this esteemed gallery. May I assume you will do the same for me if I follow your wishes rather than those of Little Sister?"

Eldest Brother stepped in close to the acting director, looming over her. He said, "You are not a member of our family, acting director. You will refer to my younger sister properly, as an outsider should. You will never again refer to her as Little Sister or as Bing-jade. She is Younger Sister to you. Do you understand?"

Fong's spine tightened. She nodded and said, "I meant no disrespect. Please forgive my fleeting lapse of judgment."

Eldest Brother yielded no ground to Fong's accommodating statement. He continued to intrude on her physical zone of comfort and loom over her. "You will not cooperate with the *low faan*," he said. "Must I repeat myself, acting director, or do you understand?"

Linda Fong stared at her feet and said, "I understand, Honorable Bing-wu. Please forgive my unintentional impertinence."

"You will not mention this conversation to anyone, including Younger Sister."

"Yes, Bing-wu," she said, still looking at her feet. "I understand perfectly. Thank you for your clarification."

Chapter 41

SOCRATES HAD BEEN in a coma-like sleep when he was jolted awake by the banging on his condo door.

"Stop banging on the door, damn it," Socrates yelled from his bedroom. He bolted upright, wrenched from deep sleep. He leaned over to the nightstand and looked at the clock radio. "Holy sweet mother." It was just after 2:30 a.m.

Socrates staggered into the bathroom, rubbing his eyes as he walked, slipped into his bathrobe, then hurried across the living room to the front door.

"Give it a rest, will you. I'm coming." He ignored the noise now and put his eye to the door's spy hole.

"Hold on a minute for Christ sake. You'll wake the dead," he said. "I'm here." Socrates tightened the belt around his robe, fumbled with the security lock, and opened the front door. "Do you have any idea what time it is? What the hell do you want so late in the night?"

"Socrates Cheng," Detective Harte said, "please step out into the hallway."

Socrates looked from Harte to Detective Thigpen. Thigpen looked back at Socrates and launched a feral grin.

"I repeat, Sir," Harte said. "Please step out into the hall."

"It's the middle of the night. Why should I?"

"May we come in?" Harte said.

Socrates, in a flash of recollection and self-preservation,

recalled Bar Association legal practice bulletins he periodi-
cally received in the mail as a member of the DC Bar. These
pragmatic discussions of criminal law practice were sent to
all Bar members, but were specifically intended for the benefit of those lawyers who did not engage in a criminal law
defense practice. The bulletins were intended as primers, and
described what an attorney's client should and should not do
if confronted with a situation such as the one Socrates now
faced.

The Bar Association's bulletins' advice was simple: Be polite, don't make any threatening moves, and do not mouth off
at the authorities. In fact, tell the client not to say anything at
all. If the client is asked to leave his home and step outside,
he should politely refuse. Otherwise he might be taken into
custody as soon as he steps out. Above all else, the bulletins
urged, the client must not let the police into his home unless
they have a search warrant that, at the very least, seems valid
to the client on its face. Not under any circumstances, not ever,
the bulletins urged.

Fully cognizant of this advice, Socrates — the former
corporate and real estate lawyer who had never set foot in a
courtroom except once as an eye witness to a bar fight, this
same Socrates who as the duteous son of a practicing Confucian had been taught to respect all authority — thought about
the bulletins' advice as he stood at his front door facing two
late night authority figures. Confronted at 2:30 a.m. by the reality of his situation, Socrates responded to Detective Harte's
request by casting aside the Bar's advice and all caution, and
stepping away from the entrance, permitting the detectives to
walk into his home. Socrates tightened his robe's belt and followed them into the living room.

Detective Thigpen, as before, moved behind Socrates,
and faced his back. Detective Harte stood in front of Socrates,
looking directly at him. He handed Socrates a document.

Socrates eyes opened owl wide as he looked, first at the
document in his hands, then at Detective Harte, then back
again at the search warrant.

"What's this for?"

Without waiting for Harte's answer, Socrates read the beginning of the search warrant: ". . . search for and recover . . . a

knife or other bladed instrument used in connection with the murder of one, Iris Hua, on or about . . . ."

Socrates looked back up and said, "Are you guys serious? I didn't—" He caught himself and abruptly paused. *Shut up, Cheng*, he thought.

"Wait a minute," Socrates said. "I have the right to read the entire warrant before you execute on it. I know that much from law school."

"Go for it, hotshot," Detective Thigpen said. "Take all the time you need. Our dance card's empty tonight."

Socrates read the warrant. As far as he could tell, it was in perfect legal order. "Am I under arrest?" he asked.

"Not yet, but be patient," Thigpen said, "the night's still young." He chuckled at his own joke.

Socrates looked at Detective Harte for some solace. He found none there.

"Socrates Cheng," Harte said, "turn around and extend your arms horizontally."

Socrates assumed the requisite posture and Harte patted him down.

"Are there any weapons on the premises?" Harte said.

"Only knives in the drawer out in the kitchen," Socrates said, and immediately regretted his statement, recalling the director's sliced throat.

"Stay out of the kitchen," Harte said. "Stay right here."

Harte nodded at Detective Thigpen who, with the snap of his wrist, unfurled an evidence bag and headed for the kitchen.

Harte said, "Sit on the couch while we conduct the search. Don't leave this room."

Socrates lowered himself onto the sofa, then said, "I want to call my lawyer. I want him here." He wasn't sure who he'd call.

"I thought you was a lawyer," Thigpen said, calling out from the kitchen. "Aren't you good enough to handle your own case?"

"Make the call," Harte said before Socrates could respond to Thigpen. He tilted his head toward the telephone sitting on the foyer table. "Face me while you call and keep your hands where I can see them."

Socrates swallowed his pride and called his former law partner, criminal law defense specialist, Boswell Smyth III. Smyth arrived at Socrates' home a little after 3:45 a.m.

Smyth first conferred privately with Socrates, then he read the search warrant. Next, he spoke with Harte.

"Are you arresting my client?" Smyth asked. "Charging him with . . . ." He paused and frowned. "With what, I must ask?"

"With nothing. Not yet," Harte said. "For now, we're just conducting the search."

"Did you read him his rights?"

"Not necessary, counselor, as you know. He's not a person of interest or target. He's not in custody either. Not yet."

"Of course," Smyth said. "Silly of me to ask."

He looked over at Socrates and raised his eyebrows.

Socrates shook his head.

Five hours later, Thigpen walked back into the living room, caught Harte's eye, and cast an infinitesimal shrug at him. He wagged his head once.

Harte nodded back, almost imperceptivity.

"I take it you found nothing, that you're done here," Smyth said, turning to face Thigpen.

"For now," Thigpen said. "We'll just take these with us for the lab." He held up several clear evidence bags containing Socrates' kitchen knives.

"In that case," Smyth said, "if you'll itemize what you're taking and then close the door on your way out, I have things to talk to my client about." He looked hard at Harte and Thigpen. "Now, detectives. Leave the receipt and take off unless you're going to make an arrest."

Chapter 42

FOUR HOURS AFTER Bos Smyth left him, Socrates, still infused with pumping adrenalin and unable to fall asleep even though he'd been awake since 2:30 a.m., pushed open the door of the THREE PROSPERITIES CHINA ARTS GALLERY and walked in. He was determined the acting director would not brush him aside this time with her stew of belligerence and studied indifference.

He saw Linda Fong standing in the alcove across the exhibit room. She had her back to him, and likely had not heard him enter since she did not turn around at the sound of the door's overhead bell. Socrates stood by the entrance door and waited.

Fong hunched forward and cradled a rotary dial telephone receiver between her right cheek and shoulder. Her left hand sliced the air with staccato rhythm as she emphasized her point to the person on the other end of the call. Her voice was pitched high. She spoke loudly enough for Socrates to unavoidably eavesdrop on her conversation.

"I don't care," she said, speaking in Mandarin. "He was here yesterday morning. Of course it was a threat. I just told you." She paused to listen. "It was not my imagination." She shook her head. "I'm telling you he threatened me. I heard his words. You did not. What I want to know from you is, what are you going to do about it?"

Socrates remained by the door and continued listening.

"No," Fong said, "you pay attention to me. I am doing everything I am supposed to. Now you must live up to your end and do what you agreed to do."

She ended the call and slowly turned toward the exhibit room. Her face pinched when she saw Socrates standing by the entrance. Then, almost imperceptivity, Fong shifted into her sales persona, smoothed her A-line skirt by running a palm over each hip, and straightened herself up so she stood slightly taller. She headed across the room to Socrates, taking quick mincing steps.

"What is it now, Mr. Cheng?" She addressed Socrates in a soft voice, betraying no animosity. "I thought I made myself clear. I have nothing to say to you."

"You were clear all right, Ms. Fong, with me and with the police." He waited a beat, then said, "Give me a few minutes of your time, then I'll go. Just five minutes, is all."

She shrugged. "Say what you want for five minutes. It will remain a monologue. Then leave."

"As I see it," Socrates said, "you had plenty of reason to ruin the exhibit, discredit the director by doing so, then maneuver to take her place. That sounds like a good motive to me to get rid of her."

"What is it you are accusing me of, Mr. Cheng? Causing the director to lose face? Killing the director? If you are . . . ."

"Maybe the director didn't take enough heat after the burglary to satisfy you. Maybe her loss of face and inevitable downfall were uncertain or moving too slow to satiate you."

Fong's nostrils flared and she stomped her foot. "You dare come into my gallery and insult me! . . . You must leave," she said, pointing to the door. Her voice grew louder as she spoke. "You go now or I will call the police. You have no right—"

"I don't think you want to do that," Socrates said, intentionally speaking softly and slowly. "You don't want to bring in the cops and call attention to yourself."

"Go now, Mr. Cheng. I have nothing to say to you. You now are a trespasser here."

Socrates ignored Fong's implied threats and protestations. "You had the best reason of anyone to want the director out of the way," Socrates said. He made no move to leave. He waited for some response from Fong, a subtle tell in her facial expression or some other clue in her body language that would tip him he was onto something. But Fong offered him nothing to work with. She merely stared back at him, standing tall and facing Socrates like a cobra eyeing its prey just before its strike.

Socrates shrugged. "If I figured this out, so will the cops. Once they decide it was you, they'll never let go. I'm your best hope for avoiding that if you're innocent."

Fong said nothing. She turned away and walked back across the exhibit room to the alcove. She headed over to her desk, opened a drawer, and reached into it. As she started to extract something, she turned toward Socrates and looked him over, slowly, very conspicuously, up and down. Then she straightened up and put a cigarette into the corner of her mouth, slammed the drawer closed, and walked back across the room to Socrates. She handed him a plastic Bic lighter.

"Please," she said, leaning in toward his hand.

Socrates fired up Fong's cigarette and handed the lighter back to her.

Fong stepped away from Socrates, paused briefly to inhale, then streamed smoke from her nostrils, aiming her chin at the ceiling.

Socrates watched the smoke collide with the acoustic ceiling tiles and scurry away in all directions.

"The director never permitted me to smoke here," Fong said. "It supposedly damages the art. But now, I am in charge." She placed one hand on her hip and held the cigarette chest high in the first two fingers of her other hand.

"Listen carefully, Mr. Cheng, I am struggling to have this gallery operating again after the disruptions caused by the crimes committed here. I am under great pressure to open the exhibit in less than two weeks, with or without the stolen objects as part of it. I do not have time to waste with you." She paused to let Socrates take in and register her subtext: *Even if I had the time, low faan, I wouldn't help you.*

Socrates resisted the urge to comment on what he intuitively knew she was saying to him.

"If you must persist in being a nuisance," she continued, "come back tomorrow night. I work late every evening to prepare for the opening. I will permit you fifteen minutes of my time at 9:00 p.m. That is all. I likely will not answer your questions in any event." She paused and looked Socrates in his eyes. "You can take it or leave it. It is of no concern to me what you decide. But, that is it. After that, we are through."

Chapter 43

SOCRATES ACCEPTED FONG'S offer, such as it was. He said he'd be back at 9:00. The offer to meet after hours didn't surprise him. He'd had similar experiences over the years when he tried to sell historic documents to galleries. He often was told to bring the documents back after hours so the gallery's operator could examine them when no customers were around.

Socrates left the gallery and walked the two miles to the Embassy of the People's Republic of China located in the Kalorama section of Washington, not far from the National Zoo and not far from Jade's condo. If matters at the Embassy went as he hoped, he would learn the Embassy's official position concerning the burglary. He also might gain some insight into why the Embassy thought the nineteen stolen objects were targeted and the other two hundred and fifty-six on display were left behind.

Socrates pushed the button located adjacent to the front entrance and watched a small security camera installed above the entrance silently rotate and zoom in on him. He nodded at the lens. A squeaky female voice, coming from a pocket-size speaker box located above the doorway, asked him in barely serviceable English to identify himself and state his business at the Embassy. Socrates looked up at the speaker box, smiled for the camera, and explained his mission in general terms.

After a few minutes, a woman in her early twenties, dressed in a navy blue American-style two piece business suit, opened the door and admitted him into a wood paneled anteroom. The woman politely, but coldly, asked Socrates to wait where he stood until she returned. She bowed, then left him standing just inside the entrance door, keeping company with an armed guard who seemed to ignore him. In less than a minute, the woman returned and handed Socrates a printed questionnaire to complete and return to her.

Socrates took a seat behind a small desk and completed the form. Then, as he had been instructed, he pushed a desktop button to indicate he was finished. The woman reentered the room immediately, as if she had been standing on the other side of the closed door waiting for his signal, and took Socrates' questionnaire and driver's license from him. She left the anteroom, but promptly returned and handed Socrates his driver's license. She departed again without saying anything to him, leaving Socrates and the guard staring together at the same blank wall across the room.

A few minutes later another door opened and a different woman walked into the anteroom. She was in her early to middle thirties and dressed in a solid bright green, traditional silk dress that covered her from just below her chin to her ankles. She bowed briefly from her waist, did not smile, and asked Socrates if he would expand upon the answer he'd written on the questionnaire, specifically, if he would describe in more detail his purpose for coming to the Embassy.

Socrates was curious about her frosty demeanor, which seemed to be imbued with hostility rather than mere formality, but he quickly shrugged it off as unimportant in the scheme of things. He explained his written answer, this time giving more particulars. He even went so far as to mention Bing-fa's name in this account of his mission.

Socrates thought the woman's reserve increased ever so slightly as he elaborated on his reason for being there. Her forehead wrinkled as she listened to him.

When Socrates finished, the woman said, "Unfortunately, we cannot help you. Thank you very much. Please have a nice day." She paused as if waiting for Socrates to respond affirmatively to her dismissal, thank her, and then leave with a smile on his face.

Socrates frowned, but didn't say or do anything. He made no move to leave.

The woman seemed puzzled by his lack of response. She tilted her head slightly, then offered an explanation for her statement. "The reasons for the selections of the objects in the exhibit were known only to our cultural attaché and to the honorable Li Bing-fa. They made the choices together. No one here has the information you seek. Thank you and good day."

She again paused as if waiting for Socrates to depart. Once again he stood firm. After a few seconds of shared silence, the woman resumed her explication, describing in very broad terms the role of the cultural attaché in selecting the objects and photos to be exhibited and included in the catalog. She concluded with a statement referring to the murder of the cultural attaché on the streets of Chinatown as she walked back to the Embassy after having dinner at a restaurant. She added, flashing a condescending smile at Socrates, that such violent crime is unknown on the streets of Beijing.

Socrates vaguely remembered reading the story of the murder in the *Washington Post*, but he hadn't focused on it at the time or later connected it with the THREE PROSPERITIES CHINA ARTS GALLERY and the proposed cultural exhibit.

So, Socrates thought, *the cultural attaché could not help him.* He had hit another dead end.

Chapter 44

AS SOON AS he returned home from the Embassy, Socrates grabbed Reginald Hallard's book he'd borrowed from the library and for the next two hours immersed himself in a survey study of China's early 20th Century history. He read with a specific question in mind.

The buzzing of the intercom interrupted his research.

Socrates walked over to the intercom panel on the wall. "Who's there?" The filtered, crackling response brought him fully alert.

"Mr. Cheng, my name is Special Agent Ingram. I'm with the Federal Bureau of Investigation. I'd like to come up and speak with you."

Socrates hesitated, then said, "No, not yet, Sir. I'll come down to the lobby and meet you by the doorman's desk. Show me your government ID. If it's in order, we can come back up here."

Ingram's official ID was in order. Socrates led him up to his condo unit and into the living room.

The special agent thanked Socrates in advance for his cooperation and advised him of the standard admonition required in situations like this, that there were severe penalties for lying to or for misleading a Federal officer. He described the penalties, then said, "I understand you visited the People's

Republic of China Embassy earlier today. What was the purpose of your visit?"

Socrates felt a chill pass through him. He hesitated. After a few seconds, he said, "I'll be glad to tell you, Special Agent, if you'll first tell me why you want to know. Why is a citizen's innocent visit to an Embassy, whose government this country recognizes, cause for the FBI to show up on his doorstep?"

"Sir," Ingram said, "I would appreciate your cooperation. Please answer the question."

Socrates stiffened. An internal alarm kicked in. "I'll answer you," he said, "in the spirit of being a good citizen, but only if you promise that afterward you'll tell me why you're interested. I think I'm entitled to know that much in return for my cooperation."

"Fine, Sir, I agree. Now, what was the purpose of your visit?"

Socrates answered the special agent's question and described his brief conversations inside the Embassy. When he finished, he said, "Now, Agent Ingram, it's your turn. Why's the FBI interested in what a citizen does exercising his First Amendment rights?"

Special Agent Ingram closed his notebook, then said, "I am instructing you not to return to the People's Republic Embassy or otherwise attempt to contact any of its personnel in connection with your prior inquiry." He paused, and when Socrates did not respond, said, "Have I made myself clear, Mr. Cheng?" He looked hard at Socrates as if daring him to protest the instructions or to ask another question.

"If you fail to comply, you may be subject to arrest and prosecution for obstruction of justice and for hindering a federal investigation. Do you understand?" He paused again and stared at Socrates.

When Socrates still failed to say anything, Ingram continued. "I asked you, Mr. Cheng, do you understand what I've told you and the consequences to you if you ignore it?"

"I understand what you want me to do or, rather, not do, Special Agent, but you haven't told me *why*, which you agreed you would."

"Thank you, Sir," Ingram said. "Since you understand my

instructions, I'll leave now. I hope we will not have cause to meet again on this matter."

Socrates showed the special agent out of his condo and closed the door behind him. He was furious. He'd been suckered by a member of the nation's police force.

As Socrates walked back to his chair to return to Hallard's book, his cell phone rang. It was Youngest Brother. Socrates answered the call.

Something had come up, Youngest Brother told Socrates, and Bing-fa wanted to meet with Socrates as soon as possible.

Chapter 45

TWENTY MINUTES LATER, Socrates and Bing-fa met in Bing-fa's small office at the Golden Dragon.

"I have again been contacted by the person who sold me the substitute writing instrument," Bing-fa said. "This time he offered to repatriate the priceless Northern Sung Edict."

Socrates considered how he wanted to respond to this information. He hadn't forgotten how his candid words before had affected Bing-fa. Speaking softly, he said, "How much will it cost you for this priceless object?"

"A mere $44,000 U.S."

"At this rate," Socrates said, "you could go broke buying back the burglars' loot, piece by piece. You told him *No*, didn't you?"

"I did not. Obtaining the return of this national treasure is worth more to me than my family's resources."

Oh, right, Socrates thought. *You mean restoring your face and consequent family honor is more important to you than your family's monetary fortune.*

"It's your money," Socrates said. "You're free to waste it without regard to what I think. But tell me this, Bing-fa, why do you think you can trust him this time after the way he cheated you, that he's not running another scam against you?"

Bing-fa said nothing, but Socrates thought he looked annoyed.

"Who is he," Socrates said, "this mysterious caller of yours? Any idea?"

"He was the same person I spoke with before. I recognized his voice. That's all I know," Bing-fa said. "As for your other question, I don't know he hasn't, as you say, run a scam against me again, but I had no choice because you haven't fulfilled your responsibility to recover our treasures."

Socrates felt his anger well up as Bing-fa placed the blame on him, but he held his emotions in check because an alarm had sounded in his head. He looked sharply at Bing-fa as he processed what he'd just heard.

"Wait a minute, Bing-fa. What you just said: You hope he *hasn't* run a scam against you again. Not, you hope he *won't* run a scam against you again."

Past tense? Socrates thought. "Is this a done deal?" he said.

Bing-fa sat up a little straighter. "You are correct. I have the Northern Sung Edict in my possession. I would like you to examine it for me to determine if the document is the genuine Edict."

Socrates shook his head. His emotions raced the gamut from anger to surprise. *Some people never learn*, he thought.

"Sure. Why not," he said. "I'll look at it for you, but you need to know what I can and can't do for you when it comes to documents. It's not like with pens."

Socrates did have some experience examining documents of the type the FBI and the police referred to as questioned documents — documents whose fundamental authenticity was questioned or documents that were genuine, but which might have been altered.

To the extent he'd engaged in the document examination process at all, Socrates had approached it only as a hobbyist, not scientifically. And yet he did possess some skills, such as his ability to read Mandarin, that could prove useful in an examination of the Northern Sung Edict. But he had his experience and knowledge deficiencies as well. For example, Socrates was not familiar with the type of parchment or with the ink used by Imperial calligraphers or with the writing style or types of wax seals prevalent in the Northern Sung royal court.

"My inability to evaluate the Imperial ink, seals, parchment and writing style will be serious shortcomings," Socrates said. "The best I can do will be to use my knowledge of written Mandarin to compare the Edict with its counterpart document illustrated in the exhibit catalog."

Bing-fa nodded.

Socrates continued to explain how he would approach his examination of the Northern Sung Edict.

"I'll examine the Edict's text and other visual contextual indicia — pictographic stroke by pictographic stroke — and compare the shapes of the symbolic words, the punctuation, the external spacing of the pictographs, and the internal spacing between the characters, against the 1:1 scale color photograph of the catalog's document. If the Edict is a fake, some deviation in its text from the text shown in the catalog's illustration should reveal itself."

Of course, he thought, *if the Edict exactly matches the photograph, but the document in the photograph is itself a fake, then I'll be delivering a false positive result to Bing-fa . . . . Well*, he thought, *so be it. Bing-fa has been warned of my limitations in this area.*

THE NEXT MORNING, Socrates returned to the Golden Dragon. He sat across the table from Bing-fa. The Northern Sung Edict lay between them.

"What have you concluded?" Bing-fa asked.

"It looks like the same document as the one in the catalog," Socrates said. "It matches visually. Other than that, you know from what I told you there are aspects I cannot confirm."

"This will do," Bing-fa said. "This is the first step in recovering our national treasures. This precious Edict will be displayed when the cultural exhibit opens. We now must repatriate the other stolen objects."

Socrates looked away, lost in thought. A dense silence cloaked him and Bing-fa.

"You are bothered by something?" Bing-fa said.

Socrates thought Bing-fa sounded more irritated than curious.

Socrates frowned. "Something doesn't make sense. I'm not sure I'm going to say this right because it isn't fully clear yet in my own mind. I don't want to put this in a way that might offend you again."

"Speak candidly."

"What's nagging at me is that someone went to all the trouble of selling you a substitute Mandarin Yellow, yet these same people then sold you the genuine Northern Sung Edict rather than create a forgery of it and sell that to you?"

Bing-fa frowned and shook his head. He seemed confused.

"I'm not making myself clear," Socrates said. "What puzzles me is this: Why didn't the caller sell you the genuine 1927 Mandarin Yellow instead of the substitute, and use that to stoke your appetite to retrieve more? Once he'd hooked you with the pen, he could sell you a forged Edict, which wouldn't be that difficult to create. Instead, he did it the other way around." Socrates paused briefly, then said, "Something about this doesn't ring true to me."

"I understand your concern after the last . . . ."

Socrates held up his palm to quiet Bing-fa. He wasn't ready to let this go.

"Think about it this way, Bing-fa. If they didn't want to keep the genuine Edict to sell later to someone else, to double dip, why not sell you both the genuine pen as well as the genuine document?" *The key term here being 'genuine',* Socrates thought.

"Introducing the substitute Mandarin Yellow into the mix makes no sense and could only raise your suspicions about all subsequent sales. If they'd sold you the genuine Mandarin Yellow right off, you would have assumed all subsequent sales were also bona fides and relaxed your scrutiny of later objects you retrieved. *That is unless the thieves know you better than I do,* he thought.

"I see your point, Mr. Cheng. Perhaps the thieves were not able to create an adequate forgery of the valued Edict." Bing-fa said.

"Maybe," Socrates responded, "but I suspect there's more to it than that." He shook his head slowly, then said, "It's as if I'm not seeing something right in front of me. Something obvious. And that really bothers me."

Chapter 46

THE FOLLOWING MORNING, Socrates sat at the kitchen table reading the previous day's *Washington Post* when his cell phone rang. He looked at the cell's LCD readout.

"Morning, Brandon," he said.

"Back at you, ol' buddy. I'm meeting with my broker in a few minutes. I'll be finished with her in about half an hour. I thought we could catch an early lunch and you can fill me in on how the super-PI's doing."

Socrates winced. Why did both Brandon and Jade insist on teasing him about the investigation by calling him Sherlock or other names?

"I'll meet you, but I won't eat, I'll just have coffee," Socrates said. "I'm meeting Jade for lunch in a few hours. How about somewhere in Georgetown so I'm not too far from Jade's office when we finish?"

They met at Clyde's, a white tablecloth restaurant and bar located on M Street in the heart of Georgetown's tourist and retail district.

Socrates told Brandon about the deteriorating condition of his father's mental health and his father's problem with the IRS. Brandon was shocked. Because his own father traveled extensively in connection with family business and had rarely spent time with him as Brandon was growing up, Brandon over the years had come to view Socrates' father as his own surrogate parent.

Socrates walked Brandon through his investigation so far, including the two break-ins at his condo, the visits and threats from Eldest Brother, the FBI special agent's deceptive visit, and his anticipated meeting later that night with Linda Fong. He forgot to mention the sale of the substitute Mandarin Yellow and the return of the genuine Northern Sung Edict document to Bing-fa.

"To add insult to injury," Socrates said, "I think I might soon be a suspect in the director's murder, if I'm not already. Can you believe that?"

Brandon laughed. "Looks like you stepped into a pile of shit this time. Do you really plan to go back tonight and see the Fong woman?"

Socrates nodded. "You better believe it. I'll take my allotted fifteen minutes, whatever that might turn out to be worth, if I can get it. You never know where it might lead."

"Any reason to think you won't be wasting your time with the woman?"

"Probably will be, but I don't know anything better to do with her at the moment. I'll have to play by her rules if I want her to cooperate with me."

"What makes you think she'll even talk to you tonight," Brandon said, "that she wasn't just blowing you off to get rid of you? Sounds like you landed on the lady's bad side and can't move beyond it."

"I don't know," Socrates said, "but it was her suggestion. I don't have much to lose by going."

Brandon nodded and looked across the room, but said nothing more.

"What? Socrates said.

Brandon remained silent.

"What," Socrates said again. "What're you thinking?"

Brandon slowly turned back to face Socrates. "I have an idea," he said. "It sounds like you really pissed the woman off and need my help." He waited for Socrates to agree. When he received only silence and was met by Socrates' puzzled look, he said, "What if I go there tonight in your place. I'll talk to the lady. Maybe she'll react differently to a fresh face with a bright smile. Frankly, I think you have nothing to lose and it could pay off."

Socrates knitted his eyebrows together. "I don't know if . . . ."

"I'll just need you to tell me what you'd like to know, what I should ask her," Brandon said.

"I'm not sure it's such a good idea because Bing-fa—"

"Worst case, she won't tell me anything," Brandon said, "and you'll be back to square one with her. On the other hand, maybe not since I'm not you and won't bring along your baggage you have with her." He shrugged and paused. "It was just a thought."

"I don't know," Socrates interrupted. "I'm not comfortable with it. I probably should check with Bing-fa first. He's weird about his privacy and . . . ."

Socrates let his protestation trail off. He stared at Brandon for a few seconds, then broke into a big grin. "Screw it. Who am I kidding? I'm not getting anywhere with the lady. Why not have you try?" Socrates thought about the idea for a few more seconds, then said, "Do it. The hell with Bing-fa. Here's what I'd like to find out from her . . . ."

AFTER OBTAINING BRANDON'S promise to call him as soon as he finished meeting with Fong, Socrates hurried to Georgetown University to meet Jade for sandwiches.

He'd covered only three blocks when his cell phone rang. The call was from the IRS's revenue officer who was handling Socrates' father's case for the New York field office.

In response to the revenue officer's question, Socrates explained who he was and why he, rather than his father, had called earlier in the day. He agreed that when he returned home in the afternoon, he would FAX his father's signed Power of Attorney to the revenue officer authorizing Socrates to speak to the IRS for his father. Socrates said he would call back late that afternoon to discuss the details of his father's case after the revenue officer had received the authorizing FAX.

Approximately two and one half hours later, Socrates was on the phone again with the IRS.

The revenue officer agreed to halt levy and collection proceedings against Socrates' father while Socrates arranged payment of the tax debt. He also agreed to transfer the case from the White Plains, NY field office to the Washington field office since Socrates parents eventually would be moving to Washington and, in the meantime, Socrates would be handling the case for them from Washington.

Socrates considered this last concession to be a good strategic result for his father. The new, substitute revenue officer in Washington would not bring to the table all the baggage deposited by Socrates' father with the New York field office when he repeatedly ignored the IRS's letters and telephone calls. Socrates and the DC revenue officer would begin their dealings with a relatively clean slate.

That small, but significant victory having been achieved, all Socrates had to do now was figure out where he would find the money to pay the tax debt for his father since his parents did not have the resources to do it. He wanted to talk with his mother about this.

BRANDON CALLED SOCRATES a little after 10:30 p.m. He sounded as if he'd been drinking. Socrates could hear ice clinking against the side of Brendon's glass as well as other bar noise in the background.

"You nailed it, my friend," Brandon said. "The woman completely blew me off, wouldn't talk to me at all. In fact, she was pissed you sent me in your place. Said something about not wasting her time listening to me if you didn't think meeting with her was important enough to come yourself."

"Damn it. I knew I should've gone," Socrates said. "How will I dig myself out of that hole? I still need to talk with the lady."

"Not to worry," Brandon said. "I fixed it up for you, but it wouldn't have made any difference if you'd been there. Even after I told her I was your boss and I came today in your place because I thought talking with her was too important to delegate to my subordinate, she still had nothing to say to me, although she did relax a bit."

Socrates groaned. "She had nothing to say? Nothing at all?"

"You got it. Zilch. Nada. Nothing at all," Brandon said. "But get this. She tilted her head back and her eyes suddenly rolled up into her sockets like she was having a fit or something. I almost freaked, I was so creeped out. All I could see were the white parts of her eyes. Then she undid it and told me to leave. I'll tell you, Socrates, I've never seen anything like that before and I hope I never do again. That lady really scared the hell out of me."

Socrates smiled. He'd have to explain *giving white eyes* to Brandon sometime, but not right now.

"Thanks for trying. The question now is, how will I deal with her from now on, given what happened?"

Brandon ignored Socrates' rhetorical question, and said, "I'm at The Guards drinking. Come over and join me. We can hoist a few beers in honor of the assistant director and her resolute pig-headedness."

"Not tonight," Socrates said. "I'm beat. I'm sacking out soon, then hitting the pavements tomorrow morning. I'll go visit our friend, Fong, and see if I can somehow get her attention for a few minutes."

Chapter 47

SOCRATES WAS DEEP within a dream and deeply irritated by the dream's storyline because in his dream someone was relentlessly banging on his condo's door.

He opened his eyes to escape, but the pounding continued. It gradually penetrated Socrates' groggy consciousness that this was not a dream at all. Someone *was* pounding on his door.

Still in the grip of sleep, Socrates cautiously stood up. After a few seconds, he grabbed his robe and lurched toward the foyer and front door.

"Dial it down," he yelled. "I'm coming."

He jerked open the door and started to say, 'What the hell do you think you're doing in the middle of the night,' but swallowed his words and caught his breath.

"Oh!" he said, and instinctively took a step back. He suddenly was fully awake.

Detectives Harte and Thigpen stood in the hallway facing him.

Thigpen put out his arm and blocked the door from closing in case that was what Socrates had in mind as his next move.

"Now what?" Socrates said. "Haven't we already been through this? Do I need to call my lawyer again?"

"Remember us, Mr. Cheng?" Harte said. He held up his gold shield as if Socrates had never seen it.

"I told you everything I know about the director's murder. I have nothing else to say. Why are you harassing me?"

"Sorry you think that," Harte said. "That's not why we're here. Something else has come up. May we come in?"

Something in Harte's body language and tone of voice resonated with Socrates and caused him to cast aside his anger and caution. He stepped away from the door and motioned the detectives into his apartment. As before, he followed them into the living room.

"You look like something the cat dragged in," Thigpen said. "Been out playing tonight?"

Socrates glared at the detective, but didn't take the bait and respond to him.

"A body's been found in Georgetown," Harte said.

"What's that have to do with me?" Socrates said.

"Maybe nothing. You tell us."

Socrates was confused. "I don't get it. Why are you telling me this?"

"We think you might know the vic," Harte said. "Your name was in his BlackBerry. He called you earlier tonight. And your name was the only one we recognized in his contacts."

Socrates frowned, confused. Slowly, the significance of what Harte had said took hold. He gasped. Socrates felt his stomach twist into a knot.

"The vic's throat was cut, he was stabbed, and the perp left him in an alley," Thigpen said. "He'd been hitting the bars and smelled like a leftover glass of scotch the morning after, when you go to clean up the mess. But you probably already know that, don't you."

Socrates cut Thigpen a withering look, but said nothing. His stomach churned as his recognition of the situation gradually fell into place.

"It wasn't a mugging," Harte added. "The vic still had his money, wallet and watch on him."

"Detective . . . ." Socrates said tentatively.

"There's something else," Harte said. He reached into his sports jacket's inside pocket and pulled out an evidence bag. It held a piece of paper.

"This was rolled like a scroll and shoved in the vic's mouth, halfway down his throat. Do you know what it is?" Harte said. He held out the evidence bag so Socrates could look at it.

"Oh, shit," Socrates said. "I know what it is." Socrates sank down onto the sofa. The paper was a photocopy of the Northern Sung Edict.

Thigpen took a step closer to Socrates. "Talk to us, Cheng," he said. "Tell us why you killed him."

Socrates ignored Thigpen and explained the significance of the Edict and that the photocopy connected the killing to the burglary at the gallery.

Harte glanced over at Thigpen who raised an eyebrow and smiled.

"It might be my friend," Socrates said. "It sounds like it's Brandon. How could this happen?" He dropped his face into his palms and convulsively shivered once.

"Where were you last night," Harte said, "after Midnight?"

"Here. Sleeping. Alone. And, no, you don't have to ask: No one can vouch for me."

Harte nodded. "The vic's a Caucasian male about your age. It could be your friend. We'd like you to come with us to the ME's office, see if you can ID him."

FORTY-FIVE MINUTES LATER, Socrates stood in front of the glass window at the District of Columbia Medical Examiner's office staring at a fully covered body lying on a waist-high gurney on the other side of the window pane.

Detective Harte looked at Socrates and raised his eyebrows. "Ready?"

Socrates closed his hands into fists and said, "No, I'm not ready, but do it anyway." He took a deep breath.

Harte signaled the ME. She pulled back the white sheet as far as the tip of the victim's chin, revealing Brandon's gray, waxen face.

"Take your time," Harte said.

"Oh, fuck," Socrates said. "No . . . no." He closed his eyes and leaned his weight into his arms, bracing himself against the windowsill. He breathed quickly, soon veering toward hyperventilation.

Harte put his hand on Socrates' shoulder. "Are you all right?" he said.

Socrates raised his head and straightened up. "No, I'm not all right. Why would I be?"

Harte spoke formally now. "Mr. Cheng, can you identify the body?"

Socrates nodded. He took a deep breath and paused. "It's . . . It's Brandon, my best friend, Brandon Hill." He wiped his eye with his sleeve.

Harte made a circular motion with his hand, signaling the ME to cover the body. He led Socrates away from the viewing area, out into the corridor. "We'll need your signature on the form indicating you've ID'd Mr. Hill," Harte said.

"I don't understand," Socrates said. "How'd this happen to him?"

"Stabbed. Thirteen times," Thigpen said. "I guess thirteen wasn't his lucky number." He grinned, then added, "And his throat got slashed from one ear to the other. Looked like a big smile." He glanced over at Harte, then back at Socrates. "What he do to get you so pissed at him?"

Harte frowned at Thigpen, shook his head once, but said nothing.

Socrates turned away from Thigpen and faced Harte. "This happened because of the burglary at the THREE PROSPERITIES CHINA ARTS GALLERY, because of my investigation. That paper in his mouth shows the connection."

Socrates moaned softly and slowly drew in a deep breath. "It should've been me dead, not Brandon," he said. "He went to the gallery in my place . . . for me. That was the extent of his involvement. Brandon had nothing to do with any of this except for the visit last night."

"What are you saying, Cheng," Harte asked.

"Don't you get it?" Socrates said. "The document shoved down Brandon's throat was a photocopy of one stolen in the burglary at the gallery, the crime I'm investigating." He slowly wagged his head. "Brandon wasn't the target at all. I was. Indirectly. Brandon was killed as a warning to me to back off."

Chapter 48

SOCRATES SPENT THE next two hours at the 2D with Detectives Harte and Thigpen retelling his version of events from the day before and answering the detectives' questions, including questions about Brandon's background and habits. He indentified Brendan's parents for them, gave the police their home telephone number, but said he believed Mr. and Mrs. Hill were not currently at home in Philadelphia, that Brandon had said they were vacationing in the south of France.

When the detectives finished taking his statement and he'd reviewed and signed it, Socrates left the building in a daze. He felt emotionally battered.

He headed toward Georgetown. He walked very slowly, shuffling along more than walking, looking at the pavement in front of his feet as he meandered west.

He pulled out his cell phone as he walked and called Jade, trying her landlines first at her office and then at home, then trying her cell. He left the same message all three times: Call me as soon as you get this. I need to talk to you. I just learned the worst possible news you can imagine.

Socrates thought about what he would do with himself until he and Jade connected. He didn't want to be alone at his store or alone at his condo. He also didn't want to be with his parents. Not right now, maybe later tonight. They would mean well, and would be concerned for him and solicitous of his feelings, but they also would ask too many questions about his obvious withdrawal, and that would drive him crazy. He wasn't ready yet to tell them what had happened and to explain the context in which Brandon's murder had occurred. He still had to get used to it himself before he'd be ready to do that for his parents.

SOCRATES WALKED TO The Guards, the bar/restaurant Brandon had called him from the night before. The Guards had been a fixture in Georgetown since the early 1970s, popular among Washington's upscale business and professional drinking crowds. The combination bar and New York City-style steakhouse was located between 28th and 29th on M.

Socrates hadn't been to The Guards since he resumed dating Jade because Jade, unlike Socrates who found the atmosphere of dimly lighted bars relaxing, did not enjoy immersing herself in bar ambiance. But today, Socrates decided, he needed this hideaway. The twilight-like aura of The Guards would be the perfect place for him to hole up alone while he struggled to bring his emotions under control and tried to come to grips with the reality of Brandon's death.

He entered The Guards slowly, paused just inside the entry doors, and looked around. The bar area, located two steps down and to the left of the double doors as you entered, was just as wholesome and inviting as he remembered. The long mahogany wooden bar and the rich, matching dark stained walls softly glowed in the warm amber light cast by lamps strategically placed around the room.

Two customers sat at the bar, both seated up front near the entrance, spaced five or six stools apart from one another. None of the nearby tables was occupied. Socrates settled onto a bar stool at the far end of the room, facing the entrance, as far away as he could be from the two men drinking alone.

The tender appeared in front of Socrates almost as soon as he settled himself onto the stool.

"Hey, Socrates, my man, longtime no see. How're you doing?" He dropped a wafer-like paper coaster onto the lacquered bar surface in front of Socrates.

Without giving Socrates a chance to answer, he continued his patter. "What'll it be? The usual?"

"Not today. Give me something stronger than beer, much stronger. A single malt, a McCallum, double over ice." Socrates smiled feebly, then added, "It's been a while, Boxer, hasn't it? See you shaved your beard."

The tender had already walked away and was pouring Socrates' drink before Socrates' had finished his question.

Socrates stared down at the paper coaster. He looked up again when his drink arrived.

"You okay? You look bad," Boxer said.

"Remember Brandon, my friend from school? Tall, good looking, preppie type with blond hair. My college roommate. Used to come in here sometimes with me." He paused and sipped his drink. "Somebody cut his throat and stabbed him last night. I just found out."

"Holy Jesus, Man, that's terrible. I'm sorry. Can I do anything for you?"

Socrates shook his head. "I'll have this drink," he said, tilting his head at the McCallum, "then go home. I feel like crap." He dropped his forehead into his palms and rested his elbows on the bar.

"YO! BOXER, OVER here. Bring another one," Socrates said. He held up his empty glass as if offering a toast.

The tender walked over to Socrates, leaned across the bar and said softly, "Socrates, my pal, don't you think you've had enough for tonight? I know you're upset, but you've been hitting it now like a couple of hours. Why don't you go home and sleep it off? I'll buy you a cab on me."

Socrates stiffened and pulled away. He straightened up on his stool, threw back his shoulders and assumed a drunk's affectation of dimly remembered sober gravitas.

"Who the fuck you think you're talkin' to?" Socrates said. "Don't tell me how to take care of myself, damn it. I'm the customer, you're the bartender. If I want another God damn drink, you'll get me another drink! Understand?"

SOCRATES WOKE SEVERAL hours later. He ran his scaly tongue across his top row of teeth and winced as he scraped off some unidentifiable scum. His mouth felt as if it was stuffed with sour tasting cotton balls.

He no longer was at The Guards. He was behind bars, lying on his back on a rock-hard bench in a jail cell at DC's Central Cellblock at 300 Indiana Avenue. The police had arrested him at The Guards and charged him with *unlawful entry* — Washington's name for criminal trespass — because he refused to leave the bar when Boxer ordered him out after Socrates scuffled with another customer.

Socrates, too embarrassed by his behavior to call his former law partner, Bos Smyth, decided to quietly accept the consequences of his behavior. He agreed to the informal court procedure called *Elect to Forfeit*, a process tantamount to pleading guilty which avoided the publicity and expense of a full blown trial. The court fined Socrates $350, the maximum fine for unlawful entry. The judge, who sternly lectured Socrates about his responsibility as a member of the Bar, graciously spared him the opportunity to serve up to six months in jail, another possible consequence of the *Elect to Forfeit* plea. The court was influenced in its decision, the judge told Socrates, because this was his first offense, because of the extenuating circumstances of his best friend's murder, and because Socrates seemed fittingly contrite.

Unfortunately, Socrates did not have either $350 in cash or a check with him. He called Jade and, eventually reaching her, asked her to bring the cash to Central Cellblock. He said he would explain everything later.

"DID YOU CALL my parents and tell them?" Socrates said.

"Of course not," Jade said. "I thought you should be the one to tell them, not me."

Socrates wheezed a sigh of relief.

"Good. I'll do it later when the time's right. I still have to get used to this myself. It hasn't really sunk in yet."

When they left Central Cellblock, Jade, who had cancelled classes for the day after receiving his call, insisted that she and Socrates go back to her condo. Socrates readily agreed. Once there, he shaved, showered, and dressed in fresh clothes he kept in Jade's spare closet for nights he stayed over.

After he finished cleaning himself up, Socrates walked out to the kitchen. Jade was setting the table. She looked up and smiled as he entered.

"Now, that's the handsome, clean cut, non-violent Socrates Cheng I remember and love. You almost look human again, except for your hangdog face."

Socrates held up his palm. "Not so loud, just whisper. My head's killing me."

Jade smiled and nodded, then continued, *sotto voce*, "Are you all right? I'm sorry I teased you. You had quite an afternoon and night."

"I guess so. I don't really remember much." He buried his face in his palms, waited a few seconds, then looked up again. "No, I'm not all right. Brandon's dead. I feel like crap. I guess I had too much to drink."

"Good guess, Darling," Jade said. "I called The Guards while you were in the shower and paid your bar bill with my AMEX card. It was a whopper of a bill. You owe me big time, my friend. You might have to take out a second mortgage on your condo just to reimburse me for your bar tab."

"What happened, anyway? The last thing I remember was holding up my glass to order another drink."

"Apparently, you did that several times. You also got into a shouting match with some guy when he stepped up to the bar and nudged you aside. Then you wouldn't leave when the bartender told you to go." She waited a beat. "There's more. You threatened to punch the bartender when he insisted you leave." She waited for Socrates to say something, but he just slowly shook his head, groaned, and closed his eyes.

"Oh, sweet Jesus," he said. "I don't believe I was such an ass."

"Oh, you were, my love. Heard enough or do you want the rest?" Jade continued to smile.

"I don't know," Socrates said warily. "Is there more?" He paused and took several breaths. "What the Hell. Go on, tell me everything. Get it over with so I don't have to hear it later when I'm not hung over and will be even more embarrassed."

Jade nodded and chuckled.

"The police came and ordered you to leave. You refused. That's when they arrested you." She paused, then said,

"There's still more. Sure you want to hear it?"

Socrates nodded.

"When I called and paid your bill, there was a note from the bartender stapled to your check."

Socrates shook his head. "Oh, no," he said. He blew out a stream of air.

"The bookkeeper read it to me," Jade said. "I wrote it down. Do you want to know what it said?"

"I don't know if I do. You tell me if I should want to know it or not."

Jade grinned and shrugged.

"Never mind," Socrates said, "tell me. Get it all over with at once."

Jade pulled a piece of paper from her pocket and looked at it. "The note said, 'Tell that sonofabitch he's been 86ed until further notice, which won't happen as long as I work here. Boxer." Jade folded her note and handed it to Socrates.

"What's that mean to be 86ed?" Jade asked.

"It means I've humiliated myself, made a major ass of myself, is what, and I've been banned from The Guards. The word will spread from bar to bar all over Georgetown. Everyone I know will know about it. If I try to come into The Guards again, they'll immediately call the cops and I'll be arrested, no questions asked." He paused, then added, "If you like bars, it's like having bar leprosy."

"Oh," Jade said, "is that all? Well, that's all right. You know I don't like bars anyway."

- Part Three -

Chapter 49

SOCRATES WAS STILL buzzed the next morning, Tuesday, when he set out to find Brandon's killer. He started with Linda Fong.

He walked into the gallery at 11:30. He intended to establish some ground rules this time and, if necessary, have it out with Fong once and for all. He was determined, among other things, that she would retract the misleading statement she'd made to the police about him.

Socrates looked around inside the entrance while his eyes adjusted to the soft interior light. What he saw when his vision cleared stopped him cold and caused him to forget all about the purpose for his visit.

He saw Jade.

She and Fong were deeply involved in conversation. Neither woman seemed to have heard him enter. Or so he thought.

In a delayed reaction to the jingle of the door's overhead bell, Jade and Fong broke off their conversation and slowly turned, in tandem like Busby Berkeley dancers, to face the entrance.

"Oh, Socrates," Jade said, as her eyes met Socrates' eyes. She smiled briefly, then turned her head away, back toward Fong.

Socrates quick-stepped across the showroom to the alcove. He never took his eyes off Jade as he crossed to her.

"I didn't expect to see you here," he said. "I didn't even know you two knew each other." He tilted his head toward Linda Fong as he spoke to Jade.

"We don't," Jade said, "not really. I mean, we've met before, but only briefly, when my father helped Ms. Fong obtain her job here. He knew Ms. Fong from when she worked at the Chinese Embassy as the assistant to the former cultural attaché."

"What are you doing here, Jade?"

"Talking to Ms. Fong, if you must know," she said, an edge now in her voice. She glanced quickly in the direction of the acting director, then, just as quickly, darted her eyes back to Socrates. "What about you, Socrates? Are you here checking up on me?"

Socrates looked over at Fong, nodded once to acknowledge her, then said to Jade, "You know why I'm here. For Brandon and your father." He waited for Jade to say something. When she didn't, he continued. "You still haven't said what you're here talking to her about."

Jade's face flushed. She grabbed her pocketbook from the desk, placed the folded sheet of paper she'd been holding into it, and turned her back to Socrates. She said to Linda Fong, in a voice Socrates could barely hear, "Thank you for your help. I look forward to seeing you tomorrow night."

Jade turned back to Socrates.

"I know you're upset, Socrates, and you're not yourself because of Brandon so I'll overlook your bad manners. But I don't have to explain myself to you or anybody else.

"Just because you're working for my father now doesn't mean I'm answerable to you or that you can tell me where to go or not go or who to talk to or not talk to. Even my father can't do that anymore." She nodded abruptly.

"I'm leaving now, Socrates," she said, "and I want you to know I don't appreciate your attitude, not even after what you've been through. I have every right to be anywhere I want, including here." She paused, stared at Socrates, then said, "I'll talk to you later." She walked around him, strode quickly to the door, and exited the gallery.

Linda Fong looked at Socrates and laughed out loud.

Socrates bolted from the gallery and hurried after Jade, catching up with her half a block up P Street.

"I'm sorry, Jade," he said. "I know you have the right to be anywhere you want. It's just I was surprised to see you, is all. I didn't expect to see you again today once we parted this morning, let alone here."

Jade slowed her pace and looked at Socrates. She continued walking, but with less persistence now. "You never answered me, Socrates. Were you checking up on me for my father?"

"Of course, not. If I was spying, I wouldn't have been surprised to see you, would I?" Socrates took a deep breath. "Please stand still a minute. I can't talk to you when you're walking away like this."

Jade slowed her pace again, but did not stop walking.

Socrates said, "I was there to put pressure on Fong about the burglary and Brandon's murder, to see if she would talk to me."

He put his hand on Jade's elbow, and stopped walking. "I also wanted to convince her to take back her lie she told the police about me." He waited for Jade to say something, but she remained silent.

"Come on, Jade," he said. "Let's not argue. I was surprised to see you there, nothing else." He took her hand. "I don't want to fight. This was just a stupid misunderstanding."

Jade beat a rapid tattoo with her foot. She frowned briefly, seemed to think over what Socrates had just said, then let go of her anger, smiled and nodded. She looked at Socrates with softened eyes.

"All right," Jade said. "If you must know, I went to see Fong for you, two times in fact, to ask her to cooperate with you. I know how frustrated you've been with the investigation, and now with Brandon and all . . . ."

Socrates narrowed his eyes. "Why would she agree to help me if she hardly knows you, Jade?"

"Because she would like my help in return. Or, rather, she wants my father's help. So I offered a trade. If she cooperates with you, I'll have Youngest Brother approach our father with a good word for her, telling him Fong helped him by helping you with your investigation."

"What did you mean when you said you'd see her tomorrow night? What's going on?"

Jade sighed. She was frustrated by Socrates' continued grilling of her. "There's a reception at the gallery tomorrow after it closes. Fong is giving it. She says it's in memory of the late director and to celebrate her own promotion to the position of acting director."

Jade leaned in close to Socrates and whispered from the corner of her mouth, "If you ask me, she probably wants to use the occasion to remind influential folks that she's available to permanently fill the director's vacant slot. It's good politics."

"You're going?" Socrates said.

Jade nodded. "I am. So are my father and brothers, and people from the Embassy. Several community leaders, too."

Socrates said nothing. His eyes remained fixed on Jade's eyes.

"The event is limited to local community Chinese who support the gallery and to others who can influence the choice of the new permanent director." She stroked her finger across Socrates' cheek. "I assume Linda Fong put together the invitation list. There won't be any outsiders as far as I know so I can't bring you as my escort."

Socrates stiffened and pulled away.

"Oh, dear! I'm sorry, Socrates." Jade blushed. "I didn't mean that the way it came out. You're not an outsider, you know that, not as far as I'm concerned."

Socrates let it pass. "I'm surprised you're going since your father and brothers will be there."

"That's exactly what we were talking about when you barged in on us — if it would make me and my family uncomfortable to all be at the gallery at the same time. But between you and me, I think Fong was having second thoughts about how my father might respond seeing me there, worried he would adversely associate my presence at the reception with her. I think she hoped I would offer to bow out and not come tomorrow night."

"Why didn't you?"

"Why should I? I still have to live my life even if my father doesn't want to admit I have one to live." As she finished explaining this, Jade leaned over and kissed Socrates' cheek.

"I have to go now, Sweetie," she said. "I have things to do before tomorrow. We'll talk later. Call me tonight — late." She turned and walked away before Socrates could respond.

Chapter 50

SOCRATES WATCHED JADE disappear around the corner. He turned back to face the gallery, now two blocks away from where he and Jade had stopped walking. He no longer was in the mood to deal with Linda Fong, especially not right after she'd laughed at him when Jade walked out. He didn't trust himself to maintain his composure with the woman, and did not want to further antagonize her by saying something that might momentarily be satisfying, but in the long run would be self-defeating. He would have his showdown with Fong, he was sure of that, but it would be on another day, on his terms. Right now, he had something else to do, something that would likely prove to be more productive than engaging in verbal jousting with the acting director.

Socrates called Bing-fa and asked to meet with him. He said he wanted to talk to him about a sensitive aspect of the investigation, and thought they should do this privately, without any of Bing-fa's sons present. They agreed to meet at Bing-fa's home rather than at the Golden Dragon.

When Socrates arrived at the White Plum Blossoms apartments, he rode Bing-fa's private elevator to the top floor where the Great Room was located.

The elevator cab opened into a 15′ x 15′ anteroom that distinctly reflected Bing-fa's Confucian values. The spare walls were painted dark green and were totally unadorned. An antique burgundy, hand-knotted rug, with a simple white lotus petal design, overspread the stained wood floor, exposing a one-foot wide border of dark wood surrounding the rug's perimeter.

The only furniture in the anteroom consisted of an eighteenth century A-shaped, five meter high rosewood cabinet and a pair of eighteenth century yoke back rosewood chairs, one on each side of the cabinet. A cricket cage dangled from the end of a brass chain attached to the ceiling in the southeast corner of the room.

An Oriental doorkeeper, wearing a teal ankle length silk gown, stood in the archway that separated the anteroom and the Great Room. He motioned for Socrates to follow him, then turned and walked across the Great Room, over to Bing-fa who was sitting in a *Jia Jing Dynasty* chair.

Bing-fa looked up as Socrates approached. He set aside the abacus that teetered on his lap, reached up and straightened his cap and collar, then stood to greet Socrates. He bowed slightly.

"Welcome to my home. You honor me by your visit," Bing-fa said as he smiled.

Bing-fa led Socrates into his scholar's studio, closed the door, and indicated that Socrates should sit. He settled into his chair across the desk from Socrates.

Socrates thought about what he wanted to say. He didn't want to cause problems in the Li household, but he wanted Bing-fa to know what he was up against with respect to his sons and other people. He hesitated while he gathered his thoughts. "This is awkward, Bing-fa, but . . . ."

"Please speak frankly." He stared at Socrates and waited.

"The problem is with some of your sons," Socrates said. "They've threatened me if I continue to help you. I assume you didn't know."

Bing-fa shifted in his seat. He narrowed his eyes. "Which sons have disgraced me?" He burrowed his hands up his sleeves and crossed his arms.

"They also broke into my home twice. Eldest Brother and your middle sons did."

Bing-fa frowned. "My sons will once again be instructed to give you the assistance you desire and to immediately
cease threatening you or interfering with you. Rest assured,
Mr. Cheng, this time they will obey me."

SOCRATES WALKED AWAY from the White Plum Blossoms
apartment building toward Georgetown. He was reasonably
satisfied Jade's brothers had now been neutralized and now
would neither harm him nor again interfere with his investigation.

His cell phone rang. It was the IRS revenue officer in
Washington, the agent now in charge of his father's case. She
wanted to meet with Socrates.

THE NEXT MORNING, promptly at 8:15, Socrates sat across
the desk from the revenue officer at the IRS's regional head-
quarters office on North Capitol Street in Washington. The
revenue officer, a woman named Lydia McCants, was polite,
bureaucratically formal, and quite firm in her position that
the IRS expected Socrates' father to promptly pay his entire
tax indebtedness, including all penalties and interest, without
any compromise of the amount owed.

Socrates responded, "I know you've heard it all before,
Ms. McCants, and I told you I will pay the full amount my father owes. Still, I'd appreciate it if you'll let me tell you something about my parents. Please."

The revenue officer frowned as if she was gauging
Socrates' level of candor by reading the lines in his face. She
nodded her consent and leaned her chair back on its hind legs.
She crossed her arms over her capacious breasts and looked
beyond Socrates, staring at the distant intersection where two
walls and the ceiling met.

"I won't offer any excuses why my father didn't make the
employer's payroll tax deposits. He was wrong not to, and he
knows it. He's said it to me several times this week. But if you
levy against my father and take my parents' bank account and
property, you'll wipe them out, the debt to the IRS won't be
paid because they'll have no means to repay it, and they'll

be too old to start over. It would kill them." He nodded at the revenue officer and paused when it became clear to him she wanted to say something.

"That won't happen, not if they pay what they owe," McCants said. "I thought we settled that."

"We did. I'm just saying, is all."

The revenue officer raised her eyebrows and shuffled some papers. She looked down at the case file, then back up at Socrates. "When will the full indebtedness be paid? You can't delay it."

"What I propose," Socrates said, "is full repayment by me on my parents' behalf, but on an installment basis. I'll take on the legal obligation for them so the IRS has the security of my condo and my other assets for its lien. What I'll ask in return is for the IRS to release the lien from my parents' house and bank accounts so they can sell the house and move to Washington. I'll also need an agreement that the Service won't touch the sales proceeds."

Socrates paused for McCants' reaction. Seeing none, he said, "My condo's equity value alone is more than enough to protect the IRS' debt under the lien while I'm paying it down."

McCants shook her head. "There's a problem with your proposal. The Service usually won't agree to installment payment plans in cases involving payroll taxes. That approach usually is reserved for income taxes. But if you want to go ahead on that basis anyway and take your chances, you can submit a formal request for an installment plan. Apply in writing through me."

Socrates considered her statement. "What happens in the meantime while the IRS considers my request?" he asked.

"Interest and penalties will continue to accrue. Other than that, nothing will happen, not if you don't delay submitting your proposal. I'll put your father's collection case in suspend status until your proposal either is accepted or rejected. In the meantime, the lien will stay in place."

Socrates said he would proceed that way and would file a written proposal for an installment plan sometime in the next few days. As he left the meeting, he again wondered how he would come up with the money to pay for this.

Chapter 51

JADE ARRIVED AT the THREE PROSPERITIES CHINA ARTS GALLERY on Wednesday evening at 5:00. She briefly stopped inside the entrance and looked around. There were approximately twenty people standing in small clusters, holding drinks and talking. She knew most of these people through her father. A few others she recognized on sight, but had never been formally introduced to.

She had come to Linda Fong's reception to fly her colors. She would be seen there by her father and brothers, and, with that courageous and defiant act, initiate the slow and arduous process of eroding, and eventually eliminating,the familial quarantine that shrouded her. Her presence at the reception would be the first step in Jade's calculated attempt to reconcile with her father and bring about her own rehabilitation. All this, of course, without knuckling under to her father's command that she terminate her relationship with Socrates.

Jade cut across the room, nodding and smiling as she made her way, and crossed to the bar which had been set up near the bead-covered doorway. She decided that under the circumstances of her father's presence she could be forgiven a temporary lapse in her Kobudo health regimen and could indulge her need for liquid fortification. She ordered a tall Stolichnaya and soda over ice.

Jade sipped her drink and looked around the exhibit room, holding her glass to her lips as she peered over its top edge. She swept her eyes back and forth across the room.

She saw the Twins standing across the room, huddled together in a corner, talking excitedly and gesticulating with their hands, acting as if they were the only ones present.

That's my Twins, Jade thought, *forever and symbiotically narcissistic.* She smiled at her clever, but accurate, turn of phrase.

She saw Youngest Brother standing alone, his back against a wall, staring at her. He made no move to cross the room to her when their eyes met.

Jade nodded once and smiled, but resisted walking over and hugging him. She didn't know how Youngest Brother might respond to such an overt show of affection, not with their father and brothers present at the reception. She stood her ground, winked once at Bing-enlai, and smiled at him again.

Youngest Brother smiled back and briefly bowed his head.

He looks so sad, so forlorn, Jade thought.

All at once Jade changed her mind and took a step toward him, but immediately yielded to reason and thought better of it. She stopped herself. She could feel her face grow warm as she blushed.

Jade again stared at Youngest Brother. She leaned her head to the right slightly and cocked one eyebrow, seeking with her silent gestures his permission for her to cross the room and join him.

She watched as Youngest Brother correctly interpreted her intent from her body language. He threw her a kiss, using only his pursed lips, and then almost imperceptivity shook his head, No. Then he looked off in another direction. Jade took a slow, deep breath and sighed it back out. She had her answer. It had been foolish for her to have hoped otherwise.

Thwarted by her closest sibling, Jade again eyeballed the room. She saw her father staring at her.

Bing-fa did not flinch or break off eye contact when Jade looked back at him. His gray eyes remained reptilian cold, his overall bearing that of a rigid and unapproachable Marine Corps drill sergeant. Bing-fa stood with his chin thrust forward, watching Jade.

Jade reflexively took a half step back and bumped into the wall. Then she lowered her head briefly.

Bing-fa turned away without acknowledging her.

Jade took another deep breath and let it out as a slow, soft moan. Her exhalation was interrupted by a tap on her shoulder. She turned and found herself staring into the face of her hostess.

"Good afternoon, Ms. Fong," Jade said, donning a wan smile.

"Welcome to my reception, Bing-jade," Fong said, speaking Mandarin. "You honor me with your presence."

Jade nodded and smiled. "I congratulate you on your recent promotion," she said, speaking vernacular Chinese, not Mandarin. "You will make a fine acting director. May you have the good fortune to be elevated one day to the position of permanent director."

Fong smiled and lowered her eyes. "That also is my wish," she said. "I hope your father will favor me with his assistance so I might achieve that worthy post. I trust his presence today is a favorable sign."

Jade shrugged slightly and remained deliberately inscrutable with her response. "My father's intentions and thoughts remain unfathomable to everyone, as always. He will reveal his intent when he believes it is appropriate for him to do so, if ever." She smiled through closed lips as if to say, *Nice try.*

"Thank you, Bing-jade," Fong said. "As always, your remarks have been most interesting." She turned her head and briefly looked around the room, then looked back at Jade. "Now, if you will pardon me, I must greet my other guests." She turned away and walked across the room.

Jade again looked around the room.

She saw Eldest Brother standing near the entrance talking to two women she did not recognize.

Eldest Brother briefly fixed his gaze on Jade, looking at her over the shoulders of his two companions. He caught Jade's eye, nodded once, then turned his back to her and reentered the conversation with the two women.

Chapter 52

SOCRATES FINISHED HIS meeting with Revenue Officer Mc-
Cants and spent the balance of the morning again canvassing
the gallery's immediate neighborhood, knocking on the doors
of homes of people he'd missed the first time around.

He also kept his eyes open for people walking dogs. One
of the library books had made the point that people with dogs
tend to develop dog-walking patterns and, at least with respect to these walks, often were creatures of habit. Socrates
hoped he might run into some dog walkers who had noticed
something out of the ordinary during one of their habitual
sojourns the night the burglars hit the gallery.

Socrates interviewed three dog walkers as they stood on
the sidewalk watching their dogs sniff the landscape. This
achieved nothing for him. The entire trip back to the neighborhood achieved nothing for him.

After lunch, Socrates stopped at Georgetown Tobacco on
M Street near Wisconsin Avenue and treated himself to a Partagas cigar. He smoked cigars once every six or seven months,
according to his mood and circumstances. He'd smoke this
one tonight at home unless Jade planned to come over. She
disliked the scent of cigars, even the fragrance of high quality
cigars such as the Partagas.

Socrates left the tobacco shop with two cigars in hand,

walked home, and booted up his computer. He again performed a data search among the records of stolen objects. He
continued to believe that the answer to the burglary and the
clue to the path he must follow to recoup the genuine Mandarin Yellow and the other stolen objects would be found in
some theme or pattern woven among the objects themselves.

Socrates worked at this until almost 8:00 p.m., but, as before, no theme emerged from his efforts. He quit the computer
for the night because he was starving.

He left his condo and walked to the Sign of the Whale,
a combination bar and restaurant on M Street, just around
the corner from Starbucks on 19th. He was in the mood for a
beer, a tossed salad, a juicy NY Strip steak, green beans and a
baked potato. His weight was under control from jogging so
he would allow himself to indulge tonight.

Socrates ate a quiet meal, drank two Peroni beers, and
finished up with a piece of apple pie. He was proud he'd had
the willpower to turn down the waiter's offer of a scoop of
vanilla ice cream to go with the pie. It was a minor victory,
perhaps, but a victory nonetheless.

He felt good and looked forward to smoking his cigar
when he returned home. Afterward, he would call Jade and
talk for a while. He paid his check and left the Whale. The
time was just after 9:30 p.m.

He strolled north up 19th Street, walking past the closed
Starbucks toward Dupont Circle. He would take the long way
home, he decided, would walk directly through the park that
comprised the Circle, then walk up Connecticut Avenue to Q
Street, and then back over to 19th again, heading home. This
would give him a chance to stop at KRAMERBOOKS & AFTER-
WORDS to browse through its books.

Socrates bought two trade paperbacks at KRAMERBOOKS,
one a noir — a recent reprint of David Goodis' 1954 novel, THE
BLOND ON THE STREET CORNER — and one hardboiled — a reprint
of Paul Cain's 1936 novel, FAST ONE.

After he finished at Kramer's, Socrates resumed his lei-
surely stroll home. He decided that when he arrived at his
condo, before he forgot to do it or something else came up,
he'd go online to Amazon and would download two eBooks

he'd been meaning to read: Gerald Lane Summers' new novel, MOBLEY'S LAW, and David Bishop's latest novel, THE BEHOLDER. Between these two well-regarded books and the Goodis and Cain he just bought, his reading would be set for a month or so.

HE WAS ALMOST home, still walking on 19th Street just west of the Circle, when he heard footsteps behind him, approaching fast in his direction. He moved off the pavement, out of the way so the runner could dash by him. As he turned to watch the runner go, something hard crashed into the side of his head.

The pain was sharp and searing.

Socrates swooned, then staggered a few feet forward like a drunken sailor.

The last thing he remembered was thinking that the Saturday morning TV cartoons had gotten it right after all. You really do see flashes of colors and exploding stars. He thought about this just before everything went dark.

Chapter 53

SOCRATES SLOWLY SWAM back into consciousness. He was
stretched out flat on his back. His head ached with migraine
intensity.

He kept his eyes closed and remained still, listening
to his surroundings, trying to buy time before his assailant
knew he was awake, straining to sense his attacker's location
so he could defend himself. He heard nothing that might offer
him a clue. He had no idea if he was alone or in danger again.
He had no sense how long he'd been laid out on the street, a
few seconds or a few hours. The night air smelled antiseptic
to him.

After a few minutes like this, hearing nothing, not even
usual street noises, Socrates cautiously opened his eyes. His
vision was clouded as if he had suffered a concussion and was
viewing the world filtered through a sheet of wax paper.

Now he was confused. He had no idea where he was, but
he could tell he was indoors, not on the 19th Street sidewalk.
He cautiously lifted his head to look around. The movement
made him dizzy and he let his head flop back down. A vice
squeezed his skull. He moaned softly.

He squinted, trying to bring his surroundings into focus,
but he could only see his most proximate world. He raised his
head again and the effort exacerbated the throbbing. Frustrated, he tried to sit up, and leaned on one elbow to support him-

self. He became dizzy again and let himself drop back down. He ground his teeth together in frustration.

"I wouldn't try that again if I were you," a woman said. "Not yet, anyway. You had a nasty knock on your head. Took seven stitches to close you up."

Socrates jerked up his head and turned to face the source of the voice. He immediately regretted his abrupt movement.

"Where am I? Who are you?" Socrates saw a woman dressed as a nurse standing about six feet away from him. She was out of focus. "What's goingon?"

"You're at the George Washington University Hospital. I'm the Duty Nurse. The ER sent you up to us."

"What happened?"

"What happened is," the nurse said, "somebody smashed you on the side of your head. Somebody else found you on the street and called 911. The EMS unit brought you to the ER where you were sewed up and then sent to us for observation. We'll monitor your brain activity for tonight. Maybe tomorrow, too."

"How long have I been here?"

The nurse picked up Socrates' chart from the foot of his bed and looked at it. "According to this, from the time you came in to the ER until now, is," she looked at her watch, "I'd say, about ten hours."

Socrates groaned and started to ask the nurse another question when someone across the room said, "I need to talk to him now, nurse." Socrates turned his head in the direction of the voice.

Detective Harte nodded at Socrates as he walked over to the bed and gradually entered Socrates' clouded field of vision.

"That's a nasty bump you got there, Cheng. Probably'll hurt like a sonofabitch for a few days. How'd it happen?"

"What are you doing here?" Socrates said. "How long have you been here?"

"Long enough to know you got a major snoring problem and long enough therefore to be glad I'm not a woman dating you. What do you remember?"

Socrates shook his head. "Ouch," he said, " I shouldn't have done that . . . . I don't remember much. Almost nothing."

He squinted as if trying to see what he couldn't readily dredge up from his memory.

"I was walking home after dinner. I'd been at Kramer's and bought two books. I heard someone running toward me from behind."

He closed his eyes trying to recall the scene. "I turned to see where they were so I could get out of their way.... I think I was hit with something, but I'm not sure. Then I woke up here." He closed his eyes trying to recall more, then said, "How'd you get here, Detective? How did you even know about this?"

"The ER doc called me. Seems he found my business card in your wallet when they were looking to ID you. He called me because this little item here aroused his curiosity."

As he said this, Harte reached into a large manila envelope and pulled out a sheet of paper enclosed in a clear plastic evidence bag. He walked it over closer to Socrates.

Socrates blanched when he saw what Harte held. "Where'd that come from?" he asked. "Jesus . . . ."

"It was pinned to the front of your shirt when the EMS team found you," Harte said. "Any idea who'd do that or why?"

"It's the . . . ."

"I know what it is, Cheng." Harte took a step closer. "That wasn't my question." He waited for Socrates' answer, but Socrates remained quiet. "What I want to know from you is why someone played *Pin the Tail on the Donkey*, with you as the ass?"

Socrates looked up at Harte and shook his head.

"So you're telling me you have no idea why somebody would rip the cover off an art exhibit catalog — for a show that never took place, at a gallery where a murder occurred — and then pin that cover to your shirt after splitting open your skull?" Harte shook his head. "That doesn't sound right to me. Help me out here, Cheng. Help yourself out."

Socrates again shook his head. "I don't know why, Detective. Honest."

"Funny thing," Harte said. "That's what I bet my partner a week's worth of powdered donuts you'd say." He looked across the room at Detective Thigpen, who grinned, nodded, and threw Socrates a two-fingered salute.

THE HOSPITAL KEPT Socrates overnight and discharged him late the next afternoon. Once back home, he called Jade at her office, but, as usual, didn't reach her. He left a voice mail message inviting her to come over that evening for dinner. He said that he had some interesting, but disturbing, even bizarre, events to tell her about.

Jade called back a few minutes later.

Socrates described the attack against him on 19th Street and walked her through his conversation at the hospital with Detective Harte.

"Oh, Darling," she said, "you should have called me sooner. I would have cancelled classes and come right to you."

"Thanks, but I didn't see the point of ruining your work day. Anyway, I'm all right now, I guess." He paused to sip ice tea. "How about coming over now. I'd love to see you. We can make dinner. I think I'm up to doing that much."

"I wish I could, but I can't right now." She paused a beat. "Oh . . . maybe I'll just skip the play and come over . . . . Yes, that's what I'll do. You need me. Okay, it's settled."

"Don't skip anything on account of me," Socrates said. He paused, hoping Jade would insist that she cancel her plans and come right to him notwithstanding his remonstration otherwise. When she said nothing, Socrates said, "Skip what play?"

"At the New Playwrights' Theater on Corcoran. It's opening night and the Twins have the leads. I was going to see them perform."

Socrates hesitated, then said, "You should go. I'll be fine. We can get together after," he said. "But I'm surprised the Twins invited you. Won't your father and other brothers be there?"

"They didn't invite me. Youngest Brother told me about it. I don't plan on letting my father or brothers know I'm there, except maybe Youngest Brother."

———

WHEN THE PLAY ended several hours later, Jade skipped the opening night post-performance cocktail reception for the playwright, cast, crew and their guests, and arrived at Socrates' condo a little past 11:30 p.m.

The table was set for a late dinner for two. Socrates had prepared Fettuccini Alfredo and a tossed Italian salad for them. He opened a bottle of D'Abruzzi Amarone, vintage 1984, and for dessert had purchased a fresh fruit tart from Firehook Bakery on Q Street. After they finished eating, they settled on the couch in the living room.

To the limited extent he could, since he did not yet know all the facts, Socrates described for Jade how he'd landed in the hospital. He also told her about the assailant's bizarre act of pinning the catalog's front cover to his shirt.

"That's really weird," Jade said, "really weird. Were you robbed?"

"I didn't find anything missing. Anyway, a mugger wouldn't have decorated me with the catalog's cover. It wasn't a robbery, it was a message. Probably from the same person who broke into my bedroom and left the catalog leaning up against my pillow. The same sick person who shoved the photocopy of the Northern Sung Edict down Brandon's throat after killing him."

Jade frowned. "That's sick," she said. "What kind of message do you think it is?"

Socrates paused, stared across the room for a moment, then looked back at Jade, and said, "I think I know, but I want to be sure before I say. If I'm right, I'll tell you later."

"What's that supposed to mean?" Jade stiffened. Her whole demeanor reflected her felt rejection.

"It means, be patient, Jade. Please. Give me some time to work out some things, then we'll talk."

Before she could reply, Socrates said, "How was the play?"

He watched Jade's body language shift and her whole persona relax as she imbibed and then digested his question.

Jade smiled and patted the back of Socrates' hand. "Okay, counselor, you win. Time to change the subject." She sat up a little taller. "It was nice. Very nice, in fact. A good production with good acting all around. I'm glad I went. The boys are good actors, always have been."

"What was the play? You never told me."

"*Romeo and Juliet*," she said.

Socrates nodded. "Oh, I see," he said. Then he frowned.

"What's going on, Socrates?" Jade stared hard at him. "All of a sudden you're a million miles away."

"Nothing." He shrugged and looked away. Then he looked back at her. "Sorry."

"Don't give me that *nothing*. You should see the look on your face. I can see the wheels turning in your head."

Socrates looked at Jade, opened his mouth to say something, but thought better of it. "I'll tell you another time, Jade, I promise. Something you said made me think of something I need to do, is all. That's what you were seeing, nothing else. I want to check out something. If I'm right, I'll tell you all about it."

With that, Socrates stood, reached over and lightly squeezed Jade's shoulder, then walked over to the bottle of Amarone. He poured them each another glass, emptying the bottle.

The next night, following up his hunch, Socrates sat in the back row of the New Playwrights' Theater and watched the Twins perform Shakespeare's play, with one Twin as Romeo and the other as Juliet.

Chapter 54

THE NEXT MORNING, with the Twins' stage play still very much on his mind, Socrates called Bing-fa. He reached him at home.

"I want to come by and meet with the Twins today," he said. "Alone though, without you or your other sons present." Socrates counted the seconds before Bing-fa responded.

"I will make my sons available at the Golden Dragon. No one will interrupt you."

"It's also important they don't know I'm coming to see them," Socrates said. "I'll be there in about an hour."

When Socrates entered the private dining room at the back of the Golden Dragon, the Twins were sitting at a rectangular rosewood table that would comfortably seat ten people. They abruptly shoved their chairs away from the table and leaped to their feet when Socrates entered the room, then moved closer to one another, and glared at him.

Socrates could feel the tension level in the room rise as he closed the door behind him. Bing-fa had kept his word and not alerted the Twins he was coming to see them.

Judging by the Twins' sour facial expressions, their furtive glances at one another, and their rigid postures, Socrates knew Bing-hao and Bing-luc were surprised to see him. They also weren't happy about it. This was exactly as Socrates wanted it to be.

The Twins narrowed their eyes into horizontal pencil lines. Bing-hao crossed his arms over his chest and scowled at Socrates. Bing-luc glowered at him and occasionally stole a sideways glance at his brother.

Socrates remained silent and wrested control of the room by taking the seat at the head of the table and acknowledging each Twin only with a single nod. He silently counted to ten, then looked into Bing-luc's eyes and said, "I saw you as Juliet in the play last night. You were very convincing."

Bing-luc said nothing in response. He shifted his eyes away from Socrates and glanced at his brother without moving his head. He then looked back at Socrates and frowned, but continue his silence.

"Probably just as convincing," Socrates said, "as when you went to the gallery wearing your female disguise and killed Iris Hua. You left part of your wig behind in the director's fist."

Bing-luc sprang from his chair as if he'd just sat on a carpet tack. He slammed his palm on the table top with a crash that caused Socrates to flinch in spite of his best efforts to appear unflappable.

The cathartic force of his bellicose gesture caused Bing-luc to regain control of his emotions. He took two deep breaths, closed and opened his eyes, and said to Socrates, speaking barely above a whisper, "I don't know what you are talking about, *low faan*. You are a fool, Cheng, just as Eldest Brother has said."

Socrates looked over at Bing-hao. He remained seated, staring at his hands which were on the table top clenched into tight fists.

"Both of you," Socrates said, pointing from one Twin to the other, "and Eldest Brother were involved, deeply involved, in way over your heads."

He paused, waiting for some reaction. Drawing none, he continued. "You broke into the gallery and stole the Mandarin Yellow and other art and documents. Later, you killed the director to cover your tracks. That much is obvious to me." He looked from Bing-hao to Bing-luc. "What I don't know yet," he said, "is why you did it." He hesitated, then added, "Or why you later thought it was necessary to kill my friend. That was a hell of a way to send a message to me."

Bing-hao said, speaking Mandarin now, "Why would we do that, any of it, assuming you are right, which you are not?"

"It is a nice theory," Bing-luc added in dialect, "but a ridiculous one. All of it. Why would we want to send a message to you?" he said.

"You are a great nuisance, I admit that," Bing-hao said, "and your involvement with Elder Sister insults our family, but you are hardly worth the trouble killing anyone to send a message. And, you fool, why would we kill Director Hua? That makes no sense."

"I'll tell you why," Socrates said. "You knew I intended to interview the director at some point because I said so when we met with your father. The director obviously had some damaging information you didn't want passed on to me." He waited briefly for a response that never came. "As for my friend, well, like I said, you were warning me away by killing him."

"The bottom line," Socrates said, "is that everything comes back to Eldest Brother. He was the motivating force behind all this. You two were just his obedient lackeys, blindly doing what he ordered. Just like the chumps you are. Twin chumps."

Bing-hao again sprang from his chair, shaking his head as if he had endured Socrates long enough. He took several quick steps toward the door as if he wanted to rush from the room, but stopped before reaching it. He turned back and faced Socrates, blocking the room's only exit.

His brother stood up and faced Socrates, who now was bracketed by the Twins, and said, still speaking Mandarin, "Eldest Brother would never have anything to do with the killings or burglary, not with any of it. Eldest Brother is just an old fool who brays his self-importance. Nothing more.

"All Eldest Brother cares about is family honor, venerating and praising our father, honoring our ancestors, and keeping traditions intact. He has wrapped himself in the past."

Bing-luc glanced at his brother, then back at Socrates. "Eldest Brother would never sabotage a display of our country's heritage by arranging for a burglary. He would never bring such disgrace to our father and family."

Bing-hao again stepped into the discourse when his brother paused. "Eldest Brother lives day-to-day in the fiction of our family's past. That fiction is his present. He glorifies a past he has never known because he cannot deal with the present he knows. It would be unthinkable for Eldest Brother to do anything to harm it."

That's pretty sophisticated thinking, Socrates thought. *I wouldn't have expected it from the Twins.*

Bing-luc spoke up again, giving Socrates the sense he was listening to a diatribe in cascading surround sound. "Eldest Brother is a throwback to decadent times."

Socrates said nothing. *The last statement also was insightful,* he thought. *Perhaps he had underestimated the Twins.*

Socrates wanted to see how this would play out if he gave them enough leeway. They clearly were becoming more agitated, the more they talked. And the more agitated they became, the more likely they would be to reveal information to him, if they didn't harm him first.

"We had nothing to do with killing anybody," Bing-hao said. "Not that part."

"Be quiet, Bing-hao," his brother said, in dialect. "You say too much."

Bing-hao noticeably stiffened at the rebuke, then looked over at his brother. "It is of no consequence what we tell this fool. We have our plan. Soon it will not matter what he knows."

This made no sense to Socrates. And what did Bing-hao mean when he said, denying their participation in the murders, *not that part?*

"If you had nothing to do with the murders," Socrates said, "there's still the burglary. Why'd you rob the exhibit, bring disgrace to your father?"

The Twins looked at one another. Bing-hao raised his eyebrows. Bing-luc shook his head.

When they didn't answer him, Socrates pushed harder. "How did Eldest Brother talk you into breaking into the gallery?"

Still, no response.

"Why would Eldest Brother want your father to lose face?"

Socrates stared briefly at the Twins, then twisted the knife he'd just poked them with: "I suppose Eldest Brother would have told you if he thought you were reliable enough to know. Even Eldest Brother must think you're too immature and feckless to keep his secrets." He shifted his eyes from one brother to the other.

The Twins scowled at Socrates, but said nothing. They were not taking his bait.

Socrates could feel his frustration rising. They were playing with him.

All right, he thought, *if that's their game, he'd play along with them, fish with them, and see what he could reel in.*

"I didn't realize you two had prior experience with burglaries and murder," Socrates said. "I must admit, you were good. You didn't leave any clues except for the tuft of wig. No trail the cops could follow. That's not how I'd expect amateurs like you to perform." He waited for some response. When none came he teased out a little more line.

"So," he said, "I assume you must have had some help. Everyone knows you're both too wrapped up in yourselves to have done it on your own." He paused, then tossed over some verbal chum for them to gnaw on. "What I can't figure," he said, "is how someone as inexperienced as you two could pull it off, even with help."

Bing-hao looked at his brother. Bing-luc smiled and nodded. Bing-hao turned back to Socrates.

"It soon won't matter what you know or think you know, *low faan*. It is as we told you. We did not have anything to do with the murders you speak of. Either one. We merely arranged for the burglary with our comrades, as we were instructed to do, and have taken possession of the stolen goods, as we agreed we would."

Arranged for? Instructed? Who else had Eldest Brother brought into this? Socrates wondered.

"Instructed by who?" Socrates said.

"*Jiao tu san ku*," Bing-luc said. "That is who," he said in Mandarin. Bing-luc looked at his brother, smiled, and nodded once sharply, using his chin to punctuate his statement.

Socrates felt his stomach tighten. His surprise must have shown on his face because Bing-hao said, in English, "Of course, as a barbarian, you have no idea what I am talking about." Bing-hao looked at Bing-luc, and arched one eyebrow.

He turned back to Socrates.

"*Jiao tu san ku* is our revered Triad," Bing-hao said. "It was our brothers in *Jiao tu san ku* who accommodated our desire to acquire the Mandarin Yellow writing instrument and other precious objects."

Socrates thought, *Now we're getting somewhere. Time to sink the hook.*

"I know exactly what you're talking about," Socrates said. "I know that *Jiao tu san ku* is the Shanghai-based criminal enterprise known in the West as the *Cunning Rabbit with Three Warrens Society.* And I know this Triad has ties with Big-eared Tu's Shanghai Green Gang."

The Twins looked at one another, then back at Socrates.

Socrates said, "So you both belong to this Triad, do you?"

"Of course we do," Bing-hao said. "As do our venerable father and Eldest Brother."

Chapter 55

SOCRATES PASSED A few seconds processing what Bing-hao had just revealed to him. He hadn't considered the possibility that Bing-fa and Eldest Brother belonged to an overseas criminal gang with ties in Washington's Chinatown. This revelation cast the two break-ins at his condo, Brandon's murder, and Eldest Brother's warnings to him in an entirely different light, all to be viewed as true threats, none to be disdainfully dismissed.

Socrates recovered his composure and said, "What I don't get is why you tried to sell your father the substitute Mandarin Yellow. You just admitted you have the original pen in your possession with the other stolen objects. You could have ransomed the genuine one to him instead of a substitute."

"Our careless Triad brother dropped the writing instrument when he removed it from the glass show case. It cracked in many places. Our father would have seen the damage and been filled with despair because he could not then return it to the art gallery and regain his lost honor," Bing-hao said.

"We hoped our venerable father and the gallery's director would not realize the difference between the original writing instrument and the similar one our Triad brothers caused to be inscribed as a replacement. We sought to restore a measure of happiness to our father by making him believe he again had the historic pen in his possession."

"What about the documents and art?" Socrates said. "Why'd you sell Bing-fa only one document? Why not the whole lot, all at once? If you care as much as you say you do about your father's feelings, then why not just get it over with quickly for him and not string him along?"

"Our Triad brothers preferred to proceed in the manner you describe to enhance their reward for the assistance they had given us. They believed our father would not object to the aggregate cost of reacquiring everything if he paid for the objects one at a time, rather than in one large payment."

Socrates nodded. There's some logic to that, Socrates thought, twisted as it is.

"In this way," Bing-hao continued, "we also would extend our father's pleasure by dribbling the objects out to him until the end when we would return to him the three most precious historical objects — the Xi'an Agreement and its two Secret Protocols.

"Our father would then have everything back in his possession. His relief at having his honor restored would be inestimable." Bing-hao looked at his brother and smiled. Bing-luc nodded and smiled back.

Socrates tensed. He'd noticed that even as Bing-hao spoke to him, Bing-luc had surreptitiously moved in closer. Socrates continued to face Bing-hao, but he peripherally watched Bing-luc's furtive advance toward him.

Socrates said to Bing-hao, "Why'd you do this in the first place if you cared about your father's happiness and the restoration of his face, as you said?

"Why'd you have your Triad brothers break into the gallery and ruin the exhibit, destroy your father's honor, and bring your father such despair?"

Bing-hao said, "You know nothing, *low faan*. The answer to your naive question is found in the Xi'an Agreement and its Secret Protocols. If you are as smart as Elder Sister thinks, read the three documents and determine this for yourself. You will receive no more enlightenment from us."

Chapter 56

SOCRATES WAS AT a loss to understand what Bing-hao meant when he referred to the Xi'an Agreement having two ancillary Secret Protocols, rather than one.

He turned toward Bing-hao, pointed his finger at him, and said, "You don't know what you're talking about, not if you say there are two Secret Protocols. There was only the one described in the exhibit catalog."

"Ah," said Bing-hao, "that shows how much you know, or rather, how little. You speak to us as if we are ignorant adolescents." He looked over at his brother, and nodded.

"It so happens we have both Secret Protocols in our possession with the other treasured objects given us to safeguard by our Triad brothers. So who's the unknowing fool now, *low faan?*"

Socrates thought about Bing-hao's insistence on this point and also about what he'd recently read. According to Hallard's book, when it became publically known after the death of Mao in 1976 that the long-rumored Xi'an Agreement actually existed, it was sought out and eagerly studied by sinologists around the world. But there had been no mention of a Secret Protocol, nor any rumors referred to in Hallard's book, suggesting its existence, let alone the existence of two such secret agreements.

The first mention of the Secret Protocol that Socrates was aware of occurred in connection with the publicity for the exhibit when the People's Republic Embassy in Washington unveiled the existence of the document, although it had not disclosed its contents. That disclosure was to await the document's debut at the exhibit. The exhibit's publicity neither mentioned nor hinted at the existence of a second Secret Protocol.

Socrates debated giving the Twins a short-course history lesson about the Xi'an Agreement and the temporary, pragmatic truce it described, but decided against it. There was no telling how they might react in their present state of mind to being lectured by him.

Instead, he said, "You claim you have two Secret Protocols. How do I know that? If you have something in your possession you think is a second Secret Protocol, it must be something else. In that case, you're even more naive than I believed."

Bing-hao took a quick step toward Socrates, but pulled up short and glared at him.

Bing-luc said, "You are the fool, Cheng, if you think that. You have no way of knowing what we have."

Okay, Socrates thought, *now let's see, boys, if you'll swallow this lure.*

"That's right," he said, "I have no way of knowing since I don't have the documents here to examine." He paused to let the implication of this statement sink in.

When the Twins didn't respond, Socrates said, "What I do know is what the relevant literature and the exhibit's own publicity said about the Secret Protocol. Knowing that, I know you two are dead wrong. There was only one secret document."

Bing-hao stomped his foot and looked at his brother, then back at Socrates. "We will prove it to you, *low faan*. I will bring the documents here for you to see for yourself, all three."

He turned and faced Bing-luc, and said in a local dialect intended to keep Socrates in the dark, "We will show this barbarian we are not to be mocked and trifled with. I will go to our home and retrieve the documents and bring them here. It soon will be over, my brother, for him and for us."

Bing-hao sneered at Socrates. "You will see for yourself who is the fool and who is not. We will bring you the three documents."

He turned back to his brother. "Do not let him leave before I return."

Chapter 57

THE ROUND TRIP from the Golden Dragon to the White Plum Blossoms apartments and back to the restaurant took Bing-hao fifteen minutes. He said to Socrates, as he handed over the three documents, "Now, see for yourself, *low faan*, who is the fool and who is not." He looked over at his brother and bobbed his head once in a sharp, knowing nod.

Socrates ignored Bing-hao and turned his attention to the Xi'an Agreement. He quickly read through the document and saw there were no surprises in it. The document was consistent with what he remembered from his college studies, from the library's history books he recently read, and from the *Washington Post*'s brief mention in the article reporting the burglary.

He finished with the Xi'an Agreement, placed it on the table, and looked over at the Twins. He motioned with his head in the direction of the two other documents, indicating he now wanted to read them. He received assenting nods from both brothers.

Socrates tried to visualize the photograph of the Secret Protocol he'd seen in the exhibit catalog so he could determine which of the two documents now before him had been illustrated, but his memory of the photograph was wispy, at best. He thought about how to proceed since he had no reference baseline to start from.

He recalled an article he'd read in college when he first started collecting historic documents. The author had offered a simple technique for amateur collectors to use as a quick, albeit not foolproof, way to compare and test the authenticity of two or more questioned documents which, to all appearances, seemed to be the same. The author had written that when you had no other basis for proceeding, when, for example, you could not test the ink or the paper or the official seals of the documents, the examiner should turn to the text itself. Look to the words, the article's author had written, for the clues they might offer you.

Socrates would follow that advice. He would first perform a rough comparison of the texts of both Secret Protocols to see if they differed from one another. He would do this by *slugging the documents,* a tried and true procedure used for centuries by proofreaders in the newspaper trade when newspapers were still printed on presses using slugs of movable type.

To do this, Socrates placed one document on top of the other, text sides up, and arranged them so only the first word of each line of the bottom document showed beyond the left margin of the top document. He then arranged the first sentences of both documents so the sentences lined up on the same horizontal plane.

If no changes had been made to either document that either added or subtracted words, the first and the last lines of the two documents would line up perfectly. But if words had been added to or subtracted from one document or the other, the last sentences of the documents would not line up.

This simple, quick test would not reveal the nature of any changes that had been made to the document. Socrates still would have to read both documents to find out the substance of specific differences. But the test would alert him to look for such divergences.

Socrates slugged both Secret Protocols and saw that the last lines of the documents did not line up. In fact, the two Secret Protocols not only were not the same, he noted, they weren't even close. The last lines were at far different levels. Much had been changed in one Secret Protocol or the other.

Socrates, oblivious now to the Twins' presence, ran his finger down the left edge of the top document, between the parallel sets of first words, line by line, and compared the first words of both documents. When he spotted a discrepancy, he knew something had been changed in that line or in its counterpart in the other document. When this revealed itself, he stopped slugging and read the offending lines in both documents to see what the differences were.

When he finished slugging both documents and had read all the lines that did not match their counterparts, Socrates was left with a good sense of how the two Secret Protocols differed. Now he needed to read each document from end-to-end so he could obtain a contextual understanding why there were two seemingly similar, but actually disparate, Secret Protocols.

He set one document on the table and began reading the other.

This document, purportedly created in 1937, provided that after Mao's and Chiang's armies defeated the invading Japanese enemy in the War of Japanese Aggression, the truce between Mao and Chiang described in the Xi'an Agreement would end, and their indigenous armies would resume fighting one another for control of China.

No shocking disclosure there, Socrates thought, *except perhaps for the fact that the resumed combat between Mao and Chiang was not only anticipated in the document as likely, but seemed to be anticipated or required.*

He glanced at the Twins. They stood side by side, not more than five feet away, watching him. He acknowledged them with a terse nod, then turned his attention back to the Secret Protocol and read its next section.

Socrates stopped reading when he completed this part of the document, and softly whistled his surprise. He thought about the implication of what he'd just read.

This section provided that after Chiang and Mao had restarted their internecine hostilities, Chiang would intentionally lose the resumed Civil War against Mao, and would flee from Mainland China with his army, family and other followers, to the offshore island of Formosa. Once there, a seemingly defeated Chiang would establish an opposition government-in-exile which would continuously claim legitimacy as the true ruler of Mainland China.

To bolster his claim to legitimacy as the rightful heir to Sun Yat-sen's 1911 revolution and to the creation of the 1912 Mainland Republic, Chiang thereafter would unremittingly threaten to invade the Mainland with his army, destroy the Communist forces, and take down Mao's government.

Socrates thought about this. Other than the requirement that Chiang deliberately lose the Civil War, the Secret Protocol's description of what Chiang and Mao had secretly agreed to accurately reflected the way events had actually unfolded in China after World War II: Mao had won his staged victories; Chiang had fled to Formosa in 1949; the Communists had ruled Mainland China from then on; and, Chiang had constantly threatened to invade the Mainland, right up until the day he died in 1975.

Socrates paused to frown at Bing-hao who had interrupted his concentration by lighting a cigarette.

Why, Socrates wondered, *would Mao and Chiang agree to such an elaborate deception?*

Socrates found his answer in the next section of the Secret Protocol. What he learned blew apart much of what he thought he knew about China in the Twentieth Century.

Chapter 58

WHAT SOCRATES HAD had just read amounted to nothing less than a detailed description of a massive embezzlement scheme entered into in 1937 among Mao, Chiang, Madam Chiang, Big Eared Tu, and Joseph Stalin, as one of the components of their clandestine conspiracy to fix the Civil War.

Under their secret arrangement, after Chiang deliberately lost the Civil War and fled to Formosa, he and Mao would engage in vociferous threats and posturing for the sole purpose of generating financial aid to Chiang from the United States Congress, aid that would be intended by the United States to sustain Chiang and his government-in-exile until the day he would make good his threat to return to the Mainland and wrest control of the country from the Communists.

In return for this choreographed enmity, Chiang and his wife would be permitted to skim millions of dollars each year from the inflowing financial aid and would keep the major portion of the stolen money for themselves. They then would give a small share of it to Big Eared Tu — Chiang's financial benefactor — and to Stalin — Mao's financial and political benefactor. None of the embezzled foreign aid would go directly to Mao. His agreed-upon payoff would be in the form of his assured military and social victories over Chiang and his unchallenged and continuing right to rule Mainland China.

Socrates glanced up at the Twins. They were watching

him intently from only a few feet away, having quietly moved in close to him while he concentrated on the Secret Protocol. Socrates ignored their proximity to him and turned back to the document.

He next read through a paragraph which explained that Madam Chiang Kai-shek's role in the conspiracy would be to tour the United States on Chiang's behalf and exploit her American education, her physical beauty, and her learned charm, all in an effort to spread goodwill and generate millions of dollars in funds from Congress and private funding sources, all under the guise of supporting Generalissimo Chiang's government-in-exile and ultimately defeating the Communist rule of China.

Socrates skipped the balance of the document which seemed to be legal boilerplate and mulled over the implication of what he'd just read. The genius of the scheme it described was that as long as Mao and Chiang maintained the public illusion of their mutual hostility and the ever-present possibility that Chiang might invade the Mainland, United States aid dollars would keep rolling in. And as long as the aid flowed to Formosa, the Chiangs and their fellow conspirators could continue to loot and share among themselves millions of dollars in stolen aid.

In spite of the simple logic of Chiang's plan, Socrates found himself reluctant to believe what he'd just read. The entire arrangement was so audacious in its conception and so contrary to the teachings of established history in the West that his instinct was to dismiss it as creative historical revisionism by someone, for some reason, that he did not know and could not imagine.

And yet, Socrates had to admit, the Secret Protocol did have a strong ring of truth to it based on how public events had actually unfolded in China after World War II, at least as the West understood China's history.

Perhaps the events described in the Secret Protocol actually occurred, Socrates thought. As outrageous as it seemed, Socrates recognized that the Secret Protocol might be an accurate reflection of the motivations, as well as the actions, of Mao and Chiang, without altering the West's conception of China's history from the late 1930s through the 1950s. Socrates' head spun with possibilities.

He set the document on the table next to the Xi'an Agreement, and looked over at the Twins. They continued to hover close by, intently watching him. They seemed content to allow him to keep reading and didn't object when Socrates said, speaking in haltering Mandarin, "I'll read this one now," as he held up the other copy of the Secret Protocol.

Socrates quickly read through the second document, skipping words he didn't know, not trying to puzzle out their specific meanings from their context. He was interested in an overview of what this version of the Secret Protocol said about the conspiracy. He didn't need to understand the meaning of every word in this version of the instrument in order to identify the ways it differed from the other Secret Protocol.

The first thing Socrates noticed was that this document and the other Secret Protocol seemed, at a casual glance, to be very much alike, even though the results of his slugging exercise had indicated they were not alike.

The second thing he noticed when he read one document completely through, followed closely in time by a full reading of the other, was that the two Secret Protocols were anything but alike in any way that mattered.

Socrates thought about this. Although the substantive differences between the two documents were unmistakable, when read and considered as a single unit, the two Secret Protocols formed a well-wrought mosaic whose ingredients disclosed the motivation behind the burglary at THREE PROSPERITIES CHINA ARTS GALLERY.

That motive was not at all what Socrates had anticipated, but now that he understood what it had been, almost everything else fell into place for him, including why the gallery's director and the cultural attaché had been murdered.

Chapter 59

SOCRATES PUSHED BACK his chair, stood up, and walked across the room, away from the Twins. He reached into his back pocket, pulled out his cell phone, and pushed the speed dial button he'd set up for Detective Harte. The call was forwarded to the desk sergeant.

"The detective's in a meeting right now," the desk sergeant said. "Is there a message?"

"Get him out. Tell Harte it's Socrates Cheng, and it's important we talk right away. Tell him I know who broke into the gallery and why. I also know why the director was murdered and that . . . ."

The blow came without warning. It slammed directly into Socrates' kidneys. The pain was excruciating, like predator's teeth ripping into raw nerves and tearing off chunks of naked flesh. Fire raced down Socrates' back and loins until it reached his testicles and crushed them in its savage grip, dropping him to his knees. A wave of nausea swept over Socrates as he collapsed. The room swirled as he lay on his side doubled up, a thirty-eight year old fetus imitator.

When the punch landed, Socrates' cell phone rocketed from his hand, hitting the wall and dropping onto the carpet at exactly the same moment Socrates' chin hit the floor.

The passing seconds seemed an eternity as Socrates fought nausea and struggled up onto one knee, balancing himself with both palms on the floor. His kidneys and testicles screamed at his futile effort to stand.

Socrates saw movement from the corner of his eyes. He tensed and looked up just in time to glimpse Bing-hao's upraised arm as it swung down and smashed a steel-hard rubber truncheon against his forehead. Everything in Socrates' life went dark.

SOCRATES OPENED HIS eyes and slowly lifted his head. He was on the floor, on his stomach. His lower back and groin screamed pain. His head throbbed. He fought back the urge to throw up.

He rolled his wrist over toward his face and looked at his watch. He'd been out for almost forty minutes. He looked around, turning his head, but not his body. The table's nearby legs, the only objects within his limited field of vision, shimmied like distant air currents above a macadam highway on a hot summer day.

The circumstances of his situation came back to him in a rush. He panicked and bolted upright into a sitting position, causing a stabbing pain in his head and back. He cautiously looked around for the Twins. He was alone.

Socrates lifted his hand and tentatively flattened his palm against his forehead where the truncheon had hit him. He sported a tender lump the size of a small egg, but his skin hadn't split open. *Lucky me*, he thought. He wouldn't need stitches this time.

He managed with difficulty, because he was dizzy and nauseous, to leverage himself up onto his feet by leaning his weight into the palm he flattened against the seat of a nearby chair.

He wasn't surprised the Twins had taken off and left him alone in the private dining room, but he was surprised no one had looked into the room, found him unconscious, and helped him. At least he'd like to think no one had looked in and then ignored him.

He thought about the events just before the Twins had cold cocked him, and about the Xi'an Agreement and the two Secret Protocols.

He assumed the Twins had taken the three documents with them. Any rational person would have. But, he realized, he was dealing with the Twins, not with mature, rational beings. He looked around for the documents. All three sat on the table just as he'd left them right before he started his call to Detective Harte.

Socrates rolled each document into a long, loose cylinder shape so he wouldn't accidentally damage it. Then he retrieved his cell phone from the carpet and redialed Detective Harte's number.

"It's about time you called back, Cheng. Were you playing me, dragging me from a meeting, then hanging up? I was pissed, though not for long. The meeting sucked." Harte chuckled. "That was an interesting message. Anything to it or was it bullshit?"

"I know who committed the burglary and the identity of the murderer of the director and cultural attaché. And I know why the burglary occurred and why the director and cultural attaché were killed," he said.

"Okay, I'll bite, Cheng. Why was it done? And who's the bad guy?" He waited for an answer. Receiving none, Harte said, "And by the way, what's a DOA in a Chinatown alley got to do with any of this?"

"Not *who's the bad guy*, Detective, it's *bad guys*," Socrates said, "plural, not one. Three bad guys, but maybe not all three as guys. Maybe as two guys and a wannabe woman."

Socrates realized he probably sounded like someone who had just been smashed over the head and still was suffering from its effects.

"What the hell are you talking about, Cheng? You're not making any sense," Harte said.

Socrates breathed deeply and tried to organize his thoughts so Harte could follow them. "The Li Twins," he said, "Bing-hao and Bing-luc, are who. With their elder brother's instigation and with help from their Triad.

"One of the Twins — Bing-hao — disguised himself as a woman when he murdered the gallery's director," Socrates said. "The hair from his wig was what was in the director's fist when I found her."

"What's your proof?"

"The Mandarin Yellow fountain pen and the rest of the stolen art and historic documents are at the Twins' apartment on H Street. At the White Plum Blossoms apartment building. The same building as their father's penthouse, but on a lower floor. Your proof's there."

"I'll need more than that to get a warrant, Cheng. I need probable cause. Help me out here."

"The Twins admitted most of it to me," Socrates said. He talked Harte through the scenario in the Golden Dragon's private dining room, but held back a few things for now such as the Twins' adamant denial they'd been involved in the murders.

When Socrates finished, Harte asked him some questions, then said, "Are the Twins at that apartment building now? What about their older brother?"

"I don't have a clue where any of them are," Socrates said.

"You'll have to come in to the 2D as soon as possible," Harte said, "and do an affidavit for the warrant." Harte waited for Socrates to agree to come in, then said, "Is there anything else you want to tell me, Cheng, anything else you *should* tell me?"

Socrates looked over at the table at the three rolled documents. "No, Detective, nothing else. Nothing else at all."

- Part Four -

Chapter 60

"HARTE HERE," THE detective said into his desktop phone.

"Detective, it's me, Socrates Cheng." Socrates cradled his cell phone between his shoulder and neck as he strained to see his watch. Five hours had passed since he'd gone to the 2D, signed the affidavit, and then headed home. "Did you get the search warrant?"

"We got it," Harte said, "for all the good it did."

Socrates detected an edge to his voice. "I don't understand. Did you pick up the Twins and Bing-wu?"

"We got him, the big brother, not them other two," Harte said. " Those two are in the wind. We tracked them to the Chinese Embassy. According to our contact at the State Department, those two took asylum, even renounced their U.S. citizenship. I wouldn't be surprised if by now they're on a slow boat to China, not that it matters anymore where they are. They're history, useless to us."

Socrates hadn't expected that, but it explained the Twins' willingness to confess their roles in arranging the burglary. It didn't explain their refusal to admit their roles in the murders.

"I'm not following you, Detective. How'd this happen?"

Harte cleared his throat and paused as if trying to decide if he wanted to discuss this with Socrates. After several seconds, he said, "We went to their apartment and recovered the stolen items you told us about. At least you got that part right.

"We'll sort through what we picked up and compare everything to the list of stolen items the gallery gave us," Harte said. "If anything's missing, we'll hit the pawn shops and usual fences. Eventually, we'll get most of it back."

The implication of this was clear to Socrates. *This effectively brings an end to my participation,* he thought. *No matter what else happens, the stolen objects will be tagged as evidence and left sitting in lockdown in the 2D's Evidence Control Branch. The stolen objects will not be in the exhibit when it opens next week.* Socrates took a deep breath and reflected on the futility of all his efforts. *So much for restoring Bing-fa's face and earning my way into his good graces. I'll have to break the bad news to Jade.*

"What about Eldest Brother?" Socrates said. "You said you picked him up?"

"Of course we did. And we questioned him and eventually cut him loose. He had nothing to say to us and we didn't have enough to hold him. Just your general allegations."

Socrates frowned. That didn't make sense. "My statements weren't too general, Detective. You were able to get a warrant with them," he said. "Eldest Brother is involved all right. He pulled the strings and manipulated the Twins." Socrates waited for Harte to say something, but Harte didn't respond.

"You should've held on to him, Detective. Now you'll probably lose him too." Even as he said this, Socrates realized he probably had just overreached with the detective.

Silence hovered between them for almost half a minute.

Harte finally broke the silence. "Listen, Cheng, unless you know something we should know, something you held back, I don't appreciate your attitude, and that includes you lecturing me." Harte waited a few seconds for Socrates to confess that he'd held back information. Then he said, "Do you?"

"Do I what, Detective?"

"Know something else we should know, something you should have spilled before?"

"No, Detective, I don't. I wish I did."

"If you want us to pick him up again, that older brother, and be able to hold him this time, I need something concrete we can take to a judge."

"Okay," Socrates said. "How's this for concrete? Bing-wu threatened me, more than once, said I'd be sorry if I continued my role in the investigation. I think he even left me a threatening note the first time he broke into my home, before I was attacked on 19th Street. I still have the note."

Socrates expected Harte to congratulate him for offering the evidence the police needed to go out again and take Eldest Brother back into custody. Instead, Harte said nothing. After ten seconds of strained silence, Socrates said, "It wasn't my imagination, Detective. Those were threats he made. And the note's real. He's probably also the guy who assaulted me and pinned the catalog cover to me. I wouldn't be surprised if he's the one who murdered my friend."

Socrates paused again to let Harte respond. When the detective still didn't say anything, Socrates said into his cell, "That should be enough for you, shouldn't it, enough to pick him up and hold him this time?"

"When did this break-in happen?" Harte asked.

Socrates brought Harte up to date. He admitted, when pressed by the detective, that he hadn't filed a police report with respect to the first break-in and that he had no proof Eldest Brother was responsible for either break-in or for the note or catalog without its cover, just his suspicion. He also admitted it might have been the Triad, not Eldest Brother, but in that case, Socrates insisted, the Triad likely was acting under Eldest Brother's orders.

When Socrates finished, Harte said, "It would've helped if I'd known this before we picked him up the first time." Harte clearly was annoyed. "Are you prepared to swear out a formal complaint against him? Or are you just blowing smoke up my ass again?"

When Socrates didn't answer, Harte said, "These are serious allegations, Cheng, if they're true. Don't waste my time with just your word against his. Were there witnesses?"

"His sister, Jade Li, saw the note and she was there when he threatened me at her condo." He paused, then said, "I'll swear out a complaint, if you think it'll help."

Socrates didn't want to file a formal complaint if he could

avoid it. Having Eldest Brother arrested based on his formal arrest complaint would not sit well with Jade or Bing-fa. On the other hand, agreeing to file a complaint could have some immediate collateral benefits for him with the cops, and that was a sufficient reason for him to seem to agree to do it even if he had no intention of following through.

"Come back to the 2D, Cheng. We'll do the paperwork," Harte said. "Then we'll bring this Wu character back in for some specific questioning."

"Actually, Detective, it's 'Li, not Wu," Socrates said. "Wu is part of his first name, Bing-wu, with a hyphen. Li Bing-wu's his full name."

"Whatever," Harte said, his impatience clearly noticeable in his tone. "You know who I was talkin' about."

"Tomorrow, Detective. I have some things I've got to do today. I'll come by tomorrow and file the complaint." Socrates ended the call before Harte could object.

Those twenty-four hours, Socrates hoped, would buy him all the time he needed to accomplish what he had in mind.

Chapter 61

AFTER SOCRATES ENDED his call with Detective Harte, he
headed to his desk. He knew, based on his experience when
he was a fledgling lawyer, exactly what he needed to do at
this stage of his inquiry to move his investigation along and
to give him perspective. He would follow the advice he had
received as a young lawyer, just weeks out of law school, when
he'd complained to a senior partner in the law firm that he
could not see any pattern in the complicated facts of the legal
problem he'd been assigned. The partner had stared briefly
at him as if making up his mind how to advise Socrates, then
merely said, 'Follow the Titans.'

Young Socrates' response had been to think, *What's he
talking about, telling me to follow a professional football team?* But
he didn't say that. Instead, Socrates responded, 'What do you
mean, Sir?'

The partner smiled condescendingly, and said, "Not the
football team, young man, the ancient Titans, the Greek gods
who ruled the cosmos before Zeus and the other Olympians
came to power. Specifically, follow Kronos, the Titan god of
time."

That was all he said, and he left Socrates standing there
feeling as if he'd somehow missed out on an important part
of his Greek heritage and education. Later that night when he
used Google and Wikipedia to research Kronos, whose name

gave us the word *chronology*, Socrates understood the partner's advice.

Socrates followed the advice and prepared a chronology of all facts and events in the legal transaction, the chronological and temporal equivalent of the contemporary investigatory strategy known as *follow the money*.

Now, today, following this same strategy, Socrates settled in at his desk and wrote out a detailed chronology of everything he knew about the burglary and the murders. It took him fifty minutes and several discarded drafts before he had prepared a timeline that satisfied him. He read the final draft several times, made some minor refinements to it, thought about what the timeline revealed to him — which was much more than he'd expected — and placed the paper in the desk drawer for now.

That's step one, he thought.

Next, Socrates called Bing-fa and asked to meet with him. Bing-fa, Socrates thought, did not sound very enthusiastic about meeting.

WHEN SOCRATES AND Bing-fa were alone, Bing-fa said, "I have lost my middle sons because of you. Bing-hao and Bing-luc are gone from my life."

Socrates acknowledged he was aware of this from his recent conversation with the police. He didn't know what else to say that wouldn't sound as if he was making excuses for exposing the Twins, or not sound as if he was gloating that he'd flushed them out. So he merely said he was sorry things had turned out the way they did with the Twins, but he didn't feel he was to blame for any of it.

"I didn't involve them in the burglary or murders," he said. "Eldest Brother did that. And besides, the Twins had choices. They could have said *No*."

Bing-fa shook his head. "I should not have allowed you into our family's matters."

"I don't think it would've made any difference in the long run, with or without me, Bing-fa. That's the reality of it," Socrates said.

"I no longer require your services," Bing-fa said. "I will arrange to have the Embassy deliver the promised gift to you. We will then be finished with each other."

Socrates felt his face grow hot. Bing-fa's abrupt dismissal of him did not sit well with him. He didn't warrant this treatment.

He reined in his anger, and said, "Eldest Brother's part of this, too, Bing-fa. A big part. You can't hide from that by blaming me and getting rid of me. Bing-wu's role is going to come out, one way or another."

Bing-fa adjusted his arms up his gown's sleeves and seemed puzzled. He frowned and stared at Socrates. "Explain yourself."

Socrates explained to Bing-fa that he believed Eldest Brother had maneuvered the Twins into arranging the burglary through their Triad, then led them into committing the murders.

Bing-fa listened without interrupting. When Socrates finished, he said, "Why would Bing-wu do these things you accuse him of?"

Socrates considered how blunt he wanted to be in responding to Bing-fa's request. The answer came easily to him as he remembered he'd just been fired and would never be able to ingratiate himself with Jade's father.

"I suspect Eldest Brother acted under a misguided sense of tradition and family honor, is why," Socrates answered. "He probably hoped to prove his worthiness to you by seeming to recover the stolen objects from the burglars, who he'd set in motion, in time to restore your face and your family's diminished honor. That way he could be your hero, Bing-fa, if not in your eyes, then maybe in some perverse way, in his own eyes."

Socrates paused to consider whether to pursue the other aspect of Eldest Brother's motivation. Raising it now might be tantamount to him *thumbing his nose* at Bing-fa.

What the hell, he thought, *this is no time to tiptoe around the issues.*

"I also believe Eldest Brother thought it was a desecration of tradition for Bing-jade to be romantically involved with me," Socrates said. He paused to see if Bing-fa would deny this. Bing-fa remained silent.

"You, in particular, should understand this point, Bing-fa," Socrates said. "After all, you set the tone for your children. You consider me to be *low faan*."

Bing-fa remained silent. He continued to stare at Socrates.

Socrates described the two break-ins at his condo and the threats Eldest Brother had made against him. This time, he described the threats in more detail than he had when he first alerted Bing-fa to them earlier in the week. He stressed he was not speculating about the nature of the warnings. "They *were* threats," Socrates said.

Bing-fa shook his head and said, "Bing-wu should not have threatened you. That is not the way of a devout Taoist. He has brought additional shame upon me." His eyes narrowed and his nostrils flared. Socrates watched Bing-fa's cheeks and forehead redden.

Socrates was taken by Bing-fa's formality when speaking with him now. Bing-fa either was very worried about his three sons or was very angry with Socrates for what he perceived to be Socrates' role in their current situations. Or, most likely, both.

Bing-fa changed the subject.

"Do you know where we can find the genuine Mandarin Yellow writing instrument, the original one, and the stolen art and documents? I remain anxious to return everything in time for the opening of the exhibit next week."

"The police have most of the stolen objects. They recovered them from the Twins' apartment. Everything's official evidence now. You'll have to deal directly with the cops."

Socrates deliberately didn't mention his own role in helping the police take possession of the contraband. Nor did he tell Bing-fa that the likely effect of this was that the stolen objects would not be released in time to be included in the opening day of the exhibit. He reached into his pocket and retrieved Detective Harte's business card from his wallet. He handed it to Bing-fa.

"Call this detective. He'll help you."

Bing-fa looked at the card, looked up at Socrates, then again read the card. He placed it in a fold inside his gown.

"One thing you should know," Socrates said. "Although the police have possession of most of the stolen items, they don't have the Xi'an Agreement or the two Secret Protocols. They don't even know about them. I have them. The Twins left these three documents with me."

Bing-fa wrinkled his forehead, genuinely confused. "You are mistaken. There is only one Secret Protocol, not two."

Socrates nodded at Bing-fa. "I know that, Bing-fa, and you know that." He paused a beat, then said, "But the fact is, I have two of them."

Chapter 62

SOCRATES LEFT HIS meeting with Bing-fa, toting mixed feelings home with him. He certainly didn't like being fired, but he understood why he had been. He hadn't achieved the one thing Bing-fa had brought him on board to do — recover the stolen Mandarin Yellow and the stolen art and documents in time for the rescheduled opening and in time, therefore, to rehabilitate Bing-fa's tarnished image. He also had exposed the Twins' criminal activity and made some serious allegations against Eldest Brother. None of this was calculated to win Bing-fa's favor. Nonetheless, Socrates felt wrongly used, discarded and unfairly judged.

SOCRATES WAS IN his kitchen making a grilled cheese sandwich when his cell phone sounded. He looked at the digital readout to identify the caller. The LCD screen displayed the phrase, 'Unknown Caller.' He answered the called anyway.

"Mr. Cheng. This is Revenue Officer McCants. I'm calling about your father."

"Ms. McCants?" Socrates said. "That was quick. I just submitted my installment payment proposal to you yesterday. I didn't expect such a quick turnaround."

"I'm not calling about your proposal," she said. "A new

problem's come up. I certainly hope you didn't know about this when we met, because if you did . . . ."

"What new problem, Ms. McCants? I did exactly what you said to do. How can there be . . . ?"

"Your parents haven't filed a personal income tax return for the last three tax years, Mr. Cheng. That problem."

This news hit Socrates hard. He felt as if he'd been blind-sided by a sledge hammer after the bar fight was over. His stomach twisted into tight knots.

Socrates slumped back against the kitchen wall and slowly slid down to the floor. He rested his forehead against his raised knees, and closed his eyes as he considered the import of what the revenue officer had just said.

How could this possibly be right? What the hell was going on with his parents? he wondered. *No, make that, what was going on with his father since his father always prepared his parents' joint returns? Three years, maybe more, without filing their taxes?*

Socrates' thoughts drifted back to his mother's recent comments concerning his father's nascent dementia, about her growing concern for her husband and his decreasing ability to function on a day-to-day basis.

Had this been going on for three years or more? If so, how had he and his mother missed it for so long?

"Mr. Cheng, are you still there?" Revenue Officer Mc-Cants said. There was a hint of annoyance in her voice.

Socrates snapped out of his wandering thoughts. "Sorry. Yes, Ms. McCants, I'm here. I was thinking about what you said and the poor state of my father's mental health."

He thanked the revenue officer for alerting him to the problem. He told her to forget about the installment plan proposal he'd just filed, and assured her he now would make arrangements to promptly pay off the entire payroll related tax debt in one payment, then would address this new problem.

After he ended the call, Socrates telephoned his former law partner, Maxwell Pogue, the new firm's tax specialist, and set up a meeting for later that afternoon for himself, Pogue, and his parents. Next, he called his father. He didn't go into any detail, but told his father to be ready to go to lunch with him, to wear a suit and tie, and to be prepared to be tied up all afternoon on a new tax matter that had just come up. As back-up, Socrates spoke with his mother, passed along the same message to her, but also explained the situation to her based on his conversation with the IRS.

When he finished with the call, he went for a short, furious run to unwind.

AFTER MEETING WITH Max Pogue and his parents, Socrates walked his father and mother back to the Westin Grand. He waited until his father announced he was going up to the room to take a nap, then suggested he and his mother talk. They settled into chairs in a small furnished alcove away from the hotel's main lobby so they could have privacy.

"I don't understand how I missed this the past three years," his mother said. "I should have seen it coming. Maybe I didn't want to."

"No point beating yourself up, Mom. It is what it is. We'll deal with it and get through it," Socrates said. At least he hoped they would. He spoke with more confidence than he felt.

"Do you think we could go to jail? Or, your father might? Isn't it a crime not to file taxes?"

"No, not in this case," Socrates said, "not given dad's medical condition. Max will work something out. Jail's not going to be part of this." He didn't say everything he was thinking, that what really worried him was that although dementia should be a good defense against jail time for his father, how would Max rationalize for the United States Attorney that Socrates' mother hadn't questioned why she hadn't signed a tax return for at least three years? What could her defense possibly be?

AFTER HE LEFT his mother, Socrates returned home and called Jade. They hadn't spoken for a while, although not from his lack of trying to reach her. He had left messages on her landline voice mail recorder at her condo, two on her cell phone voice mail, and several on her office phone voice mail, but Jade hadn't returned any of his calls. Jade clearly was avoiding him.

This time, however, Jade picked up.

Socrates sensed a change in Jade's voice. Her tone suddenly crackled with uncharacteristic chill. It was clear Jade already knew about her brothers' situations and was not happy about it, that she was, like her father, blaming Socrates for a condition her siblings had visited upon themselves.

"Yes, Socrates, how are you?" she said, then she paused, although not long enough for Socrates to respond. "I know what you did to the Twins and Eldest Brother," she said, "so you don't have to tell me."

"What I did? Wait a minute, Jade," Socrates said. "How did I . . . ?"

Jade cut him off. "We all would have been better off if you hadn't become involved in my family's affairs. I don't understand why you hate my brothers and wanted to harm them. I thought you loved me."

Socrates forced himself to speak slowly, delivering each word in deliberate isolation from the two words bookending it.

"I . . . became . . . involved, . . Jade, for . . . you, . . . for . . . us. I became involved so your father would eventually approve our relationship. You said you wanted me to help him when I asked you."

Socrates paced the living room as he spoke. He clenched and unclenched his hands. *How could Jade act as if she'd forgotten their discussion about this?*

"You were wrong to accuse Eldest Brother," she said. "He was only looking out for our family. Now he will hate me because of you."

Once again, Socrates carefully weighed his words before he answered. In spite of his mounting anger at Jade's lack of faith in him and her convenient amnesia, he did not want to say anything he might regret later. He loved Jade in spite of her taxing family and her myopic view of them.

"I didn't want it to turn out this way, Jade, believe me," he said, "but this wasn't my fault." He hesitated, then added, "I think you already know that."

"What I know," Jade said, "is that I must talk with Eldest Brother as soon as possible to repair the damage you caused our family. Goodbye, Socrates."

Chapter 63

SOCRATES SLEPT POORLY that night. He tossed and turned while his mind ran a movie reel featuring his father's dementia, his parents' problems with the IRS, Brandon's death, and his disastrous conversation with Jade. He finally nodded off a little before 4:45 a.m.

He woke at 6:30 a.m. in a pool of sweat and went for a short run in Rock Creek Park. He brought his iPod NANO with him, and listened to the audio recording of Shakespeare's *Richard II*. His run went well considering how badly he'd slept. He felt less stressed when he returned home.

After a shower, he stopped by the Wachovia/Wells Fargo Bank branch at 19th and M Streets — across the street from Starbucks and The Sign of the Whale — to put the original Xi'an Agreement and two Secret Protocols into his safe deposit box. He would use the computer scans and printouts he'd made the night before as his working copies.

While at the bank, he also began the process of obtaining a loan which would be secured by the equity in his condo unit. He planned to use the loan proceeds to pay off his father's payroll tax debt in one lump sum. He also discussed with the loan officer the possible need to expand the loan's principal amount because of the second IRS issue. He would use the additional loan proceeds to pay for his parents' tax indebtedness for the years they hadn't filed returns once Max

Pogue resolved that problem. These were the two solutions Socrates and his mother had agreed to when they talked it over after the meeting with Max Pogue.

When his mother protested that Socrates should not go into debt to resolve their problems, Socrates put his arm around her shoulders, squeezed lightly, and said, "You and pop took care of me when I was young. Now, it's my turn to take care of you."

Socrates finished at the bank and walked across the street to Starbucks. He commandeered a corner table on the patio away from other customers, and settled in with a cup of coffee, a chocolate donut, and the printed copies he'd made of the Xi'an Agreement and its two Secret Protocols. He opened the Chinese-Mandarin/American English dictionary he'd brought with him and slowly read the Xi'an Agreement, this time paying attention to every word.

He sipped his coffee and slowly worked his way through all three printouts, making marginal notes in pencil and comparing and contrasting the contents among the documents, taking care to check unfamiliar words against the dictionary. When he finished, he was satisfied he now understood the convoluted relationship that existed among the Xi'an Agreement, the two Secret Protocols, the burglary, the Mandarin Yellow, and the murders of the gallery's director and the Embassy's cultural attaché. He was pleased that the timeline he'd recently prepared was fundamental to his understanding all this.

Socrates finished his coffee and was gathering everything together so he could leave Starbucks when his cell phone sounded.

"I'm still waiting for you to come in and do the affidavit, Cheng," Detective Harte said. "We can't get the warrant and pick up that older brother without it. You need to get your skinny ass in here."

Harte paused, apparently, Socrates thought, waiting for him to offer his *mea culpa* and agree, once again, to come in to the 2D. But Socrates didn't say anything. He wasn't sure how to respond. He knew he wasn't going to show up to prepare the affidavit so he chose passive-aggressive silence as his best response right then, allowing Harte to draw his own inferences from Socrates' failure to answer.

Harte picked up on Socrates' strategy. "You can't avoid this by saying nothing, Cheng. I'm not bluffing. There's a killer out there." He paused to let Socrates respond. When Socrates said nothing, Harte added, "Let's get this done so we can get him off the streets."

Socrates relented, cast aside his passive/aggressive strategy, and quietly said, "Not yet, Detective. I've developed a theory about the case. If I'm right, I'll step away and tell you everything I know. If I'm wrong . . . well . . . I suppose I'll step back then, too, and tell you everything. I won't leave anything out. It won't make any difference at that point, either way."

Socrates' intransigence tested Harte's patience. "Tell me now," Harte said. "Don't play games with me, Cheng, because if you do, I promise you'll be the loser."

"No games, Detective, but not yet," Socrates said. "Later. Very soon, I hope." Socrates became silent and waited. He could hear Harte breathing heavily into the telephone's mouthpiece.

"What's going on, Cheng?" Harte said after a long pause, speaking softly, all suggestion of threats and intimidation now absent from his voice. "Talk to me."

"I will, but later. Tomorrow, Detective."

The edge in Harte's voice returned. "Not good enough, Cheng, Tell me now."

"Tomorrow. You have my word." With that statement, Socrates abruptly ended the call before Harte could protest.

As soon as Socrates ended the call, his cell phone rang again. He didn't bother looking to see who was calling. He was pretty sure it would be Detective Harte calling back. If not, he'd find out later when he picked up his voice mail.

He walked to Jade's condo. He intended to clear up her belief he was to blame for her brothers' situations or to go down in flames trying.

Chapter 64

SOCRATES WALKED THE distance from his condo to Jade's building in half the time it usually took him, pushing himself hard to burn off nervous energy. When he arrived, he stood outside trying to decide if he should follow some resident in through the front door and go up to Jade's condo unannounced, as he had the other day, or if he should push the intercom button, announce himself to Jade, then wait for her to buzz him in, giving her the leeway, if she wanted it, to keep him out. Thinking back on the angry reception he received the other day when he arrived at her door unannounced, he opted for the conservative approach and pushed the intercom button.

He waited almost half a minute for Jade to respond. The intercom sputtered static, and Jade's filtered voice crackled through.

"Who's there?"

"It's me, Jade. I'm downstairs, out front. We need to talk. I'd like to come up."

Socrates tried to imagine the range of feelings that Jade, hearing his voice and knowing he was downstairs, might be experiencing at that moment. He gripped the front door handle and waited for the telltale buzzing and click to indicate that the door's lock had disengaged and he could enter. Seconds passed without any sound. He kept one hand on the door handle and rocked back and forth from one foot to the other.

The intercom exploded again with static. Socrates looked over at the device on the wall as Jade's voice again sparked through.

"This isn't a good time, Socrates. Come back later."

"I'm here now, Jade. Is that a problem? If you don't want to see me, just say so."

"It's not that." She paused. "This isn't a good time for you to come up. Eldest Brother is here right now."

Socrates hadn't considered this possibility. "Damn it, Jade. I don't care if he's there. I have things to say to you, to him, too, since he's there. Buzz me in."

He decided he might as well unload everything on his mind, not just absolve himself from Jade's misperceived assignment of culpability.

SOCRATES STEPPED OFF the elevator and fast-walked toward Jade's apartment. He could see Eldest Brother at the far end of the hallway, his arms crossed over his chest, standing sentry in front of Jade's door. Jade was nowhere in sight. Socrates locked eyes with Eldest Brother as he walked closer to him.

"Tell Jade I'm out here," he said.

Eldest Brother continued to stare at Socrates and block the doorway. He said nothing.

"Jade, I'm out here," Socrates called out.

"Let me by, Eldest Brother," Jade said from inside the condo.

Socrates noted that she did not tell Eldest Brother to let him into her condo. *Not a good sign*, he decided.

Eldest Brother stepped aside.

Jade kept her distance, standing away from Socrates, her back close to Eldest Brother.

"Socrates," Jade said, "I told you. This isn't a good time. I wish you would respect my feelings about this. Eldest Brother doesn't want you here. I'm not sure I do either, at least not right now I don't. Come back later and we'll talk then. It will be better all around."

"This won't wait, Jade," Socrates said, "unless what you're

really telling me is you don't want to see me at all. If that's it, just say so and I'll go. Otherwise I'm staying. It's your call." His heart raced in anticipation of what her response might be because he knew which answer he didn't want.

Jade looked away, said, 'All right," and nodded toward Eldest Brother, who stepped aside, opening a narrow path through the entryway into Jade's foyer.

Socrates brushed past Eldest Brother and crossed the foyer to the living room, walking quickly over to the bank of windows overlooking Connecticut Avenue. He wanted to put some distance between himself, Jade, and Eldest Brother while he sorted through his thoughts. He glanced down at the street, then immediately turned back to face Jade and Bing-wu.

"I really don't appreciate you accusing Eldest Brother of committing crimes, Socrates. He told me what you said to the police. You had no right to say those things."

"Oh, really, Jade?" Socrates said, anger now gripping his voice. "Why don't I have the right? Bing-wu threatened me. Twice, maybe three times. Then he assaulted me. I'd say I have every right."

"That's preposterous, Socrates. Eldest Brother wouldn't do those things, not any of it. He's not violent unless you directly threaten him. He's a Taoist, for God's sake. You know that." She paused, then spoke again, but in a gentler voice this time.

"You're wrong about Bing-wu," she said. "You've always misjudged Eldest Brother and assumed the worst about him just because he doesn't want us to be together. I understand why that bothered you, but it wasn't fair of you to accuse him of the things you said to the police and our father." Jade turned and looked at Eldest Brother, and smiled.

Her smile vanished when she faced Socrates again. "If you're going to continue to misjudge Eldest Brother and tell lies about him, we have nothing more to say to each other. I want you to leave." She crossed her arms over her chest.

Socrates looked over at Eldest Brother, and said to him, "Am I wrong, Bing-wu? Tell me in front of Jade. Am I wrong, am I making up stories about you?"

Eldest Brother yielded nothing to Socrates. He briefly shifted his eyes and glanced at Jade, then immediately looked back at Socrates. His head never moved. He remained silent, his face expressionless, his overall demeanor serene. His continued silence bewildered and unnerved Socrates.

Socrates turned back to Jade briefly, then looked again at Eldest Brother.

"Was it my imagination, Bing-wu, that you threatened me with the note you left in my condo or the other time when you left the coverless catalog on my bed?"

Socrates no longer expected answers from Eldest Brother. His questions now were rhetorical, offered for Jade's benefit.

"Was it also my imagination you later assaulted me on 19th Street? Tell me in front of Jade, have I been wrong about you all along?"

Eldest Brother looked at Jade, then back at Socrates, but still said nothing. His silence was heavy with ambiguity and latent possibilities.

Socrates turned back to Jade, and said, "I think you give Eldest Brother too little credit for being human, for having conflicting feelings. I suspect he's capable of a lot more harm than either of us knows."

"I don't understand what you mean by that, Socrates, but I know Eldest Brother. He could not — no, correct that, he would not — do the things you accused him of." She turned toward Bing-wu and nodded.

Socrates decided this verbal ping pong was getting them nowhere. All he was doing by rehashing his feelings about Eldest Brother was putting off what he'd planned to say to Jade in a few days, after he completed some additional investigating to close up a few loose ends that still lingered. But circumstances had changed. It was time to stop avoiding the real issue now that the three of them were together.

Socrates looked over at Eldest Brother, who continued to stare impassively at him.

"I didn't come here to accuse you of anything, Eldest Brother. I didn't even know you'd be here," Socrates said. "In fact, I'm not accusing you of anything now. I was just putting some things in context and testing the waters with my questions." Socrates glanced at Jade, then back at Eldest Brother.

"Your sister's right about one thing. I don't think you did the things I just described. Not anymore, I don't. I don't see you as an actual threat to me, but it took me a while to understand that. It took the Twins to convince me."

He paused and glanced at Jade, then looked back at Bingwu. "The worst thing you're guilty of, as best I can sort everything out, is making some empty threats against me and being imprisoned in a time warp."

Eldest Brother looked over at Jade, then back at Socrates. He continued to stare at Socrates as if Socrates was a blank wall.

"Then why, Socrates, did you — " Jade said, as she walked across the room toward him. Her face had softened and she tilted her head slightly to the left as she looked into Socrates' eyes. She smiled and extended her arm as she approached him, her palm up, inviting Socrates to take her hand.

Socrates raised his palm to stop Jade's approach to him.

"It took me some time to get it, Jade," Socrates said, "but I eventually did, with the unintentional help of the Twins. Eventually, it all came together for me." His voice was heavy and solemn, more sad than accusatory.

Jade stopped walking and raised her hand to her mouth, covering her lips with her fingertips. She bit her lower lip, then ceded Socrates a nod so slight and so tentative as to be almost unnoticeable.

"I don't know what you mean," Jade said, speaking quietly through her splayed fingers.

"What I mean, Jade, is that it was you the whole time, not Eldest Brother. You. Right here under our noses."

Socrates paused and looked first at Eldest Brother, then back at Jade, waiting for some response. Obtaining none, he continued. "You killed both the director and Brandon."

He paused and locked eyes with Jade. He took a deep breath and slowly let it out. Then he said, "And I know why."

Chapter 65

JADE ABRUPTLY STOPPED walking toward Socrates. She raised her right arm and pointed her finger at his face. She stepped back, slowly moving away from him.

"That's bizarre, Socrates, even for you. I don't know what you're talking about. Apparently, you don't either. I had nothing to do with any of that. The Twins confessed to you, you said so yourself."

Socrates said nothing. He watched Jade closely as she dissembled.

"I don't know why you think these horrible things about me," she said. "How can you believe what you said, Socrates, after all the time we've known each other?"

She canted her head slightly, stepped closer to him, and looked into Socrates' eyes.

"You know me better than that, Darling." Her voice now was an octave higher than normal, almost child-like and barely audible.

Socrates shook his head and remained silent. Seconds passed with no one saying anything. He maintained eye contact with Jade the entire time.

Jade's suppressed rage suddenly exploded.

"Damn you, Socrates . . . Damn you to Hell. " She again pointed her accusatory finger at Socrates' face.

"Who do you think you are accusing me like that? First

the Twins, then Eldest Brother, now me. Where do you get off accusing me like that!"

Socrates held up his hand to silence her. "I'll tell you where I get off, Jade." He spoke far more gently than he felt. His stomach was in turmoil.

"I admit when I thought about the Twins' involvement, it took me a while before I understood they were too immature and self-absorbed to plan the burglary and killings by themselves.

"They might have committed the crimes, if told to do so, but I can't see them instigating or planning anything. The Twins are drones."

"You underestimate my brothers," Jade said, "all of them, not just the Twins. You always have."

"Not the Twins, I don't," Socrates said. "Maybe Eldest Brother, I do, but definitely not the Twins." He looked over at Eldest Brother, then back at Jade.

"I was bothered when they admitted setting up the burglary through their Triad, but continued denying being involved in killing anyone. Their insistence didn't track for me then, and it still doesn't, especially now that I know they were planning all along to flee the country and escape punishment." He paused a beat and looked into Jade's eyes.

"The Twins had no reason not to admit their role in the murders if they were involved." Socrates looked over at Eldest Brother. He hadn't moved.

"It took me a while to understand," Socrates said, "but it slowly dawned on me. If the Twins were telling the truth about the burglary, if they were just the middlemen in arranging it through the Triad, then someone else had to be involved in the instigation and orchestration of it all. Naturally, that person would also be involved in the killings." He paused to pull together his thoughts.

"You're just guessing, Socrates. You're desperate and fishing," Jade said. "The Twins were the ones. They said so. You should pay attention to what you know and stop reaching out for what you don't know."

Socrates ignored Jade. "Actually," he said, "I thought about your father as a possibility, but eliminated him because of his age and because I couldn't come up with any motive for him to sabotage the exhibit and undermine his own reputation and honor. His arranging for the burglary would have been an act against his own self-interest, cultural and political suicide."

Socrates paused and looked again at Eldest Brother. *Still a safe distance away,* he thought. He turned back to Jade. "I eliminated your father as the one responsible." He wondered why Jade had shrugged, almost imperceptivity, or was it just his imagination?

"Until recently, I thought Eldest Brother had pulled the strings, that he might even be the murderer himself. He certainly fits the physical profile, but I couldn't see any reason for him to do it.

"As far as I know, Eldest Brother had no reason to shame your father and your family. And, anyway, it doesn't fit his cultural profile, not unless he secretly hates your father and the rest of you, which I don't think he does, not based on what I've seen and been told by you and the Twins. Besides, Eldest Brother had no reason to assault me. Certainly not just because you and I were romantically involved."

Jade started to say something, but stopped when Socrates abruptly shook his head. "Let me finish," he said, his impatience clear in his voice.

"I know Eldest Brother wanted tradition to prevail, wanted to restore your father's sullied honor, but scuttling the exhibit and committing the murders wouldn't achieve that. It would have brought about just the opposite."

Jade stepped toward Socrates. She flicked the back of her hand dismissively. "I guess that leaves only Youngest Brother or me as the evil villain," she said, her voice laced with contempt, "that is, if you're keeping it all in the family."

Socrates nodded. "Right," he said, "and it wasn't Youngest Brother."

Chapter 66

JADE PURSED HER lips and wrinkled her forehead as if seriously thinking about what Socrates had just said. She shook her head. "Okay, Sherlock, " she said, her contempt now palpable. "I'm listening. How'd you come to your brilliant conclusion?"

"It's what they say in TV crime shows, Jade. You were the only one with the motive, the means, and the opportunity. All three."

"This should be interesting," Jade said, turning her head toward Eldest Brother and speaking to him. Her tone was laced with sarcasm.

Socrates, too, looked over at Eldest Brother. He hadn't moved from the foyer into the living room.

"Let's start with Brandon," Socrates said. "I was emotionally too close to his murder to see the truth. I couldn't be objective. So I made the mistake of approaching his murder backwards by making a natural, but wrong assumption about it.

"I assumed Brandon had been killed because he went to meet with the assistant director in my place, that either I was the actual target or his murder was meant to warn me to drop my investigation.

"But that's what I was supposed to think, what we all

were supposed to think. It was classic misdirection. It's why the catalog illustration was shoved down his throat, to lead us all down that wrong path."

Socrates watched Jade shrug one shoulder and raise her eyebrows.

"But there was no reason Brandon should have been murdered for taking my place because there was no reason to eliminate me. I wasn't a threat to the burglars even though I was making progress in my investigation. Not only that, the stolen items were being repatriated by Bing-fa, one at a time, at least they were until the police took everything into custody as evidence.

"The upshot," Socrates said, "was that nothing I might do going forward would pose a threat to the thieves, so why bother warning me off? Or why bother killing me or killing Brandon in my place? The answer is, there was no reason."

He paused to glance over at Bing-wu. Eldest Brother hadn't moved any closer.

"Once I understood this, I also understood that Brandon had been the target all along. His killing had nothing to do with the burglary or its aftermath. His murder was a crime of convenience, an opportunistic crime." He paused to gauge Jade's reaction, but she remained impassive, staring at him as he spoke, her arms defiantly crossed over her chest.

Socrates pointed his finger at Jade, but he softened his voice. "You knew Brandon was going to the gallery in my place to interview Linda Fong because I told you at lunch that same day." He now stared hard at Jade.

"No one else knew," he said. "Just me, Brandon, and you. This gave you the perfect opportunity to eliminate him later that night and make it seem as if Brandon's murder had something to do with the burglary.

"That's why you stuffed the reproduction of the Northern Sung Edict down his throat." He waited for Jade to say something, to deny this, but she merely shook her head dismissively.

"The reason you killed Brandon was just because he *was* Brandon, because you've hated him ever since college. It was an opportunity you couldn't pass up."

Socrates watched for some sign, either of acknowledgment or demurrer by Jade, but saw nothing, just the stolid face of a stone cold sociopath. He took a deep breath.

"You used your Kobudo blade skills to slash Brandon's throat, just as you did with the director. Then for good measure or for rage, I don't know which and I don't care which, you stabbed Brandon thirteen more times."

"If we assume you're right, Socrates — and you're not, by the way — what about the rest of it? Are you saying I was involved with everything else, that I had the Twins arrange for the burglary with their Triad?" She looked over at Eldest Brother and rolled her eyes.

Jade looked back at Socrates, and pointed her finger at him. "What you're saying makes no sense. Think about it. I'm trying to work my way back into my father's favor, not further alienate him by screwing up the exhibit and subverting his honor."

Socrates nodded. "That's what I thought, too, until recently. It was a reasonable assumption, but it was wrong."

Socrates looked at Eldest Brother. He still hadn't left the foyer. He turned back to Jade. "The burglary had nothing to do with your father. I know that now. It just seemed that way. That was another fortunate opportunity for you, Jade, and you took advantage of it."

Socrates saw movement from the corner of his eye, and quickly turned his head in the direction of the foyer. Eldest Brother had moved in closer. He now stood behind Jade, off to her left, looking over her shoulder at Socrates. He scowled when Socrates caught his eye.

Socrates tensed, then looked back at Jade, and said, "It began to come together for me, although I didn't realize it at the time, when the Twins referred to two Secret Protocols, rather than just one, as secret addenda to the Xi'an Agreement. That puzzled me because what little I knew about the Secret Protocol referred to only one such document, not two.

"Your father reinforced my confusion when I later referred to two Secret Protocols in a conversation with him. He jumped all over me as if I was an idiot, and said there was only one Secret Protocol." Socrates noticed Jade flinch at the mention of her father. She recovered quickly.

"As you can imagine," Socrates continued, "I was confused because the Twins had given me two documents, each purporting to be a legitimate Secret Protocol. But when I read them both and compared them side-by-side, my confusion disappeared. I understood why the burglary had occurred and the reason for the director's and cultural attaché's murders. And that information led me to you, Jade, although I wish that hadn't been the case."

Socrates waited for some response from Jade, but she said nothing.

"You should have destroyed the first Secret Protocol when the burglars took it, Jade. Then there wouldn't have been two documents for me to compare. Without both, I never would have figured everything out."

"This is fascinating, Socrates," Jade said. "I can hardly wait to learn what you think you figured out." She looked over at Eldest Brother and again rolled her eyes.

"You can roll your eyes and mock me all you want, Jade," Socrates said, "but one of the things I discovered, the most interesting of all, was your motive for the burglary and the murders. And, unfortunately, it all fits."

Chapter 67

JADE INTERLACED HER fingers and placed her hands on her chest. She tilted her head slightly to the side and lowered her eyes. Her beatific ensemble evoked memories for Socrates of a Raphaello *Madonna*.

Jade's voice, when she spoke, now was elevated an octave and seemed to Socrates to be contrived to replicate the voice of an innocent young girl. Socrates didn't buy Jade's posturing.

"You know how I hate being kept in the dark, Socrates," Jade said in a sing-song voice. "Please enlighten me. What so-called motive of mine do you think you uncovered?"

Socrates stared into Jade's eyes and hesitated. He wasn't sure he wanted to continue. But he realized he had no choice. He'd already committed himself with his prior statements and, in that measure, had eviscerated his relationship with Jade.

"Before the publicity for the exhibit, very few people knew the Secret Protocol even existed, let alone what it looked like or what its contents disclosed. I certainly didn't even though I'd been infused with China's history during college. I'll bet you didn't either, Jade.

"When I compared the two Secret Protocols," he said, "I realized you had orchestrated the burglary so you could get your hands on the original Secret Protocol, the one intended to be exhibited, the one illustrated in the catalog."

"That's absurd, Socrates. Why in the world would I want to do that?"

"So you could substitute a second Secret Protocol for the original one."

Jade turned toward Eldest Brother and shrugged. Then she looked back at Socrates and said, "Oh, really, Sherlock? And why would I want to do that?"

"Because the second Secret Protocol," Socrates said, "was a forgery created for you, probably by *Jiao tu san ku*, and made to your specifications, is why."

"This is absolutely fascinating, Socrates. I never realized you had such a vivid imagination. You clearly missed your calling being a lawyer and a pen salesman. You should have been a novelist creating mysteries or other imaginative fiction."

"This isn't a joke," Socrates said, his voice hardened now. "People died because of you."

"So *you* say." Jade glanced briefly at Eldest Brother, then looked back at Socrates. "Okay, I'll play along with your fanciful script. What reason would I have had to want to steal the exhibit's Secret Protocol and substitute a forged one for it?"

Jade turned briefly and again looked at Eldest Brother. She shook her head and shrugged her shoulders. Then she turned back to Socrates and said in a tone impregnated with contempt, "I'm sure Eldest Brother also would like to hear your theory before I tell him to throw you out of here."

"You wanted to substitute the forged Secret Protocol because the original Secret Protocol described, as part of an overall mosaic, an agreement between Mao and Chiang to continue a contrived Civil War against one another after the Japanese were defeated."

"That's preposterous, Socrates," Jade said, "but even if it was true, why would I care? Why would anyone care?" She shook her head in disgust and sighed. "You're talking ancient history. Besides, two armies couldn't stage fake battles and get away with it. This is absolute nonsense."

"They could and they did," Socrates said. "Most of the engagements between Mao's army and Chiang's were fought in the countryside, away from populated urban areas, away from the few foreigners, especially Western journalists, who were allowed to be in China.

"No one outside China would ever know anything about how the Civil War was staged and being fought, except for what might be reported in the press — the press controlled by Mao and Chiang in their agreed-upon spheres of influence."

"Have it your way," Jade said. "Assuming Mao and Chiang could get away with it, so what? Again, who cares? Especially now in the twenty-first century. It's irrelevant in today's world."

Jade chuckled disingenuously and looked at Eldest Brother.

"I have a feeling we're about to come to the good part, Eldest Brother," she said to Bing-wu, "the part why Mao and Chiang faked the Civil War and the part telling what my so-called motive was for arranging for the burglary and substituting a forged Secret Protocol for the original one. Pay attention. Socrates might want to give us a quiz later."

Socrates gave Jade a pass on her sarcasm and continued as if she hadn't just mocked him.

"The first Secret Protocol, the one originally intended to be displayed in the exhibit, provided that Chiang, after he fled to Formosa, would remain a vocal foe of the Communist government to generate American foreign aid to Chiang"

Jade again turned toward Eldest Brother and said with raised eyebrows and a jackal's grin, "I can feel the drama, the tension rising, Eldest Brother. I just know we're coming to the good part."

"You're right, Jade," Socrates said, "we are getting there. Now comes the interesting part, the reason you cared and your motive for the crimes that followed."

Jade placed both her palms over her heart and mimed a swoon.

"The first parts of the conspiracy didn't particularly interest you, Jade," Socrates said. "The staged Civil War, Chiang's willful defeat, Mao's rule over the Mainland, and Chiang's and Mao's vocal enmity afterward, were all prelude to what you cared about."

Jade glanced at Eldest Brother, smiled, and nodded once.

"But here's what you did care about," Socrates said. "The original Secret Protocol had specifically assigned the responsibility for enticing the United States into sending Chiang millions of dollars in foreign aid to Madam Chiang Kai-shek, your longtime idol, Jade, Madam Chiang."

Socrates waited for Jade to say something, but she remained quiet.

"As we both know, Jade, Madam Chiang performed her part very well. She returned to Wellesley College after the end of the Second World War and achieved great and favorable publicity for herself, her husband, and their hypothetical cause. She did it again in Washington when she addressed the United States Congress. This performance, itself, generated huge amounts of economic aid that continued to flow to Chiang for decades afterward."

"So what, Socrates?" Jade said, her voice growing louder and derisive. "That's common knowledge. Everybody knows it. You and I learned this as China Studies majors at Penn State. What's your point? Nobody but you cares about this."

"I'll tell you *so what*," Socrates said. "The point is, *you* cared, Jade. You cared very much. Too much, in fact. That was your problem." Socrates glanced briefly at Eldest Brother, then looked back at Jade.

Why, Socrates thought, *am I telling Jade what she already knows?* Having posed the question to himself, he, of course, knew the answer. He still held out hope Jade would deny her role in the crimes in some credible way that would convince him he was wrong about her. He didn't expect this to happen or, if it did happen, that it would remedy the damage already done to their relationship, but he hoped it might, so he had to try.

"What history didn't tell us," Socrates said, "was that the 1937 Xi'an Agreement negotiated by T.V. Soong and Madam Chiang to free her kidnapped husband came with the original Secret Protocol as part to it.

"And, of course, history couldn't tell us about the existence of the forged, second Secret Protocol because it didn't exist until recently when the *Cunning Rabbit* Triad created it for you with key information eliminated from it." He paused and silently counted to five while he stared into Jade's eyes.

"History also couldn't tell us what it was that had been excluded or why it had been omitted."

"Okay, Socrates," Jade said, "you know I'm a sucker for a good puzzle. What was it you think I wanted removed from the original Secret Protocol?"

Chapter 68

SOCRATES PAUSED TO organize his thoughts.

He took a deep breath, held it briefly, then let it seep out slowing between clenched teeth.

"You wanted to remove all mention of Madam Chiang's role in the decades-long conspiracy and massive embezzlement," he said. He paused again and looked for some reaction from Jade. He saw none. She remained impervious to the implications of his statement.

"That's what you caused to be left out of the forged Secret Protocol," Socrates said. "Those parts of the original document that referenced Madam Chiang's role in the deception and graft."

He waited for Jade's explosive reaction, but she didn't react at all, and that worried him.

"The forged document removed all references to Madame Chiang. She no longer appeared anywhere in the Secret Protocol, not even by implication.

"The forgery became the mirror image of your scissored copy of Madam Chiang's wedding photograph. The forgery cut out Madam Chiang and retained her husband in the picture of corruption, placing all blame on the Generalissimo. Madam Chiang became the innocent spouse, missing now from the portrait of embezzlement and collusion participated in by everyone else still reflected in your forged Secret Protocol."

Socrates suddenly became aware that Jade had moved in closer to him. He tensed. Sweat pooled in his underarms and his shirt stuck to his back.

"If you're suggesting what I think you are," Jade said, "that's crazy, Socrates. Even for you."

"No, Jade. That's not what's crazy." He paused to decide if he really wanted to say what was now on his mind and would likely provoke Jade's anger. He decided he'd play it out, let matters take their own course. There wasn't any turning back at this point. He glanced over at Eldest Brother who hadn't moved from his position behind Jade.

"What's crazy, Jade, is a college-aged woman — and the same woman more than a decade and a half later — still engaging in obsessive celebrity worship."

He pulled his handkerchief from his trouser pocket and wiped his neck. He stepped to his right, creating more distance between himself and Jade.

"What's crazy is you, now in your late thirties, still displaying autographed photos of Madam Chiang in your home and keeping laminated copies of her speeches and her mutilated wedding photograph on display." He pointed at the framed wedding photo sitting on the boxwood corner table across the room.

He wiped his forehead again and gingerly stepped to his right.

Socrates spoke softly now. "What's crazy is you still wearing your hair exactly as Madam Chiang wore hers more than sixty years ago when she addressed Congress."

He hesitated, then said, "That's what's crazy, Jade. That and all the other things you did, that you still do, to emulate and honor Madam Chiang."

Jade smiled, shook her head, and made her disparaging *tsk, tsk, tsk* sound.

"This is becoming more and more interesting, Socrates," she said, "although it's all bullshit." She stepped closer to him. "So, tell me, under your scenario, why would I have killed the director?"

Socrates examined Jade's eyes briefly, looking for some tell, but, seeing none, said, "The director worked with the Embassy's cultural attaché to prepare the exhibit. Together they created the catalog from photographs of the objects to be displayed, including the historical documents." He hesitated briefly, then said, "Including the original Secret Protocol."

He paused to let the implication of this sink in.

"You had to assume, because of this, that the director might have become familiar with the original Secret Protocol, either from seeing the actual document or, more likely, from working with a photograph of it for the catalog.

"That meant she posed a potential danger to you and your scheme because she might have recognized the forgery for what it was, a spurious document substituted after the burglary for the original one illustrated in the catalog."

Socrates wiped his neck again. "You couldn't take that chance, Jade, so the director had to go."

He paused briefly, sucked in some air, then added, "I assume, too, that's why the cultural attaché was murdered on her way home from a restaurant in Chinatown. She also had worked on the catalog and worked with your father to select the objects to be exhibited. This means she also might have spotted the forgery. She, too, had to be eliminated."

"Anything else you want to say, Monsieur Poirot?" Jade asked. "It seems your little gray cells have been working overtime, even running amuck."

Socrates wasn't used to Jade's sarcastic side. He'd rarely known that aspect of her personality. But, he realized, he apparently hadn't known her at all. She certainly wasn't the person she had seemed to be, the woman he'd loved.

Socrates dumped these demoralizing thoughts and continued. "That's also why the gallery planned to return the exhibit catalogs to the printer and wouldn't sell me one. The pretext was that the color was wrong, but it wasn't wrong, was it?" He eased a few more inches to his right. Jade moved in lockstep with him.

"The reason for returning the catalogs," Socrates said, "was that you couldn't risk displaying the substituted, forged Secret Protocol in the exhibit at the same time people would be walking around the gallery holding catalogs that illustrated the original Secret Protocol. Someone eventually would have noticed the difference. It was easier to have the original

catalogs replaced with new ones that would contain a photograph made from your forged, substituted document."

Jade shook her head. "See what I mean about your under-
valued fiction writing talents, Socrates? You imagine a good
tale."

"There's more," Socrates said, "if you'll be quiet." He
waited until she nodded her agreement. He could see steam
hissing from her ears.

"Once I understood this, I wondered why you encouraged me to help your father. Then it came to me.

"You wanted me to return everything to Bing-fa, including your forged Secret Protocol, because you assumed that by
the time I found the stolen objects, that you or the Twins — or
maybe the Triad — would have substituted your fake document for the original Secret Protocol among the stolen, but
later recovered, objects.

"No one would have had any reason to know that the recovered Secret Protocol, the one your father would have inno-
cently returned to the gallery along with the other recovered
stolen works, wasn't the same document as the one stolen."

Jade shook her head very slowly as if she was dealing
with very unintelligent or stubborn child.

"There's a flaw in your otherwise twisted reasoning,"
Jade said. "You didn't recover anything. The burglars started
selling the objects back to my father until the police impound-
ed them."

"True," Socrates said, "but that wasn't important in your
overall scheme of things because the substitution had already
been made." He again edged a few inches along the window
sill, moving away from Jade.

"It didn't make any difference to you whether the Triad
returned the Secret Protocol to your father by selling it to him
or if I returned it to him by recovering it from the thieves. In
either case, the substituted Secret Protocol would then be the
one to appear in the exhibit."

Jade moved in closer to him.

"I must admit, this nonsense is really interesting, Socrates.
But if you're right, then what about the Mandarin Yellow? You
seem to have forgotten all about it. I thought the pen was sup-

posed to be the object of the burglary and the focus of your investigation. You and my father certainly acted that way."

"Stealing the Mandarin Yellow," Socrates said, "was a calculated misdirection intended to make people focus on it, rather than focus on the provocative Secret Protocol, because of the Mandarin Yellow's pre-exhibit publicity. The purpose of the misdirection was to conceal the real reason for the burglary — the theft of the Secret Protocol."

"That's not so," Jade said. "Your assumptions are wrong. It was my father, not me, who wanted you to find the Mandarin Yellow. So how could that be a misdirection by me, even under your analysis?"

"Good point, Jade. I know it was Bing-fa, not you, who brought me into this matter to specifically find the pen," Socrates said. He frowned. "I also know this doesn't quite fit with my analysis, and that bothers me. It's something I'll have to work out later," he said. "But it doesn't invalidate anything else I've said."

"Nonetheless," Socrates said, "in spite of that gap in the story, I believe this: In addition to the original Secret Protocol, which was the real target and the real purpose of the burglary, the Mandarin Yellow was the only other object that absolutely had to be taken by the burglars. In that way the pen could become the focal point of the post-burglary publicity and recovery effort, keeping everyone's eyes off the stolen original Secret Protocol.

"In fact," Socrates said, "it didn't matter what else the burglars removed from the gallery as long as they took the Mandarin Yellow *and* the Secret Protocol. Everything else taken was mere camouflage randomly selected by the burglars, nothing more than protective coloring. That's why I wasn't able to see any pattern or theme among the stolen objects," Socrates said. "There wasn't any."

Jade shook her head and made her *tsk, tsk, tsk* sound again.

"Oh, Socrates, my love, why couldn't you have left well enough alone?"

She reached behind her back with her right hand.

Socrates' stomach tightened. He gripped the window sill behind him. His knuckles turned white.

"Damn you, Socrates," Jade said, her voice hardening and becoming louder. "You ruined everything."

She pulled an eight inch, double-edge *Kobudo* knife from behind her back, from beneath her blouse, and took a step toward him.

Socrates froze, his eyes fixed on Jade's weapon.

Chapter 69

WITH HIS EYES still locked on Jade's weapon, Socrates' long-ignored *T'ai Chi Chuan* training instincts — rusty and dormant, but present nevertheless as latent muscle memory and technique knowledge — kicked in and gained fleeting control over his fear. He stepped away from Jade, sliding along the window sill, his body's movement markedly relaxed and fluid now.

Jade followed him, step-by-step, as if they were running along parallel train tracks.

Jade held the blade waist high in front of her in traditional *Kobudo* style and moved the weapon from side to side in a slow, rhythmic harvester's arc, taunting Socrates, preparing to launch the classic *Kobudo* underhand blade thrust.

Socrates' lack of martial arts' practice ultimately prevailed, and fear wrested its control of him. His stomach knotted. He had only seconds to disarm Jade or become her next victim.

Socrates edged along the bank of windows. The wood window sill behind him, touching his waist, acted as his blind guide. He never took his eyes from Jade's eyes. He watched her, looking for some nuanced signal that she was about to attack. He needed to put distance between himself and Jade while he figured out what to do.

Jade rhythmically arced the blade in front of her, having

no doubt about the fated outcome. She steadily moved closer to Socrates.

Socrates' choices for survival were almost non-existent. He was no match for Jade's up-to-date *Kobudo* training. His opportunity to save himself, tenuous as it was, was slipping away with each passing second. He had to neutralize Jade's weapon hand before she initiated her attack or he wouldn't stand a chance against her double-edged blade.

"I love you, Socrates. Why couldn't you just mind your own business and left well enough alone? We would have been so happy together."

Socrates said nothing. He had no desire to fuel Jade's anger with anything he might say. The hair on the back of his neck stiffened when he saw Jade's pupils dilate.

Jade stepped in half a step closer, sweeping her blade back and forth in ever shorter, ever faster lateral arcs.

Socrates maintained eye contact with Jade and slowly side-stepped to his right until his thigh bumped the couch. He was cornered, caught in the intersection of the couch, two walls and the bank of windows.

Jade shifted her legs, moving them from their side-by-side posture to a new position, so that one leg now was behind the other, forming a straight line that pointed directly at Socrates.

She leaned forward and emptied the weight from her back leg, pouring its weight and *chi* into her front leg, leaving her back leg almost weightless and her both legs in the full-empty posture.

"You know I love you, Socrates. Tell me you know that. I need to hear it."

Socrates remained quiet, hoping with his silence to buy precious seconds. He continued to watch Jade closely, looking for some subtle warning she was about to attack.

Chapter 70

JADE WAS WELL trained in her Kobudo discipline. She yielded nothing to Socrates he could use to anticipate her attack. Nothing in Jade's body language or in her face, eyes, posture, or initial fluidity helped him. All remained inscrutable to Socrates.

But then he saw the tell.

Jade, almost imperceptibly, had arched her eyebrows.

Seconds later, she raised the blade above her head and poured her weight from her front leg into her back leg as she prepared to leap into a flying, overhead attack.

Socrates instinctively squeezed back deeper into the corner, trying to make himself smaller. Neither his former martial arts training nor his common sense offered him any reason to believe this movement might help him, but his primitive survival instinct prevailed.

Socrates raised his arm chest high, hoping to achieve what all his reading knowledge and limited practice of *Kobudo* told him he would not achieve, hoping to block Jade's blade thrust with his forearm, counting on the brief distraction this might provide to give him valued seconds to use his other hand to grab Jade's wrist, all while trying to avoid having his defending hand and arm badly slashed.

He knew his defensive parry was a long shot, a Hail Mary move, a pallid measure likely to fail. He also knew he had no other choice. He was operating on instinct and raw fear.

Jade held the blade in two hands and stretched her arms above her head as high as they would reach. She angled the blade downward toward Socrates' forehead. She slowly, as if replicating a ballerina's movement, raised herself up onto the ball of her left foot and lifted her right knee until her right thigh was parallel to the floor. She stood perfectly still, correctly balanced, a *Kobudo* flamingo poised in a bayou.

Jade inhaled slowly and fully. She closed her eyes briefly and quieted her breath.

Socrates recognized this step. It was the one he'd been dreading. The end was near. Jade was internally preparing herself to attack. She was pre-visualizing her thrust and Socrates' attempt to parry it, and was seeing her ultimate triumph over Socrates as she plunged the blade into his forehead. Pre-visualization was an important part of success in *Kobudo*.

Socrates' eyes darted from left to right and back again looking for some way out. There was none. He shrank back deeper into the corner, futilely trying to compress himself, to offer up the smallest possible target. He held up his arm as if shading his eyes from the sun.

Jade stretched higher on her pedestal leg, her muscles now taut.

She inhaled slowly and deeply.

Her eyes narrowed.

Socrates saw no way out.

Then the unexpected happened.

The swift leg-kick abruptly swept in from behind Jade, took control of her pedestal ankle, and whisked her pedestal leg out from under her, eliminating the immediate threat to Socrates. The attack caught both Jade and Socrates by surprise.

Jade crashed to the floor, smacking the carpet with a solid thud. She instantly rolled to her left and shifted her weight with practiced ease, promptly gaining purchase. She pushed off the carpet with both legs and leaped up, fully righting herself, all in one fluid motion.

Jade ignored Socrates now and confronted her assailant.

Jade looked directly at Eldest Brother's flushed face. She sucked in short fast gulps of air. Her face and neck burned scarlet with rage. Her eyes had become fuming slits.

"How dare you, you . . . ." Jade shrieked.

"Be quiet, Bing-jade," Eldest Brother interrupted, speaking Mandarin, speaking softly but firmly. "You have forfeited your right to address me. Your actions have shamed our family and ancestors beyond all time."

Eldest Brother reprimanded Jade so softly, Socrates could barely hear him.

"Put down your blade, Little Sister. Do it now." Eldest Brother held out his open palm to receive the weapon from Jade.

Eldest Brother's subdued, modulated tone, juxtaposed with his swift, powerful leg sweep and his predatory, narrowed eyes and words, chilled Socrates.

Socrates moved away from the corner, careful not to attract attention, and slipped in behind Eldest Brother. He looked over Bing-wu's shoulder, watching Jade, and waited. He had never before seen her eyes like this, a potpourri of surprise, sorrow, and rage.

Eldest Brother stepped toward Jade and again extended his hand. "Give me your weapon, Little Sister."

Jade's body noticeably relaxed. She nodded once and moved closer to Eldest Brother. She bowed her head in acknowledgement of his more eminent familial status, and dangled both arms by her sides, signaling her submission to traditional Confucian authority.

Eldest Brother nodded once at Jade and extended his open palm out farther, beckoning the weapon with his fingers.

Without warning, Jade cast aside her submissive posture in one explosive movement. She raised her head and straightened up, then swept her knife along a lethal plane, cutting to the left and back again, slicing Eldest Brother's chest with each pass.

Eldest Brother staggered backward, clutched his bleeding chest with both hands, then plummeted to the floor. He laid on his back with his eyes and mouth wide open, gasping for air. A crimson blot slowly overspread his chest, staining his beige silk gown.

Jade moved in and loomed over him. The corners of her mouth turned down. She breathed slow, rhythmic breaths, trained *Kobudo* breaths meant to anticipate the delivery of the fatal blow.

Jade stood over Eldest Brother, straddling him with one foot on each side just below his armpits. She held her weapon with two hands and slowly raised the blade above her head, an imagined Aztec princess about to perform a ritual human sacrifice.

"Forgive me, Eldest Brother." she said softly.

She inhaled deeply, closed her eyes and tensed her arms, but never completed her rite. She never had the chance to. Instead, she collapsed to the floor, falling swiftly, coming to rest among the ceramic dust and small shards that erupted from the table lamp Socrates had just smashed against her head.

Chapter 71

SOCRATES, WITH THE aid of Eldest Brother who dismissed his chest wounds as superficial, ripped two electrical cords from table lamps and trussed Jade in the traditional Chinese method of subjugation so that her bound wrists and ankles were joined together at the small of her back. Everything else was held in place by a long chord that also tightened around her neck. If Jade moved too much, she would strangle herself.

Jade lay on her side on the carpet like a roped steer. Her eyes remained open and followed Socrates' movement as he walked to the farthest corner of the room.

Socrates called Detective Harte. "We won't have to get together tomorrow night, Detective."

"Wait a minute, Cheng, we had an understanding," Harte said. "I told you, I expect you to bring me up to date, then get the hell out of the investigation. Didn't I make myself clear?"

"You did, Detective, perfectly clear, but you didn't let me finish. The investigation's done. We have the killer, we caught her and have her tied up here."

Before he could complete his statement, Socrates heard Jade shout, "No, Eldest Brother. No. Don't . . . ."

Socrates spun around to face Jade and Eldest Brother.

Jade laid on her side with her mouth wide open in a soundless scream. Blood soaked the front of her white silk blouse. Foam burped from the gash in her windpipe, forming percolating bubbles that morphed into elongated teardrops and clung to the open wound in her throat until they burst under their own weight, spraying a fine pink mist on the carpet below.

Socrates watched, frozen in place, as Jade's eyes rolled back in her head until all he could see were the white of her eyes.

Socrates took a tentative step toward Jade, but stopped when Eldest Brother held up his palm, silently insisting that Socrates stay away.

Socrates nodded his assent, stopped walking, and warily watched Eldest Brother, ready to defend himself against attack, if necessary.

Eldest Brother looked hard at Socrates and held his gaze, then let go of the blooded knife, dropping it to the floor. He turned away from Socrates and back to Jade, looked down at her, and said in Mandarin, speaking quietly, "You brought unforgiveable shame to us all, Little Sister." He lowered himself to the floor, lifted Bing-jade by her shoulders and rested her head on his lap.

Socrates turned away and walked to the other side of the living room. He picked up his cell phone from the carpet, saw that he still was connected to Detective Harte, and said, "Detective, are you still there?"

A woman responded. "This is Sergeant Mooney. Detective Harte's on his way to the general location of your call. We triangulated on your location from cell phone towers, but I need you to tell me exactly where you're at, what's the address, so I can relay it to the detective in his vehicle."

After Socrates finished his call, he looked over at Eldest Brother. Socrates nodded and fanned out his palms in a respectful and submissive silent inquiry.

Eldest Brother nodded his acquiescence.

Socrates walked over to Eldest Brother, and lowered himself onto the carpet next to Jade. He sat there, alongside brother and sister, and gently stroked Jade's insensate cheek, while he waited for the police to arrive.

Chapter 72

SOCRATES' RETURN TO some semblance of a normal life after Jade's death was slow, but steady. He gradually came to terms with the discrepancy he'd experienced between the Jade he thought he knew and loved and the Jade he uncovered.

He questioned if he should have anticipated Jade's role in the burglary and murders, if he had been in denial, and had turned a blind eye to the pathological nature of her celebrity worship he'd been aware of since college. He ultimately concluded that Jade's obsessive adoration of Madam Chiang had been susceptible to varying interpretations and that he could not have anticipated the deadly consequences of her fixation.

He considered reopening his pen store, but decided not to. Selling collectible fountain pens now seemed too trivial after what he'd been through.

BING-FA, TOO, EXPERIENCED a difficult time after Jade's actual death and the Twins' and Eldest Brother's symbolic deaths.

The police eventually returned the stolen objects to him. Bing-fa, in turn, delivered these items to the People's Republic Embassy, although not in time for Linda Fong to include them in the rescheduled opening of the exhibit.

Bing-fa's repatriation of the cultural treasures did not restore his face in the eyes of the People's Republic government or among the inhabitants of Washington's Chinatown community. Bing-fa's honor, the grail he had engaged Socrates to locate and retrieve for him, appeared to be irrevocably lost, not only because the burglary and postponement of the exhibit had occurred under his stewardship, but also because of the roles his children had played in the events.

A DISTRICT OF Columbia grand jury indicted Eldest Brother for the crimes of First Degree Murder and the lesser included offense, Voluntary Manslaughter, in connection with Jade's death. Bing-wu refused to speak up and enter a plea during his arraignment. The court, therefore, entered a Not Guilty plea on his behalf for both felony charges.

Bing-fa hired Bos Smyth as criminal defense counsel to represent Eldest Brother at his trial. He selected Smyth because Socrates, in a brief but unanswered note he sent Bing-fa shortly after Eldest Brother's arrest, suggested Smyth as one of the best criminal defense lawyers in Washington.

Much to Socrates' surprise, after a two day trial the jury found Eldest Brother not guilty on both counts.

Socrates recognized the verdicts for what they were. It was a clear, but understandable, case of jury nullification, Socrates decided.

Eldest Brother returned to Bing-fa's penthouse suite to live.

IN THE WEEKS following Jade's death, Socrates became increasingly alarmed as he uncovered more and more evidence that his father's dementia had started much further back in time than either Socrates or his mother had realized.

In the course of working through his father's latest tax problem, Socrates came across many of his parents' bills that had not been removed from their envelopes and were left unpaid in the back of a desk drawer. He also discovered several telephone messages from physicians' and dentists' offices concerning his father's missed appointments.

Worst of all from Socrates' point of view, because he knew how sharp and vital his father's mind had been not all that long ago, were the many examples of his father's increasing difficulty performing common, everyday cognitive functions. Most telling to Socrates was his father's inability to remember how to use the automatic drip coffee maker to set up coffee for the next morning, a task he had routinely performed every night for himself and his wife for as far back in time as Socrates could remember.

Socrates retained Max Pogue to head off criminal tax proceedings against his parents and to try to have the tax penalties and interest waived by the IRS. Pogue, based on significant medical evidence that Socrates' father had been in the nascent stages of dementia when he failed to file tax returns, resolved the issues with the United States Attorney's office to avoid having them pursue criminal prosecutions. He could not, however, persuade the IRS to waive the penalties and interest since Socrates' mother had not raised an alarm over the three years she had not signed tax returns. Socrates considered this outcome to be an expensive gift, but a gift to his parents nonetheless, a small price to pay in return for the authorities' agreement to not pursue criminal charges.

Socrates borrowed additional funds from his bank to pay off the second tax debt. He had no qualms about doing this for his parents. All he had to do now was to take the next step necessary for him to earn sufficient income to repay the expanded bank loan. In this regard, he had a few ideas about what he wanted to do, so he turned to that step next and placed a telephone call.

Chapter 73

"HELLO, TODD. IT'S Socrates." He hesitated. "I've thought about what you said. I want to return to law practice."

"I'm pleased, but surprised," Todd said. "I thought when we talked before you said that . . . ."

"I know, but circumstances have changed since then." Socrates took a deep breath. "I'd prefer to be part-time at first, to make sure it's right for me and for the firm, but I'd like to give it a shot."

Todd said nothing.

After several silent seconds, Socrates said, "What do you think?"

"We can have an office ready tomorrow morning if you want," Todd answered.

SOCRATES DID HIS best to make his reentry into law practice work for him and the firm, but it did not come easily. At first, his heart wasn't in it, but after the passage of several months, little by little, Socrates slipped into the day-to-day routine of going to the office, and latched onto the many rituals of daily law practice. Eventually, he found comfort in the regularity of his days and in the social contacts that being present at the law firm offered him.

Yet this evolving comfort belied an underlying, contin-

ued disquiet that gnawed at him. Something as yet unarticu-
lated eroded Socrates' peace of mind. And though it was as yet
undefined, whatever it was, it definitely had its unshakable
grip on Socrates, and would not let go of him.

Chapter 74

EIGHT MONTHS AFTER he began working at the law firm, Socrates dialed Bing-fa's private telephone number at the Golden Dragon and arranged to meet him at the restaurant. This was their first communication since Jade's death except for the brief, but unanswered note Socrates had sent Bing-fa recommending Bos Smyth as Eldest Brother's defense counsel.

Bing-fa was sitting behind his desk when Socrates arrived. He didn't stand to greet Socrates as he'd done in the past. Instead, he motioned Socrates over to a chair facing him.

At first, Bing-fa and Socrates remained silent while they sized each other up, each being suspicious of the other's inclination toward him. They were like two aged, reunited prize fighters who long ago had fought a contentious match that had ended in a hotly disputed decision and had generated such controversy that all these years later it continued on unresolved in the minds of both the match's victor and the loser.

Bing-fa finally broke the silence. Speaking in Mandarin, he said, "Your presence here uproots memories I prefer to leave buried."

Socrates, replying in English, said, "This isn't pleasant for me either."

"I am grateful for your help concerning Eldest Brother's trial," Bing-fa said, "although I do blame you for the misfortune that befell my family."

Socrates felt his insides knot. He slowed his breathing and resisted the urge to engage in verbal jousting with Bing-fa, even under the circumstances that motivated his visit today. He knew Jade would have disapproved of any such breach of etiquette by him toward her father, and somehow, for reasons he did not understand, but acknowledged, what Jade would have thought if she were still alive, still mattered to him. So he said nothing and didn't challenge the accusatory premise underlying Bing-fa's statement.

"Tell me why you have come here today," Bing-fa said.

Socrates paused even though he'd rehearsed his opening statement dozens of times over the previous few hours. He straightened up in his chair, looked into Bing-fa's eyes, and said, "I've come to realize there was more behind the burglary than ever came out. Much more."

Bing-fa shrugged. "I do not know what you mean, "he said.

"Actually," Socrates said, his voice laced with irony, "I think you know exactly what I mean."

Socrates' words, his oblique accusation, words intended to shock Bing-fa, had their intended effect. Bing-fa noticeably stiffened. He placed his hands on his lap, formed a tepee with his fingers, and frowned.

"Explain yourself," he said.

"After Jade's death, I found myself with too much time on my hands for my own good, too much time to brood over what had happened. I decided to take on a project to occupy myself. I decided to write a magazine article about the Secret Protocol, the original one, not Jade's substitute document. It would be a popular history piece for *Smithsonian Magazine* or perhaps for *National Geographic*.

"The first thing I did was to see if there was anything unrelated to the gallery's exhibit known about the document. I researched it on the Internet, but found nothing.

"I also met with several sinologists and museum curators at the Smithsonian's Freer and Sackler Galleries here in DC to ask them what they knew about it. And I sent e-mail inquiries to China scholars around the world.

"I asked everyone the same two questions: Had they ever

heard of the Secret Protocol before the publicity for the exhibit and, if so, under what circumstances?

"I expected someone to write back saying he'd seen the document himself or knew of someone who'd seen it. If not that, then I anticipated, at the very least, being told there had been rumors of its existence over the past sixty-five or so years.

"But none of that occurred. I received the same response from everyone: No one had seen the document, knew anyone who had seen it, or had ever heard rumors of its existence before the publicity for the exhibit." Socrates paused, to let this sink in.

"Don't you find that curious?" Socrates said.

"No," Bing-fa said, "I do not. You have read too much into the replies, looking for some sinister meaning where none exists. The answer is obvious if one looks at this objectively, is it not?"

"Really?" Socrates said. He strained to control the sarcasm he felt. "And what would that obvious answer be?"

"That the existence of the document was a well guarded *state secret,* and therefore the document was purposely hidden in the Chairman's secret archives, away from outside knowledge. That is why the document is known as the *Secret* Protocol." He smiled and nodded, punctuating the correctness of his statement with a sharp chin thrust.

Socrates arched an eyebrow, but let the comment pass. He continued with his rehearsed statement.

"I did something else to fill-in my free time," he said, "while gathering information for my article. I reworked the written timeline of events I had prepared when I investigated the burglary.

"This time," Socrates said, "I described everything I remembered about my involvement, as well as everything I'd read about the various stolen objects. By creating this expanded chronology, I generated new questions for which I didn't have answers. One question, in particular, bothered me."

"What would that be?" Bing-fa asked.

"Why you recruited me, why you didn't just wait for the cops to do their job."

Bing-fa smiled condescendingly from the corners of his closed mouth.

"I answered that question the first day I spoke with you at your writing store. You obviously have forgotten."

"I didn't forget," Socrates said, "and it's still a question for me."

"Then I will answer this for you once again. I engaged your assistance because the Embassy and I preferred to keep the matter private, just as I told you."

Socrates shook his head as if dismissing Bing-fa's self-evident response.

"At the time," Socrates said, "when you said that, I didn't think about your answer. My focus was on how helping you might help my relationship with Jade and help expedite Jade's reintroduction to her family.

"Looking back now, I realize your answer begged the question: *Why* did you want to avoid publicity and have the investigation pursued privately? What was it you didn't want discovered and disclosed in public?"

"And do you have an answer to your question, Mr. Cheng?"

Socrates nodded. "As a matter of fact, I do."

Chapter 75

SOCRATES INHALED SLOWLY, taking a very deep breath and briefly holding it to center himself.

"You didn't want the authorities to be the ones who recovered the stolen objects and took possession of them as evidence, at least not until you finished doing what you planned to do with them.

"You wanted me to recover all the objects so I'd return them directly to you. This was important because there was one item you didn't want the police to recover and focus their attention on. Once I delivered everything to you, you intended to remove that object from among the others before the police took custody of everything as evidence."

Socrates and Bing-fa cast cold gazes at one another.

"I didn't see it at the time," Socrates said, "but it all makes sense in hindsight. It was Jade's forged Secret Protocol that clued me in." He paused briefly to gather his thoughts.

"You didn't want the authorities to get their hands on the original Secret Protocol," Socrates said, "the one supposedly found among Mao's private papers."

"You are merely speculating," Bing-fa said. "You have no basis for making these statements. Why would I care?"

"You cared, all right, and I know why. We both know why. And it had nothing to do with Jade's forged document. It had to do with your own agenda, an agenda that preceded the exhibit by decades."

SOCRATES CROSSED HIS arms over his chest and paused to slow his breathing. He locked his eyes on Bing-fa's eyes. Neither man blinked.

"You cared," Socrates said, "because the original Secret Protocol, just like Jade's substitute Secret Protocol, was itself a fake."

Bing-fa showed no surprise, no disagreement, and no anger at Socrates' provocative assertion. He merely shrugged his indifference, and otherwise expressed no discernible reaction to Socrates' statement.

"You have an admirable intellect, Mr. Cheng, but your overly fertile imagination misdirects it."

Socrates shook his head. "I don't think so," he said. "Contrary to what you led me to believe, the Mandarin Yellow was not the principle target of the burglary.

"My search for the Mandarin Yellow was a deliberate misdirection intended by you to entice me into helping you so I would recover all the stolen items, including the original Secret Protocol. That way I would unknowingly achieve your real goal by redelivering the original document to you as part of my recovery of the entire cache of stolen objects."

"Why would I want to create such a misdirection as you imagine?" Bing-fa said.

"To stoke my interest in helping you, then to keep me focused on the Mandarin Yellow, all the while deflecting my attention from the real purpose of the burglary."

Socrates looked at Bing-fa for some clue indicating Bing-fa admitted Socrates was correct. He saw none.

"Nothing about the burglary except getting your hands on the Secret Protocol mattered to you," Socrates said. "Not the Mandarin Yellow, not the other stolen objects, and not the postponement of the exhibit. Not even your so-called loss of face. The only thing that mattered was getting back the original Secret Protocol so you could destroy it before the authorities got their hands on it and discovered it was a fake."

Bing-fa dismissed Socrates' explanation with the flick of his hand and the shrug of one shoulder.

"As I said, Mr. Cheng, your imagination is overly fertile."

Socrates ignored Bing-fa's cavalier dismissal and continued.

"To avoid this possibility, you wanted to recover the Secret Protocol yourself so you could destroy it. But to do this and not be exposed, you also needed to recover most of the other stolen objects. That way you could destroy several of them, including the original Secret Protocol, and place the blame for their destruction on the burglars. No one would ever consider the possibility that all you really wanted destroyed was the Secret Protocol, or that you, not the burglars, was responsible for destroying it."

"That is nonsensical," Bing-fa said. "Why would I want to engage in such a preposterous act?" Bing-fa's face flushed. "I have constantly striven to rescue and preserve my country's cultural patrimony and national treasures, not destroy them."

"We both know the answer to that," Socrates said. "Don't we."

Chapter 76

SOCRATES RELAXED FOR the first time since arriving at the Golden Dragon. He crossed one leg over the other and folded his hands together on his lap, interlacing his fingers. When he was sure he had Bing-fa's full attention, he said, "You were willing to destroy the original Secret Protocol and a few other cultural artifacts because you knew that Secret Protocol wasn't a national treasure, knew it, too, was a fake." He paused, then said, "You couldn't take the chance anyone else might find out."

Bing-fa's eyes narrowed. "This is very interesting," he said softly, "but nothing more than your imagination. Do you have evidence to support this brash accusation?"

Socrates shook his head.

"No evidence, Bing-fa, just common sense, some logic, a bit of intuition, and the realization that this is the only explanation that makes sense, the only way all the pieces fit together."

Bing-fa raised an eyebrow, but said nothing. He locked his eyes on Socrates' eyes.

"The fake original Secret Protocol must have been salted among Mao's private papers sometime before the public announcement of the proposed exhibit," Socrates said. "That's why no scholar I contacted had ever heard of the document until the exhibit's publicity. Before that, the Secret Protocol didn't exist except in the mind of the person who commissioned its creation."

Socrates stood up, turned his chair around and straddled it, facing Bing-fa. He rested his arms over the top of the chair's back. He felt more in command of the situation sitting this way.

"When the archivists discovered the Secret Protocol among Mao's papers, the document achieved instant provenance, as well as historical and cultural legitimacy, because Mao's private papers, until their selection for the exhibit, had remained under lock and key since his death. It was natural no one suspected that a fake document had been placed among the Chairman's legitimate, locked-up papers.

"The unraveling of the scheme started because of the burglary," Socrates said. "I assume you were caught off-guard like everyone else by the break in, but once the burglary occurred, you had no choice but to retrieve the Secret Protocol before the police did. That's where I came in. I was your means to retrieve it, your protective coloring, your stalking horse.

"I suppose you knew from Jade's stepmother I collected fountain pens. You used that information and the presence of the Mandarin Yellow in the exhibit to suck me in by pretending that recovering the pen was the focus of your efforts.

"You further fed my interest by implying that if I was successful, you might change your position concerning my relationship with Jade."

"I did no such thing," Bing-fa said. He frowned.

"That's exactly what you did. That's why you suggested I talk with Jade before I decided about helping you. How else should I have interpreted that statement, if not that way?"

Bing-fa shrugged.

"The irony is Jade obviously didn't know the original Secret Protocol was a fake. That's why she felt compelled to have the Triad steal it for her and why she intended to replace it with her own bogus version."

"Assuming what you have said is true, are you suggesting I am responsible for my daughter's death?"

Ah, Socrates thought, *so now she's your daughter again.*

"Yes, I am. And for the events that followed, including the other deaths, although I admit the burglary and murders were unintended consequences of your scheme," Socrates said. "You had no way of knowing the original fake Secret Protocol would fuel Jade's obsession with Madam Chiang and give rise to the unplanned outcomes that followed.

"If Jade had known that the original document was a fake, she could have exposed it for the forgery it was and rescued Madam Chiang's reputation from the damning text without orchestrating the burglary and causing the other disastrous events that resulted.

"So, yes," Socrates said, "that's what I'm saying. The planting of the original forged Secret Protocol among Mao's papers inadvertently brought about Jade's death, the director's death, the death of the cultural attaché, and the death of my friend, Brandon, as well as the symbolic deaths of the Eldest Brother and the Twins."

Chapter 77

SOCRATES LOOKED FOR some affirmation from Bing-fa, but he saw none so he proceeded to argue his brief.

"When the original Secret Protocol was secretly placed among Mao's papers and then brought to light in the exhibit's publicity and catalog, you couldn't have anticipated that Jade would believe it was genuine and would set in motion a plan to substitute her own sanitized forgery in its place."

Bing-fa shook his head slowly. "You are speculating, Mr. Cheng. That is all this is."

Socrates ignored Bing-fa's statement. "By substituting her forged Secret Protocol for the exhibit's original document, Jade believed she could protect Madam Chiang's reputation and still leave intact in the forged document those references to Chiang that were the very reason for the creation of the original Secret Protocol."

Bing-fa clearly was losing patience. "And that reason would be what, Mr. Cheng?" he said with icy contempt.

"To thoroughly discredit Chiang Kai-shek once and for all. To tear apart and render his reputation fully damned in the eyes of history. To drive a wooden stake through the heart of his reputation."

"Assuming you are correct, Mr. Cheng, how would the original Secret Protocol have achieved this since it already was widely known that Chiang was a thief, that he stole millions of dollars from Unites States foreign aid? Indeed, his international nickname was the *Little Bandit*."

Socrates, against his better judgment, smiled at this reminder of Chiang's nickname. Then he said, "By putting on public display a previously unknown, but fictitious aspect of Chiang's corruption — his fabricated collusion with Mao to intentionally lose the Civil War. As we both know, Bing-fa, there was no such agreement between Chiang and Mao."

Bing-fa slowly and deliberately rearranged the sash that tied his gown. He ran his palms across his lap and smoothed out the silk covering the top of his legs. Then he looked back up at Socrates.

"There is another fatal flaw in your theory, Mr. Cheng. Both Secret Protocols also discredit Chairman Mao's glorious reputation." Bing-fa paused, looked into Socrates eyes, then smiled victoriously.

"If the original Secret Protocol was a fake, as you claim," Bing-fa continued, "if it was intended to discredit Chiang, why would the creator of the document, who obviously would have been an enemy of Chiang to do what you claim he did, also discredit Mao in the document, since Mao and Chiang were sworn enemies? I believe such a person would not do any such thing to undermine the resplendent reputation of the glorious Chairman."

"Fair question," Socrates said. "The answer's found in the publicity for the exhibit, specifically, in the catalog's printed description of the original forged Secret Protocol."

"Meaning what?" Bing-fa said.

"Meaning that the catalog's authors, the cultural attaché and the gallery's director, neither of whom would have known that the original Secret Protocol was a fake, wrote in the catalog's description of the Secret Protocol that the document demonstrated Mao's integrity because Mao, unlike Big-Eared Tu, both Chiangs, and Stalin, did not accept cash embezzled from the stolen foreign aid.

"The cultural attaché and gallery's director also wrote that the Secret Protocol demonstrated Mao's great pragmatism because his participation in Chiang's scheme enabled the Chairman to defeat Generalissimo Chiang and obtain the complete rule of China for the Communist Party for a price paid to Chiang, not by the workers and soldiers of China, but by the United States, in the form of stolen American foreign aid. The catalog's caption went on to laud Mao for his cleverness and to deride the West's myopia.

Bing-fa shook his head. He seemed to Socrates to be tiring of this discussion and its many twists and turns.

"You still have not answered my previous question, Mr. Cheng. If what you have said is true, why would someone go to such efforts to discredit Generalissimo Chiang? His very existence carried its own disgrace. Who would care enough to take such unnecessary and extraordinary measures as you suggest against him?"

"Who would care?" Socrates repeated, nodding his head matter-of-factly. He again fixed his stare on Bing-fa's eyes.

"Perhaps," he said, "someone who believed that the lives of his parents and siblings had been destroyed by Chiang's parasitic economic policies after the end of the War Against Japanese Aggression, by Chiang's egregious corruption, and by the resulting hyper-inflation in China that destroyed the country's middle class.

"Perhaps someone whose family members, not able to live with their loss of face and the shame of their imposed poverty, brought additional disgrace to their children and ancestors by committing suicide."

Socrates took a deep breath. It was all out on the table now. There was no more for him to say. He felt better for having said it.

Bing-fa studied Socrates' face. "Why did you come here today, Mr. Cheng? What did you hope to accomplish other than to stir up matters better left dormant?"

"I wanted to see."

"See what?"

"See if you would admit your role in initiating the chain of events that destroyed your current family, yet failed to avenge the destruction of your former Shanghai family."

Bing-fa looked hard at Socrates as if studying him. Then he said, "Goodbye, Mr. Cheng."

Bing-fa stood up and walked over to the door, opened it, and stood by silently as Socrates walked out.

—

ONCE OUTSIDE THE Golden Dragon, Socrates stood on the sidewalk and watched the sun set behind a building across H Street. After a few minutes, he walked toward home.

He hadn't gone far when he reached into his sports jacket pocket and removed a printed form he'd been carrying with him for days. As he walked, he read through the District of Columbia's application to obtain a private investigator's license. He mentally filled-in its blanks as he walked.

His plan was simple. He would sit for the licensing exam, obtain his PI's license, and continue to work at the law firm during the day, while at night and on weekends he would build an independent PI practice. Then, when he'd obtained enough regular business to sustain him, he would leave the law firm and become a fulltime PI, perhaps even performing occasional investigations for his former law partners.

Socrates smiled as he approached Dupont Circle. Who would have ever guessed he'd become a PI? Certainly not him. He wouldn't have taken that bet, no matter what the odds given him.

The End

About the Author

Steve Roth has been a student of Chinese culture, philosophy and history for more than two decades. He is a contributing writer to *Kung Fu Taiji* magazine and the editor of several books on Chinese martial arts. Steve is a published historian with more than 100 published articles and monographs to his credit. He also is a longtime pen collector. Steve owns a 1927 Parker Pen Company Duofold Mandarin Yellow.

Steve holds a bachelor's degree in philosophy and history from Pennsylvania State University and a law degree from Duke Law School. Steve is a freelance writer focusing on computer technology. He lives with his wife, Dominica, in Washington, DC.

You can contact Steve at StevenMRoth.Auhor@gmail.com or through his web page at http://www.StevenMRoth.com. You also can reach him on Facebook, Twitter and LinkedIn.